The Emperor's Knives

Empire: Volume Seven

ANTHONY RICHES

HODDER

First published in 2014 by Hodder & Stoughton
An Hachette UK company

First published in paperback in 2014 by Hodder & Stoughton

3

A CIP catalogue record for this title
is available from the British Library

Paperback ISBN 978 1 444 73195 8

Typeset in Plantin Light by Palimpsest Book Production Limited,
Falkirk, Stirlingshire

Printed and bound by Clays Ltd, St Ives plc

Hodder & Stoughton policy is to use papers that are natural,
renewable and recyclable products and made from wood grown in
sustainable forests. The logging and manufacturing processes are expected
to conform to the environmental regulations of the country of origin.

Hodder & Stoughton Ltd
338 Euston Road
London NW1 3BH

www.hodder.co.uk

Acclaim for EMPIRE

'A damn fine read . . . fast-paced, action-packed.' Ben Kane

'Stands head and shoulders above a crowded field . . . real, live characters act out their battles on the northern borders with an accuracy of detail and depth of raw emotion that is a rare combination.' Manda Scott

'Riches has captured how soldiers speak and act to a tee and he is very descriptive when it comes to the fighting. It is a novel full of power, lust, envy, violence and vanity. The very things that made Rome great and the very things that would lead to its downfall. If you like historical novels, read this book.' *NavyNet* on *Arrows of Fury*

'With *Wounds of Honour* Anthony Riches has produced a terrific first novel that focuses on the soldiers of the Roman Empire in great detail. He vibrantly portrays the life in an auxiliary unit.' *Canberra Times*

'This is fast-paced and gripping "read-through-the-night" fiction, with marvellous characters and occasional moments of dark humour. Some authors are better historians than they are storytellers. Anthony Riches is brilliant at both.' Conn Iggulden

EMPIRE

Wounds of Honour
Arrows of Fury
Fortress of Spears
The Leopard Sword
The Wolf's Gold
The Eagle's Vengeance

About the author

Anthony Riches holds a degree in Military Studies from Manchester University. He began writing the story that would become the first novel in the *Empire* series, *Wounds of Honour*, after visiting Housesteads Roman fort in 1996. He lives in Hertfordshire with his wife and three children.

Find out more about his books at www.anthonyriches.com

For Jennifer and David

ACKNOWLEDGEMENTS

When I first began to contemplate actually writing the story that has become *The Emperor's Knives* – as opposed to the previous musing on how fascinating it would be to get Marcus back on his home turf and turn him lose to seek bloody revenge – it quickly became very clear to me that I had a major disadvantage in any attempt to set a novel on the streets of Rome. I had no real knowledge of the streets of Rome. I knew the Forum, the Colosseum and the Palatine, at least as much as is possible from their remains, and I still get goosebumps from my memory of first touching the stone on which Julius Caesar was cremated, but the ancient city beyond that tiny portion was a mystery to me. Finding the internet less helpful than is usually the case, I was fortunate to enjoy one of those serendipitous moments of discovery that we tend to put down to luck, and perhaps ought to credit to the power of a focused mind instead. Seeing a review of *Dans La Rome Des Cesars* (translation: *In The Rome Of The Caesars*) I made a swift purchase, waited impatiently for its arrival, then settled down to pore over the most amazing book on the city I've ever read. I can't understand much of its text, being far from fluent in written French (there is no translation), but I can assure you that the pictures and maps are enough to make up for that lack of fluency.

Gilles Chaillet has written a labour of love, a gorgeously illustrated map book of the fourth-century city apparently based on the plaster model built by his countryman Paul Bigot – Le Plan De Rome – which now resides in the University of Caen. The French Amazon blurb calls the author 'Stakhanovite' (a 1930's Soviet Russian term for overachievement), and I can see their point, given the 5,000 hours of work that went into writing it (and the 3,000 hours of artwork by his collaborators Chantal Defachelle and Isabelle Brune). Trust me, if you have one iota of interest in the eternal city, you owe it to yourself to purchase this magnificent book. And if you can read French, so much the better!

With Rome's street map at my fingertips, the second subject I needed to understand better was the brutal, ignoble, but occasionally dazzling spectacle of gladiatorial combat that was a staple of Roman entertainment for a good five hundred years. While it would be fair to say that I have consulted at least a dozen works on the subject, from the mildly sensationalist to the deeply academic, the book that I found to be of the most value was Philip Matyszak's marvellous *Gladiator – The Roman Fighter's Unofficial Manual*. As with his other short, pithy but detailed packed works, Philip has excelled in bringing crisp understanding to a sprawling subject, a book both learned and yet wearing its erudition lightly enough for the reader who just wants to be informed. If there's a fact worth knowing about the arena's bloody trade, some of it amusing, some of it truly horrifying, then it's in this book. I cannot recommend it highly enough. As usual, should you find any factual errors you can rest assured that they are all my own work. Oh, and there's a signed first edition waiting for the diligent reader who can find the quip I've reproduced from Maty's book in connection with entry to the gladiatorial life – but only one. The first person to contact me on Facebook gets the prize if they have the right answer.

With those two recommendations made, it only remains for me to say my thank you's. To my wife Helen, my agent Robin, and to my editor Carolyn and her assistant Francine go my gratitude for your continued support, tolerance and gentle chivvying. To my beta readers, David, John and Viv, thanks for pointing out plot errors and inconsistencies. And to you, reader, goes the biggest thank you, simply for getting Marcus and the Tungrians this far. This is the book I had in mind when my young protagonist was following Dubnus up the road to the north from York, long before *Wounds of Honour* was complete, so thanks for helping me to realise that ambition. And stay with it, if you're of a mind for more – we've a long way to go, you, me and the Tungrians.

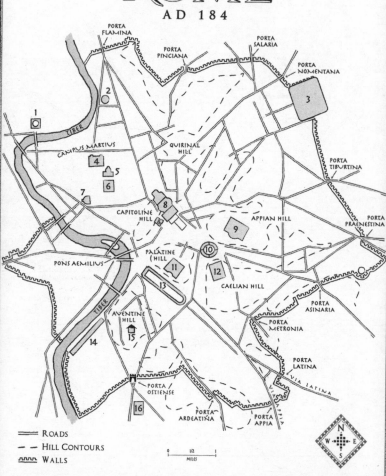

MAP OF
ROME
AD 184

Roads
Hill Contours
Walls

0   1/2   1
MILES

N W E S

1. MAUSOLEUM OF HADRIAN
2. MAUSOLEUM OF AUGUSTUS
3. CAMP OF THE PRAETORIANS
4. BATHS OF NERO
5. PANTHEON
6. BATHS OF AGRIPPA
7. THEATRE OF POMPEY
8. IMPERIAL FORA
9. BATHS OF TRAJAN
10. FLAVIAN ARENA
11. IMPERIAL PALACE
12. TEMPLE OF CLAUDIUS
13. CIRCUS MAXIMUS
14. PORTICUS AEMILIA
15. FELICIA'S HOUSE
16. BARRACKS

MAP OF
CENTRAL ROME
AD 184

FORUM

CAPITOLINE HILL

BATHS OF TRAJAN

APPIAN HILL

BATHS OF TITUS

LUDUS DACICUS
(DACIAN SCHOOL)

TEMPLE OF VENUS & ROME

FLAVIAN ARENA

LUDUS MAXIMUS
(GREAT SCHOOL)

PALATINE HILL

LUDUS GALLICUS
(GALLIC SCHOOL)

SPOLARIUM

IMPERIAL PALACE

TEMPLE OF CLAUDIUS

LUDUS MATINUS
(MORNING SCHOOL)

CIRCUS MAXIMUS

CAELIAN HILL

N
W · E
S

ROADS
HILL CONTOURS
CLAUDIAN AQUEDUCT

0 ___ 1/2
MILES

Prologue

'Excuse me for bothering you sir. Do I have the honour of addressing Sextus Dexter Bassus?'

The man in the doorway nodded, playing a forbidding look over the two men standing before him in the small but neat front garden of his house, rendered private from the main road that climbed the Aventine Hill by a substantial wall that ran all the way around the property's modest grounds. His look of irritation was due in no small part to the fact that the unexpected callers had summarily dismissed the slave who had opened the door to them, peremptorily telling him to fetch his master on the apparent grounds of the matter at hand's 'sensitivity'.

'You do. And you are?'

The taller of the two men, who seemed to be doing the talking for them both, smiled in a self-deprecating manner.

'Me? A man of no great importance, although this may help to establish my bona fides in the matter I am desirous of discussing with you.' The caller lifted the end of his belt to display a stylised tri-form spearhead decoration in polished silver. 'This, Dexter Bassus, is the badge of a beneficiarius, a man chosen to give trusted service to one of his military superiors. In my own humble case I am just such a man, in the service of an extremely high-ranking military officer. His absolute need to stay nameless in this matter means that I am in turn required to nurture a similar desire for anonymity. I'm afraid that all I can tell you here, on your doorstep, is that my visit concerns events that occurred in the province of Britannia a little over two years ago.'

Bassus leaned forward, his eyes narrowing.

'If this is about my brother—'

A raised hand stopped him in mid-sentence, the self-assured nature of the unnamed messenger's gesture making him start backwards a fraction despite himself.

'There's nothing more to be said out here, I'm afraid, Dexter Bassus. If I might just come inside for a moment, I'm sure that everything will become clear . . .'

Bassus looked past the beneficiarius at the man waiting patiently behind him who was, if not completely ragged in his state of dress, demonstrating a robust attitude towards the requirements of both fashion and the regard of his fellow citizens. His eyes were roaming the modest garden with a faraway look, as if he'd never seen such a thing in all of his life.

'And who's this? Another one of your "high-ranking officer's" men?'

The other man laughed, evidently amused with the idea.

'Silus? Not likely! Silus is a man of the streets, and not accustomed to the workings of the Palatine, *if* you take my meaning?'

Bassus's eyebrows raised at the mention of the hill upon which the imperial palaces and the throne's sprawling bureaucracy had taken root.

'The Palatine?'

The caller smiled thinly.

'I can say no more. As to my companion here, I keep him handy whenever I travel through the city alone, especially at this time of the evening. And there are risks connected with my visit to your house that go well beyond the simple danger of robbery with violence. I can make it no plainer for you, I'm afraid – either we discuss this matter in a more private place, such as your study, or both Silus and I will simply vanish from your door, never to trouble you again. I will tell my sponsor that you chose to be uncooperative, and he in turn will resign himself to your never knowing the truth about what happened in Britannia. It really is very much up to you.'

Bassus thought for a moment, clearly torn between caution and curiosity.

'You can come in, but that man has a look to him that I don't care for. He can wait in the garden.'

Silus smiled, a disquieting vision given the state of his teeth, and his employer mirrored his expression with a nod of agreement that was almost a bow.

'How delightful for him! Silus is enormously fond of gardens, given his rather plain accommodation in the Subura district. I'm sure he'll be more than happy to enjoy the fruits of your gardener's labour in this pleasant evening's warmth, while you and I discuss our business with a little more privacy than can be achieved on your doorstep.'

Bassus waited until the bodyguard had strolled away to sit on one of his stone benches before ushering the mystery visitor through the doorway and into the cool of the house. The man took two steps and stopped, looking about him with evident approval.

'Very nice, Dexter Bassus, very nice indeed! Someone in your household clearly has the most exquisite taste in interior decoration . . . The lady of the house, perhaps, or possibly a particularly talented slave? Whoever it is, you're a lucky man!'

Bassus grunted a perfunctory agreement and ushered the visitor into his private office, scowling at the room's door as it creaked loudly on its hinges. He indicated a chair facing his desk, behind which he installed himself while the other man lowered himself into a sitting position with a slight grimace.

'My back isn't all that it used to be, I'm afraid. All those years on horseback criss-crossing the empire at the emperor's behest have quite taken the spring out of me, as you can see . . .'

He waited a moment, as if inviting Bassus into his conversation, but the other man only stared at him in bemusement.

'I know, not the subject you invited me in to discuss, and I apologise. A man who has previously enjoyed robust good health does have the irritating habit of sharing the smallest aches and pains with all and sundry when they eventually catch up with him.' He smiled into his host's darkening frown. 'Yes indeed, to business! You are, Sextus Dexter Bassus, the brother of one Quintus Dexter Bassus, are you not?'

Bassus shook his head, his voice laced with irritation.

'We've already established that!'

The visitor leaned back in his chair with a smile, steepling his fingers.

'Forgive my unavoidable disagreement, but in point of fact, Dexter Bassus, we have *not*. When I mentioned Britannia out there on your doorstep, you promptly asked if your brother was involved, but you didn't ever actually mention his name. Precision is a quality for which I am known, and I cannot afford to allow that reputation to be sullied by a moment's inattention. So—'

'*Yes!*' Bassus sat forward, slapping the desk and fixing his guest with a hard stare, his patience clearly at its limits. 'I am the youngest brother of Quintus Dexter Bassus, who was, before you spend another lifetime working your way around to the question, the tribune and commanding officer of the Second Tungrian Cohort in northern Britannia. He died two years ago in the uprising that overran the frontier wall built by the Emperor Hadrian, and he left me, his only surviving sibling, as the owner of this house. Does that cover all of your questions?'

'Not quite.'

Bassus sat back again with an expression of dismay that was bordering on something more than irritation.

'I think I should have you thrown—'

The messenger spoke over him without any change in his expression.

'Yes, I think you probably should, Dexter Bassus, but you're not going to show me the door, not yet. For one thing, you don't know to which of the empire's esteemed military men, a well-regarded senator by the way, you might be giving offence, and for another . . .' He smiled faintly at the big man. 'The circumstances of your brother's death were never made clear to you, were they? Or, indeed what happened to his wife, your sister-in-law. You'll remember her quite well, I'd imagine, given that this was *her* house?'

Bassus looked at him with a different expression, his anger of a moment before replaced by something approaching horror.

'No . . .'

The visitor pursed his lips and shrugged without any discernible sympathy for the man sitting opposite as his bad news sank in.

'Well, as it happens, very much *yes*, I'm afraid. The lady in question survived the barbarian attack quite neatly, and as you would expect, eventually remarried. Her new husband is an officer in the First Tungrian Cohort, a nice young man, indeed in point of fact, more of a gentleman really, the son of a senator. He's almost supernaturally skilled with just about any weapon you can name; the result, I am reliably informed, of his having trained with both a soldier and a gladiator throughout his youth. Recently, however, he's fallen on hard times . . .' The beneficiarius leaned forward to confide in his host, lowering his voice to a stage whisper. 'His father was unfortunate enough to get himself executed for treason, you see. You might recall the excitement in the city at the time, when Appius Valerius Aquila was accused of plotting against the emperor? There was no truth in it, but since when did that ever stop an emperor like Commodus when he takes a fancy to a man's estate? I believe the Aquila villa was even possessed of a small private arena, which I would imagine made it impossible for the young emperor to resist, given his known predilection for a gladiator.'

He sat back again with a smile that was bordering on the beatific.

'So, to sum up, your brother dies, by his own men's swords I should add – he seems to have been a little too keen on the stricter aspects of military discipline from the sound of it – and leaves his young wife, the legal owner of this house, a widow. She then marries a rather dangerous young man who seems to go through anyone and anything that gets in his way, like a spearpoint through tunic wool, and they manage to survive the rest of the war with the tribes. Not to mention at least one attempt by the imperial authorities to bring him to justice. And now they're here.'

Bassus jerked bolt upright in his chair.

'*Here?*'

'Well not here, as such, but they are less than a mile away, living in the military transit barracks on the Ostian road. And yes, I can only imagine what must be going through your mind . . .'

A loud crash echoed through the house followed by the sound of a woman's voice raised in protest from the room above them. The beneficiarius raised his eyebrows, tipping his head to the study door.

'Trouble in the kitchen, from the sound of it! Mind you, I expect your wife will be on top of the problem. Probably better if we leave her to it?'

The sound of footsteps sounded on the floorboards above them, and then down the stairs as the woman of the house evidently came from whatever she had been doing to investigate. Silence fell, and the beneficiarius leaned forwards again with his eyebrows raised in question.

'So, Sextus Dexter Bassus, the question is this: what do you think we should do about this change in your circumstances? After all, it probably isn't going to be very long before this rather excitable young man appears at your door with his wife and demands that you vacate *her* property . . .'

Bassus looked down at his hands for a moment.

'I'm not like my brother . . . he was always the forceful one. Do you think . . .'

'Do I think what, Dexter Bassus? Do I think I could help? Possibly. You want this whole problem to go away, I presume? It wouldn't be cheap.'

The answer was instant.

'I have money! Not enough to buy a house like this, but enough to reward you generously for any help that you could provide in . . . relieving me of this problem. Would five . . . no, *ten* thousand sestertii be enough?'

The beneficiarius shook his head with a hint of sadness.

'More than enough to employ a man like Silus, much more, but then a man like Silus isn't going to be capable of dealing with this problem. This will require a team of men, and one in particular with the cunning to lure this young man into a carefully designed trap. A man like me, to be precise.' He inspected his fingernails for a moment. 'And I have a sum more of the order of twenty-five thousand in mind.'

The room was silent for a moment while Bassus digested the offer, and silence hung over the house beyond the study's stout wooden door. When he answered his voice was edged with incredulity.

'*Twenty-five thousand sestertii?* But that's—'

'Everything you have? Not quite. At this point in time, you have this lovely town house, and your good health to boot. There might well come a time not far in the future when you have neither, unless this young man is stopped from carrying through his plans to dispossess you of his wife's property.'

Bassus nodded disconsolately.

'Very well, half now and half when the job is complete and proven to my satisfaction.'

He stood, shaking his head and muttering under his breath, going round the desk and stooping to prise a floor tile up from its place, reaching into the gap beneath it to pull out a good-sized purse. To his surprise the visitor stood up, stretched with a grimace and then called out in a loud voice.

'Very well, Silus, we're in here!'

With the same slow creak of hinges in need of oil, the study's door opened, revealing the bodyguard standing stock-still in the frame. His face and tunic were spattered with blood, and a long dagger dangled from his right hand in an almost nonchalant manner. Bassus gaped at him, finding his voice after a long pause.

'You . . .'

Words failed him, and the nameless messenger nodded helpfully.

'Killed your cook, her husband the butler, their daughter the kitchen servant and lastly your wife? That does seem to be the inescapable conclusion. And yes, *obviously* you're next, now that you've paid to have young Marcus Valerius Aquila murdered. Your desire for the problem to go away will be honoured in full, but just not for your benefit. More for mine, really.'

Bassus shrank back against the wall behind him, his face twisted in terror as Silus advanced into the room, looking to his master for the signal to make the last kill.

'You . . . you were just waiting for me to show you where the money was!'

The anonymous visitor smiled again, shaking his head with a sad smile.

'Not really. Did you not wonder how my price just *happened* to coincide precisely with the amount of money you have left from that which you inherited when your brother died? There actually was enough there to buy you a nice place, wasn't there? Not quite this pleasant, but good enough and in a respectable area. Greed got the better of you, I'd imagine. Why buy a house when you already had one, since your brother's wife showed no sign of returning home, eh? I've known what you're worth down to the last sestertius for a while now, and where you hide the money, but robbery was never my aim. I didn't want to steal your money, I wanted you to pay me to deal with the Aquila boy, a job which I can assure you I'll carry through to the full extent of your rather heavy purse and beyond, if need be.'

Bassus shook his head in disbelief.

'So why . . . ?'

He waved a hand at the bloody knife, his mouth opening and closing silently.

'Why kill you all? Because I need this house as part of the plan to fulfil your last orders, that's why, and you and the rest of your household would at best have been inconvenient loose ends.'

A waved hand set Silus in motion, walking slowly around the desk with his dagger held ready. He raised the knife, speaking to Bassus in a matter-of-fact tone that was clearly calculated to soothe the panicking victim in his last moments.

'Keep nice and still mate. It'll be a lot quicker and less painful if you do.'

Bassus looked about him frantically for a way out of his predicament, but before he could make any move the knife man stepped forward quickly, whipping his dagger up and thrusting it deeply into the point where his cowering victim's neck and shoulder met in the classic street executioner's stroke.

'*Ah!* You bast . . .'

Clutching reflexively at the wound with blood squirting between his fingers, he tottered, stepped forward one seemingly drunken pace, and then stopped, swaying on the spot. Eyes rolling upwards as consciousness failed, he slumped to the floor and lay still, a puddle of blood spreading from the wound with one small rivulet trickling down into the underground hiding place from which he had taken the purse. The beneficiarius looked down at him with an expression of pity.

'How disappointingly stupid. He fell for the beneficiarius story the moment he saw this meaningless piece of silver.' He lifted the belt end, smiling down at the faked symbol of patronage. 'Even when whatever it was that broke during your struggle out there hit the floor, he still wasn't bright enough to realise what was happening until you came through the door.' He shook his head. 'Never mind. Clearly we perform a service to the gods on days like these, ridding this world of the more credulous of our fellow citizens and leaving more room for clever fellows like you and I, eh Silus?' He slapped the blood-spattered murderer on a relatively clean section of his arm. 'And well done for a neatly concluded job! Let's get all that blood washed off the floor and walls shall we, and decide what to do with the bodies?'

The gory bodyguard stood and looked at him for a moment before speaking.

'Doesn't it worry you to be alone with a murderer and more gold than I've ever seen in my life, with no one else to hand or even knowing that we're here?'

His employer raised a sardonic eyebrow, half his face shadowed in the dim evening light filtering through the study's high window.

'You only ask from curiosity, of course?'

Silus looked down at his bloody knife.

'That's right, only my curiosity.'

'Well in that case I shall enlighten you as to the source of my boundless confidence with regard to your continued flawless execution of my orders. And it really is *very* simple. Once a day, every day, I report to a very, very important man. I provide him with the information I glean as I go about my job, information which is *particularly* important to him. He expects results from me, Silus, and I expect that he would be more than vexed if the admittedly small matter of my death were to get in the way of my achieving those results. Be assured that he knows all about you, and indeed all about the seemingly immeasurable number of family members whose main breadwinner you would appear to be – how many children is it that you have?'

'Seven.'

His employer clapped his hands together softly.

'Seven indeed, and they all survived the plague the last time it stalked the city? That really is quite astonishing good luck! I know of whole families that were wiped out in less than a week. You're a lucky man, Silus, but it might just be that you've used up all that luck. Were I to go missing, even for a day, this man is the type to assume the worst and set investigators on my trail. A trail which I have ensured will lead straight to your door. So, were you to make this simple and entirely understandable mistake, you would soon enough find yourself and every one of your seven children, and that fat wife of yours and her brother, and his wife and children too, all enjoying a brief unscheduled trip to dark rooms buried far beyond any thought of rescue. There are men who ply their trade in those badly lit places, Silus, who make a simple schemer like me and a murdering thug like you appear to be men of the highest virtue. Your family, once in their power, would be abused, degraded and tortured in ways that even a man with your broad experience of the world cannot begin to imagine, since these men's depravity is limited only by the bounds of their particularly savage imaginations.'

He stared at the killer for a moment, opening his arms wide.

'So if you'd like to play through that possible future for your family, you go right ahead and put the knife into me.'

Silus shook his head.

'No, my curiosity is quite satisfied. Funny though . . .'

His employer raised an eyebrow.

'What is?'

'I was just thinking that you're not quite right in the head, if you don't mind me saying so.'

The other man smiled at him broadly.

'Many men have tried to offend me Silus, it's in the nature of my business to attract insults, but very few of them have ever succeeded. After all, none of this is personal, it's simply business. And trust me, there is a method in my apparent madness. I have a plan that will bring this man Aquila to justice at last, and in doing so more than likely perform the other task that my rather impatient sponsor wishes to see completed. So, let's be about it shall we? These bodies aren't going to bury themselves.'

I

Rome, September AD *184*

'Close your mouth, Dubnus, or something will fly into it.'

The heavily built and bearded soldier walking alongside Julius, senior centurion of the First Tungrian Cohort, gave his superior officer a disparaging look before resuming his perusal of the inhabitants of the Aventine district through which they were progressing. When he spoke his voice was awestruck, as if he could barely believe the scene before him.

'But they're bloody everywhere, Julius! Bar girls, shop girls, girls on the street, girls on the corner, girls writing graffiti on the wall about how their clients made them scream with pleasure!' He pointed to a prostitute leaning against the door of a house, her pitch marked out by several lewd and enticing statements as to her abilities and offerings scrawled on the wall behind her. 'That one will even . . .'

He swallowed, and shook his head in amazement at the debauched act that was apparently on offer for the price of a decent meal.

'Yes, the city can be rather overpowering for the first-time visitor, but then you would insist on accompanying us. Perhaps you should concentrate on the architecture instead?'

Julius turned and nodded to his tribune who was walking a few paces behind the two centurions, resplendent in a pristine toga and with his hair cut and combed to glossy perfection, even if his clean-shaven face was in defiance of the latest fashion. Dubnus drew breath to speak again, managing with some reluctance to drag his attention away from the prostitute who was so enticingly crooking her finger at him while lasciviously teasing the digit's end with her tongue, but was rudely interrupted by Julius before he could open his mouth.

'That's a good idea, Tribune. That way he won't embarrass the rest of us by walking round with a damp spot in the front of his tunic. You're not wearing armour now Dubnus, look to your decency man!'

The big Briton gave his friend a hard look before gazing up at the buildings on either side of the road along which they were walking, craning his neck to stare up at the five- and six-storey insulae towering over them.

'You're the funny man today, are you Julius? As it happens, I was just thinking that I still can't get used to the idea that people actually live in those things. Imagine having to climb all the way up there and then discover that you've forgotten something. And what happens if there's a fire on the ground floor, and you're all the way up there?'

Tribune Scaurus laughed grimly.

'In that case, Centurion, you would at least have the gratification of knowing that you would be the last to burn, unless of course the screams of the better-off tenants in the lower floors gave you the time to ponder the choice of a slow death by fire or a quick one by impact with the ground. In the event of fire, I believe the rule of thumb is that the lowest tenant usually gets out with at least some of his possessions, the next highest occupant usually escapes with his life, and the next highest, *if* they're blessed by Fortuna's smile. After that it seems to be a simple question of either burning to death or jumping.'

The man walking beside Scaurus followed up on the tribune's comments in a more serious tone of voice. Equally formally attired and groomed, he was tall and limber in appearance, muscular in an athletic way rather than any tendency to the hulking power of the centurions walking before him. His skin, darker by contrast than that of his fellow officers, advertised the fact that he had not been born in Dubnus's native Britannia.

'Of course these days, now that they're mainly built with brick rather than timber, the main risk isn't fire, it's collapse. People lie in bed at night in those things listening to the building creaking around them, and wondering if they'll be crushed to death if someone sneezes too loudly and brings the whole thing down. The bases aren't broad enough for the height they build them up to, you see, since no one bothers to obey the height regulations.'

Scaurus raised an eyebrow at the younger man, and his reply carried an undisguised sardonic undertone.

'Crushed under several tons of bricks? Much what anyone seeking to bother me this afternoon might feel like, I expect, given the number of escorts we managed to collect between my quarter and the transit barracks' main gate.

One of the three obviously barbarian men bringing up the rear shook his head in disgust.

'It's a good thing I heard you discussing this little afternoon stroll with Centurion Corvus, before you had the chance to sneak off into this cesspit on your own.'

Scaurus shook his head in irritation without looking back.

'Indeed, Prince Martos, what *was* I thinking? Why in Jupiter's name would we have wanted to make our way to our meeting with one of Rome's most influential senators in a discreet and, dare I say it, sober manner, when instead we could be preceded by a pair of swaggering centurions with obvious hard-ons for anything female under the age of sixty . . .' He shook his head at Julius's wounded expression. 'I saw you eying up that little blonde, First Spear, so stop pretending you're immune to the attractions of the opposite sex now that your woman has your balls firmly clamped between her thighs. Now, where was I . . . ? Ah yes, preceded by a pair of priapic officers and trailed by a trio of barbarians, at least one of whom is equally intent on impressing every working girl we pass with the glory of his manhood.'

He shook his head with amused irritation.

'If I've told you once Arminius, I must have told you a hundred times in the last ten years, they simply will not have sex with you without payment, no matter how muscular you are or, for that matter, how much you attempt to demonstrate that you have a penis that would make a donkey feel inadequate.' He paused for a moment, listening for any retort, before continuing. 'As for the need to protect us, Centurion Corvus here and I both walked these streets for years without ever attracting anything worse than an unkind glance, and that was when we weren't in the company of the five biggest and ugliest men under my command. But no matter, you have at least provided us with some measure of entertainment during our walk. And here we are – this is our destination.'

He waved a hand at a sizeable domus, a rich man's house set in enough ground for the construction of half a dozen of the towering insulae, each side of the large detached property shielded from casual view by mature trees that had grown almost as high as the neighbouring apartment buildings.

'Perhaps you'll all be a little less bumptious now that we're no longer at such imminent risk of being robbed and murdered? And remember, we're here to provide the senator with some consolation for the death of his son, so just mind your manners or you'll have the pleasure of a long wait on his doorstep.'

An apparently imperturbable butler greeted them with an impressive lack of any reaction in the face of so large a party of men, most of whom were clearly disreputable types to judge from their scars, tattoos and in one case the absence of an eye, even if the barbarians among them were all dressed in clean tunics and had well-polished boots. Bidding them to remain in the house's entrance hall, he withdrew to inform his master of their arrival, leaving the party to consider the murals that adorned the room's walls. Dubnus leaned closer, admiring the detail in a representation of a goddess frolicking in a woodland glade seen through a window painted onto the plaster.

'Nice work.'

Julius raised an eyebrow at his friend, shaking his head in apparent bafflement.

'Nice work? Since when, oh Prince of the Axe Men, have you had any ability to recognise the difference between good painting and that done by a Greek pot painter using a brush poking out of his arse to slap the colours on? All you're doing is admiring her tits, you dirty bastard . . .' He leaned closer, pursing his lips in approval. 'Although on closer inspection I'm forced to agree with you that they are a most lifelike representation, what with—'

Dubnus interrupted him, pointing at the view through another 'window'.

'I know. And look at what this satyr's doing to the maiden he's captured! I swear he's got it up her—'

A voice from behind them had the two men start.

'Greetings, esteemed visitors. I sometimes have to leave my clients waiting here for hours, given the number of visitors I routinely receive, men seeking either my favour or assistance, and these murals provide them with some small measure of distraction. Given long enough, I'm told, it is possible for the diligent hunter to discover over two hundred such visions of loveliness around the room, although I must confess I've never found the time . . .'

Scaurus stepped forward with a solemn expression, bowing deeply to the toga-clad man who stood in the doorway that linked the hall to the rest of the house.

'Greetings, Senator Sigilis. Please accept our humble gratitude for your kindness in agreeing to meet with us.'

Their host returned the bow, albeit in the more cursory manner due to a member of the equestrian class from a senator, the taut smile of greeting on his face the expression of a man who had not shown genuine pleasure for a long time. He was as tall as either of the Tungrian centurions, although his body was whip thin by comparison to their muscular bulk, and his hair was silver-grey over a lean and heavily lined face.

'The gratitude is mine, Tribune, for your kindness in expressing the desire to speak with me of my son's last few weeks of life. I would imagine that most soldiers would prefer to forget the men they have left on the battlefield, much less actually come face-to-face with a grieving parent. Please come this way, and do bring your, ah . . . *familia* . . . with you.'

They followed the senator through the archway into a large garden in which a pair of slaves were tending the already immaculately manicured plants and flowers.

'Over here.'

He led them to a seating area at the garden's far end, stone benches arrayed around a flat gravelled area large enough to act as a small stage, or for a group of musicians to play their instruments, and protected from the sun's heat by a circle of carefully planted cedar trees. At the butler's command, the gardeners went into the domus and carried out a padded chair, into which the senator lowered himself with a grimace, then vanished back into the house leaving only the butler, who, satisfied that his master was comfortable, retired out of earshot.

'Forgive my ostentation. A decade ago good honest marble would have sufficed for my backside, but these days I find the stiffness in my joints eased a little by a touch of luxury. I thought we might best speak out here in the garden, given that walls frequently hear more than would appear possible, even, I suspect, in my house.' Sigilis played his bleak stare over each of them, his eyes assessing every man in turn before moving on. 'You bring a large party with you, Tribune, larger than I expected, and yet you provide me with some small distraction by doing so. If I might speculate as to the origins of your people . . . ?'

Scaurus smiled back at him.

'By all means, Senator. We must present something of a mixed bag.'

'Indeed you do, although some of you are easier to read than others.' He looked at the tribune. 'You, of course, are already known to me, Rutilius Scaurus. I remember your father well, and the disappointment we all felt when he was obliged to take his own life after being landed with the blame for that shabby little affair on the other side of the Rhenus. I am, of course, on excellent terms with your sponsor . . .' He smiled thinly. 'I find it ironic that his fortunes should be recovering so strongly with the praetorian prefect's death, while my own seem to be in a terminal decline, but I can't hold it against the man. He tells me that you've grown no less headstrong for your years of service. He also tells me that you've been dabbling in politics of late?'

Scaurus shook his head.

'Not me, Senator, I'll leave that to men with more ability and stronger stomachs than mine.'

Sigilis raised an eyebrow.

'So it wasn't you that marched ten boxes of gold into the palace and got the praetorian prefect murdered by the emperor a few nights ago?'

The younger man shrugged, his face commendably impassive.

'I was no more than a small part of that night's events, Senator. Most of the hard work was done by your colleague Clodius Albinus, in league with the emperor's freedman Cleander.'

Sigilis chuckled mirthlessly.

'How very self-effacing of you. You carried a cargo of gold, proving the praetorian prefect's ambitions to take the throne all the way from the northern frontier . . . Where was it again?'

'Britannia, Senator.'

'Yes, all the way from Britannia, along, I'm reliably informed, with the lost eagle of the Sixth Legion, which you then used to tip Commodus over the edge to murder his own praetorian guard commander. Somewhat to the amazement of the hapless Clodius Albinus, I would imagine, and much to the delight of that conniving snake Cleander.'

Scaurus returned his level gaze in silence, until the senator nodded slowly.

'Just as your sponsor intimated to me. You're shot through with granite, aren't you Tribune, and a dangerous man to cross for all of your modesty and self-effacement?'

He turned his stare to the younger man sitting next to Scaurus.

'And what have we here? Early twenties, Roman in appearance, and muscled like a man used to carrying the weight of weapons and armour on a routine basis. I did my time in the service, and, believe it or not, I once had much the same build. You're fresh from battle too, if appearances are any indication, unless of course you did that shaving . . .' He raised a hand to point at the scar across the bridge of Marcus's nose. 'It looks too light to have been a sword. A spear, perhaps?'

Marcus tipped his head in recognition.

'Yes, Senator. I didn't get my head out the way fast enough.'

Sigilis pursed his lips.

'You were still lucky, that's a scratch compared with some of the facial wounds I saw serving as a tribune with the Thirtieth Legion in Caesarea. Well, scar or no scar, you remind me in your manner of a man I used to know, a highly respected fellow senator who was clearly too well thought of to survive under this regime. He died a good three years ago, and his entire family with him, dragged from their beds at night and carried away to a fate the thought of which makes me shudder. Only the older son remained unaccounted for, or so the informed gossip from the palace had it. He had been serving with the praetorian guard as a centurion, but vanished only days before his father was arrested and was last seen heading for Ostia with orders to take ship on a courier mission – or at least that was the story that got him out of the praetorian fortress.'

He locked gazes with the centurion.

'Your name, young man?'

The Roman rose from his seat and bowed.

'I am known as Marcus Tribulus Corvus, Senator, Centurion, First Tungrian Cohort, but I am indeed the fugitive son of your friend Appius Valerius Aquila. You now hold my life, and that of my family, in your hands.'

Sigilis smiled back at him with apparent genuine pleasure.

'Rest assured that your secret is safe with me. It is indeed an honour to make your acquaintance, Marcus Valerius Aquila. The letters my son wrote before he died in Dacia made generous mention of you, although he was clever enough to do so in veiled terms that he knew only I would understand. And now you have returned to Rome with the fire of revenge bright in your eyes, even though you have no idea where to find the men upon whom you would visit your violence?'

The young Roman's tone hardened, no longer deferring to the status of the man to whom his words were directed.

'I will find them, Senator, with or without the help your son told me you would be able to offer. And *when* I find them, I fully intend to subject them to the same indignities my father, my mother, my brother and my sisters suffered before they died.'

Sigilis sat back and stared at him with grim amusement.

'That's more like the way I'd expect a man of your class to express himself, under the circumstances. So, a tribune with a propensity for righting old wrongs, and a centurion set on vengeance for his dead family. That would be a combination to strike fear into the men responsible for the destruction of your family, I'd say, *if* they were to find out that they were being hunted. And what sort of supporting cast do we have for this pair of furies?'

He looked across the remaining members of the party with an expression turned bleak again, locking gazes with each man briefly before speaking.

'Two more soldiers, officers to judge from their apparent confidence, both scarred and both with the look of killers.' He smiled grimly at Julius and Dubnus. 'Some men find themselves unable to kill, even when their lives are at risk in battle, and others kill but are for the most part unchanged by the experience, apart from the inevitable nightmares and regrets that will trouble them until they come to terms with the fact. And there is a third type of man, gentlemen, men whose eyes lose just a hint of what they were before once they have stood toe to toe with other men and taken their lives, while also gaining something else that's impossible to define. I saw battle more than once with the Thirtieth, and I saw sleepy farm boys become executioners in the space of one swift engagement, once they'd undergone their blood initiation. Their eyes were just as yours are now, windows on souls with some small part torn away and replaced with something else, no more evil than they were before, just with a fraction of their humanity excised. They scared me more than the enemy we were fighting, if I'm honest with you . . .' He smiled bleakly. 'Which was the point at which I realised I probably wasn't fitted to military service.'

The senator laughed grimly, shaking his head and turning his attention to the remainder of the party.

'And a trio of barbarians, each of you bigger and uglier than the last. Now that isn't something a man sees every day, not without chains and collars at any rate. You, with your hair worn in a topknot, you are a German I presume?'

The slave nodded.

'I am Arminus, Senator. I was taken prisoner by the tribune in battle, and he saw fit to spare my life and bind me to his service. Now I guard his back when he is foolish enough to leave it uncovered . . . which is often.'

Sigilis snorted a laugh.

'A slave with a sharp tongue in his head, and yet unmarked by any sign of the lash. Either your master is a gentler man than I'd imagined, or your service to him has value that outweighs such minor irritations. And beside you, a one-eyed man with more scars than I've ever seen on a warrior, looking back at me as if I am the subordinate in our brief relationship. Royalty?'

His question was directed at Scaurus, but Martos answered the question directly, gesturing to the tribune.

'I was a prince, before I was betrayed to this man by a mutual enemy who took my throne and abused my people. The tribune spared me from the execution that was my fate by rights, and now I am an ally of Rome.'

'And the eye?'

'I ran amok among my enemies when we recaptured my tribe's capital, and I lost my reason to an unthinking rage for their blood. When I regained the ability to think clearly I was painted from toe to hair with the blood of a score of dead and mutilated men. My eye was the price that my god exacted for that revenge, it seems . . .' He paused for a moment, shaking his head sadly. 'I would have traded every life I took to have found my son alive, but my betrayers had already thrown him from the highest rock to feed the crows, and caused my woman to take my daughter's life to spare her the indignity of their abuse. She killed herself . . .'

'And you felt unable to remain in the place where your family was destroyed as a consequence of your having trusted this betrayer?'

Martos nodded.

'I have entrusted my future to these men.'

The senator nodded, turning his attention to the last of them, taller than either of the other two barbarians by a head and whose body was almost a parody of the human frame, such was its size and musculature.

'And you, the giant. Who are you?'

The big man's voice rumbled a one-word reply.

'Lugos.'

He pondered Scaurus's turned head and raised eyebrow for a moment before speaking again.

'My pardon. Lugos, *Lord.*'

Sigilis chuckled, the flesh around his eyes crinkling with the pleasure.

'There's no need to call me "Lord", barbarian, I do not expect you to obey the formalities of our society since you are so clearly a newcomer to our city, although a simple "Senator" would suffice if you feel such a need.'

Sigilis returned his attention to Scaurus.

'And now, with our introductions made, perhaps you will indulge the wishes of a grieving father and tell me how it was that my son came to die in Dacia? I received the official communication, of course, and my senatorial colleague Clodius Albinus was able to fill in a few of the gaps given that he was in command of the Thirteenth Legion in Dacia, but you are the first men I've met who were actually present when he died. Tell me all about that day, if you will, and provide me with some feel for the way in which my Lucius went to meet our ancestors?'

The second of the audience chamber's two doors opened, on the other side of the wide airy room from which its four occupants had entered. They had been ushered one at a time into lamp-lit opulence by the stony-faced praetorians who had escorted them through the palace, then left to their own devices with the politely delivered, but nonetheless firm instruction to wait for their host. A single man dressed in a formal toga stepped inside, glancing around the table at which they were sitting waiting for him. All four stirred in their seats at his entrance, even the gladiator who prided himself on his self-proclaimed imperturbability shifted his position minutely, and the newcomer smiled at their reaction, opening his hands in greeting.

'Gentlemen, my apologies for keeping you waiting. Affairs of state, you know how these things are . . .'

The squat, ugly man sitting at the table's far end cracked a slow, lazy smile.

'We know, Cleander. There's not one of us that hasn't kept a man waiting for one reason or another, to make him nervous or to piss him off.' He gestured to the man beside him. 'Even our gladiator here has been known to toy with a man for a while before taking him down with a single sword blow. The old tricks are the best, eh?'

The imperial chamberlain smiled back at him.

'Indeed, although I'm not exactly here to have one of your fingers cut off for refusing to pay your protection money, am I Brutus?'

The other man shrugged, but before he could answer another of them spoke, his voice crisp with authority, clearly used to issuing commands and having them obeyed without question. He had removed his armour when he received the summons to attend the gathering of the Knives, but his red praetorian tunic and the vine stick lying on the table before him told their own story as to his role in the palace.

'He's right though, isn't he, Chamberlain? My tribune, the praetorian prefect above him, you, you're all in the game of imposing your will on other men. We used to work for the praetorian prefect, but now that the Emperor's stuck the blunt end of a spear through him and left him to bleed to death in the dark, we work for *you*. That's the point you're making, I assume?'

Cleander dipped his head in a sardonic acceptance of the truth in the centurion's statement.

'You assume correctly, Fabius Dorso, since I will certainly be the man keeping your new prefect waiting from now on, when I feel the need to impress him with my authority, since I shall be his master in all but name.'

The praetorian dipped his head in return and kept his mouth shut, wisely deciding to let his fellow conspirators mount any further challenge to the chamberlain's apparently unquenchable ambition. Unsurprisingly, it was the man sitting opposite him, resplendent in a spotless toga of the very finest quality wool, who took up the unspoken challenge. His voice was acidly sardonic, a weapon perfected over years of debate.

'However will you find the time to manage the detail of such a large and important role, Aurelius Cleander?'

'Ah, well you know how it is as well as I do, don't you, Senator?' The chamberlain smiled back at him with a shrug. 'Some men, Asinius Pilinius, have a talent of making a life's work out of something that needs nothing more than a swift decision and the right delegation. There's always someone with the right skills and motivation to carry out your orders, if you look hard enough for him, and I seem to have the skill of finding that man and putting him to work. I'll answer the big questions and leave the people that I select to enact them to work out how best to achieve my desires. A bit like the way we'll be working from now on, in fact. I'll decide which men are deemed to have committed treason, and you four can deal with them in the usual fashion, take your share of the spoils, have your fun and make sure that the throne receives the condemned man's assets. Speaking of which . . .'

He unrolled a scroll, stretching out the silence as he read down the items listed. At length he looked up again, gazing around the table at each man in turn, his stare level and direct.

'Gentlemen, I think it's important that we have a clear understanding at the start of this new relationship. It seems to me that you may have become used to taking a little more than your agreed share under Prefect Perennis, to judge from this inventory of the proceeds of his estate.' He raised the scroll. 'There's nothing *really* valuable missing of course, all of the major assets are accounted for, but there seems to be a disappointing amount of portable wealth that has, for want of a better term, gone for a walk.' He looked up at the four men around the table, pursing his lips in amusement at his own joke, although not one of them had showed any sign of reaction. He shrugged. 'Here's an example. There seems to be a suspiciously small number of slaves available to sell, and none of them, it appears, the prefect's family members. Which is disappointing since, as we all know, the children of the rich and famous command such high prices from the men who appreciate that sort of thing.'

The praetorian's eyes flicked momentarily to look at the senator, and Cleander smiled inwardly at the realisation of one of his suspicions.

'Yes, there are a great many valuable items that we expected to recover which seem to have gone missing, which has piqued the emperor more than a little. A rather splendid collection of antique swords which apparently dated back to the time of Alexander, for one thing. He had his eye on those, as you can imagine. There were some rather splendid marbles that seem to have vanished too, rather pornographic in nature and, while not all that valuable they were, it seems, on the list of things that the emperor expected to receive as his compensation for the former prefect's treason. Their absence has left him somewhat piqued, and a piqued Commodus is not a safe man for any of us, you can be assured of that. So, given that the safe delivery of the Perennis estate to the throne was your collective responsibility, I think the fairest solution to this problem is for you all to waive your fees and percentages for the job on this occasion, as a means of reassuring the emperor that you remain his loyal and attentive servants and that you intend to protect *his* property somewhat better next time. I'm sure that you can see the sense in that, or would anyone like to argue the point? You would like there to be a next time, I presume?'

The gladiator Mortiferum stirred indolently in his chair and brushed a crease from his perfectly tailored tunic before speaking, casting a sidelong glance at Pilinius, and the chamberlain shuddered at the lack of life in the younger man's eyes.

'You want me to accept the loss of my share because our senatorial colleague here and his cronies like to play their games with the wives and children of our victims?'

He hooked a thumb at the subject of his words, who stared down at the table's highly polished surface without any sign of emotion. Cleander shrugged, affecting disinterest in the swordsman's statement.

'No, I expect *you* to accept the loss of *your* share because *you* failed to ensure that *your* side of the bargain was honoured.'

The gladiator's head turned slowly until his eyes were boring into the chamberlain's, and while Cleander knew that the deliberate movement was all part of a well-practised persona, he was unable to suppress a shiver of fear at the malevolence that radiated from the man's expression.

'You know that I could be over this table and breaking your neck before you could summon your guards?'

Forcing a smile onto his face, Cleander shook his head.

'I think not. I gave very explicit instructions before entering this room with exactly such an act of foolishness in mind. If any of you offer me violence, then you will *all* be physically restrained, at whatever the cost in guardsmen since they are a commodity of which I am blessed with a fairly inexhaustible supply. Not killed, gentlemen, but rather deliberately kept alive and imprisoned, after which all of your families will be gathered here to watch you being crucified in a private arena. And then, while each of you twists and writhes on his cross, your loved ones will be violated in the most appalling ways you can imagine in front of you, before being ripped to pieces by savage animals which will literally eat them alive. Not the usual lions and tigers though, I have something far more entertaining in mind for that eventuality.'

He paused, enjoying the silence that had fallen across the room.

'The dog, while far less effective as an instrument of execution than a lion, is a far more terrifying prospect when employed in numbers. All one needs to do for a really good show is to paint the most sensitive parts of the victim's anatomy with a nice thick paste of blood and set half a dozen ravenously hungry animals loose upon them. Need I describe the unendurable agony that your family members will undergo while their helpless writhing bodies are being torn apart under such loathsome circumstances? I would have thought that you in particular might enjoy the irony involved in that image, Senator Pilinius.'

The praetorian, the senator and the gang leader were all in his pocket, that much was evident from their stunned expressions, although the gladiator merely sat back, his malevolent stare steady on the chamberlain. Cleander grinned back at him.

'And there it is, eh Death Bringer? To have control of brutal men it is simply necessary to promise the application of even greater brutality to those they cherish. And nobody does brutality quite like the Roman state, which makes the whole thing rather simple. But that's not enough for you, is it? You have no family other than your brother, do you, nobody for me to threaten with the most degrading of deaths? You think you're immune from this leverage. So for you, great champion of the arena, I have a different fate planned. You and your brother will both be crucified, but you'll be cut down from your crosses before you choke yourselves to death, to ensure that you'll be compos mentis for what will follow. You will be cut to pieces very, very slowly, one thin slice every hour over a period of months. Imagine, first your fingers, one coin-thin piece at a time, then your toes, and then, one cut after another, your limbs, with each wound promptly cauterised to prevent you bleeding to death. I'd imagine that it might take the best part of a year for you to die, and all the while you'll be cursing yourself for succumbing to a moment of anger. When you're not screaming in agony and then babbling out your insanity, that is.'

He raised an eyebrow and waited, keeping his face utterly immobile as the gladiator stared back for a moment before nodding slowly.

'Good. I'm glad we understand each other. Be clear, gentlemen, that should any mysterious fate befall me, no matter how innocent you may all seem in the matter, the punishments that I've described will be delivered with swift and brutal efficiency. Call it my last wishes.'

He stood, rolling the scroll up.

'And let's have no recriminations, eh? The missing items are more than enough to cover your respective shares, so sort it out between you and prepare yourselves for the next time the emperor calls upon your services. After all, I think I can state with some assurance that you don't really do the things you do for the money, do you?'

'So, Centurion, my son died an honourable death?'

Sigilis had waited until the story of the battle on the ice had been fully recounted before swiftly turning to Marcus, knowing that Scaurus would be more inclined to protect him from any unpalatable facts. Well aware that he would be likely to face the question at some point, Marcus had long since rehearsed the answer that would disguise the fact that the senator's son had died with a spear in his back.

'He died in combat with overwhelming numbers of the enemy, Senator, beset on all sides. Your ancestors will have been proud to receive him into their company.'

Sigilis stared hard at him, and the young Roman fished inside his toga, pulling out a heavy gold pendant which he held out to the older man.

'When I was able to recover his body, this was still around his neck. I expect he would have wanted it to be returned to you.'

The senator looked down at the yellow disc lying on his palm, the finely detailed representation of the god Mars standing on a field of vanquished foes. He swallowed, shaking his head slowly.

'That pendant has been in my family for generations, all the way back to the conquest of the Dacians, when Trajan decided to bring that accursed land into the empire. My grandfather had it made with gold he took from a nobleman he killed on the battlefield, and passed it on to my father when he served. I wore it in Caesarea, and Lucius took it in his turn when he joined his legion. He was my only surviving son, after the plague from the east took both of his brothers from me, so there are no members of my family left to bring it further honour. Wear it for me, and every time you remember my son you will perpetuate his memory.'

Marcus nodded, folding his fingers around the heavy metal disc.

'Your son wrote something on the ice before he died, using his own blood. Something he wanted me to remember . . .'

Sigilis raised an incredulous eyebrow.

'With his *blood*?'

Marcus nodded soberly.

'As I said, Senator, he was a strong-willed man. He was dying, he knew that much, but he was determined that I should act upon something he had told me a few days before. It was—'

The senator's voice was suddenly cold.

'Did this by any chance involve a group of imperial assassins who call themselves "The Emperor's Knives"?'

'Yes sir.'

Sigilis pursed his lips.

'I didn't intend for him to overhear my discussions on the subject of the revival of that most despicable of imperial habits: the murder of wealthy men under the pretext of their having betrayed Rome, followed by the confiscation of their assets.' His lip curled. 'Confiscatory *justice*. I feared – and I still fear – that my estates would eventually attract the attention of the men behind the throne, and I wanted to spare him from having to live under the shadow of that threat. But, with all the persuasive power of an only son, he somehow managed to convince me that he should hear what it was that my informant had to say—'

Scaurus interrupted.

'Your *informant*? I believed that you had employed an investigator?'

The senator shook his head slowly.

'You've evidently been away from Rome too long, Tribune, and paid too little attention to your history lessons as a younger man, I suspect. There is a ruinous state of affairs that is forever waiting its time to flourish under the absolute power of imperial rule. It happened under the emperor Tiberius, when Sejanus came to dominate the city, it happened twice more, under Nero and Domitian, and now we see the same bloody horror rear its head once more under this dissolute fool Commodus. It is rule by the informant, gentlemen, a rule that terrorises the worthy man of good character who commits no other crime than to be wealthy, when the empire is as near to bankruptcy as it can be without actually collapsing. We invaded Dacia back in Trajan's day, and the failed attempts before that, simply because it had enough gold to sustain the empire for a century or more, enough to allow five emperors to rule equitably because they had the riches of the Dacian mines to support their rule, and therefore had no need to indulge in underhanded methods to support their budgets.'

He sighed, shaking his head.

'And now? Now the empire has fallen prey to the eastern plague, and the population is reduced in size so drastically that tax revenues are falling too fast for the mines' output to compensate. Add to that an emperor who spends gold on his own pleasure like water, and the recipe was almost complete. All that was needed then was for someone in a position of high power to realise that the only thing standing between the emperor and anything he wanted were the limits of that man's conscience.'

His gaze flicked up to Marcus, an apologetic grimace playing across his face.

'Your father was a man of such impeccable character as to have earned his passage to Elysium several times over, and yet he was one of the first victims of that unrestrained absolute power, as Perennis started down the path of blood that has led us to where we are now. His wealth was well known, and besides that Commodus openly coveted his villa on the Appian Way. After all, it had its own baths, water supply by aqueduct, even a hippodrome. What more could any emperor want from a country residence!'

His laugh was bitter.

'And now we members of the senatorial class live in fear that we will be the next to face false accusations, to find ourselves blinking in the torchlight in the middle of the night when Commodus's hired killers come for us and our families. Yes . . .'

He nodded at the look on Marcus's face. 'The *Knives*. So you pull a face when I say the word "informer", Tribune, and yet that is what Rome has become once more, a city in the merciless grip of the informers. There are more than enough men of this craven nature within the Senate itself for me to be utterly confident in predicting that this emperor has sowed the seeds of his own downfall, creating a monster that must eventually eat itself. And so I have suborned one such man, a well-placed individual who spends most of his time listening for the tiny whispers of dissent that can be used to accuse an innocent citizen of treason for a crime no greater than discussing the days of the republic, before that misguided genius Octavian declared himself Caesar Augustus because he saw no other way to liberate Rome from its apparently endless cycle of civil wars than by concentrating absolute power in the hands of a single man. I pay my informant well, and in return he ensures that I know exactly where the Knives will make their next visit.'

He signalled to the butler, who in turn made his way back to the house and opened a door behind which a hooded figure had been waiting. As the informer made his way across the garden, Sigilis turned back to the Tungrians with an apologetic grimace.

'I didn't want to introduce you to him until we had the rest of our business out of the way. He tells me that you parted on less than ideal terms when you last met.'

Marcus's eyes narrowed in suspicion as the informer stopped before them, his face almost invisible in the shadow beneath the hood.

'*You?*'

Arminius started as he realised who the senator's man was, surging off the bench with a snarl only to find himself face-to-face with Scaurus.

'You are a guest in this man's house, Arminius, and still my slave to command! You *will* respect his hospitality!'

The hooded man laughed softly.

'How very decent of you, Tribune Scaurus. It seems that the senator's trust in your sense of Roman manners was justified . . .'

The voice was unmistakable in its lazy drawl, and Marcus was shocked to find his thoughts snapped back to a woodland clearing two years before, in the wake of a victory over the fearsome Venicone tribe. He looked at the informer in disbelief as the man reached up and pulled back the hood to reveal a face that Marcus had never expected to see again.

'Well now, centurion, are you Tribulus Corvus or Valerius Aquila today?'

The young centurion spat out the man's name through bared teeth, seething at the sight of the man.

'*Excingus!*'

'Let's make one thing clear, shall we?'

The gladiator put a finger firmly on Brutus's chest, prodding him hard enough to put a scowl on the other man's face.

'Keep your bloody hands off me! You want to be a bit more careful who you—'

'No, I really *don't*.' Mortiferum leaned in closer, his voice pitched low so that his words were only barely audible, and the praetorian took the senator by the arm and drew him away until they were well out of earshot. 'Don't imagine that just because your thugs have scared a few shopkeepers and pimps into submission I wouldn't go through you and your muscle like a hot poker though a week-old corpse.' He prodded the gang leader's chest again, the smaller man's body jerking with the force of his gesture. 'Try me, and find out just how many of your men are willing to stand against me and my followers. The people of this city worship me and my brother, and I reckon that they'd tear a man to pieces just for raising a blade against us outside of the arena. I might be wrong, of course, but that's a calculation for you to make. You two, come here!'

The guard centurion strolled up with the senator following slowly behind him, and the gladiator looked about him at the three of them.

'I've been denied my fee from the other night because you three couldn't keep your sticky fingers to yourselves. Dorso!'

He pointed at the praetorian, who returned his stare levelly.

'You're probably the least of it, but even you had your share. You and those two guardsmen who follow you round, you carried away enough of Perennis's antiques to more than cover your fee, if you were to sell them on.'

The soldier nodded.

'That's true enough.'

The accusing finger turned to point at the senator, who pouted back at him with an expression of haughty disinterest.

'And you, Pilinius. I counted thirty or more slaves being led away by your men, not to mention the prefect's wife and children. I don't care what perverted games you get up to with them, but that many bodies represent a lot of gold. More than your share, in fact.'

The patrician shrugged.

'I think you'll find that possession is the guiding principle here, my friend.'

The gladiator grinned savagely, reaching out and taking a handful of the other man's toga to pull him close.

'And I think you'll find that the guiding principle is in fact a foot of sharp iron, if you're not careful, Senator. Think on it.'

He pushed the suddenly white-faced Pilinius away from him with a grimace of disgust, spinning back to push his finger into Brutus's face.

'But you, *fool*, are the stupidest bastard of the three of you. Only you could have taken the simple task we've been given and turned it into an act of wholesale robbery!'

'What—'

The gladiator poked him again, harder, looking round the three of them with a snarl of anger.

'Do you think I'm truly stupid, just because I choose to live in a ludus cell, rather than buying out my contract and splashing my money on a big house and a dozen slaves? I'm the smartest of all of us, you pricks, because I keep my head down and don't attract attention to myself, something you might do well to consider. You . . .' He poked the guardsman. 'With your antiques collection hidden in that private museum no one's supposed to know about. You . . .' He turned to the senator. 'Slaughtering the families of the nobility for the fun of your gang of upper-class perverts! And you!' He snapped down on the gang leader, his expression so fierce that the other man was unable to avoid recoiling. '*You*, you stupid bastard, slinking back once we'd all left and bribing the guards who'd been set to keep the Perennis house intact to look the other way. Since when were you interested in *art*?'

He looked around him in disgust.

'Which is why, gentlemen, you're all going to dig in your purses and come up with my share, or you'll all live to regret it. Work it out any way you like between you, but make sure that gold's in my hands before sunset tomorrow or there'll be excitement. And trust me, you'd much rather life remained dull.'

He turned and stalked away, leaving the other three staring at each other with a combination of calculation and bemusement.

The informer smiled and bowed, opening his hands in welcome.

'Tiberius Varius Excingus, to remind you of my full name, former centurion in that exalted corps of spies, blackmailers and murderers that masquerade under the title of "Grain Officers" – and now, given my rather abrupt and vigorously enforced resignation from my former employment as a result of failing to bring you to justice, Centurion, present-day informer. Funny how things turn out, isn't it?'

Scaurus stared at him for a moment before turning to their host with a look of polite disbelief.

'I'm not sure you understand quite how dangerous this man is, Senator. The last time we crossed paths with him, he was in the company of a praetorian centurion, a remorseless murderer, and they were tracking down my centurion here on orders from Prefect Perennis. They abducted his wife with the intention of using her both as bait to ensure his compliance and distraction to make his murder easier. This man Excingus threatened my family here in Rome, and if he had not made his escape in the confusion of the resulting fight, one of us would undoubtedly have put a sword in his guts and left him to choke out his last breath in a puddle of his own blood.'

The former frumentari shrugged, nodding equably as Sigilis replied.

'That's more or less as he's already related to me, as it happens.' The senator fixed Scaurus with a penetrating stare. 'I won't make any excuses for his previous behaviour, Tribune, but neither will I apologise for using him to my own ends. Varius Excingus is without any shred of doubt quite the most amoral man I've ever met, but that complete lack of any decency provides me with information that has already saved lives.'

Marcus shook his head in incredulous disbelief.

'And you *trust* him?'

The senator laughed, and pointed a finger at Excingus.

'Trust? *Him?* Do you take me for a madman?'

The informer shrugged again and pursed his lips, nodding sagely.

'I'll answer that one, if you'll allow me the liberty, Senator?'

Sigilis gestured for him to continue, and Excingus smiled at Marcus as broadly as if their previous encounter had ended in vows to meet again someday, rather than with a bloodbath of the men sent to find the younger man and kill him, with the grain officer only managing to escape with his life by the narrowest of margins.

'No, Centurion, the senator would indeed be most unwise to repose any trust in a man with my singular lack of principles. But I'll remind you of a discussion we had the last time we met, when you asked me how it was that I could live with the things I do. You may not recall my answer, since I'd imagine that you had bigger matters on your mind, but I know what my response was because it's the same one I give every time I'm asked the question. My only guiding principle, Valerius Aquila, is to make the best of this life in any way that I can. And if that eventually means that my informal provision of information to Senator Sigilis comes to an end, then so be it. For now, however, the senator's generous rates of payment are more than sufficient to ensure my complete discretion.'

Scaurus shook his head.

'I wouldn't trust you any further than I could see you, and even then I'd be keeping my sword to hand. But if the senator has chosen to employ your services I'll go this far and no further: while you're under his protection I will not seek to harm you in any way . . .' He turned and played a hard stare across the men behind him. 'And neither will any of my men. However . . .' He stepped closer to the informer, until their noses were almost touching. 'If I so much as suspect that you're planning to sell us out, then I'll personally see to it that you vanish without trace.' He turned away to retake his seat with a disbelieving shake of his head. 'I doubt you'd be missed.'

Excingus nodded equably.

'Exactly as I would have expected. And perhaps I can lighten the moment a little?' He fished in a pouch attached to his belt and held out an iron key to Marcus. 'Here.'

The young centurion stared at it for a moment without making any move to accept the offering.

'A key? To what?'

The informer smiled back at him, reaching for his hand and pressing the key into the palm.

'Ask your wife. And now gentlemen, if you've come in search of information, perhaps we can get past the initial awkwardness and get down to business. Senator?'

He held out a hand, and the older man nodded, signalling to his butler once more. The slave reached down into a wooden box that had been concealed in the shrubbery, taking out what appeared to be a purse. Crossing the garden with the same impassivity he had displayed before, he placed it in his master's hand with a bow. Sigilis acknowledged him with a grave inclination of his head.

'Thank you. I expect you have pressing duties to attend to in the house? Please don't allow this inconsequential matter to impede you in their completion.'

The butler bowed again, and to Marcus's eye it seemed that a look of relief crossed his face as he turned to make his way back through the garden and into the domus. Excingus held out a hand.

'Poor man. He's more than intelligent enough to understand the heat of the fire you're playing with by employing my rather dubious services, isn't he?'

The senator dropped the purse onto his level palm with a resigned expression.

'I suspect he looks askance at having to pay you to provide information to these men for which you've already received a substantial sum.'

Julius frowned at the informer, still far from happy with such an unexpected turn of events.

'You make him pay simply to talk to us?'

'I do. And so would you, in my place. Every additional person I share my knowledge with presents an additional risk of my being betrayed . . .'

The first spear barked out a laugh.

'And wouldn't that be ironic!'

Excingus simply continued speaking, ignoring the barb.

'. . . tortured for as long as I could stand the pain without descending into insanity, no matter what truth and lies I babbled in extremis, then summarily executed and dropped into a deep pit to rot, unmourned and most certainly unlamented.'

Sigilis coughed as if clearing his throat.

'And so, having been paid . . . ?'

The informer nodded.

'Apologies, Senator, I was on the verge of becoming maudlin. As you say, to business.' He turned to address the Tungrians. 'I suggest that you abandon your prejudices, gentlemen, and pay especially close attention to what I am about to tell you, for I doubt that anyone else in Rome has either sufficient knowledge or courage to provide you with this information. There are four men who form the heart of the emperor's policy of propping his treasury up through "confiscatory justice" . . .'

He paused, waiting for any of them to comment, but none of the men sitting around him responded.

'These four men bring a particular combination of skills and experience to the services they perform, not to mention their shared disregard for the humanity of their victims. They are, in different ways, intelligent, driven and successful men in their own fields, positively charming in one case, and none of them displays any overt signs of mania, and yet they are all, in their own ways, just about the most dangerous men in the entire city. Perennis gathered them to him when it became clear that the throne would not survive without financial assistance, reasoning that his own praetorian guard might be likely to draw the line at being ordered to slaughter a man and then either kill or enslave his entire familia. He gave them whatever it was that he believed would motivate them, but we can simplify that down to two things. Firstly he offered them money. A lot of money, for a relatively small amount of effort. And secondly, he extended to them the opportunity to do exactly as they pleased with some of the most respected families in Rome. Think about that for a moment, and then ask yourself how many men in the city would jump at the chance to have free licence with the women of a household like this one. Never mind the novelty of taking the mistress of the house by force while her husband's corpse is still cooling on floor, think of the possibilities for a man with that inclination. Daughters, female slaves . . . more than enough helpless female flesh for everyone, eh?'

He met Marcus's stare of hatred with an equally frank gaze.

'I won't ask for your forgiveness for pointing out the obvious, Centurion, since I know that your own family was one of the first to suffer such a catastrophic end, but I *will* point out that I'm simply explaining these men's motivation. Hate me for doing so if you like, but at least recognise the realities of what you're dealing with. You might find that understanding of some value, once you've mastered your repugnance at the knowledge.'

He shrugged in the face of the young centurion's obdurate stare.

'Anyway, as I was saying, there are four of them. So, where shall we start?' He mused for a moment. 'Perhaps with the most dangerous of them, a gladiator who fights under the name of Mortiferum . . .'

The Tungrian party left the senator's house in the late afternoon, Excingus having departed via a well-disguised and heavily built door in the garden wall that opened into the storeroom of a shop on the other side of the wall. Senator Sigilis had stared at the departing informer's back with the expression of a man who urgently needed to wash his hands.

'I rent the shopkeeper his premises for next to nothing, on the condition that the occasional person comes and goes in a rather more discreet manner than knocking at my front door. Of course, using it to admit a man like that means that I can't rely on it for a discreet exit myself, should the need arise, but then it's not the only secret way out of the property, as I'm sure you can imagine.'

The Tungrians had taken their leave of him with much to consider, and even Dubnus was uncharacteristically quiet as they made their way back towards the Ostian Gate. Less than a hundred paces from the gate's massive archway, a pair of men stepped out onto the cobbles before them, one of them instantly recognisable as Senator Albinus, Scaurus's former commander in Dacia and, since the confrontation in the emperor's throne room that had ended in the praetorian prefect's death, his sworn enemy. The other was Cotta, a muscular man with a weather-beaten face and the leader of Albinus's personal bodyguard. A former legion centurion, he had established a small but effective team of bodyguards composed of the pick of the soldiers retiring from his legion and had been bankrolled by Albinus, to whom he therefore owed a considerable debt in both money and gratitude. The tribune stepped forward to meet them, holding up a hand to halt his men.

'Senator Albinus. Centurion. To what do we owe this unexpected pleasure?'

The big man stared back at him in silence for a moment before waving a hand and calling out a command that rang out down the suddenly empty street.

'Bring them.'

As he strode off down a side street, ten or so men emerged from the shops to either side and behind the Tungrians, another half-dozen strolling out into the street behind Cotta and blocking the road to the gate. Each of them was carrying a tight role of cloth, and Julius raised a hand waist-high, waving it downwards in a clear signal to his men to refrain from reaching for their knives. Cotta smiled easily at Scaurus, gesturing to the side street.

'Best if you come with us, Tribune. The senator wants a word with you, and it's probably best not to have the plebs gawping at us while he's doing it, eh?'

He shot Marcus a knowing glance and then raised a questioning eyebrow at Scaurus, who looked appraisingly at the men encircling his command.

'Your men *are* armed, I presume, Centurion Cotta?'

The retired soldier snapped out a terse order.

'*Swords!*'

Each of his men pushed a hand into their roll of cloth, pulling a short infantry gladius from the fabric. Scaurus shrugged, his glance at Marcus eloquent, then turned to follow Albinus up the street. Thirty paces brought them out into the shade of a small square surrounded on all sides by insulae, and the burly senator waited silently in its middle until his hired swordsmen had herded the Tungrians into the enclosed space, grinning as Julius and Dubnus looked about them with expressions promising swift violence, clearly restrained only by the weapons that hemmed them in on all sides.

'Perfect, isn't it? I own the buildings around us, of course, which is why there aren't idlers dangling out of every window!'

Scaurus looked about him with thinly disguised amusement.

'Always one for the theatrical, aren't you Senator?'

The big man smiled broadly back at him, revelling in his domination of the situation he had so clearly engineered.

'Oh, I wouldn't call this theatrical, Rutilius Scaurus, I'd be using the term *gladiatorial*.'

The tribune shook his head in bemusement.

'Gladiatorial? What, do you intend to turn your men loose on

us in some sort of pitched battle? What do you think the urban
cohorts will make of that? I'm sure they'll be along soon enough,
given the spectacle you made back there with so much illegal iron
on the street.'

Albinus shook his head, his smile widening.

'Oh, I doubt it. The local tribune has managed to get himself
rather deeper into debt than might have been sensible, so once
I'd purchased that debt it was relatively easy to persuade him to
keep his men clear of the area for rather more time than I need
for this carefully constructed scenario to play out. Centurion?'

Cotta stepped forward, dropping a sword at Marcus's feet with
a clang of iron on stone, and shot him another pointed glance
that narrowed Julius's eyes with a sudden suspicion. The senator
pointed to the weapon, his voice taking on a triumphant tone as
he barked out an order.

'Pick up the sword, Valerius Aquila! Pick up the sword, and
prepare to fight for your life!'

Scaurus stepped forward, his expression hardening, and a pair
of Albinus's ex-legion bodyguards moved swiftly to block any
attempt to approach their master.

'What the fuck are you playing at, *Decimus*?'

Albinus grinned back at him from behind his protectors.

'Nice try, Rutilius Scaurus, but no amount of impudence is
going to distract me from delivering this lesson to you. Perhaps
the death of your pet centurion will teach you to exercise a little
more humility with your betters. Now, pick up the sword, *boy*, or
I'll have my man here kill you anyway, defenceless or not.'

Marcus smiled tolerantly in the face of the insult, bending to
take the sword by its hilt.

'Be warned, Roman . . .' Martos stepped forward to stand
beside Scaurus and raised a finger to the senator, his expression
murderous. 'If this man is harmed here while you hide behind
those swords, I will find you and tear your heart from your body
with my bare hands!'

Albinus raised his eyebrows in mock terror.

'And how will you make that happen, when a word from me

will see you dead on the cobbles beside him? Would anybody else like to consider volunteering for a place in the closest refuse pit? No? Let's be about it then! Centurion!'

Cotta stepped forward, reaching forward to tap Marcus's blade with his own with an evil grin.

'You ready to fight, youngster?'

Marcus looked at Scaurus with a helpless shrug, discarding his toga on the square's cobbles for one of the senator's bodyguards to remove.

'This has been coming ever since this man and I laid eyes on each other that night on the Palatine Hill, Tribune.'

Scaurus nodded in reply, and the two men dropped into fighting crouches, each of them watching the other as they circled slowly. Cotta looked his opponent up and down, nodding reluctant approval at the younger man's muscular frame.

'You're a fighting soldier, from the look of you. Britannia, was it?' Marcus nodded, focusing intently on the other man's eyes as Cotta shook his head in apparent disgust. 'Full of tunic lifters and arse pokers, Britannia. It's a shame your old man didn't send you somewhere character-forming before they murdered him.'

The younger man feinted forward with the point of his gladius, watching in cold amusement as his opponent stepped back and parried easily.

'What, somewhere like Dacia?'

Cotta snorted his ridicule.

'Dacia? Land of cock suckers. And don't bother telling me about Germania either, the whole province is riddled with queers. No boy, if you want to be a real soldier then you need to get sand in your crack!'

He advanced swiftly, testing Marcus's defence with half a dozen swift strokes, grinning as the Tungrian retreated closer and closer to the men guarding the exit from the square. As his seventh cut sliced in low, aimed at Marcus's left thigh, the younger man tossed his sword into his left hand and parried it wide, stepping quickly forward and twisting to punch a half-fist into Cotta's right bicep and then straightened his body, using the momentum to swing a vicious back fist at the grimacing centurion's face. Cotta barely managed to duck out of the blow's path, giving the younger man all the time he needed to swivel to his right and hook the veteran's leg with his extended left boot. The older man fell back onto the cobbles with a grunt of expelled breath, the sword falling from his nerveless fingers.

'Get at him! Kill him while he's down!'

Ignoring Dubnus's bellowed encouragement, Marcus bent to pick up the fallen weapon, watching as Cotta recovered his footing and took a sword from each of the two nearest men. The veteran stood out of sword's reach for a moment, breathing hard and appraising his opponent with a new respect.

'I heard you were taught to fight by a soldier and a gladiator. Which one of them taught you that little move?'

Marcus closed the distance between them, scraping the soles of his boots across the cobbles.

'The soldier, as I recall. He wasn't up to much when it came to swordplay, but he knew more than enough dirty tricks.'

Cotta raised his blades.

'Sounds like my kind of man. The gladiator must have been a faggot if he taught you to fight with two swords.'

Marcus shrugged again, his eyes locked on the points of Cotta's blades, stepping closer still until the tips of their swords were touching.

'He made a start. I perfected the style in a few battles that you might have heard of while you were lazing around Rome protecting fat-arsed politicians from their own stupidity.'

Both men lunged forward at the same time, their swords meeting each other and pushing wide as the soldier snapped his head forward to butt Marcus in the face, but the younger man was ready for the attack, ducking his head and then wrenching it back up to deliver a heavy blow to Cotta's chin. The former soldier staggered backwards, spitting blood from his bleeding tongue and spluttering with laughter.

'You cheeky young bastard!'

Marcus held his swords out ostentatiously wide of his body, then dropped them onto the ground with a clatter of iron on stone.

'Shall we go to bare knuckles then, Cotta, or have you had enough?'

The older man shook his head, tossing his own weapons aside and feeling his jaw.

'Fuck that, I think you've already broken one of my teeth.'

Albinus bridled, pointing at Marcus with a face contorted with rage.

'What the *fuck* are you doing, Cotta?! *Kill* him!'

The ex-centurion wiped the blood from his mouth, shaking his head with a tight smile of warning.

'If you want him dead so badly, Senator, you feel free to try to kill him.'

The senator put his face inches from the veteran's, his features twisted by a snarl of rage.

'I paid well for you to set up this cosy little business, Centurion, which means that I *own* you. Either you do as I tell you, and leave this traitor's spawn bleeding here in the street, or I'll have you . . .'

Something within Cotta snapped, abruptly and without warning, and Scaurus pursed his lips as the ex-soldier took a handful of his sponsor's toga.

'Paid me well, did you?' He reached into his belt purse and dropped a handful of gold coins onto the cobbles. 'There's your money, Senator!' He pulled the toga down until Albinus's head was level with his chest, bending to snarl into the terrified man's ear, grinding his words out through gritted teeth. 'And you'll have me what? Killed?' He laughed down into the senator's face. '*Hah!* I'll disembowel any man you send after me, and then I'll strangle you with the bastard's guts!'

Scaurus strolled forwards, patting Cotta on the arm.

'I think your point is made, Centurion.'

Albinus staggered back, propelled by a push from Cotta's broad hand, pointing a trembling finger at the former soldier.

'If I can't buy you, I'll buy your men! Ten gold aurei for the man that puts his iron through that treacherous bastard's guts!'

There was a moment of silence as the former soldier stared at him with naked disgust, until at length he spat bloody phlegm across the coins scattered at his feet. When he spoke his voice was cold, as if his anger had burned out and been replaced by something harder and more implacable.

'You could offer them fifty apiece and I doubt you'd have any takers. We've something in common, these men and I, which is that we've all faced the empire's enemies together, and bled, and lost our mates, while all *you've* ever done is sit on the back of a horse and come up with a succession of good ways for us to risk our lives to bring *you* glory. So I'll give you two choices, Senator. You can leave now, with an escort of my men to protect you from the kind of scum who'll take your purse and slap you about if you're lucky, and drag you away never to be seen again if you're not. Or you can open your mouth to say any words other than "*thank you, Cotta*" and then you'll find out what it's like to walk home alone with me following ten paces behind you, making sure every pimp, thug and murderer on the street knows just how vulnerable you are.'

He stood and stared at the white-faced Albinus, his expression still taut with anger.

'Just three little words. Any *fucking* time you like, Senator . . .'

As the silence stretched out, Dubnus turned to a grinning Julius with a look of confusion, shaking his massive head in puzzlement.

'Am I missing something here?'

2

'Was it the dream again, my love?'

When Felicia awoke the next morning she found Marcus sitting by their quarter's window, his eyes fixed on the lights burning on the walls of the city, the impending dawn still no more than a smudge of grey on the eastern horizon. She had lived with him for long enough to know what would have awoken him early, and the answer to her whispered question was already clear in her mind even as she asked it. He nodded, smiling across the room at her in the light of the single lamp burning in the corner, although his expression was more haunted than happy. She beckoned him with a crooked finger.

'Come back to bed then, before Appius wakes up.'

He padded softly across the room and slid in behind his wife, warming his feet on her calves despite her quiet protests, pulling her to him and cupping her breasts in one hand.

'Our meeting with Lucius Carius Sigilis's father yesterday seems to have inspired the ghosts of my family to greater efforts. Twice last night and again this morning they came to me in my dreams, showing me their injuries and entreating me to take revenge for our family's slaughter.'

She snuggled back against him, reaching a hand up to stroke his face.

'My darling, you know that this is just—'

'Just my sleeping mind, working on the events of the day and tortured by my guilt at having survived such horror?' Felicia turned to face him, her expression growing more troubled as she realised that he was staring at the wall behind her. 'That may well be the case, but I cannot live the rest of my life haunted by these dreams, whether they be my family's ghosts or simply my mind's way of coping with the reality of their horrific murders while I escaped from their killers. And now that I have the names of the four men who murdered my father, my brother, my sisters, and probably sold the rest of our household into slavery, I am bound to act against them.' He paused before speaking again, knowing that his wife had to know the news he had kept to himself the previous evening. 'A gang leader, a praetorian, a senator and a gladiator: Brutus, Dorso, Pilinius and Mortiferum. We got their names from an unlikely source though.'

Felicia frowned at something in her husband's voice and sat up in bed, turning to look down at him in the light of the lamp burning by their son's cot.

'Unlikely?'

Marcus looked up at her, clearly trying to gauge her possible reaction before he spoke again.

'Excingus.'

Her eyes opened wide with shock.

'*Excingus?!* The grain officer who kidnapped me and tried to murder us both?'

'The same.'

'And you didn't . . . ?'

'Kill him? He was under Senator Sigilis's protection. And taking my knife to him wouldn't have changed anything, although it would have prevented me from learning the identities of the men who killed my father.'

Felicia looked back at him with a grave expression.

'And if he hadn't told you, you wouldn't be planning to kill them all, would you? This can only end badly Marcus . . .'

He smiled back at her.

'I understand your fears, but I really don't have any choice in the matter. And besides, I have Cotta and his men behind me now.'

'Yes . . .'

Her tone was dubious.

Marcus laughed softly. He and Cotta had grinned at each other in the square the previous evening, both of them deaf to Albinus's furious protests as he'd been led away, and the veteran centurion had wrapped him in a bear hug that had squeezed the breath from his body before pushing him away and looking him up and down.

'I thought you were dead, boy, but look at you, scars and all! You can join my little team of lads any time you like!'

Marcus had stared dumbly back at him, smiling through unexpected tears and was unable to reply. After a moment's silence, Scaurus had coughed politely behind him.

'Ah . . .'

Cotta had straightened, throwing a salute at the senior officer. 'Tribune, sir!'

'There's no need for all that, Centurion, given that you're retired.'

The veteran had shaken his head dismissively.

'A man leaves the legion when his twenty years are up, Tribune, but the legion never really leaves the man, does it, sir? Tattoos, scars and memories of dead friends, they're all still there until the day you die, and since me and my lads are time-served veterans for the most part, we can recognise a fellow professional when we see one. Which means that we'll be saluting you, and calling you "sir" just as long as we're working alongside you.'

Scaurus had stepped forward, regarding Cotta from beneath raised eyebrows.

'As long as you're working beside us, Centurion? Whatever gave you *that* idea?'

Cotta's return stare had been utterly unabashed, the tolerant gaze of a career soldier when challenged by his less-experienced senior officer.

'The fact that me and my lads know Rome a damned sight better than your boys, no disrespect intended, First Spear.' Julius had nodded his head gracefully, a corner of his mouth lifting in a wry smile at his tribune. 'The fact that I've burned my bridges with one of the most powerful senators in the city by failing to obey his order to kill the centurion there. And the fact that I've been beating common sense into this officer of yours since he was half the age he is now, although to little avail given the stories I've been hearing about him from your soldiers, once they've got a few cups of wine down their necks. Put simply Tribune, you need us. And I'm not about to allow that silly young bugger to get himself killed in Rome, not when he seems to have made a tolerable job of surviving everything else that's been thrown at him up to now.'

Once the usual dawn officers' meeting was out of the way, Julius went to report to Scaurus as to the two cohorts' strength, gathering Marcus and Dubnus to him with a glance as he left the transit barracks' cold and slightly dingy headquarters building. The tribune greeted them cheerfully, inviting them to join him at his breakfast table where, Marcus was unsurprised to discover, Cotta was already busy ploughing his way through a plate of bread and honey. Scaurus gestured to the empty seats around the scarred and stained table.

'It isn't often that a man gets to eat fresh bread of quite such good quality, and the honey's excellent. Help yourselves, gentlemen.'

He turned to the silent Arminius, who was doing his best to avoid attention in the room's corner.

'Don't you have a young pupil to be teaching the martial arts?'

The German gave him a hard stare before shrugging and making for the door.

'I'll find out what you're planning soon enough, don't worry.'

Cotta raised an eyebrow at the door as it closed behind him.

'You're not beating that slave enough, Tribune.'

Scaurus shrugged.

'I tried it, in the early days of our relationship, but it seemed to make no difference to his attitude, and it all proved to be rather a lot of energy expended to little effect, so I stopped bothering. He means well enough . . .' He took another piece of bread and popped it into his mouth, looking at Marcus with a quizzical expression, and when he spoke again his tone was deceptively soft. 'So, are you determined to see this through then, Centurion?'

Marcus heard the edge of formality that underlaid his tribune's apparently disingenuous question, and straightened in his chair.

'Yes Tribune.'

Scaurus shook his head, his lips pursed in grim amusement.

'Relax man, I'm not intending to try to stop you, far from it, I just want us all to be very clear on the likely consequences of taking action again these men. For a start, there's our new friend Cleander to consider. I'd imagine that the imperial chamberlain will smell a rat pretty quickly if we start killing the men whom the emperor depends on to carry out the task of confiscating the assets of the wealthy, wouldn't you? And that's before we ponder what the reaction of the remaining members of the group might be when they realise that they're being hunted. If so much as a hint of our involvement in the deaths of any of these men becomes known, then we can expect a violent reaction, to say the least, and even if there's nothing to point to us, they're all going to get paranoid very quickly when the first of them dies.'

The young centurion nodded earnestly.

'Exactly my thinking, sir, and I wasn't planning on any sort of assistance from anyone within the cohort. This is my debt to pay, and I'll—'

'Really?' Julius shook his head in disbelief. 'You were expecting that we'd happily sit here getting fat on too much wine and spicy food, while you blunder round this cesspit of a city in search of revenge? What were you going to do, rely on that arsehole Excingus to see you right? That bastard would sell you out in a heartbeat; this man Cleander's thugs would snap you up and you'd never be seen again. Is that what you were planning?'

Marcus shook his head.

'No Julius. Credit me with a little intelligence. I know Rome as well as any man, and I have more friends in the city than you might imagine.'

Scaurus pursed his lips, tilting his chair back.

'All the same, the idea that you might dispose of four men with that sort of profile on your own is perhaps more than a little ambitious. I don't doubt that your man Cotta here will be able to provide you with some assistance, but perhaps it might be worth reviewing what Excingus told us yesterday and apply a little thinking as to just how hard they're going to be to kill, shall we?'

He raised a single finger.

'Let's start with Senator Pilinius. The man lives in a veritable fortress, far better protected than Sigilis's domus. Entrants to the place come through the front door in the main, past enough of his bodyguards to weed out any attempt at infiltration without very much effort. If they don't want to be seen participating in that sort of entertainment, and they're of sufficient importance, then they slip in via the back door, where his men will all be armed to the teeth with much less work to do and therefore twice as vigilant. Given how Pilinius and his cronies get their enjoyment, I'd imagine that they'll be more than a little jumpy too. All of which would tend to indicate that he might be easier to get to on the street, but then as I recall it, Excingus told us that the senator goes everywhere with at least half a dozen bodyguards, which means that we'd have to attack him with twice that many men to be sure of getting to him. And I don't know about you, but the idea of a running knife fight on the streets of the capital doesn't really fill me with any enthusiasm for the likely success of such a desperate roll of the dice, or for our anonymity being preserved for that matter.'

He raised a second finger alongside the first.

'Then there's Dorso. As a serving guard officer he lives in the praetorian fortress which, I hardly need to remind you, contains several cohorts of soldiers, only one of which is on duty in the imperial palaces at any time. Getting into the fortress will be hard enough, but killing Dorso without alerting anyone else, and then getting out of the place undetected? That's a rather tall order.'

Two fingers became three.

'Then there's Brutus, who would be the worst of them if it weren't for Mortiferum, but let's worry about the gladiator in a moment. His "Silver Dagger" gang must number at least a hundred men, and that's before we factor in loosely affiliated members of dozens of the smaller gangs that he tolerates in return for payoffs and instant obedience when he demands it. As soon as he hears of the deaths of any of the others he'll shut himself up in whatever slum bolt-hole it is that he uses when the heat's on, with enough men gathered about him to make anything less than a full-blooded attack nothing more than a waste of effort and lives. And there's no way I can take the cohort on to the streets of Rome, we'd bring the Guard down on us like a hod full of bricks falling from a sixth-floor building site.'

Cotta puffed out his cheeks, shaking his head at the scale of the difficulties they faced.

'And as you say, if the other three are going to be hard . . .'

Towards the end of their briefing the previous day, Excingus had turned the conversation to Mortiferum, shaking his head at the very prospect of getting to the man.

'It can't be done, gentlemen, because the Death Bringer, crafty sod that he undoubtedly is, hides himself away in the very last place on earth that he's going to face any threat. He spends all his time, when he's not out slaughtering rich families for the emperor that is, in the Dacian Ludus.'

Marcus and Scaurus had nodded their understanding, exchanging gloomy glances, but the remainder of the party had stared back at him blankly.

'The Dacian Gladiator School? No? I see I'll have to explain. There is an arena in Rome, gentlemen, of which you might have heard. It is the Flavian Amphitheatre, built by the emperor Vespasian a hundred years ago, the foremost arena in the empire and big enough to allow sixty thousand people to watch the games that are held there. Thousands of gladiators fight in that arena every year, and each one of them has to be trained and prepared for his moment on the sand, which is why there are four official training schools for gladiators clustered around the building. There's one called the Gallic School, where they turn out the heavy boys, fish men, hoplites and the like; there's the Morning School, where they train men how to fight wild animals . . .'

'Why the *Morning* School?'

The informant had shrugged at Dubnus with an expression of irritation, his tone sarcastic.

'Perhaps it's because the beast fights tend to take place in the morning?'

The Briton had shrugged back as he replied, clenching a massive fist.

'And perhaps I'll impose on the senator's hospitality just a little. Don't forget that I can still remember the stink of the shit running down your legs from the time I missed killing you by no more than a dozen heart beats.'

Excingus had nodded, his smile suddenly dazzling.

'A fair point, Centurion, and well made. Shall I continue?'

He'd waited for a moment and then resumed his lecture.

'Then there's the Great School, which turns out all of the smaller fighting specialisms, spearmen, chariot drivers, net fighters and so on, and last of all, there's the Dacian School. With a name like that their specialism's rather obvious, I suppose: lightly armoured sword fighters, originally Dacian prisoners when Trajan set it up since he'd just conquered the province. And if the other three members of this very exclusive gang look hard to get to, just consider how hard it'll be to get to a man who lives in a cell alongside another two hundred or so like him, all of them worshiping him as the deadliest fighter in the place . . .'

Marcus nodded at Scaurus, taking another piece of bread from the breakfast table.

'Excingus was probably correct yesterday when he said that getting to the gladiator's going to be impossible. I think it's probably for the best to concentrate on the others for the time being, and wait to see if Fortuna offers us any way to get to this "Death Bringer".'

Dubnus shifted in his seat.

'And if you're right, then the violent death of the first of them will alert the other three that someone's coming after them.'

Scaurus nodded.

'It seems likely, Centurion. After all, it's not as if there's any shortage of men with a motive, even after their victims' households

have been torn apart. Distant relatives who weren't actually quite
so distant, friends determined to have revenge for the dead . . .
there must be a fair few men in Rome who'd be more than happy
to catch any one of these men off guard.'

The bearded Tungrian stared at the map for a moment.

'It seems like we'll have to make sure that the first couple of
deaths look like accident or incident then, won't we . . . ?'

When Marcus had given his wife Excingus's key earlier that
morning, her first reaction had been stunned silence. After a
moment, he realised that she was welling up with tears.

'That's the key to your father's house in the city?'

His wife's reaction was wordless, a tear trickling down her cheek
as she fought for composure, and Marcus spoke gently into the
silence.

'And now a calculating animal like Excingus hands it to me
with a smile. What to make of that, I wonder?'

Taking a deep breath Felicia managed to speak, her voice
trembling with emotion.

'I doubt it would stand much comparison with what you were
used to when your father was still alive, but it's a quiet enough
little place, and I was *so* fond of it before we left Rome. I grew
up in that house, and it's my last link to my mother and father.
When I married that bastard Bassus, he took the key off me and
sent it to his brother. He said that we would live in it when he
was posted back to Rome, but that we might as well get some
use out of the place in the meantime. I'd all but forgotten it, with
everything that's happened since, until you put this key in my
hand. But *how* did that awful man come by it, I wonder?'

She fell silent again, lost for words at having the means of
access to a house she had long since abandoned to the wreckage
of her previous marriage. Marcus shook his head.

'He wouldn't tell me, but I doubt there was very much subtlety
to his taking possession of the place. Where is the house?'

'It's up on the Aventine Hill.'

He wiped her tears away and took her hands in his.

'I'll ask Cotta if a few of his brighter men might escort you into the city later, and you can go and have a look around the place and decide what you want to do about it. Half a dozen scar-faced veterans ought to be enough to deter the most determined of thieves. Why not take Annia with you, and make a morning of it? After all, there are plenty of shops on the way, and you were saying that you needed to find some better clothing than the stuff you've been wearing for the last few months. Why not treat her, and buy the children something new to wear as well?'

Rummaging in his purse, he'd spilled a handful of coins onto the bed between them, eliciting a tearful smile from his wife.

'Well now, Centurion, what a nice idea! It'll make a change from all of our money going to fund exotic swords and the latest fashion in helmets . . .'

When Marcus had requested Cotta to lend him a few of his men to escort Felicia and Annia into the city, and explained the real purpose of the expedition, the veteran's response had been swift and unequivocal.

'That's a job for me. If your women and children are going to set foot outside of this barrack then I'll be the man escorting them, me and a few of my *choicest* lads, the best combination of bright and nasty, if you know what I mean. If Senator Albinus wanted you dead to teach the tribune here a lesson, then I can't see him hesitating to kill or abduct your wife if he sees the opportunity. And from what you've told me about this Excingus character, he won't hesitate to inform the senator about your circumstances if he gets to hear about our little falling out with Albinus. So I think I'll take a careful look around the place before there's any talk of moving in, shall I?'

The Tungrian officers watched as the small party headed for the barracks' gate before turning back to their training duties. Scaurus and Julius had decided to maintain the two cohorts' fitness and weapons skills regimes while the Tungrians were in barracks awaiting their next orders, reasoning that whether they were sent back to Britannia or elsewhere in the empire, they were likely to be in the thick of the action soon enough. The hulking first spear nodded happily at the sight of his men working hard at their weapons skills.

'Not bad, if I say so myself. Not bad at all.'

The transit barracks' parade ground had been converted into a training area, with dozens of pairs of men sparring with wooden swords while others looked on and offered derisory advice before taking their own turn. A piece of open ground alongside the barracks had been commandeered, with twenty wooden posts having been erected at one end. In front of each post a tent party of seven or eight men took turns to hurl their spears at the man-sized wooden target from twenty paces; those men who missed being detailed off to run the field's perimeter with the offending weapon held over their heads before rejoining their comrades.

'Infantrymen sweating their bollocks off in the sunshine. What an agreeable sight!'

The three centurions turned to see who was addressing them to find themselves under the scrutiny of an amused-looking man in an anonymous tunic, his boots scuffed and battered from continual heavy use and only cursory attention. Every inch as tall as Dubnus, if nowhere near as massive in build, his heavy beard was flecked with grey, and his brown eyes were set in a face whose skin resembled aged leather.

'And you are?'

The newcomer nodded to Julius, ignoring the harsh tone of his question with a good-natured smile.

'Avidus, Centurion, Third Augusta. You?'

The first spear stared at the other man for a moment with his eyes narrowed, and for a moment Marcus spoke quickly, convinced that Julius was on the verge of setting about the stranger with his vine stick.

'You're not an infantry officer, are you Avidus?'

The weathered face turned to look at him with its amused expression untroubled by Julius's glare.

'Infantry? *Fuck* no! I, sonny, am one of that glorious band of men who get the opportunity to march at the head of the legion.

I'm a pioneer, gentlemen, or to be more precise, a surveyor in command of a detachment of pioneers.'

Dubnus looked at him for a moment with an expression of growing glee before finding his voice.

'You're a road mender!'

Avidus rolled his eyes, shaking his head in disgust.

'And here was me thinking that I might receive a more sympathetic reception from a member of the auxiliary forces, but clearly one bone-stupid grunt is much like every other, whatever armour they're wearing.'

Julius found his voice, putting out his hand.

'Julius, First Spear, First Tungrian Cohort. I was going to beast you for being out of uniform but since you've clearly got a pair on you, I won't waste my breath. What brings you to a transit barracks on the road from Rome to Ostia?'

The surveyor shrugged.

'You tell me. Me and my lads have been here for the best part of a month.'

'You mean you've been sent here and then left to rot?'

'You've got it. Nobody seems to know where we're supposed to be going. We were detached and shipped over here in response to a request for skilled manpower from a legion somewhere else in the empire, but by the time we got here the original request had been mislaid.' He shook his head in disgust. 'Knowing my luck, we'll end up getting sent somewhere really fucking cold where the only work going is digging out blocked latrines.'

Dubnus spread his hands in a gesture of disbelief.

'Come on though, a whole month without orders this close to Rome? Have you *seen* the whores they've got in there?'

Avidus nodded wearily.

'We felt the same, for the first fortnight or so. A different girl every night, and how long was that likely to last, so we went at it like prize-winning chariot horses until we realised that we weren't going anywhere any time soon. Now our money's more or less gone, so we're limited to the occasional walk into the city to look at the women.'

'Look but don't touch?'

The surveyor nodded knowingly.

'Exactly. A duck's arse and an unpaid whore, the two tightest holes you'll ever find.'

Julius stroked his chin thoughtfully.

'So you know the best places to go, where the value's to be found, right?'

Avidus nodded, pursing his lips in the manner of a man considering his expertise.

'You could say that. We certainly spent enough silver finding out where not to go!'

'In that case, Centurion, I think we can provide each other with some mutual service. You can tell me where best to send my lads when we allow them into the city for a wet, and in return I can ask my tribune if we can spare a little money to let you spend the rest of your time here in some degree of comfort. Which legion did you say you were from?'

The surveyor grinned, pulling up his tunic sleeve to reveal a tattoo of a winged horse.

'The Third Augusta, First Spear, Africa's finest!'

Excingus walked into Albinus's office between a pair of the senator's newly recruited bodyguards and bowed deeply, but when he raised his head the expression on his face was anything but subservient. His host waited in silence while the informant looked about him with naked curiosity.

'So, do you like what you see?'

Excingus smiled gently at the acerbic note in Albinus's voice, and inclined his head slightly as he replied.

'Indeed, Senator, you are clearly a man of some considerable learning, if I am to judge by the large number of scrolls on your shelves.'

Albinus laughed tersely.

'You understand flattery then.'

The informant bowed, his lips twitching in another smile.

'Indeed I do, Senator. And a good many other things besides.

Although the principal subject I thought to discuss with you is *betrayal*.'

The senator sat back.

'Is it indeed? My secretary gave me to believe that you have something greatly to my advantage to offer?'

Excingus pursed his lips.

'I believe that I can persuade you that the two are one and the same, Senator Albinus, if you'll allow me to explain?'

Albinus waved a patrician hand.

'I can spare you a little time.'

'Thank you. I will deal with betrayal first. As the story has reached my ears, your previous associate Gaius Rutilius Scaurus has of late chosen to play a game more suited to his own ends than those which align with your own, and without any of the respect that ought to be forthcoming from a man in his position to a man of your status. I believe that a recent attempt to teach him some manners foundered on the rock of another man from whom you might have expected somewhat more loyalty than was in fact displayed when the moment arose?'

The senator's face darkened.

'If you've come to rake over the coals of my recent disappointments then you'll very shortly find yourself on the street with a new set of lumps, *Informer*.'

Excingus opened his arms wide, tilting his head in question.

'I simply seek to establish the facts, Senator. I've found in the past that the redress of injustices is more easily achieved when all parties are clear as to what needs to be achieved.'

He waited for a moment, and at length Albinus waved a hand.

'Then continue. But move to what you have to offer to my advantage sooner rather than later.'

'Indeed. To illustrate that potential benefit, I must first point out that I have achieved a position of some influence with your senatorial colleague Gaius Carius Sigilis. He purchases information from me with regard to the activities of certain men who are, shall we say, loosely aligned with the imperial household. Men who provide the emperor with their services when the occasional need arises for prominent members of society to be removed from their positions.'

Albinus leaned across the desk.

'Sigilis buys information from you in order to understand whether he's likely to be murdered for his estate?' The informant nodded, and Albinus leaned back, looking at the ceiling as he spoke again. 'As well he might. I may be safe from such threats due to my recent services to the imperial chamberlain, but he most certainly is not, from the rumours I hear. But what does this have to do with Scaurus?'

Excingus smiled.

'The tribune has recently contacted Senator Sigilis, and indeed visited him, with the sole intention of using the information I sell to him to track down and murder each of the four men who have become known as "The Emperor's Knives". He is accompanied, as I am sure you will be aware, by a young centurion who goes by the name of Corvus, although he is in reality the son of Appius Valerius Aquila. And this young man is consumed with the need to have his revenge for the destruction of his family. It seems that now his main target is dead, killed by the emperor as a direct consequence of your recent visit to the palace bearing an obscene quantity of stolen gold, he has resolved to deal with his father's murderers in person.'

'And the benefit that this might have to me is . . . ?'

'Given that I will be feeding Scaurus and Aquila with the information they will then use to hunt down the emperor's tame killers, it would be remarkably easy to point them in the direction not of their intended target, but instead send them head first into a trap of our devising.'

Albinus nodded slowly.

'I like the way you think, Informant. And your price for delivering these ungrateful bastards into that trap would be what exactly?'

'A modest one. I'm already very well paid by Senator Sigilis. This is more of a personal matter than for financial benefit, so I can afford to make my fee for the job a modest one. Shall we say ten aurei in gold, to be paid when Scaurus and Aquila are delivered to you?'

The senator smiled.

'Two and half thousand sestertii? I would have paid a good deal more, but you know your own price. So, our interests are aligned then, it seems. Very well, come back to me when you have information upon which I can act. And in the meantime, I think it best if you do not come to my house again. Send a messenger with a proposed meeting place, somewhere public, and we can contrive to meet and talk with a lower profile than will be the case if you're seen entering my property.'

Excingus inclined his head again.

'As you suggest, Senator.'

'There's no need for you to struggle with all that baggage, Domina. My young lads will be happy to carry your purchases for you.'

Cotta had been a provider of bodyguards to Rome's ruling class for long enough that he knew the ways of the women with whose safety he was entrusted, which was why he had brought a pair of his younger recruits along on the shopping expedition. Taking Felicia's load of fresh food and clothing from her, he distributed it between the pair, giving them a significant look as he did so.

'And what you learn from this, my lads, is that you never take just enough men on a shopping trip. Someone's going to end up holding whatever it is that you've all gone looking for, and we can't allow good manners to compromise good security, can we?' He turned back to Felicia with a smile. 'Shall we be on our way to your house, Domina?'

The doctor raised an eyebrow at him.

'There's really no need to call me that, Centurion. My name will make a perfectly adequate form of address.'

Cotta shook his head with a tight smile.

'Sorry, Domina, but whether you appreciate it or not, you're the wife of a Roman senator, even if he has fallen on rather harder times than we might like. One of these days that young man's family name will be restored to its previous status, and I see no reason not to show due respect to it in the meantime. Now, where is this house of yours, exactly?'

They climbed the Aventine Hill at a pace sedate enough for the women, who were both carrying their children, until at length Felicia stopped and stared in a combination of hope and trepidation at a house of moderate size in its own modest garden, protected from casual onlookers by a six-foot-high wall. Overlooked on three sides by larger buildings, it was nevertheless clearly still the sort of residence that only a well-to-do and moderately wealthy family would be able to afford. The district was of a decent quality, with nothing more jarring to Cotta's trained eye than a pair of roughly dressed children playing with a wooden hoop on the corner. Taking in Felicia's determined expression, the veteran officer held out his hand.

'Perhaps I ought to go in first, Domina. After all, we have no idea what might be waiting for us inside. If I might have that key please?'

After a moment's thought she surrendered the iron key, and with a word to his men to stay on their toes, Cotta opened the gate and looked cautiously through it into the garden, a well-tended paved affair with flower beds and plant pots that had clearly been weeded and watered recently. Slipping though the gateway he pushed the door back into place, sliding a dagger free from its sheath on his upper-left arm as he turned to stare at the house. Padding softly across the paving slabs, he walked quickly to the window on the front door's left, peering through the glass's rippling sheet into the room behind it. Nothing was moving. Walking on round the house, he found a door, and, lifting the latch, was surprised to find it unsecured. It opened with a gentle creak that announced his presence as obviously as if he'd knocked, and, abandoning stealth, he went through the doorway with his knife held ready to fight, finding himself in a well-sized kitchen which had been left scrupulously clean by the previous inhabitants. The plates and pans were clean, and stacked in orderly piles, and there was none of the smell of rotting food he had expected. Moving through the house he found the same situation in every room, the floors clean, the furniture well ordered, but no trace at all of whoever had lived in them previously, and after a few minutes of cautious searching he shrugged, sheathed the knife and made his way to the front door.

'The place is empty, my lady, with nothing more troubling than a slightly musty smell – will you come inside?'

The two women walked into the house, Felicia looking about her with a mix of wonderment and disbelief, while Annia simply stared at the rooms' relative opulence with unabashed approval.

'Soft furniture? Glass windows? It's *lovely*, Felicia! You're so lucky to have something like this!'

The doctor nodded in a distracted manner, turning to Cotta with a questioning look.

'And there's no sign of anyone?'

The veteran shook his head.

'No, Domina, nothing to give any clue as to who was living here before the place was emptied out.'

She took a deep breath and then, with a brisk nod of her head, made a decision.

'Very well. This house belonged to my father, and since it was never transferred to my first husband's ownership whoever was living here would have known they had no claim to it when he was killed in Britannia. They were probably just hoping that I would never return.' She looked about her again with a new light in her eyes. 'This is my house, and I shall treat it as such. Centurion, would you be so good as to inform my husband that I will be taking up residence here for the period that we are in Rome, and request him to send up my clothes?'

'I will, Domina. And I'll arrange for a standing guard to be mounted on the property, to make sure that you and the child aren't bothered.'

Felicia smiled gratefully at him before turning to Annia.

'Will you stay and keep me company? It'll make a pleasant change from repairing broken soldiers, and we can pretend that we're a pair of respectable Roman matrons for a few weeks.'

Her friend looked about her for a moment before grinning at her mischievously.

'I think I can bear the hardship, *Domina*. After all, the last time I had a proper roof over my head for more than a day or two I was running a brothel, so it'll make a novel change not to have a constant stream of soldiers walking in with their pricks tenting their tunics.'

A spluttering cough behind Annia coupled with the sudden look of amusement on her friend's face made her turn back to Cotta, whose face was a picture of uncontrolled amazement. Putting a hand on his arm, she favoured him with a sweet smile of apology, patting his hand as he fought to regain his composure.

'I'm sorry, Centurion, I'd completely forgotten that you don't yet know who we are and where we've come from. You and I must sit down over a glass of wine when all this excitement is done with, and I'll explain the finer workings of a city whorehouse to you. And now, Domina, shall we go and have a look around your lovely home?'

'So tell me, Centurion, what sort of engineering tasks are you and your men trained for?'

Avidus raised his eyebrows disapprovingly.

'Which tasks, Tribune? *All* of them.'

Scaurus frowned.

'Really? I thought there was a tendency to specialise?'

The engineer nodded knowingly.

'Well there is, sir, except you have to bear in mind that we're the only legion on the entire African coast. If our bridge builders got lost in a sandstorm or ambushed by the locals, then we'd look a bit stupid when we got to the next river only to find the crossing burned out. Third Augusta has always made sure that every man in the pioneer centuries is skilled for every task, which means that when we're not on the march we don't get sent to bring in the harvest or pick stones out of the fields, we get sent for training.'

'So you can genuinely carry out any feat of military engineering?'

Avidus raised a hand and tapped the raised digits with his other forefinger.

'Road repair, mining operations, bridge building, demolition, siege machinery—'

'What, you mean you can build bolt throwers?'

He smiled at Dubnus's question.

'Yes. But not just bolt throwers. Siege towers, catapults, battering rams . . . you name it, me and my lads can do it.'

Julius walked around the desk from his place behind Scaurus to stand beside the engineer.

'The centurion here and his men have been lost in transit, from the look of it. Wherever it is they're supposed to be going, the idiots in charge of manpower appear to have mislaid the instructions. And of course, no one wants to ask the grown-ups for fear that they'll end up looking stupid. So at some point soon these poor sods are going to find themselves being assigned to a legion just to get them out of the way before they become a serious embarrassment, and they'll probably end up freezing their balls off in Germania. Or . . .'

He let the word hang in the air, and Scaurus raised a jaundiced eyebrow.

'*Or?* Or what? The last time we had this discussion I ended up taking on a half-century of disgruntled legionaries and having more than one interesting conversation with the Sixth Legion's camp prefect. It was a good thing he was feeling friendly towards us in the wake of our having rescued their eagle from the Venicones, wasn't it? And now you want me to quietly fold a century of engineers into your cohort?'

'It's only thirty men, tribune, hardly a—'

Scaurus shook his head.

'No you don't. He's a centurion, they're a century. And what makes you think that the man in charge of troop allocations won't smell a rat when you slide this man and his soldiers up your sleeve?'

Julius's face went blank, and Scaurus's eyes narrowed in suspicion.

'You've already made the deal, haven't you?'

His first spear shook his head.

'Not my place to do so, Tribune, but the officer in question tells me that he's open to reallocating Avidus to us if we're happy to make a modest donation to his temple.'

He stared at the wall behind the tribune and waited for Scaurus's reaction in silence, knowing better than to attempt any form of persuasion on a man who he knew to be stubborn in the extreme once his mind was made up.

'So you've offered him a bribe?'

Julius shook his head.

'Not at all. I simply enquired as to where Avidus's century was likely to end up, and then let slip that we'd be happy to look after them for a while. The request for the donation was all his idea. Apparently they want to put in a new altar stone . . .'

'And you, Centurion? What do you think of the idea?'

Avidus shrugged.

'I'm a soldier, Tribune. I go where the army tells me to, dig holes while unfriendly natives practise their archery skills on me, fill them in again and then start marching. As long as our pay and conditions aren't changed, my lads and I will happily tag along with you for a while. Preferably somewhere warm?'

Scaurus frowned and turned away, looking out through the unshuttered window at the barracks buildings that faced the headquarters.

'I won't deny that you'd be useful to us . . .' He turned to face Julius. 'How much does this transit officer want then?'

A knock at the door interrupted Julius before he had a chance to reply, and one of Cotta's men was escorted into the room by the duty centurion, the battered pugilist Otho. Jumping to attention, the bodyguard explained that he had been sent to inform Julius and Marcus of the fact that their women had decided to remain in the city overnight, and would they mind sending up some clothing and bedding?

'Well now, I suppose that's not entirely unexpected. I don't suppose we should expect your ladies to stay cooped up in this rather stark barracks when there's a house on the Aventine Hill going begging, should we? Perhaps we might go for a look at this place, the three of us, and you, Centurion Avidus, if you fancy a walk.'

Scaurus grinned at his officers with the look of a man relishing the prospect of a break from the usual routine.

'And who knows, if we're really lucky, we might get out of the gates without an escort of jealous barbarians.'

Mortiferum was hard at work on the Dacian Ludus's practice ground when Senator Pilinius appeared at the door of the enclosed rectangle of sand-strewn ground on which they were sparring. He looked across the ranks of trainee gladiators as they toiled at the repetitive exercises that would build their strength and muscle memory, clearly searching for his comrade in the emperor's service.

One of the three men sparring with Mortiferum noticed his glance up at the senator, and relaxed his defence on the assumption that their opponent would break off the fight to speak with such an important visitor, but the champion gladiator seized his chance with the speed for which he was famed.

'Ignore him!'

He danced forward to attack with both swords raised, parrying the man's clumsy defensive cut with one blade while flashing the other wide to his right, forcing the other two back as he swiftly stepped in closer and shoulder-barged his victim over a hooked ankle to send him reeling. As the helpless gladiator sprawled on the hard, sandy surface, Mortiferum lunged in, tapped him delicately on the throat with the tip of his heavy wooden practice sword, and then flung himself forward, somersaulting over the fallen man's prone body to land on his feet with the downed fighter between them, spinning as his feet hit the sand and raising his swords to fight, shouting a command.

'Stop!'

He looked at his remaining two sparring partners with a questioning look.

'Look where we are. You, stay down, you're dead! You two, what do you do now?'

The brighter of the trainees answered first.

'We either split and come at you to either side of the corpse . . . ?'

Their teacher shook his head.

'Not the best answer, Felix. First rule of fighting as a pair – never fight alone if you can avoid it, or a good swordsman will simply kill one of you quickly and take his time with the other.'

'Or we could come at you together around him to one side or the other . . . ?'

The champion gladiator shrugged and grinned.

'We can play at going round and round him all day, I'd say. The crowd would lose interest in that long before I would, and everyone knows what happens when the crowd gets bored.'

Felix nodded glumly.

'We have to jump the corpse together?'

Mortiferum nodded.

'That's the best approach, nine times out of ten. One of you might stop a blade, but the other ought to get a chance to return the compliment, at least against a good to average opponent. In this case, of course, you'd both be dead before you could regain your footing. So, what was the mistake that Sergius here . . .' He prodded the recumbent trainee with the boot of his toe, shaking his head at the man. 'And you can stop giving me that look unless you want me to prod you somewhat harder with my sword next time. What did you do wrong that allowed me my opening?'

The fallen man, who had propped himself up on his elbows to listen, replied, 'I followed your eyes, Death Bringer.'

'You followed my eyes. In point of fact, you all followed my eyes, but I went for *you*, Sergius, for two reasons. Firstly, because you were the closest, and secondly because you were perfectly positioned so that your corpse would put an obstacle between me and these two. Get up then.'

Sergius rolled to his feet away from Mortiferum, knowing better than to put himself inside the reach of the deceptively dangling wooden swords. The champion fighter raised one of them to point at his training partners.

'Don't I keep telling you that watching your opponent's eyes only tells you where he's looking, not where his sword's going. You need to watch the point, ladies, nothing else matters.'

Sergius cocked his head in puzzlement.

'Don't we need to watch the other man's body as well?'

Mortiferum nodded, grinning back at his training partner.

'When you're ready my friend, yes you do. The time will come, if you're good enough, that you'll know what's coming next just from the set of a man's body, the twitch of a muscle, the way his eyes flicker—'

'But you told us not to look at the eyes!'

The champion gladiator's grin widened.

'Yes. I told *you* that, because *you're* only capable of watching one thing at a time. When *I* face a man, I can see everything, every twitch and blink, every little tell as to his next move, and I absorb and understand them all without ever having to think through what's happening. I see how much blood there is on the sand behind him, and whether he might slip if I push him backwards. I see the faces in the crowd, and whether they're shouting acclaim or just baying for blood. I see the men in the imperial box and what their mood is, so I can put him down quick if they're looking forgiving or let him make a decent show of it if I think they'll need convincing that he's worth saving. I can see the wounds I've already given him, how much they're bleeding and how dark the blood is, so I know how badly I've hurt him and whether it'd be kinder to kill him clean.' He grinned again, shrugging at the skill with which he had been gifted. 'I see so much more than you do, a little of which is training, but most of which is just how I was born. And now . . .'

He raised a hand to acknowledge Pilinius's presence, knowing that to delay any longer would be an unnecessary and highly visible snub to the man.

'And now I can see that the senator would very much like me to stop what I'm doing and go to see him. And while it's tempting to ignore him for a while longer, I see no value to be had from antagonising him.'

Dropping his training swords to the floor, he walked over to where Pilinius was waiting for him, making a cursory bow of his head in place of the usual obeisance, and fixing the senator with a direct stare.

'Senator?'

If the patrician was irritated at the apparent lack of respect, he hid it well.

'Mortiferum. Our partners in crime and I have come to an accommodation as to how we best deal with your request for payment of the sum withheld by our new patron.'

The gladiator nodded.

'And?'

'And so here . . .' He took a purse from the slave standing behind him, his secretary and accountant. '. . . is your fee. Feel free to count it.'

Mortiferum shook his head.

'There's no need for such vulgar display of lack of trust, Senator. I'm happy that any need for unpleasantness has been averted. After all, you do have a rather significant event looming in your calendar. Far better not to have it disrupted by any unpleasant occurrences, wouldn't you say?'

Pilinius stared at him for a moment before responding, and when he did his voice was acerbic.

'Quite so, Mortiferum, quite so. But it seems that the details of my evening's entertainment have spread beyond the circle of men I might usually have trusted with the information. I won't ask you where you obtained that tasty morsel of gossip . . .'

Mortiferum bowed his head again, knowing that Pilinius already understood just how unlikely it was that he would ever share such a sensitive source of information.

'. . . but I would ask you to pass it no further. The powerful men with whom I share these rather singular pleasures would be far from pleased to have their tastes revealed to the city. And *their* displeasure might be rather more punitive than mine.'

He turned and walked away, his slave shooting the gladiator a swift, unfathomable glance before turning to follow him. Mortiferum weighed the purse for a moment before tossing it to an identically dressed and equipped man who had walked up behind him during the conversation.

'Here you are brother, this is the fee from the Perennis job.'

His sibling caught the leather bag and also weighed it in his hand.

'I told you they'd crumble if you applied a little pressure. Even that halfwit Brutus is clever enough to know there's not a man in the city that could stand against Velox and Mortiferum.'

Mortiferum nodded, turning back to his sparring partners.

'Indeed. And now, since that little transaction has left me feeling dirty, I think I'll work up a sweat by turning these three inside out a few times. Remember girls, watch the blade, *not* the eyes!'

The Tungrian officers walked up the Viminal Hill as the sun was approaching its zenith, Julius wiping the sweat from his beard with an expression of disgust as Cotta walked out to meet them.

'This bloody city's too hot, too hilly and too bloody full of half-naked women for my liking.'

Scaurus looked about him, mopping at his damp forehead with a handkerchief.

'At least the ladies distracted our bodyguard enough to cause them to fall behind and thus spare us the usual running commentary on the goods in the shop window.'

Marcus looked back down the hill, to see that the single prostitute their escort had stopped to talk to had swiftly been joined by half a dozen of her fellows. Scaurus grinned knowingly.

'Well now, that'll be hard for them to walk away from without incurring the wrath of the ladies. I suggest we get inside, before the shouting starts.'

Cotta tipped his head to indicate an empty shop up a side road opposite the house.

'Before we do, Tribune, might I suggest that I stroll across and find out who that shop belongs to? If the price sounds sensible my suggestion would be that we rent it for whatever period will make the owner happy enough not to ask any questions as to what we're doing with it?'

Scaurus looked across the street, sizing up the indicated building.

'What an excellent idea, Centurion! Please do.'

The officers had only been inside the domus as long as it had taken for the barbarians to extricate themselves from the clutches of the group of irascible prostitutes and walk up the hill under a hail of abuse, look around them and declare that, whilst it was clearly a very nice house if you liked that sort of thing, there was really nothing quite like a wooden hall, when there was a knock at the door. Taking the arrival to be Cotta returning from his errand, Marcus answered it only to find Excingus waiting between a pair of the veteran centurion's men.

'Ah, Centurion, how nice to find you've already made your-selves at home. I was hoping that my small gesture wouldn't go astray . . .'

The informer waited, raising an eyebrow at the young centurion who stared back in bafflement for a moment before realising what it was that Excingus was waiting for.

'Wait here, Excingus. I cannot invite you into my wife's house without her knowledge and acceptance.'

Felicia frowned in disbelief, and as she opened her mouth Marcus was certain that she was about to flatly refuse the informant access to her house, but then she closed it again, smiled at her husband and nodded.

'By all means, Marcus, invite the man in.'

Her husband stood and stared at her for a moment in disbelief before turning back to the door.

Excingus smirked at him before walking into the domus, looking around with an expression of satisfaction.

'It's nice to see the fruits of one's labours being employed to good effect.'

Felicia greeted him with a stony face, her body stiff with anger.

'If you have fond imaginings of some sort of a reconciliation between you and I, you'd be well advised to disabuse yourself of them. I'll remind you that you participated in the murder of an innocent medical orderly and the abduction of a pregnant woman, in the company of a man whose clear intent was to rape and then kill me once I'd served the purpose of distracting my husband and thereby facilitating his murder.'

Excingus nodded.

'No more and no less than I had expected, Domina.'

'And if you expect your "only following orders" act to soften my ire, then again you are doomed to disappointment. You could have discharged your duty to seek and apprehend my husband without resorting to the depravity you had planned for me.'

'And which you avoided by the less than civilised expedient of ramming a knife up into my colleague's jaw?'

Felicia's face hardened involuntarily at the memory, and Excingus was unable to prevent himself from flinching minutely at the ferocity of her expression.

'Yes. And be warned, Informant, this is the first and last time that I will willingly accept your presence in this house. The next time you set foot inside my door, whether you come bearing either weapons or flowers, the result will be just the same.'

Excingus bowed.

'Understood, Domina. But before I take my leave, might I have a brief word with your husband's commanding officer? I believe he's here?'

Scaurus stepped out of the dining room with a curt nod to the informant.

'How can I help you, Varius Excingus?'

'How can you help me? Or how might I help you, Tribune? I have information for you, news of a potential opportunity to strike at one of the Emperor's Knives.'

'And you want money for this information?'

Excingus smiled, shaking his head.

'No, Rutilius Scaurus, I'm already quite satisfied financially.

Senator Sigilis has established a generous schedule of reimbursement to reward me for the reduction in their numbers, by whatever means . . .'

Scaurus favoured him with a jaundiced look.

'I see. And you're presumably hoping that we will be the "means" by which you collect your payment?'

The former frumentari shrugged.

'I had assumed that we had a shared interest. Perhaps I was mistaken in my belief that you were burning with the desire to right the wrong done to your centurion's father, and so many other innocent victims of these men's depredations?'

Scaurus nodded briskly.

'Very well, we'll play your game, Excingus, but not here. We'll meet tomorrow morning then, as soon after dawn as you like. Come to the transit barracks on the Ostia road and ask for the Tungrians. Your safety is assured.'

'I'd rather not—'

Scaurus barked a laugh, his grin lopsided with wry amusement.

'I'm sure you'd much rather not come onto our ground, but then the choice isn't yours to make, not unless you want to miss the opportunity to collect whatever generous bounty the senator has put on our, as yet unrevealed, target's head. And now, Informant, I'd say that your welcome here has reached its limit. I suggest you leave before the doctor here changes her mind, and requests me to have you killed as recompense for the orderly whose murder you so casually ordered. It would be a request I would find hard to refuse.'

Excingus nodded dourly and turned for the door.

'If you guarantee my safety then I will come to your camp. But be aware, gentlemen, that should you break that vow I will have left a very clear trail to your door.'

'One more thing, Informant . . .'

He turned back in the doorway and made an exaggerated bow.

'How might I help you further, Domina?'

Felicia walked forward and stared into his eyes.

'What did you do with the previous occupants of this house?'

Excingus laughed softly.

'Ah, so now that you have possession of your father's house, you wonder what price was paid to allow you to walk back in. Worried that I had your former husband's family put to the knife, are you?'

She held the stare, her lip curling in disgust.

'It did cross my mind.'

His face creased into an affronted frown.

'Then put it *out* of your mind, madam. This is Rome, not the sort of frontier village you've become used to, and I am most assuredly not given to the wanton acts of murder that are the emperor's preserve. Your former brother-in-law and the rest of his family are safely tucked away somewhere not too far from here.'

He turned and left without waiting for a reply, leaving the Tungrians staring after him and the barbarians in particular fingering the hafts of the knives they had secreted about them. Julius shook his head in disbelief, raising an eyebrow at Scaurus.

'*Really*, Tribune? We're going to work with him after what he did in Britannia? He'll sell us out without any hesitation whatsoever.'

The senior officer answered, still staring at the door through which Excingus had made his exit.

'I see little choice. As of now we don't even know which of the four of them he has in mind for this "opportunity", so we either take the chance he's presenting, with an eye open to the risk he presents, or we let it pass and give up on the whole thing.'

The two men stared at each other in silence for a moment before Cotta interjected.

'I'd say that you're both right.' He gestured to Scaurus. 'The tribune has it correct when he says that there's no way we can take the vengeance we're seeking without that man. But on the other hand, the first spear is right to say that we can trust that odious bastard no further than we can piss . . . begging your pardon ladies.'

Felicia and Annia smiled demurely, and the former soldier continued with his face slowly reddening.

'Anyway . . . what I was going to say was that there might be a way to bring a greater element of trust to the relationship.'

Julius frowned in disbelief.

'Greater trust? You're suggesting that we might give that boot-scraped piece of shit the benefit of the doubt?'

Cotta shook his head.

'Not exactly. The problem is that right now we only have two choices: either to trust him blindly or to kill him. One choice is recklessly naive, while the other ends any hope we have of taking revenge for the death of Marcus's father. What I have in mind might just give us a third option.'

'You don't want to know, Marcus, leave it at that.'

Cotta shook his head firmly at his former protégée, his mouth set in a tight line of determination.

'I have to know. I need to understand just how bad it—'

The veteran cut him off with a sweeping chop of his hand.

'Just about as bad as you can imagine, for all the fact that you've seen the ugly face of war. Some things are just better not being discussed, or you'll end up going mad simply because they were here and you weren't.'

Marcus stood up and paced away across the small garden. Beyond the house's wall the sounds of the city were ever present: the slap of feet on cobbles, the shouts of shopkeepers and street hawkers rising in an incessant discordant chorus. Scaurus had taken his escort of barbarians back down the hill, leaving the young centurion to spend the evening with his wife under the watchful eyes of his friend and several of Cotta's men.

'And that's my point. I wasn't here, but they were. My entire family gone, overnight, and me never any the wiser as to what happened to them. For all I know they may have been sold into sl—' He fell silent at the look on his friend's face, as Cotta's last line of resistance crumbled. 'What?'

'Lucius.'

His face took on a haunted expression, and Marcus recalled that Cotta and the gladiator had started training his younger brother only the year before his own enforced exile to Britannia. He waited patiently for the former soldier to compose himself.

'I heard later that Lucius was sold to one of Pilinius's friends. Seems that the senator had no need of him, given the number of women who were taken from your father's villa, so he disposed of him in return for enough money to buy himself a formal toga.'

Having broken his silence he was unable to stop talking.

'Your mother and sisters were served up as part of one of Pilinius's parties. I don't know what happens behind the walls of his villa, but I do know what the end result is. One of the servants who got away in the confusion came to find me a few days later, and took me to the illegal dumping ground out past the Esquiline gate. Your sister Livia's body was lying there naked, with its eyes already pecked out by the crows. We buried her, and searched the pits for anyone else from the household, but we didn't find anything to tell us the fate of the rest of your family, or any of their household for that matter.'

Marcus looked at him for a moment, and imagined the revolting task of searching the infamous dump, strewn with rotting corpses and infested with vermin and wild dogs.

'Thank you.'

The two men were quiet for a moment.

'Your father was tortured, of course. They will have thrown his body in the main sewer to be flushed into the Tiber, I'd imagine.'

Marcus was silent for a moment longer.

'I'm going to kill them all. Each and every one of the men who did this to my family are going to look me in the eyes as they die, and realise that they are no better than wild animals. And when I've killed all four of these Knives, I'll only have one more man to deal with.'

Cotta put a hand on his arm, shaking his head slowly.

'Do you remember when I used to tell you never to back down from a fight, or a slur on your honour? To hit any man that threatened you with either first, any way you could, and to keep on hitting him until he'd stopped fighting back?'

'Yes. My father said much the same thing to me more than once, albeit somewhat less graphically.'

The veteran's face was deadly serious.

'Just this once, ignore us both. You have a wife and child, you have friends who respect you and a new life to enjoy. Take that prize and run with it Marcus, and ignore the bloody path that leads to revenge, or you'll end up losing everything! There are more important things, as you'll only find out the hard way if you go up against these men.'

He stared at his friend, and Marcus shook his head helplessly.

'I *know!* Pilinius is too rich, Brutus is too well protected, Dorso lives in the praetorian fortress and Mortiferum is too fast with a sword even if I could get to him! But I have to *try!* Can't you see that?'

Cotta nodded sombrely, his shoulders slumping in defeat.

'Yes. Only too clearly. I just wish I could make *you* blind to it.'

The first cohort's 6th Century were sitting around outside their barracks in the late-evening sun exchanging weary insults, bone-tired from a full day of exercise and training, when Qadir, the centurion commanding the 9th Century, walked around the corner with a dozen men in his wake. Quintus, the century's chosen man and its leader in Marcus's absence, leapt to his feet and bellowed for his men to do the same.

'*Attention! Get on your feet, you maggots!*'

Qadir, the only one of the cohort's officers to hail from the eastern end of the empire, waited until the soldiers were all standing erect before speaking, his heavily accented voice deceptively soft as he addressed Quintus.

'Good evening, Chosen Man, and my apologies for interrupting your evening. The tribune has detailed me to form a small unit of men for a special task, and there are one or two of your men who, your centurion tells me, should have the requisite skills for the job.'

'*Yes, Centurion! What skills are you looking for, Centurion?*'

Qadir smiled faintly at Quintus's bellowed response.

'I think the main requirement for the role would be that the soldiers in question must have absolutely no scruples, be possessed of a strong disregard for authority and be willing to do anything, no matter how unpleasant or indeed contrary to accepted standards of right and wrong. I told Centurion Corvus, of course, that he could be describing nine men out of ten in this cohort, but he replied that he had two very special individuals in mind. I presume that you have some idea of who he might have meant?'

Quintus nodded.

'Oh yes, Centurion, I know exactly who the young gentleman had in mind.' He raised his voice in a parade-ground bellow again.

'*Sanga and Saratos, front and centre!*'

3

Excingus presented himself at the barracks' front gate an hour after dawn, and was only slightly perturbed to find himself being collected from the guardhouse by Dubnus and a half-dozen of his hulking soldiers. The centurion wordlessly escorted him to the headquarters building, their path taking them past a group of twenty or so soldiers, stood rigidly to attention, who were the unhappy subjects of the long and inventive stream of invective being spat at them by an irate chosen man, while their centurion, a man of eastern appearance, stood to one side with a faint smile. The informant felt their eyes on him, every single man doubtless wishing that he were anywhere other than under the lash of the deputy centurion's tongue. The shouting died away behind him as he entered the headquarters, although the sound of impassioned disgust could still be heard as he waited for Scaurus to enter the room.

Outside, Quintus waited until the headquarters' door was firmly shut before pausing for breath, clenching a fist around the brass-bound and knobbed pole that was both his symbol of office, and his means of pushing his men into their places in the century's formation.

'So that was him, gentlemen. You all got a good look at the man, now store his face away in your tiny little minds and I'll march you away for your morning of playing at being informants yourselves.' He swept a withering glare across their ranks. 'Informants? I wouldn't trust any of you to know the crack of your arses from the cleft in your fucking chins! You'll all be back with your centuries by lunchtime! Anyway . . .'

Shaking his head in apparent disgust he took a deep breath and then reverted to parade-ground volume.

'Stand still, you *monkeys! Right . . . turn!* Quick . . . *march! Your left, your left, your left, right, left! You with the fat arse! Get in fucking time or I'll tickle your fucking piles with the end of this fucking pole!'*

Inside the headquarters, Excingus raised an inquisitorial eyebrow at Dubnus, who had dismissed his men and now waited, still silent, in a corner of the room.

'So, Centurion, do you intend to persist in this attempt at intimidation for the rest of the day?'

The massively built Briton shook his head in disgust.

'I have nothing to say to you. Shut your mouth or I'll loosen a few of your teeth and give you a reason for silence. When the tribune arrives you can talk all you like, but until then—'

Scaurus walked briskly into the room and took a seat behind the desk, Marcus and Julius following him in and taking positions to either side of their tribune.

'Sit down, Informant, and tell me what it is you have for us that presents so great an opportunity?'

Excingus wordlessly unrolled the large scroll that he had carried into the fort, and Scaurus weighted down the paper's corners while the informant smiled tightly at the men gathered around him.

'You will recognise this map as a plan of the city, Tribune, but your provincial colleagues may not share your familiarity with Rome.'

He pointed at a spot to the south of the city's walls.

'We, Centurions, are here.'

His finger moved, indicating in turn a succession of points on the map.

'This is the Palatine Hill, where the emperor has his city palaces. This is the Flavian Arena, where the gladiators fight, this—'

Julius leaned forward and put his face close to Excingus's, his voice heavy with irony.

'We know, Informant, that gladiators fight in the arena. We've seen the Palatine, and the Great Forum, and we know that these . . .' He pointed to a massive shape on the map to the north of the Colosseum. 'Are the Baths of Trajan. Dubnus had his purse stolen there and spent an hour threatening various lowlifes with violence before he gave up on the prospect of ever seeing it again. Get to the point.'

The informant smiled cheerfully back at him.

'So nice to hear that you're assimilating quickly, you'll be surprised at the number of men from the provinces who can never get past how many prostitutes there are in the city.' He met the first spear's narrow-eyed gaze with a look of innocence. 'So, without the lesson in the city's landmarks, here's the thing. This . . .' He pointed again, ignoring Julius. 'Is the praetorian fortress. I mention it because it's important, and because I very much doubt that you've ventured all the way across the city just to look at yet another fortress, although you really should. It's a rather impressive pile of stones – although I'm forgetting, Centurion "Corvus" here began his military career in there, didn't you, Centurion?'

Marcus locked stares with him, and the informant quickly decided that coming to the point might be the most sensible choice.

'Anyway, as you know, one of the men you've decided to hunt down and kill lives in that fortress. And while you might just manage to get in there, dressed in the right uniform and with a great big smile on your plan from Fortuna herself, I really can't see you getting out again, even if you managed to find and kill him which, I have to admit, I think unlikely. For one thing, you have no idea where his quarters are in the fortress, and for another, there's always the risk that the hard-eyed young centurion here will be recognised by one of his ex-colleagues as a former praetorian who left informally and under something of a cloud.'

'And?'

'And, First Spear, I happen to have come by some information that I think will provide you with a rather less risky alternative. Would you like to hear it?'

Having thanked Quintus for his part in the charade that had enabled the trackers to take a good look at their target, Qadir dismissed him back to his duties and looked about the soldiers standing in ordered lines in front of him.

'Fall out and sit down.'

He waited until they were all sitting on the ground in front of him, their expressions a mixture of curiosity and excitement at the unexpected change in their routine.

'Tribune Scaurus has a task in mind for you men, or for some of you at least. If you take it on, and if you're successful in mastering the necessary skills, then you'll all be granted immune status and awarded a rise in pay to one and a half times basic. *But . . .*' He waited until the interest generated by the last statement had died away before speaking again. 'I have to warn you, not all of you will be capable of the task the tribune has in mind. And if you don't have the skills, I will return you to your centuries without hesitation. So I suggest that you pay very close attention to the lessons that I am about to teach you, for it will be by their application that you will either succeed or fail. Follow me.'

He led the group up the transit barracks' narrow main street until they reached the stone wall at the far end.

'Divide into two groups.' Once the brief period of confusion caused by his command had been resolved, he ordered one group to stand behind him. 'The rest of you, I want you all to walk away towards the headquarters. You two, stop at the end of the first barrack. You three, at the end of the next block, and you four stop after three blocks. Is that clear?'

The soldiers shuffled their feet and looked at each other, trying to work out what was so difficult about this that they risked being sent back to unremitting sword drills and the lost chance to boast about their increased pay and status to their tent mates. Qadir stared at them in silence for a moment.

'If you spend half the day pondering the meaning of my instructions then you will all fail this test, and so you will all go back to face the inevitable rough humour that will result from your failure. So, I will ask one more time, and any man that does not answer me quickly and clearly will be our first dropout. Is that *clear*?'

The men standing before him chorused their understanding, and the Hamian nodded slowly.

'Very good. Now, when I wave my arm, the pair must hide

behind the barrack beside which they are stopped, when I wave it again the trio must hide, leaving only the group of four in view. When I call out to you then you must all return here. Clear?'

Again the agreement was swift and loud, his gently posed threat clearly having sunk into the soldiers' minds.

'Then do it. The rest of you, turn and face the wall while they do as I have bidden.'

While the second group walked back down the street, Qadir spoke to the men gathered before him, his quiet, assured tones forcing them to listen with the utmost care.

'The first lesson that we will learn is that in this game which we will be playing, distance is our friend. Every fifty paces that a man moves away from you makes him seem that much smaller and insignificant, and, unless he wears bright clothing, every step makes him that much less visible, as you will see in a moment.'

With the other men in their various places, he spoke again.

'When I give the word you may turn, just for a moment, and look over your shoulder, in the manner of a man who wishes to see if there is anyone behind him. Just for an instant, mind you, the quickest glance possible and as casually as you can manage. Now!'

The soldiers looked around, then flicked their gazes back to Qadir.

'You all saw the men one block away without any problem?'

They nodded, looks of puzzlement on all but a couple of faces. Qadir waved his arm, waiting until the closest men had taken cover.

'Now!'

The soldiers turned and looked again, a few more of them turning back with looks of understanding, and again the centurion waved his arm, waiting until the three soldiers had moved into hiding, leaving only the group of four visible.

'Now!'

This time when the men turned back from peering over their shoulders they were nodding and exchanging knowing glances as men will when the obvious dawns upon them.

'You see? The closest men stood out very clearly, the next closest were obvious enough, but the third group?

Saratos was the first to speak, his face still thoughtful.

'They hard to see with quick look. If they tunics not red be even harder.'

The Hamian nodded approvingly.

'Exactly. Well done soldier. Now we'll repeat the lesson, and this time you men will be the ones standing in the street. Off you go, and send the others back here to me.'

'So there you have it. If you still want to mete out whatever it is that you consider to be justice to one of the Knives, you have the perfect opportunity.'

Excingus sat back in his chair and waited for a response from the officers gathered around him.

'You're *sure* that he'll visit this place of his tonight?'

The informant shrugged, pursing his lips non-committally.

'Of course I'm not *sure*, Rutilius Scaurus—'

'Let's keep this formal, Informant. There's never going to be any point in our relationship when I'll tolerate any degree of familiarity from you.'

Excingus smiled, and Marcus watched with fascination as he swallowed whatever irritation Scaurus's swift put-down inspired in him with disturbing ease.

'Of course, Tribune, my apologies for overstepping the bounds of our admittedly tenuous association. And no, I can't be *sure* he'll visit his private museum this evening. What I am sure of is that since he's been there every night when he's not had watch duty for the last week, it does seem to be a fairly reasonable bet that tonight will be no different, wouldn't you agree?'

Julius leaned forward in his chair.

'And how do you come by such good information, precisely?'

The informant leaned back, his face wreathed in a knowing smile.

'Ah, the question that every man in my trade, be he good, bad or simply indifferent, comes to expect.' He struck a pose, raising an eyebrow in a mock inquisitorial manner and speaking in the haughty tones of an aristocratic employer. '"So exactly *how* do you know this, Informant?"' Changing his position, he adopted a sly look, his voice becoming more persuasive than hectoring. '"Do tell me, my man, where *did* you come by that fascinating snippet of information?"' Sitting bolt upright, he strengthened his voice to imitate the bluff no-nonsense approach of a wealthy businessman. '"So come on then, Informant, how much do you want to tell me where you get all these secrets. What does it take for me to dispense with your services and cut out the man in the middle, eh?"'

He shook his head pityingly at the glowering first spear.

'Everyone I deal with asks me the same question, sooner or later, and I've become more than expert at giving absolutely nothing away. Do you really believe that I'll happily trot out my means of knowing where Dorso is going to be, and when? There's honest and open, First Spear, and then there's downright naivety.'

'And we understand your desire not to have your sources suborned, Informant . . .'

'And yet, Tribune?'

'Precisely. And yet, what's my guarantee that I'm not going to send my men into a trap, with or without your active participation? How do I know that you've not been fooled into accepting this apparent pattern in the praetorian's movements? What if he's a good deal more suspicious and careful than you're implying, and whoever goes to confront him in this museum of his finds a warmer reception than we might have hoped for?'

Excingus shrugged again.

'As to what's inside the place, I have no idea. For all I know, he's employed Flamma the Great himself as a live-in bodyguard. All I can tell you is that once Dorso's done guarding the imperial palaces, he takes enough time to wash and change into his off-duty uniform, and then walks down the Vicus Patricius to a little place he either rents or owns – the latter, I suppose, given all the money he must have made over the last few years – buys himself and the two guardsmen who escort him everywhere a hot meal from a nearby tavern, and disappears into the house. He doesn't come out until early the next morning, when he walks back up the hill to the praetorian fortress and goes back on duty. And as to how I know this? Just for once, given the difficult nature of our relationship, I'll give up one of my methods if it will help to persuade you of the provenance of my information. I used a gang of petty thieves and pickpockets, men I pay handsomely enough to take time away from their profession when the occasion demands their particular street skills, to tail Centurion Dorso, discreetly mind you, for the last six nights. Given that the prae-torians rotate the assignment of their cohorts once every two weeks, to give the men on night duty time to adapt properly to the change of their sleeping hours, I can see no reason for him not to repeat the same routine this evening. He couldn't be any more accommodating in his predictability if he tried.'

'And you have no idea what it is that he has in there?'

The informant shook his head at Marcus.

'As I said, I'm not entirely sure. My people can track him from one place to another easily enough, but once he's inside the house he's out of their view. We can all speculate, and my guess would be that he goes there to gloat over the highlights of his collection, but that's all my opinion is – speculation.'

'Why do we need to break into this place of his? This man has a reputation as a collector of weapons, so why don't we just put word out that we've got trophies to sell from the recent campaign in Britannia?'

Excingus smiled at the young centurion, unable to keep a patronising edge from his voice.

'If only it were that simple. If you still had that rather interesting sword you captured in Germania Inferior, for example . . .' He smiled at Marcus's narrowed eyes. 'Come now, Centurion, soldiers will talk. Yes, if you were still in possession of the "Leopard Sword" then you might have a sufficiently juicy worm to put on the hook, but a few old bits of rusty metal that you took from a tribe that no one's ever heard of? This man's a serious collector, or so it's rumoured, with weapons and other items that span the entire history of Rome and going as far back as the conquest of the Etruscans. He's even rumoured to be in possession of a sword which is supposed to be the one that One Eyed Horatius used to hold the bridge over the Tiber almost seven hundred years ago, and the gods alone know what sort of price that would command if it were to come on to the market.'

'No wonder he's so happy to participate in the murder of prominent members of society. There must be heirlooms in their houses the likes of which otherwise never see the light of day. So, how do you propose that we bring this praetorian to some kind of justice?'

Excingus raised a jaundiced eyebrow at the tribune.

'How do *I* propose? I don't intend to propose anything, Tribune. All I'm going to do is tell you where and when I expect you'll be able to get to the man. How you go about it thereafter is entirely up to you. And now, gentlemen, as far as I'm concerned my part in your scheming against Centurion Dorso is at an end. Do I need an escort back to the main gate, or shall I find my own way?'

'So, now you know the effects of distance on your visibility when you're following a man, let's consider how that works in practice, shall we?'

The detachment had gathered around Qadir at his command, and were sitting in a semi-circle around him while the Hamian centurion looked around at them, assessing how closely they were following his words.

'Imagine that we are following a single man through the city. Our task is to keep him in sight while he makes his way to wherever it is he is heading and . . .'

He paused and looked about him with a significant glance, raising an eyebrow in silent question. One of the brighter soldiers answered, summoning his courage to speak directly to the officer.

'To make sure that he don't see us, Centurion?'

Qadir nodded encouragingly.

'Exactly. For if he does, our careful pursuit will be over in a moment. Did anyone here perhaps play the game when they were children?'

The soldiers looked at each other blankly, and when Sanga spoke it was with a wry grin.

'Not really, Centurion. We was all more likely playing the "trying to get it up the locals girls" game.'

Qadir nodded, sharing his man's smile.

'Very well, allow me to share some small part of what I learned before I left my home and travelled all the way to your cold, damp and barbaric province. We are following a man – let us call him "the mark" – through the city. How far back from him should we be?'

'Three blocks, Centurion.'

Qadir looked at the man who had answered.

'Are you sure?'

The soldier looked puzzled.

'Didn't you just show us how far back we have to be to avoid being noticed, sir?'

The Hamian nodded.

'I did. But consider, what will be the effect if our man turns a corner to the left or right? You will be three blocks back, and will not know whether he plans to turn another corner at the next opportunity. By the time you reach the point where he turned, he might well be out of sight. So what must you do?'

The soldier thought briefly.

'Run?'

'Yes, you must run, and hope that he is still visible when you reach the corner in question. But then if the mark has any suspicion that he's acquired a following, might he not choose to turn back on himself and look around that corner a moment later? And if he sees you running towards him then his suspicions will obviously be confirmed. Not only will he make a point of running himself, and turning two or three corners to throw you off his scent, but he will also be looking out for you whenever he is on the street. This will *not* be a good outcome.'

He looked around him for a moment before chuckling softly at their downcast faces.

'But this does not have to be the case. The task of following the mark is much easier for one or at the most two men, and sometimes two are better than one since they can talk to each other. After all, what could appear more natural than two friends having a lively conversation when the mark takes that quick look behind him? So, one or two men follow the mark at a distance of between a block and two blocks behind, and the other men hang further back, two groups of two or three on either side of the road.'

He looked round the men with a faint smile.

'So, let's try that question again. The mark feels suspicious about those two men behind him, so he chooses to make a sharp right turn. You have no need to run, since you have men in support of you, but what *do* you do? After all, he's suspicious of you already, so he has an eye open for anyone trying to follow him, and you were close enough for him to register the colour of your hair, the shade of your tunic and so on. And if he sees you again, still following him even though he has just turned two or three corners to evade just such an attempt to track him, he's likely to react just as badly as if he saw you running. So . . . ?'

'So we need to get the blokes that are hanging back to move up sharpish and take up the follow.'

Qadir applauded softly.

'Good, Sanga – but how shall we do that? The mark will, after all, be listening carefully for the sound of shouting, anything out of the ordinary.'

Saratos frowned up at him, clearly considering the question, then smiled quietly to himself.

'You, Sarmatian. I think you know the answer.'

'Is obvious Centurion. We make signal with body.'

Qadir nodded approvingly.

'Yes we do. As the man in the following role, once the mark has gone out of sight to the left or to the right, you need to signal to the men behind you that they need to do two things. Firstly, that they need to move up smartly and take up the follow, and secondly . . . ?'

He looked at the Sarmatian soldier again, and Sanga nudged his mate in the ribs.

'Secondly need to make turn to right or left.'

'Exactly.'

Sanga had his hand in the air in an instant, the question written all over his face.

'Centurion?'

'Soldier?'

'Well sir . . .'

Qadir could see the question forming, the soldier's lips moving slightly as he tried to think of a way to express his curiosity without looking stupid in front of his comrades.

'When we perform these tricks that I am training you for, Soldier Sanga, there is no stupid question except for the one you don't ask. So?'

'I was just wondering, Centurion . . .' He paused, still searching for the right words. 'How it is you know so much about spying on people?'

Once Excingus had been escorted from the headquarters building, Scaurus sat back in his chair.

'Well?'

Julius's tone was thoughtful.

'It could be a set-up, designed to lure the centurion here into a trap, but that feels unlikely to me. Excingus knows that if anything happens to any of us he'll be the first suspect, and that we're hardly likely to hesitate to put him to the knife.'

Scaurus nodded his agreement.

'The question for me isn't whether this is a genuine opportunity to take down one of these men, but how he came by the information so quickly. Yesterday he didn't have a clue as to how we could get to Dorso, or not that he was willing to share with Senator Sigilis who, as his employer, you would expect to be the first person to be informed, and yet today he knows the praetorian's movements for the last week? He's either playing his own game or there's something we're missing in all this, but whatever it is, the sooner we get our men trained and out there to start tracking him around the city the better.'

'And that's the other problem.'

Scaurus turned his attention back to the veteran centurion.

'What is?'

'Being followed around the city. I wondered yesterday, when Excingus appeared at the front door of the doctor's house so very soon after she'd arrived, but something he said just now, about newcomers being amazed at how many whores there are in the city, pretty much confirmed it for me. We might be thinking about tracking him around to see who he talks to, but our informant friend seems to have beaten us to the punch.'

'He's going to turn this time.'

'No, he not.'

'I'm telling you he'll turn, you barbarian fuckwit . . . here it comes . . . come on . . . *shit!*'

'Tell you, he no turn. Next corner.'

Sanga grimaced, speeding up his pace a little.

'Yeah, good guess Saratos, you lucky prick. Come on, get ready to run.'

Up ahead the centurion's distant figure was approaching the next cross-street, and Sanga looked quickly across the road at the two men walking on the left side, both of whom were watching Qadir with the same hungry intensity he was feeling. The closer of the two looked back at him and the Briton winked.

'You ready girls? One gets you two he'll turn right!'

The closest of them waved a dismissive hand, then tensed as Qadir abruptly turned, looked back and crossed the road from right to left, disappearing out of sight in the opposite direction to the one he'd expected. The men closely following him split up, one of them walking on past the turning as if nothing had happened to cover the next street along in case Qadir turned right again, while the other bent to tie his boot lace, his body turned to indicate the direction the centurion had taken. The men to Sanga's left smirked at him as they turned their own corner and sprinted for the next junction, knowing that they had to reach the next street along and be settled back into a walking pace before their quarry emerged in order to take up the role of his new tails.

'Come on!'

Sanga was already halfway across the road, ignoring the entreaties of a tavern owner to sample his meat stew. With Saratos at his heels, the pair crossed to the far side and hurried up the street, closing the distance to the point where Qadir had disappeared from view. They were barely twenty paces from the point where he had disappeared from sight when the centurion reappeared around the corner at a pace close to a run, looking back as if he was being pursued by furies and only seeing the two soldiers at the last moment. Nodding a brief recognition he spoke swiftly as the two men stared at him.

'I've seen you once, gentlemen, so if I see you again then this exercise is over!' Dodging around them he made off in the direction from which they had come. 'And next time try not to stare quite so obviously!'

The two men looked at each other for a moment before Sanga tapped his comrade on the shoulder and pointed at the other side of the street.

'Go!'

Walking swiftly around the corner from which Qadir had reappeared so suddenly, he ran for the far end, crouching to pop his head out at ankle level to peer down the street to his left. Seeing only the bemused-looking soldiers who had turned left to take up the follow, he bounded round the corner and sprinted past them.

'He's doubled back!'

They stared after him as he ran across the first junction, sure that Qadir would not have stopped or turned again so soon. Looking to his left he saw Saratos crossing the junction two streets away and running hard, and accelerated to match the other man's pace.

'Look at this one, he can't wait to get down to business!'

A pair of prostitutes stepped into his path, and it took all of the Briton's agility to avoid crashing into them. Looking about him he saw a stall selling rough wool tunics, and he grabbed a handful of coins from his purse.

'How much?'

The stall holder leaned back and looked up at the looming soldier, grinning at the handful of money with the look of a man who had seen his chance and intended to grab it with both hands.

'For a man your size? Five sestertii.'

Tossing the coins at the vendor Saratos snatched up a large blue tunic and ran to the next road junction, skidding to a halt and repeating the crouch-and-peep act, retracting his head quickly as Qadir turned the corner and walked purposefully towards him, shooting a glance back over his shoulder. Backtracking hastily he was still looking round for somewhere to hide himself when the older and clearly more experienced of the prostitutes took matters in hand, pushing him up against the wall and thrusting her body against his, her hands roaming under his tunic to find his hardening member.

'Come on you dirty bastard, you know you want to!'

Out of the corner of his eye he saw Qadir stride past barely half a dozen paces away, but the desultory flick of the Hamian's gaze clearly failed to register that the helpless man pinned against the wall beneath yet another of the capital's money-hungry working girls was one of his men. Finding his penis already erect, she laughed eagerly, tugging hard enough at the organ's shaft to sorely test his resolve.

'Come *on!* I'm fucking starving! Three sestertii!'

'Just . . .' He caught her hands and gently pushed her way. 'One minute, eh?'

He walked back to the crossroads and waited for Saratos who eventually came past with the look of a man out for a gentle stroll.

'Put this on, and give me yours!'

The Sarmatian ducked into the side street and pulled off his tunic, much to the amusement of the watching prostitutes, his tattoos bright blue in the afternoon sunlight. He pulled on the new garment and renewed his pursuit of Qadir without a backward glance, and Sanga turned back to find the prostitute standing behind him with a hard smile on her face.

'Soldier, are you? That explains the muscles. Well now, Soldier, since you'll probably lose your load in seconds, I'll do you for two sestertii. Which you can get by reclaiming what you overspent on that tunic . . .' She jerked her head at the tunic vendor who was looking up at them with an expression of unease bordering on naked fear. 'He usually only charges two.'

As the late-afternoon sun dipped towards the roofs of the transit barracks, a bored-looking boy dressed in a tunic cut in the military pattern wandered out of the main gate. He was wearing a belt that ensured the garment's hem hung above his scabbed and somewhat grubby knees but which also, far more to the interest of the five children sitting around and playing knucklebones on the other side of the road, carried the weight of a half-sized sword. Dressed in an assortment of clothing that appeared to be either too big or worn threadbare, they watched the child with expressions of calculation as he walked slowly towards them. After a swift discussion, the biggest of them stood up and approached him with a hard grin, but the boy's calm stare and firm grip of the sword's hilt swiftly dissuaded him from his initial idea of simply stealing the weapon.

'Who are you? We ain't seen you before.'

The child looked up and down the road before answering.

'I'm Lupus. I live with the soldiers in there.'

'Lupus? What kind of stupid fucking name is th—'

The boy was quicker than his inquisitor expected, drawing the sword and taking guard in a way that put the blade's edge within an inch or so of the urchin's neck.

'*My* name. Have you got one, or did your mother not bother?'

His inquisitor danced back with a look of alarm.

'I'm Julius! And there's no need for the sword!'

Lupus grinned at him, slotting the blade back into its scabbard.

'Maybe not, Julius, but now we all know where we stand. Arminius always says that—'

'Who's Arminius?'

'My fighting teacher. He's German.'

The children, who had gathered round him with looks of bemusement, stared at each other in further disbelief, and another of them, a boy with a long scar across his cheek, piped up in a disbelieving note.

'You ain't got no fighting teacher! You're making it up!'

Lupus simply grinned, waving a hand back at the barracks behind him.

'Want to see me training with him?'

Julius shook his head.

'We'll never get in here. That's army ground. If we even *try* to get in we'll just get a good hiding and then be kicked out.'

Lupus shrugged.

'I can get you inside, if you're not too scared to come with me.'

They stared at him in collective uncertainty for a moment, and then one of the smaller children stepped forward, pushing Julius aside. It was obvious that they were brothers, although where the older child had the look of a bruiser in the making, the younger had more of a sly look about him.

'Why?'

Lupus frowned at the question.

'Why what?'

'Why would you want to get us inside?'

'Because I'm bored! The only other children in our cohort are babies, and they've gone into the city. I've got no one to play with.'

'*Pla—*'

The scar-faced child's incredulous guffaw was cut off by a hard elbow in the ribs from the younger boy, something which to judge from the unmoving faces of the other children was nothing out of the ordinary.

'Yeah, we'll play with you. We love to *play* . . . But how do we get in there?' He shot a meaningful glance at the gate guards. 'It ain't like those bastards are going to let us just stroll in, is it?'

Lupus nodded, leaning forward to whisper quietly.

'Follow me. I know another way in.'

He walked away confidently, ignoring the risk that the children would mob him once they were safely away from the guards at the barrack's gate, and their ringleader shook his head at his companions to deter just such an attempt, muttering a quiet command to them.

'Not now. Later.'

On the south side of the barrack's encircling wall he led them to a small doorway inside an arch set in the stonework.

'I found this while I was exploring. It was bolted inside, but there's no lock . . .'

Lupus swung the door open and went in through the gate, leaving the street children standing outside looking at each other. The small child pushed Julius towards the door.

'Go on. If it's safe we'll follow you inside.'

The boy sidled up to the gateway and peered through it at the barracks buildings on the other side, taking a nervous step forward to the threshold, peering in to either side.

'I can't see anything.'

His brother stepped forward and swiftly thrust him through the gate.

'Ah, you bastard Gaius!'

His outburst was met with a stony-faced stare, as his younger brother pointed a finger at the barracks behind him.

'Stop fucking about and have a proper look!'

The child walked slowly forward three paces, staring about him wildly as he regained his equilibrium. Nothing moved, other than Lupus who raised an arm to point at the barracks.

'Half of them are empty! We could play hide and seek . . .'

Gaius walked through the gate, looking around as if he could hardly believe what he was seeing, and the remaining children followed him into the enclosed space.

'We *could* play hide and seek, but I'd rather play at looking round this place. There must be plenty of stuff we could sell back in the city, and—'

The gate slammed shut behind him, and the children whirled to find a huge bearded centurion standing behind them with his back against the wooden door.

'*Get them!*'

A dozen men sprang from the cover of the barracks to either side, their arms outstretched to prevent any of the children from escaping into the maze of buildings, but rather than looking to escape, Gaius shrugged his shoulders and waited meekly for the soldier to take him by the arm.

'Not going to run, little man?'

The child shook his head, grimacing up at the soldier.

'Nah. If you wanted to hurt us you'd have your knives or your cocks out by now, so I figure you want something from us. So let's talk, eh?'

'There's no demand for it I'm afraid. We get the odd German asking for it, but I can't make a living selling that foul muck and it doesn't keep for long either, not like wine. What's wrong with a good honest cup of Iberian, that's what I want to know?'

Marcus nodded his agreement, putting down enough coin for a flask of the good falernian that the tavern owner kept under the counter, and ushered a still-fuming Dubnus to the table to which Qadir had already laid claim. The establishment's working women, whose instincts for silver were clearly well honed, had swiftly surrounded the Tungrians on their arrival, but then equally quickly worked out that the three centurions weren't looking for the particular services they were offering. Dubnus poured three cups of wine, raising his own in a weary salute before sipping at it in a disconsolate manner.

'Bloody wine. It's all very well for you lot that grew up with the stuff, but it gives me a foul headache. Where can a man get a beer in this city, that's what I want to know?'

'You had a beer the other night, and spat it out onto the floor. Remember?'

The big man nodded, pulling a disgusted face.

'Do I? I could never have imagined that it was possible to

ferment a brew that I wouldn't enjoy, but this place just keeps on coming up with new ways to piss me off. What was it called?'

'Cerevisia. It's a Gaulish recipe, I believe.'

Dubnus shuddered.

'Well it was just *wrong*. I won't get a decent drink until we're back in Britannia, that's obvious.'

He sipped at his wine again, looking down into his cup with a resigned expression, and Marcus turned to Qadir with a question.

'So then, spy master, how many of your trackers do you think have managed to master the art of following a man through the city then?'

Qadir looked out of the window of the tavern with a small smile to where a pair of his newly trained spies lounged insouciantly against the wall of the building on the street's far side, watching the neighbourhood women walk by.

'Consider this, my brother. We take soldiers, or rather the one soldier in ten with the wit to cope with such a task. These are men who are well accustomed to making a little work go as far as possible, and to whom the art of idling and generally avoiding the attention of their superiors has become second nature. Thus it is that on the street they are most adept at blending into the background, and, when forced out of whatever cover they are using, at then giving every impression that they have no interest whatsoever in the man they have been set to follow.'

He took a sip of wine, nodding in appreciation of its quality, raising the cup in salute to Marcus and Dubnus.

'That really is very good. Anyway, later this afternoon, once we had practised tailing a mark – myself, as it happens – with mixed results, I sent them out to follow randomly selected citizens as those innocents went about their business, under my own watchful eye. Most of them did well enough, including the two men who started a fake fist fight to throw one of our marks off his suspicions. I think you can guess which two soldiers were willing to get blood on their tunics in the pursuit of authenticity?'

Dubnus snorted a quiet laugh, tipping his head towards Marcus.

'Two of *his* men, perhaps?'

'Exactly. I've never seen a couple take to the art of tailing quite as quickly. Sanga bought Saratos a different coloured tunic to wear at one point, once I thought I'd thrown them all off, and the man tracked me for a dozen blocks from so far back that I had no idea he was there, until I led him back to the rally point. Assuming that he had become lost in the city's maze, and would eventually find his way back to us, I was berating them for failing to keep me in sight when Sanga just coughed, and pointed to his fellow soldier who was lounging in a doorway and listening to it all with an expression of such innocence that it was all I could do not to burst into laughter. The ten men I have retained are all good enough to risk following Excingus the next time that we get the chance, but those two are head and shoulders the best of them. I have another idea in mind for them . . .'

The three men looked up as Cotta walked into the establishment, dropping into a chair opposite Marcus and pouring himself a cup of wine from their jug. He drank, smacking his lips appreciatively, wiped the sheen of sweat from his brow and then flashed his usual hard grin at the Tungrians.

'Well then! We, you will be pleased to hear, are now the proud proprietors of the shop around the corner from your woman's house, young Marcus. I drove a hard bargain with the landlord, given that I discovered from the neighbours that the place has been empty for almost three months. Something to do with bad drains. All we need now is something to sell from it.'

'Well that's easy enough.'

Marcus looked round at Dubnus, whose previously morose expression had clearly brightened at the thought which had occurred to him. Cotta leaned forward with a mischievous smile.

'Go on then, *spit it out.*'

The big Briton raised a weary eyebrow.

'We've already done that one, thank you. Anyway, as to what business to run in the shop, the answer's obvious.'

'Is it?'

He nodded emphatically at a bemused-looking Cotta.

'What's the one thing that a man has to have done to him no less than once a month?'

'Once a month? I like to get my leg over a good deal more regularly than that!'

'Not that!' Dubnus reached out and took a hold of the veteran officer's hair, tugging at a stray lock. *'This!'*

There was a moment of silence.

'A barber's shop?'

The big man shrugged.

'Why not? Let's face it, it'll give us a good reason for having men going in and out of the place, a few of whom can then go to your wife's house to stand guard. And believe me, we've got more than enough men who've been cutting their mates' hair for long enough that they know how not to make too bad a mess of it.'

Cotta pulled a thoughtful face for a moment.

'You know that very might well be an inspired idea. But who's going to run it?'

Dubnus's smile broadened.

'That's the best bit. I know *just* the man. Just make sure you watch him carefully. He's as slippery as an eel once there's a sniff of coin on the breeze.'

'Come along now, little one, nearly there.'

Felicia and Annia had walked down the hill in search of some fresh food once the worst heat of the day had abated, both women carrying their children as usual while a pair of Cotta's men had walked before them to clear a path through the Aventine's cosmopolitan hubbub, two more following on behind to discourage any attempt at robbery. With a bag full of fresh produce for the evening meal, they were climbing slowly back up the slope to where the house waited, guarded by another two men.

'Are you sure I can't take him for you, Domina?'

Felicia smiled and shook her head at the closest of her protectors, shifting the sleeping Appius from one arm to the other.

'Thank you, but he's asleep. And we'll be . . . home . . . soon enough.'

Annia laughed softly behind her, her own child tucked under her chin and tightly strapped to her body with a length of cloth.

'Home! You never thought you'd be saying that again, did you?'

Her friend stopped and looked up the hill, just able to make out the roof of her father's house above the walls of the houses that lined the road.

'No. And now that I can, it doesn't really feel right in my mouth. I'm really just not sure . . .'

Annia put an arm around her shoulder, shaking her head at the bodyguards who were gathering around them with faces that spoke volumes for their professional concern.

'You lot can concentrate on making sure that we're not robbed, and *I'll* look after the Domina.'

She wrapped her arms around her friend, sandwiching the two sleeping children awkwardly between them.

'Now you just listen to me. You're clever, educated and you're a success in a profession that a lot of men can't handle. Your father would have been more than proud of the way you've coped since his death, and taking that house back is no more than you deserve. You heard what Excingus said, the previous occupants weren't harmed when he made them move out, and let's face it, he's more than unpleasant enough to have had the measure of your previous husband's family. So let's just—'

She fell silent, looking down to see what it was that was tapping against her leg.

'So much for you lot as bodyguards, eh? You can't even stop a little dog from getting to us! Look at it!'

A dog no bigger than a large cat had taken advantage of their pause to make an appearance from the side alley where it had been resting out of the sun, drawn by the scent of cooked meat rising from their bags, and was pawing at Annia's leg with a hopeful look. The four ex-soldiers turned to look at her, the oldest of them stepping forward and stooping with his hand open, ready to take the animal by the scruff of its neck with a purposeful look.

'*Wait!*'

He stopped in mid-lunge and looked up at Felicia, whose

command, if softly stated, had been sufficiently terse in tone to momentarily freeze him where he stood.

'Domina?'

She bent her knees and knelt to caress the dog's neck. The animal jumped up on two legs, placing its front feet on her thigh and reached up to lick the tip of her nose.

'Such a sweet little thing.' She nodded to the bodyguard. 'Pick him up, please, but gently. The poor little man looks just about done in for lack of food; you can see his ribs quite clearly. Pick him up and we'll take him home.'

The soldier did as he was asked, holding the animal away from him with the obvious expectation that it would shortly realise that it needed to urinate.

'Are you sure, Domina? These street dogs are well known for carrying diseases, and when your back's turned he'll just be stealing food and biting the children. What if he has the madness?'

His attempt to persuade Felicia to see sense petered out as he realised that she was shaking her head in a manner that he had learned, even in his short time as one of her protectors, was utterly unequivocal.

'The madness?' She put a finger under the dog's chin and tilted its head, looking into the alert eyes with a smile. 'There's no madness here, just a bright little fellow who lacks a meal or two. Bring him along and we'll give him a little food, see if we can't fill him out a little.'

Annia bent to look at the dog more closely, dodging back to avoid an attempt to lick her face.

'You lot haven't got the sense you were born with! Call that a street dog? No wonder he's so thin, there's no way he's been able to compete for food with monsters like that one.' She pointed to an evil-looking stray that was lounging further down the alley in the deeper shade. 'If we throw him back now he'll be dead in a week. And besides . . .' Her face took on a scornful expression which Cotta's men had come to know all too well. 'Let's face it, we'll all sleep more soundly knowing that we've got a guard dog roaming the house. I wouldn't trust you lot to guard a shit house.'

Felicia smiled winningly at the veteran in whose big hands the dog was trembling, turning away up the hill and calling back over her shoulder to her friend.

'Come along now Annia, I think you've had quite enough sport with these poor men today already. Let's concentrate our thoughts on what we might call the poor little fellow, shall we?'

Annia bowed her head in a show of respect, shooting the waiting bodyguards a sideways glance.

'Yes, and what an exciting game! I vote we call him Centurion! It'll be nice to see this lot having to pay their respects to a skinny little runt like that . . .'

'All these years I've been singing marching songs about a restaurant with bedrooms up the stairs, I can hardly believe that I'm actually sitting in one.'

Marcus laughed softly at his friend, raising an eyebrow in question.

'And do you fancy making the trip upstairs?'

Dubnus glanced across the room at the trio of prostitutes who were still sulking against the far wall.

'She's too old, she's too young, and she's rather too skinny for a man with my tastes. And besides . . .' He leaned forward to confide in his brother officer. 'I've never found it easy to do justice to a woman I've had to pay for.' He looked down at his crotch with a significant expression. 'After all, I hardly need to go beg—'

One of Qadir's newly trained soldiers walked slowly past the tavern and made eye contact with the centurions in their place at the window, tipping his head back the way he had come, up the hill's long slope to where the magnificent bulk of the praetorian fortress loomed against the dusk's purple backdrop. The four men turned away and concentrated on the food set before them. A moment later, the man they had been waiting for strode past them and turned into the tavern, throwing his cloak back over his shoulder and taking a coin from the purse at his belt, slapping it down on the counter in the manner of a man long familiar with the establishment. A pair of guardsmen still dressed in their uniforms had followed him down the hill, and stood waiting at the tavern's door with expressions of tired boredom. Waving away the customary expressions of respect and greeting that he was offered by the restaurant's owner, the praetorian graciously accepted a small cup of wine from which he sipped sparingly, nodding gravely to acknowledge the acceptability of the vintage. Dressed in the red off-duty tunic of a praetorian officer, a highly polished vine stick in one hand and a knife hanging from his gleaming leather belt, his thick hair and beard were neatly cut in apparent ignorance of the imperial fashion for long, bushy facial hair. His voice was loud enough to be heard over the buzz of the other customers' conversation, and the prostitutes looked up with barely disguised boredom.

'Lentil stew again? Go on then, I'll take a pot full, and some bread to mop it up with. And the same for my men.'

Dorso leaned against the counter with the look of a man at rest after a long day, his gaze sweeping across the tavern's customers without any visible sign of interest, and Marcus was careful not to meet his eye. After a short wait the proprietor handed the waiting soldiers three small pots of food and a parcel of bread wrapped in rough cloth, bowed his thanks for the distinguished officer's custom and escorted him to the door. Marcus spooned up the last morsel of his meal and reached for the cloak in which his knife was concealed, waiting as Dubnus extricated himself from his place next to the window. While Cotta pounced on the untended wine jug, Qadir looked up at Marcus with professional concern, flattening his hands onto the table in the universal gesture for calm.

'Keep well back from him until the last moment. It would be a shame if he were to take fright at this late stage. Just remember what I told you.'

Marcus nodded.

'We're simply out for an evening stroll, nice and easy.'

The Hamian waved the two men away, and emerging into the street they found the soldier Saratos leaning against the far wall with his eyes locked on a point further down the hill. They set off in Dorso's wake at a gentle pace, their tracking of the praetorian made simple by the vivid red of his finely woven cloak and the two soldiers strolling close behind him. After another hundred paces or so he turned left, off the main street and into an narrow side street that ran away down the hill at an angle, and Dubnus slowed his pace momentarily.

'Let's not dive into the alley too quickly, or he might hear us behind him.'

Marcus nodded, reaching into his cloak to ready his knife. Emerging from the alley's shadows they saw the praetorian thirty paces or so ahead of them with his men on either side, all three of them bending over a man dressed in rags who was squatting against the wall to one side of a heavy wooden door. His powerful voice carried effortlessly to the two men as they approached the small group silently from behind.

'Ex-soldier, are you? Gods below man, but you *stink*!' He rummaged in his purse, pulling out a coin. 'Here's a denarius, which I suggest you use at the nearest bathhouse . . .'

Marcus and Dubnus had closed the gap between them quickly but silently in their leather-soled boots, Dorso's raised voice covering the faint creaking of their stitching. The praetorians never saw what had hit them as the two men struck. Dubnus smashed his man to the ground with a hammer blow from the lead-cored truncheon that had been hidden up his sleeve, the soldier more than likely already dead before he hit the cobbles, and Marcus struck his target with a bladed hand in the throat, dropping him kicking and choking to the cobbles, then put the point of his knife to Dorso's throat with a growl of barely restrained anger.

'You can die here and now, if you choose!'

The praetorian froze, but when he spoke his voice sounded more composed than Marcus would have expected, given the knife's harsh touch at his throat.

'It's true then. No good deed goes unpunished . . .'

Dubnus took the pot from his hand, reaching into their captive's cloak for the key they knew would be hanging from his belt. He opened the door and waved a hand at Sanga in dismissal.

'Let's go inside, shall we, and find out what it is that you come here to gloat over? You can be on your way, Sanga, although I'd recommend you do indeed find a bathhouse and sweat out whatever it is that's making you stink like a donkey's arse crack before you go back to barracks.'

The soldier got up and walked away, muttering to himself loudly enough for the two men to hear as they hustled the praetorian into the house.

'"*Make yourself smell bad*," he says, and then when you do all you get is abuse. Fuckin' officers . . .'

While Marcus shepherded the praetorian in through the door, Dubnus dragged the prostrate guards in behind them, closing the door and leaving no trace of the ambush before knifing both men in the throat to make sure that they were dead. In the entrance hall there were lamps set out ready for use, and a single flame left burning to light the others. The big Briton lit a pair of them while Marcus held Dorso at knifepoint. He walked forward into a wide inner chamber, then stood and stared in wonder at the sight that emerged from the shadows as the lamplight strengthened. On every side of the room there were weapons racked on the walls: swords, shields, spears and axes, variously scarred, notched and battered by their evident use on combat, each with an engraved bronze plate fastened to the wall on which it was displayed. Released from Marcus's grip, albeit with the knife still poised to strike if he attempted to fight back, Dorso turned slowly to face them, his expression strangely seeming closer to relief than fear in the dim light. The young centurion narrowed his eyes, lifting the knife close to his face, a shining bar of metal whose dappled surface gleamed in the lamplight, growling out the words he had rehearsed a thousand times as he had dreamed of the moment of his revenge.

'My name is Marcus Valerius Aquila.'

The praetorian smiled gently, spreading his arms wide in apparent surrender.

'I know it is. And I know that you intend to kill me.'

Dubnus and Marcus exchanged glances, both men perplexed

at the apparent ease with which their quarry was accepting of his fate.

'And you're just going to stand there and let it happen?'

Dorso shrugged easily, clearly not troubled by his predicament.

'You stand before me, Valerius Aquila, with a blade bared and murder in your eyes and ask me if I am ready to die?' The praetorian laughed softly. 'If I weren't, I could easily have thwarted you out in the street, set my men on you and called for help.'

Marcus's eyes narrowed at the shock of hearing his true name from the emperor's murderer.

'You recognised me?'

The praetorian shook his head in grim amusement.

'You may have forgotten your time with the Guard, young man, but I haven't. After all, I knew for several days before we received the order to kill your father that as the emperor's tame murderers my colleagues and I would be the men called upon to deal out imperial "justice". I used that time to have a good long look at you, Centurion, in readiness for the moment I faced you with a blade in my hand. I wanted to be sure that I wasn't going to get any nasty surprises.'

'And?'

Dorso shrugged.

'You were nothing that special, just another snotty-nosed senator's son who happened to be a little better trained than the average. You had the speed, and the technique, but you were still soft. You wouldn't even have seen me coming, although it might be a different story now since you seem to have hardened up a little since then, got yourself a scar or two. Your father sent you somewhere he expected you'd never be found, didn't he?'

'Britannia.'

'Yes, Britannia.' Dorso nodded and chuckled, clearly confirming something he had already known. 'Cold, wet and desolate, and forever being attacked by one barbarian tribe or another. I'll bet you've seen more fighting in the last two years than most of us get in a lifetime. And now here you are, hardened from the fire and ready to put your father's killers in the ground one at a time, eh?'

Marcus raised the knife again, showing the praetorian the pattern that ran through its fire-hardened metal shank. Dorso's face took on a reverent expression as he stared at the weapon.

'I've only ever seen that sort of metal once before, but the sword from which it was made was a deadly thing, capable of cutting through another blade with ease.'

Marcus looked about him.

'You seem fascinated with weaponry. You come here every night just to look at a collection of old iron?'

Dorso shrugged impassively.

'Not just *iron*, Valerius Aquila. This is the history of our people you see on these walls. Take that sword, for example . . .'

He pointed to a sword on the wall next to Marcus, and as the younger man turned to look at it, Dubnus put a massive hand on the praetorian's shoulder, digging the fingers into his flesh beneath the tunic, and raised his own copy of the dappled steel knife so that the blade's glinting edge was visible in the lamplight.

'Give me an excuse and I'll do the job for him.'

Marcus took the sword down from the wall, turning back to display the weapon to its owner.

'So what's so special about this then?'

Dorso shrugged again, ignoring the Briton's tight grip on his arm.

'In truth, it's really not all that distinguished, a nameless sword from the civil wars with no provenance other than its obvious age. It pales into insignificance when compared to the dagger carried by the blessed Julius's standard bearer, the man from the Tenth Legion who jumped into the surf when his follow soldiers were too frightened to set foot on the beach during the first invasion of Britannia – that's over there, behind you on the far wall. And yet you've found what used to be one of my most treasured pieces. Some poor anonymous grunt fought and most likely died with that in his hand, back in the days when the battles were massive day-long affairs with half-a-dozen legions on either side, and the fate of the republic rested on the outcome. Sometimes I just get that down and sit with it in my lap, wondering what happened to the poor bastard that carried it. After all, if he managed to survive the fighting, he'd probably have found his family starving when he got home. Too many of the middle-class men the armies depended on were killed in the civil wars, you see, and the day of the gentleman farmer was long gone by the time that Augustus put an end to it all by declaring himself emp—'

Marcus stalked back across the room with the antique sword in his hand.

'Spare me the history lesson, Dorso, before I allow this sword to taste blood one more time.'

The praetorian shook his head, the faint smile back on his face.

'You'd be better not leaving any visible wounds, wouldn't you Centurion? You need make it look like natural causes, I'd say, or the rest of our merry band of murderers will smell a rat and go to ground. I might have chosen to meet my fate head on, but I can assure you that they won't be as accommodating.'

The younger man stared at him for a moment before speaking again, his voice edged with disbelief.

'You really knew we were hunting you?'

The praetorian nodded.

'I had a fairly good idea. Unlike my fellow players in this dirty, bloody game that we play at the emperor's command, I heard the full detail of what happened in the throne room when Perennis died. You can imagine the chaos in our fortress when the guards on duty who witnessed it came back up the hill, and I was fortunate enough that the officer of the guard on the Palatine that night was a friend of mine, which meant I got to hear the full story, and without any of the interesting detail censored.'

The praetorian smiled bleakly at Marcus.

'I managed to get him on his own, once he'd been debriefed by Perennis's senior officers, and he told me the whole story, including the apparent involvement of a centurion from *Britannia*. He told me how that centurion, who, I should point out, apparently had a fresh scar across the bridge of his nose, looked as if he'd have dearly liked to have been the one that did for the prefect. And then, Valerius Aquila, just when I was wondering who that centurion might be, and why the emperor's new favourite Cleander had allowed him to vanish off into the night, my friend told me something which gave me the answers to questions I hadn't even asked. He told me that he was sure he knew that mysterious centurion from somewhere, but he just couldn't work out *where.*'

'He knew me from my time with the Guard.'

'Yes. But fortunately for both of us, the two of you didn't serve in the same cohort. He knew you as a face he'd seen around the fortress, if only he could have remembered, but he didn't make the connection I did. But then he hadn't listened as your former tribune suffered under the undivided attentions of the emperor's torturers. Having taken money from your father to send you away on the false errand that saved your life, the fool sobbed and screamed and bellowed out the place to which your faked orders had sent you, even before they subjected him to the necessary amount of agony to verify his story. And that place was Britannia. Britannia was the key to the puzzle, Valerius Aquila. The tribune told the torturers that your father sent you to Britannia, to the Sixth Legion in the province's north, and here was a centurion from Britannia bearing that legion's lost eagle *and* the severed head of its commanding officer. Your father sent you to the Sixth because of some previous relationship he had with that legatus, am I right?'

Marcus nodded.

'Legatus Sollemnis was my birth father. Appius Valerius Aquila took me on as a baby to save him the embarrassment and encumbrance of a child.'

Dorso nodded slowly.

'And so the last pieces of the puzzle slide neatly into place. And when I saw you in the tavern with that rather distinctive scar across your nose, I knew that my time to meet with Our Lord Mithras was at hand.'

Marcus stared uncomprehendingly at the older man.

'You recognised me, and yet you still chose to come here knowing that it would be your death sentence? Why?'

Dorso shook his head slowly, rubbing a hand across his face.

'Why just walk into your trap? I'm *tired*, young man. Tired of committing murder in the name of a man who isn't fit to be on the throne, tired of watching my fellow murderers indulging their sick fantasies with the innocent members of blameless families. I'm even tired of all this . . .'

He looked around at the room's panoply of antique weapons with a sigh.

'I used to come down here with a light heart, overjoyed to own such a fine collection of weapons from some of the most noteworthy periods of both the republic and the empire. See that?' He pointed to a long sword on the wall to their left. 'That's the blade that killed the Dacian emperor, Decebalus. I purchased it last year with my share from the murder of a particularly rich senator. It is an antique of almost inestimable value, and when I bought it I was filled with pleasure, and pride that a man from my relatively humble origins might own such a thing . . .' He paused, looking down at the floor and shaking his head. 'But over the last few months that pride has turned into disgust. Call it religion, call it conscience, but I am no longer able to take any pleasure from treasures purchased with innocent blood. In truth, Valerius Aquila, I'm more than tired. I'm *sick*, sick at heart, disgusted with myself for the things I allowed to happen in front of me, without intervening to offer some shred of dignity in death for so many innocents. I deserve to die, and offer some small recompense for their suffering.'

Dorso closed his eyes for a moment, then snapped them open and shot a pleading stare at Marcus.

'You will struggle to believe this, but I am at heart a decent man. My father taught me from my earliest days to do the right thing . . .' He waved a hand at the weapons that festooned the walls about them. 'But I allowed myself to be corrupted by my desire to own Rome's history, something I could never have achieved on a centurion's salary. Oh, I might have managed to buy one or two of the pieces you see before you, but I can assure you that this is the finest collection of weaponry you'll find anywhere in the city. Anywhere in the empire!' The praetorian's face, momentarily lit by the pleasure of his private museum, abruptly fell back into despair. 'And all of it tainted by the blood of those who had no need to die at all, or to undergo the suffering to which they were subjected.'

He shook his head, his lips twisted in disgust.

'Having accepted the role of imperial murderer, I quickly realised that I had already done too much and seen too much to ever be allowed to end my participation in that evil. The only way for a man to stop being a member of the Knives is for the other three to raise their blades and make a victim of him in his turn, and thereby ensure his silence. And so I participated in crimes of the most despicable nature, in the company of one man who can only be described as insane, another whose urge to prey upon the helpless is as disgusting as any vice I've ever witnessed, and a third who is only truly alive when he's in the act of killing. For all the evil that I have done, and for which I am truly disgusted with myself, I can assure you that what you will find when you track them down will be infinitely more base and revolting. I caution you, Valerius Aquila, to be careful that in dealing out the justice that you so badly desire, you do not find yourself taking on their worst character traits.'

He took a deep breath.

'And now, if you will, all I ask is that you make my end swift. When I'm gone I suggest that you burn this place, and destroy these grisly instruments of slaughter. It used to be that their antiquity, and what I assumed would have been their honourable use in defence of the city and people of Rome, provided me with some small measure of relief from the nagging self-hatred that my role as an imperial executioner caused me to feel. Now all I can feel is revulsion at the potential atrocities that may well have been committed with them in Rome's name with these weapons. Their destruction can only be for the good.'

Marcus walked away from Dorso, looking about him at the shadowed ranks of weapons that lined the walls around them.

'I had intended for you to die slowly, in an apparent eternity of agony, but it seems to me as if you've undergone much of that suffering already.' Marcus picked up the large jar of oil from which the lamps were refilled each night. 'There is a quick way for you to die, and one which will give little clue to your comrades that their destiny is upon them. Do you believe that you could tolerate the pain?'

The praetorian looked across the room at him with a grimace of anticipation.

'I can only accept the challenge. Spread the fuel around liberally though. Once I'm alight I want this whole grisly showcase to burn with me.'

Marcus showered oil across the floor in splattering arcs, soaking the thick rugs and curtains with it, then carried the jar over to Dorso. The older man took it from him, swiftly upending the clay container over his head and soaking himself with the remaining fluid. Large drops ran down his face and dripped from his beard onto the mosaic floor, and the two Tungrians backed away as he nodded at them, reaching up to take a torch from its sconce and hold the flame out before him.

'You see? I am ready to make amends for my sins, and I go to meet the Lightbringer! When next you pray to Our Lord, remind him of my sacrifice, and ask him to pardon my sins in recognition of my sacrifice in his name. And you, Valerius Aquila . . .' Marcus watched in horrified fascination as Dorso put the torch's blazing head to his tunic, the oil smoking furiously for an instant as it swiftly heated towards the point where it would burst into flame. 'Please forgive me! Forgive—' The praetorian's last word was lost in the sudden roar as the oil took fire.

His body was abruptly consumed by a column of flame that momentarily licked at the ceiling high above them. With a hideous shriek of agony the dying man tottered forward into a rack of spears and knocked it over in a toppling clatter, sprawling head-long into the puddle of the oil which Marcus had spilled at his request. With another concussive ignition, the floor around his writhing body was alight, and Dorso's screams strengthened from those of a man in agony to the pure, bestial howl of a creature from which any hint of humanity had been scoured by the flames.

Dubnus put a hand on his friend's shoulder and dragged him away.

'Come on! Before the whole place goes up, and we find ourselves having to explain to the urban cohorts why half the street's on fire!'

They fled, Marcus looking back as Dubnus pulled him into the alley and started shouting that there was a fire, seeing the flames flickering brightly at the museum's high windows. The glass popped and tinkled to the ground in a glittering shower, and Marcus realised, with a combination of gratitude and regret, that the praetorian's screaming had stopped, replaced by the fire's terrible, powerful roar.

4

'And then he simply set *fire* to himself?'

Excingus's voice, usually so carefully controlled in tone and inflection to give every impression of complete imperturbability, was as incredulous as the expression on his face. He'd appeared at the barracks' gate that morning soon after dawn, unbidden but clearly eager to know what had happened with Dorso. Marcus looked across the table at him, painfully aware that there was only a feeling of emptiness where'd he'd expected some sense of triumph in the wake of the praetorian's demise.

'As strange as it sounds, yes. From what he said before he put the torch to himself, he was suffering from an attack of conscience.'

The informer put his head to one side as if trying to work out what the word meant.

'And it sounds as if he was expecting you to make an appearance?'

The young centurion nodded.

'Yes. He'd learned enough about the circumstances of Perennis's death from the praetorians who were on duty when the prefect was murdered by Commodus to realise that I was back in the city.' Marcus grimaced. 'We were lucky. If he'd not had such a strong death wish then Dubnus and I would probably have been walking into a trap. As it was, I genuinely believe that he was marking himself for death.'

Excingus nodded slowly.

'And now you're not feeling *quite* as satisfied with the state of affairs as you thought you might, given his death, are you Centurion? You didn't want contrition, did you? You wanted a fight, and the chance to carve Dorso into ribbons with one of his own swords.'

Scaurus frowned at the informant, but Marcus shook his head.

'All I want is for the four men who murdered my family to suffer some measure of their misery and agony. And Dorso's death wasn't an easy one.'

Excingus laughed tersely.

'Apparently so. His screams were heard half a dozen streets away, I'm told. So, honour is satisfied to some small degree, and as far as the authorities are concerned it's a simple enough fire, which ought to stop the others taking fright. So, now that you've seen off one of them, are you sure you want to continue? *If,* of course, I could deliver another of them to the point of your sword?'

Scaurus's eyes narrowed.

'*If?* Share what you have, Informant.'

Excingus tipped his head to one side again, considering the tribune's demand.

'Really? I ask a question of the man seeking vengeance and you answer for him? I could wonder which of you feels the most strongly motivated . . .'

Scaurus turned to Marcus.

'He's right, loathe though I am to admit to it. This is first and foremost your concern. So, do you wish to continue?'

His centurion stared blankly at the table for a moment.

'I have no other choice. What do you have for us, Varius Excingus?'

The informant raised an eyebrow at the use of his name, but spoke quickly nonetheless.

'The gang leader Brutus has taken to the streets. It seems that there's another group of thugs who go by the name of the "Dog Eaters" encroaching on his territory, stripping away whole city blocks from his control and attacking his main business in each neighbouring block in turn.'

Julius spoke, having sat quietly throughout the previous discussion.

'And his main business is . . . ?'

'The same as every other gang you've ever run across, taking a piece of anything and everything he can muscle his way into.

Protection money, prostitution, theft . . . As their name suggests, it's a dog-eat-dog life at that level of society, and it seems that an even bigger dog has decided to eat dear old Brutus's dinner.'

'And what do you mean by "taken to the streets"?'

Excingus turned back to Scaurus.

'Exactly what it sounds like. He's fighting a war for survival, and in a war the last thing the general wants is for the enemy to find and overrun his headquarters. He's gone underground – possibly quite literally so – and is directing his army from a place that should be safe from attack since nobody knows where it is.'

'And in reality?'

The informant grinned savagely.

'I have an . . . associate, shall we say, although associating with him is a little like making a pet of a viper. He lives and practises what I will euphemistically call his trade in the Aventine district, with a loose affiliation to one of the smaller gangs that supports Brutus. It seems that they have been contracted, secretly and under threat of a slow and nasty death, to secure a secret hideout for Brutus and his senior men, somewhere from which they can direct the fight for their ground without the risk of being disturbed by unfriendly strangers. My man Silus, expensively purchased I can assure you, not only knows the location of this place, but has agreed to take a small party of men to it, when the time is right. And word has reached them that Brutus intends taking occupation of this clandestine headquarters for a day or two from tonight. He only stays in each safe house for a short time, choosing the next location at random, but with every change he has to give his men a few hours to make sure that his networks of runners and soldiers can be realigned to keep him informed and protected. So, gentlemen, tomorrow night would appear to be your best opportunity, *if* you want to put your heads into the lion's mouth?'

Later that morning, Julius looked around the shop that Cotta had rented, pulling a disgusted face at the state of the space in which he stood. The shop's floor was little more than a selection of warped and mismatched boards laid over the rough dirt beneath them, while the coating of plaster that had originally adorned the walls had long since been reduced to a few patches that clung stubbornly to the bricks, fragments of paint giving some hint as to their original bright decoration.

'What a fucking dump! This place can't have seen a copper coin's worth of maintenance since Hadrian was on the throne. And we paid *how* much for this shithole?'

The veteran centurion standing beside him grinned at their surroundings.

'Your expectations are a little out of alignment with the reality of Rome, First Spear. What we're paying per month for this place wouldn't normally cover the cost of a shop like this for a week, but then it's not really in the best spot and, as you say, it is a little basic . . .' He waved a hand at the shop's dilapidated state. 'But then we've got an asset that'll make short work of even this mess.'

The other man looked round at him with a snort of incredulity.

'You think my soldiers can sort this out? We're fighting men, not the assorted collection of plumbers and plasterers that you were chasing around in your legion cohort.'

Cotta smiled, tapping his purse.

'In which case I'll have a wager with you that we can have this place tidied, painted and ready for business inside a day, once the groundwork's out of the way. I've got just the men lined up, since your Centurion Dubnus was kind enough to find me some volunteers who are the least likely to leave a customer looking as if he's had his hair cut by a butcher. You leave me to it and I'll have the first customer in here and on his arse being asked how he'd like his hair cut before sunset tomorrow, if your ditch diggers don't hold the whole thing up. Shall we call it ten sestertii?'

The first spear shook his head hurriedly.

'No, we fucking well won't call it ten sestertii. If you're that sure you can get my lads grafting that hard then you must have some secret weapon up your sleeve. On you go then, I've got military matters to be discussing, and no time to bandy words with a man who clearly missed his way in life. A shopkeeper is what you should have been . . .'

Cotta grinned, calling out into the street for his volunteers. The soldiers filed into the shop with a barrel-chested soldier at their head, the veteran looking about him with eyes that were as alert to the possibilities of the situation as always, and his first spear raised a knowing eyebrow.

'Morban. I should have known you'd manage to find a way to get out of having to work up a sweat with the rest of your century, rather than just strutting about and pretending to be a soldier. Let's hope our new colleague here knows what he's getting into if he's going to trust this new enterprise of his to your tender care!'

The standard bearer saluted and snapped to attention with a precision that widened the eyes of the men at his back before they caught the look on Julius's face and hastily followed his example as he stalked past them and out into the street, calling to Avidus who was staring intently at the local architecture with a look of bemusement.

'Well then, Centurion, that's not a look I wanted to see on your face.'

The engineer scratched his head, waving a hand at the apartment block at whose base the shop stood.

'I'm just trying to work out whether what you want is possible. The good news is that this block looks reasonably sturdy, so it shouldn't be too difficult for us to do the work without bringing it down on top of us.' He looked up at the building with a professional's disdain. 'Although it wouldn't take much to have the whole block fall in on itself, since it's not exactly built to last. The bad news however . . .' He looked about him again, shaking his head. 'Is that I have absolutely no idea what we'll find once we get the floor up, and if it's rock we're going to make a right bloody racket.'

Julius pointed at the main road up the hill, less than fifty paces distant from Felicia's house on the far side.

'See that street? It's quiet enough now, but once it's dark it's a non-stop procession of carts, with all of the banging and crashing you could ever want to cover up any noise you'll be making, not to mention the cursing and shouting when a horse or a mule isn't pulling its weight or just drops dead from overwork. You could probably quarry out enough rock to build a bath house without anyone being any the wiser. Are your boys ready?'

Avidus grinned and then whistled sharply, and a dozen men lounging against the shop front got to their feet, their tools held ready to work.

'They're as eager as shithouse dogs with the smell of a sausage. A night in the brothel of their choice after a month of nothing better than changing hands at ninety-nine, that's enough to get my lads working up a sweat any time you like!'

Julius nodded, raising his eyebrows in silent comment.

'And it's a promise I'll keep once I've got a nice big storeroom underneath the shop, ready to fill with shields and weapons.'

'You're sure that's wise? If the Watch find out . . .'

The engineer left his statement unfinished, but both men knew the risk involved in what Scaurus and Julius were planning.

'You can leave me to worry about that. Just concentrate on getting my hole dug, eh?'

Avidus saluted ironically.

'Same old fuckin' army. Only difference is I won't have to fill this hole in once it's dug.'

The first spear turned away, his face creased by an evil smile.

'Who says you won't be filling it in again?'

Excingus met his spies at the Ostian gate, looking about him with his customary caution before squatting down to join the ragged group of children. A grizzled and filthy man wearing the remnants of a military tunic was dozing in the morning sun twenty paces away, but otherwise the scene around the gate was one of busy normality. The children's leader, a boy so worldly wise before his time that the informant was still uncertain whether to be repelled or fascinated by the urchin, looked up at him with apparent disinterest.

'We was wondering when you was going to turn up. Or *if* you was going to turn up, given what you told us to do yesterday got us caught by them bastards in the fort.'

Excingus raised an eyebrow.

'Somebody's brighter than I gave them credit for. What did they do to you?'

The child shook his head disparagingly.

'Nothing. The officer in charge offered us money to work for him.'

The informant clapped his hands together.

'Excellent! And I presume that you accepted?'

The urchin looked up at him with an expression of disbelief. ''Course I did!'

Excingus smiled at him with apparent fondness.

'You're a little brighter than your father, aren't you, Gaius? Silus must have married above himself when it came to intelligence. Very well, what was it that Julius wanted from you?'

Gaius picked at a fingernail.

'You ain't getting it that easy. Remember what you said to me when you took us on to be your eyes and ears?'

The informant smiled knowingly.

'There's a price for everything . . .'

'And everything has its price. So there you go.'

The child raised an expectant eyebrow at Excingus, who sighed and dipped a hand into his pocket.

'Here.' He placed a coin on the outstretched palm, shaking his head as the child examined it with pursed lips. 'Don't push your luck, brat. Either take the coin or consider the consequences. After all, you *have* just sold me out.'

Gaius nodded equably.

'He told me that they don't trust you.'

Excingus's face took on a pained expression.

'I'd managed to deduce that already. What else?'

'They want us to report back on where you go and what you do. Everything.'

Excingus nodded.

'Excellent. I do so enjoy the realisation of a scheme.'

The child frowned, tilting his head to one side.

'You wanted us to get caught?'

'Oh, well *done* . . .'

Gaius shook his head as the man clapped his hands together in ironic applause.

'You fuckin—'

Excingus reached out and took a handful of the boy's tunic, pulling him close and showing him the blade of a small dagger.

'Let's never forget who the real brains is here, shall we, Gaius? You think in terms of where tonight's dinner is coming from, whereas I consider how best to set myself up for the rest of my life. This is going to be the last job I ever do, if I get it right, because there's enough gold washing around for a small but nicely significant fraction of it to stick to my fingers. I dangled you outside that barracks until Julius couldn't resist taking the bait, and now I have a means of making him believe anything I want. Those idiots are going to dance to my music from now on, and you're going to make sure that they hear exactly what I want them to hear. Aren't you?'

By lunchtime the engineers were well into their task, having ripped out the shop's dingy floorboards and enthusiastically dug down into the spongy tufa beneath them at a pace, which had made the Tungrians wide-eyed with amazement.

'They're going at it like madmen!'

Cotta looked down into the rapidly deepening pit, grinning at Morban as the sweating Tungrians passed the clods of freshly hewn tufa out into the street, where it was thrown into the cart waiting at the door.

'Ah, well that's the joy of tufa, standard bearer. When you cut it out of the ground it's more like thick, spongy mud than rock, but once it's exposed to the air it hardens up like brick. These lads know that as long as they keep going, and don't give it time to set, they can have a much easier time of it. We'll . . .'

He frowned as one of a group of diggers who had been labouring hard at a spot close to the door, which was stubbornly resisting their picks, raised a hand, calling for Avidus. The weather-beaten engineer took one look at whatever it was that his man had unearthed, and looked up at Cotta, beckoning him down into the hole. Intrigued, Morban followed, only to recoil as he realised what it was that the engineers had uncovered.

'No wonder your boys were going slower in this spot, the tufa's already been dug up and replaced once. He waved a hand under his nose and grimaced.

'Stinks too . . .'

The excavation had revealed a human hand, black with putre-faction but nevertheless clearly recognisable.

'You!' Cotta pointed to one of his men. Fetch the doctor.'

Felicia arrived shortly after, and looked at the corpse for a moment before speaking, her professional curiosity softened by compassion and more than a little relief at the news that only one body had been found.

'I was worried that you might have found my former husband's brother and his family.' She bent closer to look at the now fully excavated corpse, ignoring its revolting smell. 'It's a woman's body, but she must have been dead for weeks, poor thing. Will you bury her?'

Cotta nodded at the question.

'Yes. We'll wrap her in enough material to disguise what it is we're carrying out to the cart, once we've got something to take the edge off the smell.' He looked round at Morban, smiling wanly at his green complexion. 'Make yourself useful, eh, standard bearer? Do the rounds of the local shops for a block or so. Introduce yourself as the new proprietor of this shop, and explain that we're digging out a basement for storage. While you're at it, make enquiries, gently mind you, after the owner of this place.'

Morban stared at him grimly.

'You want me to find out if he had a wife—'

Cotta raised a finger.

'*Has* a wife. Let's assume that nobody else knows about this act of concealment, in which case the lady in question might just be "visiting her mother". Or this might not be his wife, it might be a girlfriend who threatened to reveal all and paid for it with her life. So gently does it, eh? And while you're at it, buy some quicklime.'

Morban was back an hour later, the look on his face no less grim than it had been when he left, and which darkened further at the sight of the dead woman's excavated corpse.

'The locals seem like a decent enough lot, especially once they realised we're not going to give them any competition. Seems our landlord had a young wife, much younger than he is, and the first flush of love was long since over the horizon. More than one of the people I talked to found it fit to mention gladiators . . .'

Cotta and Avidus exchanged knowing glances.

'So she was over the side of their canoe and paddling vigorously with men of a more suitable age . . .'

Avidus nodded wryly at Cotta's opinion.

'And stamina.'

'As a result of which she ended up under the floorboards of his shop. I presume he was just going to give any questions as to her whereabouts a blank face, and wait for her to be forgotten.'

Morban took a foot-high earthenware pot from one of his men and handed it to Avidus.

'Quicklime. Ought to be more than enough for one little girl like that. What will you do with her?'

Cotta looked down at the corpse for a moment before speaking.

'Get her in the cart and bury her in rubble, with enough lime to stop her stinking while we take her past the gate guards, and dump her somewhere quiet.' He gestured to Avidus. 'You look after that, and I'm going for a chat with our landlord . . .'

Qadir walked into the tribune's office and saluted, standing to attention and staring at the wall behind Scaurus's head, much to Cotta's amusement. The tribune waved a hand at the spare chair, smiling at his centurion's determined expression.

'Do sit down Centurion, and relax just a little?'

Julius nodded encouragingly, and the Hamian perched on the

stool provided. Cotta resumed his story of the day's events in his usual matter-of-fact tone.

'So I went round to his house, covered in dust from the digging of course, and he came out to greet me with the usual haughty look on his face.' He grinned at the recollection. 'I asked him if he had a bad smell in his nose, and then while he was frowning at that, I tossed a piece of her tunic on the floor in front of him. A lovely colour when it was new, I'd imagine, and still recognisable as green despite the fact we had to peel it off her like it was her own skin. He went as white as a vestal's virgin's stola, the poor bastard.'

'And?'

The veteran shrugged at Julius's question.

'He stood there for a moment and then just sat down on his arse, as if his legs had suddenly given up on him. I suppose he'd been shitting himself ever since he did it, and then to have the evidence slapped on the floor in front of him without any warning was all too much for him. I helped him up, and got him inside, and then we had a little chat about it. Seems that she got a little too brazen for her own good, thinking that just because he couldn't get it up any longer he'd tolerate her parading around with her lover. Some gladiator or other. Once she was dead, he realised how deep the shit he'd blundered into was, given that her family aren't the forgiving kind, so he buried her in the shop by lamplight and then pretended that she'd run off with another man, and that he was the wounded party.'

'I see.' Scaurus leaned back in his chair. 'And what do you propose we do about this crime of passion?'

Cotta shook his head.

'Beyond using it to make sure that he gives us every little bit of help we ask him for? Nothing. He killed her in a fit of rage, he's still full of remorse three months on, and turning him over to the Watch isn't going to bring her back. I think we leave this sleeping dog to lie. Besides, I expect that we can use the leverage to good effect at some point. He owns a selection of commercial properties in some rather nice areas, so there's bound to be a favour of some sort he can do for us soon enough.

The tribune thought for a moment.

'I concur. And you, Centurion, what news do you bring?'

Qadir's Latin, as impeccable as ever, was gently accented from his upbringing in the empire's east.

'Tribune, I have a report for you from our spies in the city.'

Scaurus nodded, leaning forward.

'Julius tells me that you're to be congratulated on the speed with which you've turned some of our wilier soldiers into spies. One of these days you really must take me through how it all works, and where you learned this particular trade for that matter. You've had men following Excingus all day?'

'Indeed, ever since he came here this morning, Tribune.' Qadir looked down at the tablet he had placed on the desk in front of him. 'Firstly, the target met with the children who were detained in the barracks yesterday. My best man was close enough to hear the tone of the discussion although not the words, and he reported that it all seemed quite amicable.'

Scaurus looked at Julius.

'So either they've chosen not to tell him about your bribe . . .'

Julius shrugged.

'Or they told him and he took his usual pragmatic approach to almost anything, up to and including having a knife at his throat.'

'Yes. He does rather tend to roll with whatever gets thrown at him, doesn't he? So we'll either get accurate information from these children or be fed a pack of lies on the basis that he'll promptly outbid us on the bribery front.'

Qadir coughed gently, and the two men turned back to him.

'In either case my men will, it is to be hoped, provide us with definitive evidence of his movements. After meeting with the children, Excingus then went back into the city, and made his way to a rather unexpected location. One of the men set to tail him ran back to our usual meeting place and briefed me, and I had time to make my way to the spot in time to see him leave.'

He stood, pointing to an area on the map of the city that

Scaurus had commissioned in order to be able to plan his next steps with better understanding of the distances involved.

'He went to this place, and was inside for over an hour.'

Scaurus stared at him in silence.

'The Gardens of Sallust? You're *sure* about this? I wouldn't have had Excingus in mind when I thought about a keen botanist.'

Qadir nodded.

'And now you understand why I went to see for myself. When Excingus left the gardens, he looked more than usually pleased with himself, and I would judge from his expression that whatever business he had been transacting inside had gone very well.'

The tribune nodded.

'And the Gardens of Sallust are less than half a mile from Senator Albinus's villa. It's as we suspected, I suppose, Excingus has been making friends in high places. And after that?'

The Hamian turned to face Julius.

'After that, First Spear, he walked across the valley to a small house on the Viminal Hill. He was most cautious as he approached the location, changing direction three times and doubling back twice to expose any potential followers, but by the grace of the goddess Deasura we managed to keep sight of him. His destination appears to have been his home, as he had not come out by the time that night fell.'

Scaurus sat back with a look of satisfaction.

'Excellent. One day of your men's work has shown us who's behind him in this interesting little matter and where our supposedly tame informant lives. That's good work by any measure.'

Qadir inclined his head gravely in acceptance of the praise.

'And if I might make a suggestion, Tribune?'

'Please do.'

The Hamian assumed a thoughtful look.

'I am comfortable that we have the skills necessary to continue tracking him around the city, but I feel that we were a little lucky to have followed him back to his home without alerting him, given how thoroughly he tried to expose anyone that might be following him. I suggest that now we know where he lives we keep well clear once we know he's heading in that direction?'

Scaurus nodded.

'You're right, there's no point tipping him off that we know where he sleeps. We'll stay clear of him once he's heading for home, but perhaps we ought to watch him once he's there?'

Qadir smiled slightly.

'I have predicted this suggestion, Tribune. Rome's gutters have a new pair of beggars this evening.'

The next morning, with the new cellar excavated, a narrow, open side set of stairs dug into the rock to allow easy access, and with rather better-quality floorboards installed in the shop above, Morban's men set about renovating their establishment in preparation for its opening. Working at their various tasks under the standard bearer's guidance, jibes and cajoling, they made swift progress in re-plastering and painting the walls and ceiling.

'Get your backs into it boys, I'm working to a schedule here!'

One of the older men shot him a jaundiced look as he trowelled plaster onto his section of the wall, his raised eyebrows revealing just how aware he was of the veteran's ability to turn a profit from almost any situation.

'Got a bet on it, have you, Morban?'

His sally was met with a knowing look from the standard bearer.

'No, but I know something you don't. If we have this place working by first thing tomorrow then there's a share of the profit available to us.'

He smiled smugly as the soldiers turned to look at him with new interest.

'What sort of share?'

'Thirty per cent, and the rest to the burial club.' The men nodded to each other at the mention of the fund that would ensure that each of them would receive the proper rites and commemoration at the end of his life. 'Which means that given there's eight of you, you lot get three per cent apiece of everything we earn.'

One of the swifter brains among them worked the numbers.

'Which means you're taking six per cent?'

Morban raised an eyebrow at him.

'And . . . ?'

The man in question, a standard bearer from another century, shook his head in mock confusion.

'So we does all the work for three coins on the hundred apiece, and you does sod all for six? Doesn't seem straight to me.'

The standard bearer shook his head pityingly.

'All you've got to do is clean this place up, slap on some plaster and paint a flying prick on the wall for luck, carry in a few chairs and then laze about until we actually have hair to cut. I, on the other hand, have to keep you idle bastards working, make sure you do it right, go and find customers, take the money, count the money . . . Do I need to go on?'

Another man spoke up sardonically.

'They're letting you count the money as well?'

Morban smiled happily back at him.

'Oh yes. My counting skills will be well employed here and that's a fact.'

The soldier turned back to work.

'Better resign yourselves to *two* per cent lads, old sticky fingers is back in the saddle.'

'The fat one went off round the neighbourhood asking questions, and he bought a pot of quicklime as well. And later on, when it was quieter, they carried something out to the cart, wrapped in a sheet, and it looked wet, or at least the sheet did. Smelled rotten too.'

Excingus stroked his chin, taking a sip of his drink before responding to the child's story.

'So they were digging, and in the course of that excavation they found a body of some nature. I find the corpse of little interest, but the digging by which they discovered it is a good deal more fascinating. Why would they be digging a basement for a barber's shop, I wonder?' He pondered for a moment. 'Find out what they're up to down there, will you, Gaius?'

The child looked back at him with something close to incredulity.

'How am I supposed to do that? Just wander up and ask for a look in the new cellar?'

The informant waved a hand, dismissing the question.

'As you get older – *if* you live long enough to get older, given your constant urge to question the instructions of your betters – you will learn that the most important question a man can ask is not "*how*". If I have to tell you how you are to achieve this simple task then I might as well do it myself. I don't care how you do it, only that you do it. You don't imagine that these soldiers have rented a shop, and have redecorated it at their own cost, for the simple fun of commerce do you? They have a reason for setting up this establishment, whatever it is that they plan to sell as a cover for their real activities, and I want to know what it is, because not knowing is making me a good deal more nervous than you can imagine.'

He stood, tossing a coin onto the table.

'Off with you, and don't come back without a detailed picture of what it is that they have down there or I may be forced to find someone else to do the job. You have a meeting with my good friend Julius today?' Gaius nodded. 'And you remember the story I gave you for him?'

'You met with Senator Albinus yesterday, and agreed to sell him information about where and when he can set a trap for the soldiers.' The child frowned. 'But I still don't see why—'

'Why I would allow them to learn such a thing?' He reached forward, putting a hand over the child's eyes. 'Tell me, what can you see?'

'Well I can't see fuck all, can I?'

'Exactly. There is a city in front of your eyes, but all you can see is my hand.'

He removed the hand, and Gaius looked up at him with an expression of dawning comprehension.

'You want the soldiers looking at the hand?'

'And not the much bigger picture that it conceals. Exactly. Now be off with you, I too have a meeting to attend.'

He strode out into the street, ignoring the beggars who hailed him vociferously from the gutter, and walked away towards the spot he had detailed in his message to Albinus. Arriving to discover that the senator was already in his place, he dropped into a chair beside him, waiting until the guards who had accompanied Albinus to the gardens had withdrawn out of earshot. Since Cotta's sudden departure from his service, the senator had taken to surround himself with former gladiators, any of whom Excingus suspected would be happy enough to cut his throat just for the simple pleasure of watching a man die.

'You seem very keen, Senator. I thought I was early for our meeting, but I find you already here.'

The other man replied in a soft tone of voice, but with clear irritation.

'And I thought you and I had a bargain, Informant? Me to pay you in gold, and you to provide me with the opportunity to take Scaurus and his man Aquila unawares? And now I discover that one of the emperor's band of killers is dead? I suppose you'll try to fob me off with some story of suicide, but I—'

'Far from it, Senator.'

Excingus waited for a moment, allowing Albinus to speak again if he so wished, but the other man simply fixed him with a hard stare and raised his eyebrows.

'Continue.'

'As I said, this was no suicide. Aquila and that brute of a centurion who accompanies him everywhere jumped Centurion Dorso and his men on the street, killed the bodyguards, and dragged Dorso into his private residence. They murdered him in a most gruesome way, dousing him with oil before setting light to him.'

Albinus raised his eyebrows in horror, staring up at the trees above them.

'I heard that his cremated corpse was found in the ruins of a private house, but to have burned him alive? This Aquila has sunk to the level of the barbarians who follow him around! I'll serve him up some good old-fashioned Roman justice when I get the chance!' He shook his head, then turned back to the informant. 'So why is it, given our agreement, that you gave me no fore-warning of this opportunity to snap them up?'

Excingus raised an eyebrow.

'I would have thought that was obvious, Senator. Our deal is for the delivery of both Aquila *and* Tribune Scaurus, is it not? Were I to have set you in motion to have your revenge last night, then you would only have taken one of the two. Not only would the man who has caused you the greater offence still be alive, but he would also be forewarned, and in command of fifteen hundred men, many of whom, I am informed, feel great loyalty to this Aquila.' He looked about him at the senator's ragtag bodyguard. 'I doubt that your few men, who seem rather better muscled than they are equipped for swift action, would have much hope of holding them off if they came for you in numbers.' He shook his head and wagged an admonishing finger at the surprised Albinus. 'No, if this is to be done then it must be done correctly, and last night offered no such opportunity. When the opportunity presents itself, you will be the first to know.'

He smiled at the senator.

'*Trust* me.'

Morban looked about him at the shop's renewed decoration, the paint still drying on parts of the walls while the air was filled with the aroma of fresh plaster. A neatly painted winged phallus adorned one wall, and the chairs in which their customers would sit to receive their barbering were lined up in two ordered rows.

'Lovely.' He glanced around the group of soldiers, all of whom had changed into clean tunics, clapping his hands together and rubbing them gleefully. 'Right then! You lot, brace yourselves for business. I've got an idea how we can drum up some custom nice and quickly.'

Strolling out into the sunshine he waddled across the street, filling his lungs with a deep breath before bellowing at the top of his voice, cutting through the hubbub with the practised ease of a man who was used to making himself heard.

'*Half-price haircuts! Half-price shaves! Today only, get your hair cut in the latest fashion by trained barbers! Half-price haircuts! Impress the ladies with a smooth chin and be the envy of your friends! Half-price shaves! No more looking as if you've cut your hair with a knife, we'll leave you looking . . .*'

He grinned broadly at a man who had stopped in his tracks.

'Haircut is it, sir? Or perhaps you'd like to find out just how good you'd look after a shave from one of our expert tonsors? Walk this way, and prepare to be astounded!'

He led the bemused customer into the shop, pointing to the soldier he judged least likely to cut their first customer's throat by accident.

'You, here's a customer. Give him the closest, smoothest shave you can, and as our very first customer we'll make it gratis as long as he promises to tell his friends just how good our bargain prices are!'

The customer in question beamed happily, quickly taking his place in the chair indicated. Nodding seriously, the 'tonsor' in question whipped out a military dagger and set to stropping its edge against a leather strap. Taken aback by the weapon's unexpected appearance, the man in the chair took on an uneasy look and started to rise from his seated position only to find a powerful hand pushing him back while the soldier addressed him in a gruff voice.

'Keep still mate. I won't cut you unless you move, but if I do cut you then it'll be right nasty . . .'

He smeared a handful of olive oil around the customer's chin, quickly coating the now terrified man's beard with the slippery fluid before setting to with his blade. After a few deft strokes his potential victim began to realise that he'd not actually been cut yet, and that each pass of the knife was painlessly removing a section of what had hitherto been a stubborn growth of stubble. The soldier grinned down at him, seeing the relaxation slowly soften his tensed features.

'Yeah, good isn't it? This knife's a fucking beauty, the best I've ever had, holds an edge easy and it's good for the toughest work.

I even did a barbarian with it in Dacia last year, when I lost my sword in a goat-fuck of a fight . . .' He paused, shaking his head in irritation as a trickle of blood ran down the now thoroughly terrified customer's cheek. 'Now look what you've made me do! I *told* you not to move!'

Cotta walked into the barbers' shop shortly before dusk, nodding a greeting to Morban. His men, having shaved and tonsored the day's last customers and swept away their clipped hair, were waiting for the command to be on their way with the eagerness of men who were planning a full night's entertainment.

'On your way boys, and remember, you're all back on duty here at dawn. And no getting so pissed up that your razor hands are still shaking when you get here, eh?'

The soldiers made their exit without having to be asked twice, heading out into the city with respectful nods and half-salutes to the veteran. Morban waved a hand at the chair in front of his desk.

'Have a seat, Centurion, take the weight off while I finish cashing up.'

Cotta sat, fixing his eyes on the standard bearer and watching with interest as his hands moved deftly over the piles of coins arrayed in neat piles on the desk.

'My old man always used to say, when he wasn't face down on his bed from too much wine or chasing recruits and thrashing them with his vine stick, that the way a man looks at things will tell you a lot about him.'

Morban looked up momentarily, feigning a curiosity that Cotta could see through with ease.

'Really?'

'Yes, he did. And the older I get, the more I respect the old bastard's opinion . . .'

He deliberately went quiet, until the silence got to the other man in exactly the intended manner. Morban looked up, a sudden hint of disquiet in his swift glance, then looked back down at the money.

'There it is. Just like he said, it's in the eyes. So, Morban, you came recommended to me as a man with a magical touch with money.'

The standard bearer smiled in an attempt at self-deprecation.

'Really? That was kind of—'

'Yes.' The centurion's voice hardened. 'I was told that any money that was put in front of you would, if you were left alone with it, magically start to vanish.'

The other man reared back with an indignant expression.

'Just a minute! I—'

'Resemble that comment?'

Morban's eyes narrowed at the time-honoured put-down.

'I've counted all this money three times now: thirty-three shaves and seventy-five haircuts, which comes to . . .'

'So that's fifty-eight customers, is it?'

The veteran soldier's eyes narrowed as the deceptive lightness of Cotta's tone sank in.

'Ahhh . . . no. In fact it was seventy-two.'

He met the centurion's stare with his most impassive mask and waited for a response. Cotta shook his head slowly, and something in his impassive stare sounded a warning in the standard bearer's mind.

'Once an officer always an officer, eh? Alright it was seventy-eight . . .' The veteran centurion held his gaze steady. I'm telling you, seventy-eight customers. And that's it.'

Cotta nodded.

'Very good. I do so like it when I come to an accommodation with an experienced senior man like you.'

He held out a hand, and Morban opened the desk drawer, pulling out a purse and sweeping the money arrayed across the flat wooden surface into it before dropping the purse into the outstretched palm.

'About the lads' bonus?'

'And yours for that matter?'

The standard bearer grinned shamelessly.

'Well, now that you mention it . . .'

Cotta shook his head in feigned disbelief.

'Every time I think I've met the most barefaced crook that could ever exist in the army, someone goes and proves me wrong. You can take the bonus out of the money you're still holding back from the other fifteen heads that your lads cropped today.'

Morban gaped as the secure ground he thought he'd managed to put beneath his feet abruptly dropped away.

'How . . . ?'

Cotta stood.

'How did I know how many haircuts your boys have got through today? That's for me to know and for you to wonder, I'd say. You'll work it out in your own time. When I see your lads I'll tell them that you've got their share for the day, shall I?'

'But that won't cover it!'

Cotta grinned, bending to pinch the older man's cheek.

'No, it won't, will it? Perhaps this old dog might just have learned a new trick tonight – not to lie to a man that's forgotten more ways to make money vanish than you'll ever know. Goodnight Morban!'

Excingus dropped wearily into the chair facing Gaius, waving a hand at the landlord who promptly sent one of his daughters over with a flask of wine. Having deposited flask and cups onto the table, she fixed the informer with a sultry pout, squeezing her breasts together to make them protrude alluringly. Excingus waved the hand again to dismiss her, shaking his head firmly as her pout went from allure to disgust.

'On your way child. You're too young for me, I'm too tired to do you justice, and my young friend here doesn't have a fully functioning phallus yet. Come back in two or three years' time.'

The child frowned at him.

'How do you know my dick doesn't work!? For all you know, I could be—'

'Looking at your hairless sausage in puzzlement, I'd imagine. What did you find out for me?'

Gaius shrugged.

'About the barber's new cellar? Nothing.'

Excingus poured himself a cup of wine with an expression of profound disappointment at the child's answer.

'I give you one simple thing to find out, and all you can say is "nothing"?'

The boy regarded him steadily.

'Exactly. Nothing. There's nothing down there.'

'What?' The informer shook his head in fresh irritation. 'So you did get a look at it! How did you manage that?'

Gaius shrugged.

'You ain't the only one with money that wants to know things. We was employed to watch the place and tell that centurion that's playing at being the boss how many men went in and out.'

Excingus raised his eyes in disbelief.

'You're telling me that you were paid to count haircuts? Sometimes I wonder if the whole city has gone mad.' He shrugged. 'So, while you were counting heads, exactly how did you manage to get down the stairs?'

Gaius grinned.

'Simple. I got a haircut.'

The informant smirked.

'Yes, now you mention it, you do look a little more military than you did this morning.'

The boy ignored his comment.

'And when I was done I took a quick peek down the stairs. They never even knew I'd done it. After all, nobody gives any mind to a little boy being a bit nosey, do they?'

'And?'

'I *told* you. Nothing!'

'It is with the greatest of difficulty that I am restraining myself from taking a handful of what little hair you have left and banging your irritating fucking head on this table.' Excingus was grating his words out in a mixture of fatigue and irritation. 'What. Did. You. *See?*'

'An empty cellar. Just rough rock walls and nothing else.'

Excingus sat back with a frown.

'Why? Why go to all the trouble of building a cellar and then leaving it empty? I was sure there'd be weapons down there, but if it's just a bare storeroom perhaps that's all there is to it.' He mused in silence for a moment. 'Perhaps I'm reading too much into it after all. They *are* soldiers, and the army always likes to overdo anything it takes on . . .'

He shrugged.

'No matter. And it's time I was elsewhere.' Taking his cup from the table, he downed its remaining contents and stood. 'It's time to go and meet your father, and encourage him to deliver young Aquila's next victim. With a little luck Brutus's thugs will catch the arrogant young bastard and carve his lungs out.'

Cotta led six of his men through the Viminal district's darkened streets behind Excingus, with Marcus close at his heels, while the informant's man Silus walked cautiously twenty paces ahead of the party to check each road junction for any presence of the city's Watch before signalling that the path was clear. The veteran centurion had bluntly refused to consider Marcus's attempts to leave him behind when they had set off from the barracks.

'And besides, you'll need some men at your back if you're going to put this Brutus to the knife, or you'll never get past his men. And you can't take soldiers. Trailing Excingus around is one thing, but going up against a gang like the Silver Dagger will need men who know these streets, and how to fight in them, and that means my lads. And what about this *Silus*, eh? How likely is *he* to be trustworthy?'

The veteran soldier had predictably taken an instant dislike to their guide upon meeting him an hour or so before, when Excingus had beckoned him from the shadows of the Baths of Trajan to join their small, furtive party. To the veteran centurion's experienced eye, the informer's man had the look of a killer, the same dead look to his eyes that he saw in some of his own men.

'But whereas I know my men well enough to trust them, this Silus is a stranger to me. He can be trusted not to lead us into a fucking great trap, I assume?'

He'd asked the question of Excingus bluntly, albeit having led the informant far enough from the group of soldiers for a degree of privacy.

'No.' The answer had been equally frank, in Excingus's usual matter-of-fact tone. 'I expect he would sell us out, given half a chance, but I have him by the balls, or at least I hope so. He knows that my sponsor in this matter is fully aware of his part in it, and where his family resides. I'd like to think that he's tied to me by the fear of whatever retribution might be visited on him, and his enormous herd of children and blood relatives, but ultimately there's no denying that we're taking a risk in employing his services.' His teeth had flashed in the moonlight, the familiar smile that made Cotta want to punch him with every ounce of his strength. 'And if you have a better idea as to how we can make this happen, I am veritably all ears.'

The veteran centurion had simply shaken his head in the face of the smug smile and gestured for Excingus to carry on. Gathering the party around him, the informant's briefing had been short and to the point.

'Brutus and his men have moved into an insula not far from here. It has five floors. I can take you to it.'

Cotta had waited a moment, looking expectantly at Silus, then leaned forward to whisper a question with a disbelieving tone in his voice.

'That's it? That's all we know? We've no idea how many of them there are? Or what defences they might have installed to fend off an attack by their rivals?'

The street thug had nodded dourly.

'That's all I know. I can tell you from experience that Brutus will have at least a dozen of his best men with him, although they won't all be standing guard at the same time. And he usually puts a man on the roof to watch the surrounding streets, and another one or two at ground level to guard the entrance. After that?' He shrugged disinterestedly. 'After that it's anyone's guess. Perhaps half of them will be asleep . . . perhaps.'

Cotta had shaken his head in disgust.

'And not your problem, eh? This is going to be bloody interesting . . .'

Now they were within a hundred paces or so of the building,
and Silus's progress had slowed to a cautious creep through the
shadows of the insulae that towered over them on either side. The
streets were quiet, and Cotta's party were moving with the stealth
of men who understood that their lives might well depend on
remaining undiscovered until the very last moment. Without
warning, Silus sank into the deeper shadows, raising a palm to
warn them of approaching danger, and Cotta's men followed his
example and went to ground in the gloom.

A pair of men walked past at the street's end, each of them
carrying a heavy club.

'City Watch?'

Excingus shrugged.

'Impossible to say without asking them. And even if they are
the Watch, they'll be in Brutus's pocket, most likely, so the end
result would probably be much the same whether they were or
not. If they catch sight of us creeping about in the darkness they'll
call for help, and that'll be it.'

They waited until Silus got cautiously back to his feet, following
in his footsteps as he peered around the corner in both directions
and then slipped around it to the left. Twenty paces down the
street he stopped, gesturing for Cotta to come forward.

'The building you're looking for is fifty paces down on your
left. If we go any closer we'll probably be spotted by the man on
the roof . . . there, see?' A smug tone crept into his voice. 'Told
you so . . .'

Squinting up at the line of buildings, Marcus saw a figure
outlined against the stars, the watcher staring down into the street
for a moment before stepping back from the building's parapet.
A framework of wooden poles had been erected around the
building, the sort of scaffolding used by builders.

'Once a man's under that scaffolding he'll be invisible from
above.'

Cotta nodded at Excingus's statement.

'Exactly what I was thinking. I'll just—'

Marcus interrupted.

'No. This is my fight. I'll make the approach and get the front door open, then *you* can bring your men up.'

He stepped around the crouching men and slid down the wall of the insula in whose shadow they had taken cover. Advancing gingerly towards the safe house, he heard a scrape of cloth on brick behind him, turning to find Cotta at his back. He pointed to where the rest of the veteran's men waited.

'Go back! I told you, this is *my* fight!'

The veteran centurion grinned fiercely at his savage whisper, shaking his head.

'No one's going to thank me if I come back without you. And you're not the only one with a score to settle here.'

Marcus stared at him for a moment and then nodded, turning back to their target, then froze as he realised that the rooftop watcher had reappeared high above them, silhouetted once more against the blaze of stars. Cotta muttered quietly in his ear.

'We're close enough. When he moves again we go for the door.'

The younger man nodded, and when the lookout stepped back from the parapet once more they hurried forward, flattening themselves against the safe house's wall under the cover of the scaffolding. The window shutters were closed, and so, to Marcus's dismay, was the door itself. A hiss from the shadows made Marcus turn to look at where the rest of the party waited, to see Silus pointing back down the road. Cotta scowled at the realisation of what he was trying to tell them.

'They must be coming back!'

He waved at his men, pointing to the right in an order for them to make their escape while they still could. They hesitated, clearly unwilling to leave their chief, but he repeated the gesture again with an angry emphasis. As the two men watched, their guide led Excingus and the rest of the party away down the side street and into the deeper shadows, leaving Marcus and Cotta alone.

'What do we do now?'

The veteran grinned at his former pupil.

'Well we can't stay here, can we? We need to get into that insula, and quickly! The only thing I can think of . . .' He reached under his tunic. 'Is this!'

He directed the steaming stream of fluid at the bottom of the door, squatting to get a better angle and directing the urine into the narrow gap between door and lintel. For a moment the only sound in the still of the night was the splashing of his urine against the hard surfaces, and then Marcus's keen ears heard a sudden outburst from inside the building.

'What the fuck! Some dirty bastard's having a piss on the fucking door!'

The veteran centurion cupped his hand, filling his palm with what was left of his urination and whispered harshly to Marcus.

'*Ready!*'

With a sudden clatter, the first of the door's bolts were pulled back, and Marcus drew his patterned dagger, raising the blade and drawing back his hand. As the door swung open to reveal an angry-faced bruiser, Cotta hurled the handful of urine into his face. Before the doorman had the chance to override his instinctive disgust at the warm liquid's pungent aroma and the sudden sting in his eyes, Marcus pounced forward with the blade, stabbing the sharp iron into the doorman's neck. Cotta hurried forward, pushing the dying man back into the building and beckoning Marcus in behind him.

'*Shut the door!*'

He lowered the shaking sentry to the hallway's floor and squatted next to him, shaking his head as the guard's lips twitched in an effort to speak.

'I know. One minute you're bored to tears, the next some bastard's chucked piss in your face and opened your throat. Seems a little unfair, doesn't it?' He watched while Marcus shot the heavy door's bolts as quietly as he could, whispering to the younger man with a look of disbelief on his shadowed face. 'Well then, we're in. Although given there's only two of us, I think I've finally worked out what my old man meant when he told me to be careful what I wished for, just in case I actually got it. We can either wait for the Watch to bugger off and then try to find the lads, although the Lightbringer only knows where Excingus and Silus will have led them in their haste to get away, or we can go and see how many more of them we'll have to kill to get to their boss. You choose . . .'

Marcus raised his knife, the blade still dark with the dead sentry's blood.

'You know my choice.'

His friend nodded and stood up, pulling out his own dagger and tip toeing down the hall to the first doorway with the younger man at his back. Taking a quick peep around the door frame he shook his head.

'Nothing. Which makes sense, because if there was anyone else down here with him they'd have heard us killing him and come out to play. So where are they, I wonder?'

They climbed the stairs to the first floor, back to back, Cotta leading and Marcus staring into the ground floor's gloom as he backed up the steps behind him. The first-floor landing was just as silent, and a cautious examination of the rooms to either side of the stairs revealed nothing but empty rooms. The two men repeated their cautious climb to the second-floor landing, but found the building's next floor equally silent. Looking up the next flight of stairs, Cotta nudged Marcus with an elbow and pointed up into the gloom.

'See that?'

The Tungrian stared hard, realising what it was that the veteran was showing him. A thick wooden door, criss-crossed with iron reinforcing bars, had been installed at the top of the stairs, and was hanging half open in the building's silence.

'There'll be men on that floor for certain.'

Marcus nodded.

'There's no point to an obstacle unless you man it.'

His friend mounted the first step, placing his foot down with slow, delicate care.

'We take our time from here, and get it right. If we wake them now we might as well slit our own throats.'

They went up the stairs in complete silence, stopping with each faint creak of the treads to listen for any sign that they might have been heard, both men steeled to charge up through the door with their knives ready to fight. Reaching the door, Cotta gently pushed at it, grimacing at the hinges' thin squeal of protest as he overcame the weight of the iron-studded wood, opening it sufficiently to slip through. Standing on the landing beyond, he cocked his head to listen, grinning at Marcus as the sound of snoring reached them. Somewhere in the unlit gloom one of the sleepers broke wind and muttered something unintelligible, and the veteran soldier waved a hand under his nose with a grin, leaning over to whisper in his friend's ear.

'How's that to make you feel alive, eh boy? One cough and these slumbering idiots will be up and all over us, but right now we're walking through them like ghosts. Come on . . .'

As he turned towards the next flight of stairs a figure emerged from the half-lit gloom of the room to Marcus's left with the stiff-legged half-steps of a man more asleep than awake. He mumbled an irritated question, peering owlishly at Marcus in the dim light.

'What're you noisy bastards—'

Cotta took a single quick step and wrapped his arm around the sleepy man's mouth, driving his dagger into his back. His victim spasmed, his bare feet slapping lightly on the floorboards as he fought the dagger's cold, agonising intrusion. Marcus put the point of his own knife against the man's bare chest, looking into his imploring eyes for a moment before pushing the blade home with a single thrust. The gang member's eyes widened at the sudden intense pain, then rolled upwards as his torn heart stopped beating, the body slumping back against Cotta who lowered it slowly to the floor.

'Come on!'

His face and tunic were covered in blood, and the coppery stink filled the dank air as he beckoned Marcus on, making the Roman wonder how long it would take for the stench to awaken one of the dead man's comrades. They crossed the landing with slow, careful steps and then mounted the stairs, Cotta leading with his former pupil once more at his back. On the floor above there was quiet, and the veteran centurion took a moment to lean against the wall and blow out a long, slow breath.

'Fuck me but that was close!'

Marcus looked up at the floor above them, protected by a door like the one they had passed through a few moments before, this one closed and presumably bolted.

'Brutus should be up there, if he's here.'

His friend nodded grimly.

'And no amount of sneaking around is going to open that door. I think it's time for a more direct approach.'

He led the young centurion quickly up the stairs, ignoring the inevitable noise of their footsteps just as the gang leader's men would have done, raising his dagger and tapping smartly at the door with its handle. The two men looked at each other as footsteps thudded down the hallway on the other side.

'Who is it?'

Cotta raised a hand to Marcus, putting his mouth close to the wood and growling a response.

'Secundus.'

He winked, and bent close to Marcus's ear.

'What are the odds on there being at least one second son in a dozen men, do you think?'

The voice on the other side of the door laughed tersely.

'Hah! Only *you* would be stupid enough to forget to give the password.'

Marcus raised his eyebrows at Cotta, who shrugged, then deepened his voice again.

'Forgotten the fuckin' password too.'

The man on the other side of the door was silent for a moment, and in that brief space of time the veteran's face creased with concern as he waited for the sentry's next words.

'Fuck me backwards, surely even you can't be that—'

His words were lost in the clatter of iron as the guard drew first the topmost bolt, then its twin at floor level. The two men braced themselves to attack, only to hear a sudden shout of alarm from two floors below. Marcus could hear the uncertainty from the other side of the door as the noise reached the guard's ears. His voice was suddenly clearer, presumably as he flattened his ear against the door to hear better.

'What's that noise?'

Cotta nodded to himself and stamped at the spot where the door's catch would be located. The thin iron catch snapped under the kick's force, sending the door flying back into the sentry's face with a solid thud of wood on bone. Marcus went through the opening first, flipping his knife to catch it by the blade before whipping his hand forward to send the sliver of metal flying the corridor's length. The dagger buried itself in the throat of another gang member who was still struggling to draw the short sword from his waist, and he fell backwards, clawing at the wound as it spurted blood onto the floor at his feet. Without warning, a pair of men erupted from a room to their left, both armed with knives whose blades glinted in the dim lamplight. Cotta squared off with one of them, a vicious stab of his dagger making the other man recoil from the threat, while his companion snarled at the unarmed Marcus and drove his blade forward at the Roman with more enthusiasm than skill.

Sliding his body to one side the Roman took the extended knife arm, gripped it by the wrist and shoulder and snapped a knee up to break the elbow, plucking the blade free as his attacker's face crumpled into a gasping shriek of agony. Cotta parried a knife thrust and punched his assailant hard in the face, sending him staggering backwards, shouting back over his shoulder as he followed up with his dagger raised.

'*The door!*'

Marcus lunged for the door and slammed it closed, shooting the upper bolt as the first shouts echoed up from below, pushing its lower counterpart into place as footsteps hammered on the stairs. The sliding catch was broken, but the screaming bodyguard's fallen knife slotted neatly into its keep and secured the door well enough to afford them a moment or two of respite from the men bellowing at them from the other side of its stout defence. He turned back to the fight to find Cotta locked in a death struggle with his opponent, the younger man's greater strength slowly forcing his blade in towards the veteran's throat. Seeing Marcus advancing on him, he grunted with renewed effort, forcing the knife down by sheer brute force against which Cotta was able to do no more than deflect its path to slice a deep gash into his arm. Before the gang member could raise the weapon to strike again, Marcus was upon him, punching a half-fist into his throat and dropping him choking to the floor.

'*He's yours!*'

Striding up the corridor he felt the familiar burn of rage wash through him with the knowledge that one of his family's murderers was close at hand. Pulling his knife from the stricken swordsman's throat he tugged the unused gladius from the scabbard at the dying man's side and stood to face the last door in the corridor's short run. It opened easily, revealing a pair of hard-faced bodyguards with a squat, muscular man standing behind them.

'*Get him!*'

Both of the men were armed with swords, and at Brutus's command they advanced with the blades raised, ready to strike. Marcus threw his knife at the closer man's feet, the blade sticking into the floorboard between them and distracting his attention for an instant in which Marcus lunged forwards and stabbed the sword's point deep into his thigh, wrenching the blade free in a gush of arterial blood. The bodyguard staggered backwards, his breath whooping with shock as his life spurted from the torn limb, and the other man hesitated momentarily in the face of their attacker's bloodied blade. He turned to flee but the Roman was faster, raising his stolen gladius two-handed and ramming the long blade through the terrified guard's neck, snapping his spine and dropping him flopping to the floor. Marcus looked up to see Brutus climbing through the window with a look of abject terror as he stared back at his nemesis, and went after him with narrow-eyed purpose, snatching his knife from the floorboards.

The wooden scaffolding swayed gently as he climbed through the window and stepped out onto it, looking to his right to see the gang leader's head vanish as he climbed down through a hole in the boards with a frantic haste that shook the flimsy platform. Two big steps took his pursuer to the opening in the scaffold's rough planks, and he slid down the ladder with his feet braced against its legs to land with a thump. Brutus was in the act of climbing onto the next ladder down, squealing in terror as he realised that Marcus was gaining on him, but he was no better than halfway down the rungs when his grip on the ladder's sides was brutally broken by the impact of the younger man's booted feet. Scrabbling up from the floor, he drew a knife, but Marcus slapped it from his hand with casual ease and punched him once, a swift jab between the eyes that sent him reeling back against the building's side, momentarily helpless. When his senses returned he found himself standing with his back to the open air beyond the scaffold, held erect by a powerful hand in his hair.

'I can pay you! Whatever they've promised you, I can double it! Name your price!'

Marcus dragged his head close until the two men were eye-to-eye, his lip curling in disgust.

'This has nothing to do with the Dog Eaters, Brutus! This is *personal*. My name is Marcus Valerius Aquila!'

He held the terrified man out at arm's length for a moment, waiting while the realisation of who it was that had hunted him down sank into the gang leader's battered consciousness.

'*Aquila?* The senator's boy?'

Marcus smiled cruelly, jerking the hand that was holding Brutus upright.

'The same. I swore to find and kill you all. And now it's your turn.'

Brutus's eyes widened as he realised what was about to happen. 'No! I—'

Marcus released his hair, put the hand into his face and pushed, sending the gang leader staggering backwards until his back foot found only empty space. He toppled into thin air with a screech of terror, but only fell as far as the end of a broken scaffold pole that protruded invisibly up into the night air twenty feet below. With a horrible crunch of bone, the two-inch thick pole's jagged wooden end punched through Brutus's body, suspending him ten feet above the ground and protruding up through his back. Terribly wounded, he groaned in shocked agony as the depth of his predicament became clear, slipping down a foot as his blood lubricated the pole's wooden shaft. Marcus turned back to the ladder without a backwards glance as Cotta came down it one-handed, his other arm black with blood.

'We need to get that cut bandaged—'

'There's no time. They're breaking the door down!'

The two men hurried down the remaining ladders while voices shouted and cursed distantly above them. When they reached the ground, Marcus took a moment to look up at Brutus's body. As the two men stared upwards, he slid further down the pole's length, dropping to their eye level with another deathly moan of terror and pain, his hand ineffectually gripping at the gore-slathered wood in a vain attempt to arrest his descent. Cotta looked at the long, blood-smeared shaft rising out of the gang leader's back with a soldier's expertise, pulling a face at the monstrous wound.

'That thing's clean through his liver. Leave him. If he's not already dead, he'll soon wish he was.'

The Roman shook his head, staring dispassionately at Brutus's contorted and blood-flecked face.

'We can't risk him telling anyone else who killed him before he gives up his life.'

Cotta hefted his knife.

'Is that all that's worrying you? Here, I'll just have his tongue out then.'

He took a firm grip of the dying man's chin, but Brutus summoned his last reserve of strength and pulled his jaw from the veteran soldier's grip. His voice was no more than a ragged, choking whisper, but the hatred in his voice was unmistakable.

'*Death . . . Bringer . . . will . . . slaughter . . . you . . . all.*'

He coughed up a gout of blood, his entire body shaking with

the horrendous pain, and Marcus took his chin in one hand, pulling the gang leader's contorted face round to look at him.

'When you reach the other side of the river, if you can fool the ferryman into taking you across, you'd best start running. Because if Mortiferum does kill me, I'll be coming after you to do this all over again.'

Brutus stared at him glassy-eyed. The young Roman realised that the man had lost his grip on life, and released his hold on the corpse's jaw, allowing its head to hang loosely. He stood and stared at the corpse for a moment, feeling the same numbness that had overtaken him when he'd realised that Dorso was dead. He shook his head slowly at the absence of the elation he'd still hoped to feel in his moment of triumph.

'Come on, there's no time for that!' Cotta dragged him away from the macabre scene, shouting back up at the gang members clattering down the scaffold's ladders above them.

'*Victory to the Dog Eaters!*'

The two men hurried away into the darkness pursued by the shouts of the dead gang leader's bodyguards.

5

'Fuck me, look at that lot! Word must have got around!'

An older soldier among the volunteer barbers snorted at his comrade's observation.

'Of course word got a-fucking round, you daft bastard, that cock Morban's only offered another day of cheap haircuts.'

A queue of men had already formed outside the shop, and as Morban unlocked the door he had to put out a beefy arm to hold back the throng as his men filed inside.

'Just a moment, gentlemen, the lads'll be ready to get cutting shortly!' Holding up a hand to indicate that the man at the head of the queue should stay where he was, he ducked back into the shop, grinning at his men as they readied themselves for work. 'Now can you see why I set the price low? There's barbers all over the Aventine standing wondering where all their customers have gone, while we've got as much work as we can cope with and more. You boys are going to make a decent purse today, just as long as you can keep up with the demand, so no fucking about with the finer points, just get the punters neat and tidy, get them out of the door and put the next arse on your seat.'

He turned back to the door, gesturing to the first customer with a beaming smile.

'Come along in, sir, come and get your hair barbered in the latest style for next to nothing!'

Once his men were hard at work, he wandered off to buy a small pie from the baker two doors down, but before he'd made half a dozen paces he found himself in the middle of a small knot of traders, all eager to make his acquaintance. The baker himself took the surprised soldier by the arm, clapping him on the back with a beaming smile of welcome.

'It's wonderful to have you here! My business has been excellent this morning, with all these men waiting for a haircut and fancying a bite to eat with the money they're saving by coming to your shop!'

The other shopkeepers agreed noisily, and Morban enjoyed the unfamiliar feeling of basking in their approbation until, one by one, they drifted away with promises of friendship and offers to provide any help he might need in the future. At length only one man was left, the barbers shop's next-door neighbour, a quiet man who introduced himself as Albanus and who sold pots made, he told Morban, by his wife and son in the back room. The potter fixed him with a knowing look.

'I don't sleep too well, and I sometimes sit in the window up there and watch the street.' He pointed up at the room above the shop. 'It's not as if I have anything else to do. I saw your lads with the spades carrying in what looked suspiciously like weapons last night, when they were finished digging out that new cellar of yours. None of my business, mind you, and I won't go blabbing, but you know there's a death penalty for being caught in possession of anything longer than a kitchen knife in the city?'

Morban shrugged, warming to the man but unwilling to trust him just yet, and the potter laughed dryly.

'Don't blame you for keeping silent. No matter, you're good for business and I ain't the squealing kind. One more thing though, have you had a visit from One Eyed Maximus yet?'

He laughed at Morban's mystified look.

'You will soon enough then, now that you've got so many customers making so much noise. He'll be along for his share right enough.'

'*His* share?'

'Aye, ten per cent if he likes you, more if not. I always give him a smile and make out how pleased I am to have someone watching over my business, even though I doubt he'd lift a finger if I was being robbed, and that way he just taxes me at the standard rate.'

Morban mused for a moment, rubbing his chin.

'Best not to call him a thieving bastard then?'

Albanus laughed again, and winked at him.

'Best not. Not unless you want to be bringing those swords up out of the cellar.'

'You'll have to make out that you're Pilinius's guests, and avoid going anywhere near the man himself for fear of being exposed. No doubt he'll have other things on his mind . . .'

With predictable punctuality, Excingus had made his way to the Tungrian barracks on the Ostian road the next morning, arriving soon after the troops had been sent to their usual training session. He'd been less interested in the details of the gang leader's demise, however, than in alerting them to the prospect of an opportunity to bring retribution to the third man on their death list. Reminding them of the senator's grisly reputation for playing bloody and repulsive games with the survivors of the households destroyed by the Knives, he'd started to lay out the details only to find himself interrupted by Scaurus.

'You told us before that it was going to be nigh on impossible for us to get into one of Pilinius's parties, and now you're talking about it as if we're going to stroll in?'

The former grain officer smiled tightly, holding up a small leather pouch which Julius took from him and emptied onto a spade-like palm. A pair of square metal tokens fell from the bag, unremarkable silver plaques ornamented with a design too intricate to be discerned at first glance.

'What are they?'

'They are your tickets, Tribune, to enter the grounds and house of Senator Tiberius Asinius Pilinius. Tonight, for one night only, you have the opportunity to witness the sort of games that the senator and his friends like to get up to in private and, if you're lucky, to deal out whatever justice to him you think fitting.' He raised a warning finger. 'Although you'll have to be very good indeed to achieve that laudable aim and get out unharmed. The senator takes no risks with his safety, especially when his closest and most powerful friends come out to play, so you'll be searched most comprehensively before being allowed to enter the grounds. Any weaponry you use will therefore have to be taken from the guards.'

'I see.'

Scaurus took one of the tokens from Julius, initially frowning at it as he tried to work out exactly what the design that adorned the silver surface represented, then recoiling with a grimace as he worked it out. He tossed it to Marcus, who looked down and momentarily closed his eyes as he made the same realisation.

'So exactly how did you come by these tickets to enter the senator's night of debauchery?'

Excingus's face took on the same obdurate look he'd assumed the last time they'd asked him to reveal his sources, but before he could speak, Scaurus unleashed Marcus with a twitch of his head towards the informant, and the young Roman was across the room and at his throat, pushing him back against the building's wooden wall with a strength that Excingus had not suspected until it was too late. Scaurus and Julius stepped in close behind him, each of them regarding him dispassionately.

'You're not under Senator Sigilis's protection now, Informant, and I'm closer than you might suspect to turning you over to the delicate mercies of this rather frustrated centurion. You'll recall that he has a strong motivation to treat you with an equal lack of compassion to that you displayed towards his pregnant wife? So I suggest that you unlock that head full of secrets just a little, and be as frank as you can possibly be about what we'll be walking into tonight, if we take up this last-minute invitation to put our heads into the lion's mouth. It's either that or . . .'

Marcus reached down to his belt and pulled a knife from its sheath, raising the curiously patterned iron so that Excingus could see it. His voice was cold, that of a man barely holding on to his temper.

'This dagger has a curious history. It was originally part of a larger weapon, a sword made with an exotic iron from the east and forged under the hammer of a smith with incomparable skill. That sword would cut through armour like cleaving smoke, and when I took it from the man who was using it for evil purposes, I had it melted down and reformed as a series of knives, of which this is one. Do you see the parallel with yourself perhaps?'

Excingus snorted his disdain.

'I tell you everything, or you'll use it to cut me to pieces?'

'*Yes.*'

The informant looked into his eyes, and realised with a start that, if anything, the centurion would probably rather he remained silent. He sighed.

'Very well. You know all too well that I'm a pragmatist, especially with a blade at my throat. My man inside Pilinius's domus is his secretary.'

Scaurus raised an eyebrow at the informer.

'You've suborned the man who has every tiny detail of the senator's dirty little games in his head? That really is quite impressive, Excingus. I may not like you, but I'm forced to admit that as informants go you're straight out of the top drawer. What did you do, pay him or threaten him?'

'That's not rel—'

Marcus leaned forward and glared at Excingus, his hard-eyed stare speaking volumes as to his desire to take his knife to the man, and Scaurus smiled grimly at the informant's involuntary twitch of fear.

'Oh, it is relevant, I'm afraid. What are we to do should your man's resolve weaken at a critical moment, if he realises the inevitable consequences of his betrayal if we fail? It'll be too late to ask questions once we're at Pilinius's mercy, won't it? So I need to know what your leverage was, Informant, in order that I can use it to put him back in line if he shows any sign of turning on us. Without that we'll have no choice but to turn down this *opportunity*, and with that your usefulness to us will be at an end.'

The informant looked at him, then back at Marcus.

'I have no choice, I see. Very well.' He sighed, raising his eyes to the room's ceiling at being forced to disclose his secrets. 'I discovered, by means of tailing the man when he left the senator's estate on the private business that Pilinius allows him, that he has children by a slave in another senatorial household. It seems that their owner gave him to Pilinius in repayment of a debt when the senator decided that he needed a rather more capable secretary. They live with their mother, whose owner is a relatively soft man and has not yet sold them on. It seemed likely to me that this man would want to purchase not only his own freedom, but that of his woman and the children, and so I realised that I had two means of controlling him.'

'Money and the risk of betrayal?'

Excingus smiled at Marcus, nodding his head.

'You know, Centurion, I think you'd make a very capable grain officer. Yes, money to swell the funds with which he hopes to buy their freedom, and the threat that Pilinius might come by the information that his secretary has children. The senator's more than clever enough to realise that his man is compromised by their existence, were he ever to discover them, and quite sadistic enough to claim them from his colleague as the secretary's blood and therefore his property as the man's master. And what he might do with them once he had power over them . . . well, that's enough to give any man pause for thought.'

The tribune thought for a moment.

'So these tokens . . .' He shot a look of disgust at the metal square resting on his palm. 'Will gain us entry to Pilinius's villa?'

Excingus nodded.

'Not just into the house, there'll be plenty of people there who are only invited to attend the party that's the front for the real event. After all, there are only a very few men who gain access to the senator's real entertainment, the rest are just invited to provide the cover of an innocent night of debauchery for those select few.'

'I see. That explains the rather explicit imagery on this . . .'

He held up the shining piece of silver, and Excingus shook his head.

'Don't let that rather simple picture fool you. The reality of what the senator and his friends get up to is a good deal worse.'

'*Worse?*'

Excingus shook his head, his stare withering.

'Either you've been away from Rome for too long or you've been lucky enough in the past to avoid the sort of people that Pilinius associates with. If you're going to do this thing then you'd better be prepared to witness some sights that you might have preferred never to have seen.'

Marcus shook his head, his teeth bared.

'I've walked battlefields after the fighting's done with. I've disembowelled, decapitated, crippled and maimed. I've left barbarian warriors to die in agony, crying for their mothers. The men who killed my father not only destroyed my family's honour, they condemned me to a life of marching from the scene of one massacre to the next, listening to my soldiers weeping and thrashing about in their sleep at the horrors they have seen and done to other men, and those inflicted on their comrades. Trust me, nothing you could show me in this city comes anywhere close to the spectacular displays of massed slaughter in which I've played my part.'

The informant shrugged equivocally.

'We'll see. And now gentlemen, perhaps I ought to talk you through the domus's layout?'

The first gang members arrived an hour or so before dusk, strolling down the street with bemused stares at the queue outside the barber's shop. They stood for a moment taking in the scene, then walked in past the queuing customers, none of whom, Morban noted, cared to protest about them jumping the line of waiting men.

'There's a queue I'm afraid, gentlemen, you'll have to wait your turn with the men outside.'

The taller of the two bent to address Morban with a condescending smile, the happy expression somewhat marred by his empty left eye socket. Putting his heavily scarred knuckles on the standard bearer's desk, he sneered into his face.

'If we wanted a haircut, *Fatty*, then we wouldn't be queuing for it, and there ain't one of your customers would have the balls to stand in our way. But, as it happens, we ain't come for a haircut, we're here to give *you* one.' He looked around at his comrade with a smirk of pride at the joke. 'Ten per cent of your day's take, in return for our constant vigilance against any threat to your business. You'd be amazed what sorts of nastiness can happen when a shopkeeper chooses not to purchase our services.'

Morban nodded quickly.

'Sounds fair to me.' He reached into the desk's drawer, dropping a generous handful of coins into the gangster's outstretched hand. 'We've done alright today, so here's your share. Might I know who we're doing business with, just in case anyone else comes round trying to extort the money from us that we'll need to make payment to you?'

The big man grinned.

'We're the Hilltop Boys, old man, and there's no bastard going to dare put their feet on our turf. *My* turf! One Eyed Maximus rules this part of the Aventine, and everyone round here knows it!' He leaned closer, bending down to whisper in Morban's ear. 'I like to cut things, Fatty. More particularly I like to cut people. And when anyone . . . *anyone* . . . denies me something I want, well, I cut them, don't I? I give them a simple choice, see, I tell 'em that I can either blind 'em, or cut out their tongues, or just make the unkindest cut of them all.'

He grinned at Morban, challenging the other man to ask the question.

'You don't mean . . . ?'

'Oh yes. If they want to keep on seeing and talking then I just take the end off their cock. Just an inch or so, unless they really upset me, in which case I leave 'em just enough to piss with. Something to remember me by, and to make sure they never deny me anything ever again. So, want to stay on the right side of me, do you, Fatty?'

The standard bearer nodded slowly.

'Seems I do.'

'Once *again* it appears that an opportunity for my revenge has passed me by, Informant.'

Excingus looked impassively across the gardens, ignoring the senator's bodyguards.

'I take it, Senator, that you're referring to the news of the death of a certain well-known gang leader?'

Albinus slapped the arm of his seat, drawing glances from the nearest of the people walking through the gardens. Excingus shifted uneasily, lowering his head in apparent close examination of the tablet in his hand.

'Of course I'm referring to the murder of yet another of the Knives! Brutus was found dead in the river this morning, his death having apparently been caused by a wooden pole rammed right through his body! Are you telling me that wasn't Aquila's work!?'

The informant shook his head.

'I can't tell you anything of the kind, although I'll point out to you that Brutus is reputed to have been at war with another gang leader, some nasty piece of work who seems to be more than capable of such an act. I should also tell you that Brutus had a reputation, I've since discovered, for going into hiding whenever that sort of inevitable turf war started, and not coming out until the matter was resolved. Since none of my contacts had the faintest idea where he might have taken refuge, it does cross my mind that he might simply have been discovered by his rival? Sometimes the most obvious answer is the most obvious for a reason . . .'

He sat in silence and waited for Albinus to think it through.

'Coincidence? Is that what you're trying to tell me?'

The informant wrinkled his brow.

'I'm not *trying* to tell you anything, Senator, I am simply explaining that I knew as little as you did about Brutus's whereabouts as everyone else in the city, with the apparent exception of the man who leads the Dog Eaters' assorted thugs and murderers. I'd imagine that Scaurus and Aquila are equally frustrated!'

Albinus opened his mouth to speak again, his expression that of an unhappy man.

'*But . . .*' The informant neatly forestalled his employer's next complaint. 'Given that you pay me for information, I do have news of an event which, I suspect, will bring your former colleagues in the military to the scene like flies on shit, and provide you with the perfect opportunity. You'll be aware, no doubt, of Senator Tiberius Asinius Pilinius?'

Marcus and the tribune made their way into the city in the early evening with a discreet escort of Cotta's men, their formal clothing immaculate and their skins ruddy with health after a long session in the barrack's bathhouse. At the domus's front gate they parted company with their bodyguards, showing the tokens that Excingus had procured for them to the men controlling admission to the house's grounds. A heavy-set bruiser with a missing eye looked hard at the metal squares, nodding at them with a knowing look.

'Two for the *inner* hall!'

One of his comrades gestured to the house.

'This way sirs.'

The party was clearly already in full swing, noisy revellers having spilled out onto the wide terrace that fronted the house, and as the bouncer led them round to the left side of building a couple ran across their path and into the garden, the female looking over her shoulder at her partner with a lustful expression. The sounds of laughter and the grunts and moans of sexual activity could be heard from the gloom of the house's grounds, clearly left unlit to facilitate privacy in these encounters, and Scaurus muttered a quiet aside to Marcus.

'It's a clever tactic, to hold parties where anyone can pair off with anyone else in complete privacy, and I'd imagine Pilinius buys up half the city's most expensive prostitutes for the occasion. Any allegations about whatever it is that he gets up to will instantly be suppressed by the more powerful guests, even if they're not involved in his perversions, for fear of their own little indiscretions coming to light.'

They entered the house through a side door, finding themselves confronted by another half-dozen doormen. Knowing what to expect, they stood still and allowed the senator's men to run expert hands through their clothing and across their torsos and limbs.

'They're clean. Take 'em through.'

The man who stepped out to escort them into the house was at odds with the muscular and hard-faced doormen, with the look of someone more accustomed to giving orders than taking them, but lacking the physique to impose his will upon others. He took their tokens and examined them both carefully before exchanging a knowing glance with Scaurus, and Marcus guessed that this must be the senator's duplicitous secretary. Having led them down a narrow corridor, with the sounds of merriment leaking through the doors on their right, he paused at a flight of stairs, speaking to them in an urgent whisper.

'I wasn't sure if the tokens I gave to Excingus were going to come back tonight, but it seems that you're intent on whatever it is that you've come for. Are you thieves?'

Scaurus nodded, and Marcus kept his mouth shut as the tribune spun out the story they had agreed with the informant earlier in the day.

'We know that your master keeps his greatest treasures out of public view, the items that he picks up when he's working for the emperor?'

The secretary's eyes widened.

'You know about . . . ?'

'We know everything about it, friend. *Everything*.'

The other man frowned his incomprehension.

'But if you know everything, then you'll know that all Senator Pilinius takes from their houses are—'

'There you are, Belenus, I've been looking for you everywhere!' A bulky, toga-clad figure with a shaved head was coming up the stairs with grunts of exertion. Asinius Pilinius sent me to find you, and to tell you that his guests are ready for the show to begin.'

The secretary bowed respectfully.

'As you say, sir. I'll just escort these two gentlemen to the lower level and then—'

'No need! You go and get it all started, and I'll take them downstairs!'

Without any choice in the matter, Belenus bowed respectfully, turning away to his duty.

'Yes, Senator, as you wish.'

He made his exit, leaving the two men to the newcomer. Marcus watched him as he hurried away, returning his fearful backward glance with an impassive stare. Climbing the remaining stairs, the newcomer stuck out a hand, clasping both men in turn with a firm if slightly moist grip.

'Now, gentlemen, on behalf of Asinius Pilinius, welcome to this entertaining little event! I'm Titus Pomponius Avenus, one of his closest friends and, I should add, one of the original members of this select group of men. You're new to this, I presume? I don't recognise your faces from any of the previous times we've gathered to celebrate!'

Scaurus inclined his head with just the right degree of respect.

'Indeed, Senator, this is the first time that we've been invited to join in the fun.' Avenus raised an eyebrow and, knowing that any failure to convince the man as to their bona fides might lead to suspicions that would unravel their cover story, the tribune took on a confiding look. 'In truth, Senator Pilinius took pity on the pair of us when I expressed an interest in his events, having heard of them from a mutual friend. He issued us both with an invitation, accompanied by clear instructions to keep ourselves to ourselves on this occasion.'

Avenus nodded knowingly.

'And that's sagacious advice, I'd say. He won't want you bothering his more distinguished guests, not until you've proven yourselves as worthy members of our rather exclusive group. What is it that you both do with yourselves?'

Scaurus smiled modestly, bowing again.

'Allow me to introduce myself and my colleague. I'm Gaius

Rutilius Scaurus, and this is Marcus Tribulus Corvus. We both have the honour to serve the empire as legion tribunes. Having recently returned to Rome from Britannia, where shows such as the one the Senator is hosting tonight are by no means a rarity, I was musing to him only last week how much I missed a little, shall we say, *unusual* entertainment?'

The stout patrician guffawed.

'So you're not such new boys to our little games after all! I'll wager that you get a good deal more variety than we do though, what with all those exotic barbarian women, eh?' Marcus grinned, showing his teeth in an expression that was perilously close to becoming a snarl, but the other man was too far gone in his own fantasies to notice such a subtlety. 'I'm not sure that we've got anything quite as exciting as the entertainment you'll have seen in Britannia, but tonight's entertainment promises to be quite special. The Senator procured a large number of performers only a week or so ago, enough for everyone here to participate. And since I'm a staunch supporter of the army, I feel it my duty to take you both under my wing, so to speak. Tonight, gentlemen, you will be my companions. Come along then!'

He turned and made his way back down the stairs with the two men following behind, and after twenty or so steps, led them into a large, torchlit room.

'Quite an ingenious little play room, wouldn't you say? There's no way into it other than the staircase we just came down and a door that leads into the grounds at the rear of the house, and the wall between this and the rest of the house is so thick that I doubt you could hear a trumpeter on the other side if he were blowing fit to burst!'

Marcus looked back at the entrance to the staircase, noting that a massive iron gate stood ready to swing into the opening, with a heavy wooden bar leaning on the wall beside it. He looked about him, frowning as he recognised a pattern in the tiled floor.

'Is that a robbers board?'

Avenus grinned.

'I should have expected a military man such as yourself to have recognised it. Yes, we don't always use it, but tonight it seems we have enough participants to provide all of the pieces for a game. Isn't that exciting? Ah, and there's our host!'

They followed his pointing hand to find Pilinius deep in discussion with a pair of men who looked vaguely familiar to Marcus. Scaurus nodded, looking about him with the air of a man keen not to attract attention to himself.

'Well that's been very kind of you, Pomponius Avenus. We'll just take up a position here and watch from the sidelines, as it were. I don't want to transgress on the terms under which we were granted our very kind invitation.'

Avenus bridled.

'Nonsense! I'm sure that Asinius Pilinius simply meant for you not to interrupt any conversations whose participants don't actually know you. He may be busy now, but he'll find the time to greet you soon enough, I'll make sure of that! After all, what sort of host would fail to grant some recognition to his guests, however brief. In the meantime, let's get into a good place for the show, shall we? You can repay the favour by telling me all about these "entertainments" of yours in Britannia!'

Julius nudged Cotta, pointing at a wagon coming towards them down the street. They were in the doorway of a shop whose owner had long since closed up for the evening.

'What do you reckon?'

The former centurion peered around the doorway's stone arch.

'Could be. I'd have expected more than one wagon though, if they're going to have enough slaves for a decent . . .'

He stopped talking as a second vehicle rounded the same corner and followed the first one up the shallow hill, watching as it ground along the considerable length of the wall that separated Pilinius's domus from the street. At a prearranged signal, the gate for which they were heading opened, and the first cart rolled inside while a pair of armed guards strolled out into the street, looking up and down the hill with the bored look of men doing a job which had never once given them a reason to draw their weapons.

'It's definitely tonight then.'

Julius nodded, watching as the second wagon pulled into the domus's grounds and was lost to view.

'Looks that way. You'd better warm your lads up.'

'Distinguished guests, your attention please!'

Pilinius stepped into the middle of the hall's floor, his beaming smile playing on the men gathered about him as he raised his hands and turned slowly in a full circle, in the manner of a showman about to unveil his latest exotic beast from beyond the empire's edge. Scaurus edged to one side, putting another man between himself and the senator, grateful for the interruption to Avenus's incessant and increasingly pointed questions.

'Gentlemen, it is a delight to see you all gathered here again, ready to celebrate what I think you're going to find is a quite unparalleled collection of subjects for tonight's entertainment. Tonight, my friends, we will not be sampling the usual assortment of criminals, runaway slaves and failed gladiators that is our usual fare. *No!*'

He looked about him with a triumphant expression, raising his arms to encompass the men gathered before him.

'No, my friends! Tonight we shall be feasting upon the very best that the empire has to offer our very *particular* tastes! For tonight, for one night only, we will enjoy the fruits of . . .' He paused dramatically, milking his audience. 'The fall of the house of Perennis!'

His audience looked on in what Marcus could only construe as unabashed delight, men whispering to their fellows with huge grins plastered across their faces.

'Oh yes, we've enjoyed the *leavings* of other great houses in our time. Few of us that were present will ever forget the sport that we had from the disgrace and execution of Senator Appius Valerius Aquila!' Marcus froze at the words, willing himself not to leap forward and attack the man as Pilinius continued his speech. 'But tonight, gentlemen, we have a feast to surpass even *that* epic Bacchanalia! Behold, our stars of the evening!'

A dozen men clad and armed in the same manner as the doorman on the floor above hustled a large group of women forward and into the circle of torchlight in which the senator was standing. Half of them were dressed in white, the others in black, and the purpose of the chequered robbers board worked into the hall's floor became all too obvious.

'Here you see before you Sextus Tigidius Perennis's wife . . .' A weeping woman was led forward by a pair of his men, forced to her knees and presented to them, the men gathered around her muttering their approval as Pilinius ripped open her thin tunic to reveal her breasts. He cupped one of them, squeezing the dark-skinned nipple between his thumb and forefinger. 'Who among you doesn't want to sample this lady's charms, especially given her rather exotic birthplace?'

'She's a Dacian, you know.' Avenus was whispering to the man next to him. 'Perennis always used to boast that she was a wild animal in bed . . .'

'And here!' A girl was led forward, barely out of her childhood. 'The Praetorian Prefect's daughter by his previous marriage, young and unsullied! One of you will be taking her virginity tonight! And here, the lady's handmaid, her hairdresser, her seam-stress, and a large number of female household slaves . . .' Pilinius paused for a wave of approving comments to die away. 'Yes, gentlemen, enough women for *nearly* every one of us to get his prick wet before the night's done! And for the rest . . .' He grinned around him evilly. 'I have a smaller number of the younger and more attractive male slaves from the Perennis household.' He tapped the blade of the dagger sheathed at his waist. 'And if you're not inclined to a shapely boy, then you'll know what to do with them!'

The men gathered about him laughed, exchanging excited glances that spoke volumes to Marcus as to their intentions towards the captives.

'So, honoured guests, who wants to play robbers!'

A roar of approval greeted the question, and the guards started hustling their captives into position on the game board.

'And now, young man, tell me more about these shows of yours in Britannia. Making captured warriors fight each other in the legion arenas is all very well, but it's not the most intimate of entertainments, is it? What about the women, the female members of the aristocracy, eh? What about the tribal kings' daughters? You must have had some fine sport with *them*?'

Marcus stepped forward, inclining his head deferentially and asking their escort the only question he could think of to distract the senator's gimlet-like attention from Scaurus.

'Forgive me, Pomponius Avenus, but I'm a keen robbers player. Which rules will we be using tonight?'

Avenus frowned.

'Rules? Who the fuck cares about *rules*? It'll be the usual, I expect, pieces removed by being bracketed to either side by the enemy, the king captured by being surrounded . . .'

The younger man flicked a glance at the massive playing board, seeing that the guards had positioned Perennis's wife on the square usually taken by the white king, one man mockingly placing a rough wooden crown on to her head. The man playing the white side then stepped onto the board and pointed to one of the terrified slaves, indicating for her to be moved two spaces forward. A pair of the senator's men took an arm apiece and forced her to move to the appointed square, and Avenus barked a harsh laugh.

'Look at the stupid bitch, she clearly doesn't have a clue about the game! The most fun comes when you get a decent player as one of the pieces on the board, as you can imagine. Once one or two of them have been dragged away, *then* we find out which of the remaining pieces can actually play the game! They're the ones looking about them, working out who's likely to be next to be taken, and we even once had a man who started shouting advice at the player controlling his side of the board!' He laughed uproariously. 'As you can imagine, our man immediately started playing to lose, which caused the idiot to become ever more hysterical! It was too, too funny for words!'

Marcus leaned in closer to the senator.

'And when the pieces are taken?'

The patrician smiled at him approvingly, raising his own token and leering at its depiction of a woman being sodomised by a toga-clad attacker at knifepoint.

'Ah, so you see the point of the game! When a piece is taken, young man, a lot is pulled from that bag Pilinius's secretary is holding, lots corresponding to the numbers on the tokens that gain us entry. If your number is called then you are free to enjoy the piece that's been taken from the board in any way you like. Any way at all!' He smirked at the younger man. 'I don't know how you did it in Britannia, but here in Rome the custom is to screw the backside off her, or him, in any way you like. And after that . . .'

He drew a finger across his throat.

'Of course, it doesn't have to be a quick death, that's all down to individual choice.' He slid a slim dagger from his toga with a sly smile, displaying the evilly sharp blade before putting it back in the sheath concealed in his sleeve. 'My preference is to open them up and take wagers on how long it'll take them to die.'

Marcus stared at him, evidently aghast.

'You *murder* them?'

Avenus frowned, his expression between disapproval and surprise.

'Well of *course* we murder them! Why else would Asinius Pilinius take such great care to ensure that there are no witnesses to these exclusive gatherings of Rome's most influential men?'

The younger man leaned forward and gagged, dry retching and clinging to Avenus's toga. The senator pushed him away with a horrified expression.

'You're not really man enough for this, *are* you? You, come here!' He beckoned to one of the guards, who walked across to the three men with a well-practised look of inscrutability. 'Take this young fool outside for a breath of air, before he pukes all over someone. Take *special* care of him, you understand? Very *special* care.' He turned to regard Scaurus with a jaundiced eye. 'And *you*, tribune, are you in the wrong place, too?'

The heavily built man nodded impassively and put a hand on

Marcus's sleeve. Allowing himself to be drawn along in the guard's wake, he shot a glance back at Scaurus as the tribune shook his head in disgust, replying to Avenus's question in a disappointed tone of voice.

'It shows how much you can get to know a man and still be surprised by his reactions to the simplest things. To think, an officer who I saw stand firm in the face of a massed barbarian charge only six months ago, reduced to a useless choking wretch by the simple prospect of killing a slave. You did the right thing in telling that man to kill him, of course, I doubt he'd have kept his mouth shut about what he saw here.'

The patrician nodded approvingly, looking across the room with the evident hope of catching their host's eye. Scaurus pulled gently at his guide's toga, lowering his voice to a level that forced the older man to bend closer.

'We'll have to go and tell Pilinius what happened of course, but first let me restore a little military pride by explaining to you how we *actually* did things in Britannia. There was one particular tribal nobleman who I had beheaded in front of his wife and daughters, after which I deflowered each of the girls in turn while she watched. And when I was done with that, I went one better with their mother . . .'

The senator, his interest piqued, fastened his attention on the tribune only to have it distracted by the first piece to be captured on the robbers board. With a scream of terror the handmaiden, her eyes rolling with fear, was manhandled out from between the two black-clad pieces sweating to either side of her, and was carried away from the game. One of Pilinius's household slaves dipped his hand into a leather bag, his face impassive as he read the number carved into the wooden ball he had selected at random.

'Number seven!'

One of the guests raised his token in the air, the glint of its polished silver winking in the torchlight as he stepped forward to claim his prize, dragging the woman away by her hair.

Avenus grinned approvingly.

'Now there's a man who knows how to give us a spectacle. That one's exit from this life won't be a swift one, I can guarantee that!'

Senator Albinus presented himself at the Pilinius domus's front gate with an imperious lack of regard for the guards' demand for his invitation.

'A token? Of course I don't have a bloody token! Do I look like the sort of pervert who attends your master's debauchery? I need to see the senator urgently, as I have news of the greatest import to him!'

He folded his arms, daring any of the guards to raise a finger against him, and his bodyguards planted themselves around him with equal obduracy. The leader of the group of men minding the gate beckoned one of his men.

'Go and fetch the senator's secretary, you'll find him at the inner gate. Tell him we've got a guest without an invitation by the name of Senator . . . ?'

'Albinus. Decimus Clodius Albinus. And hurry! Senator Pilinius has unwanted guests on his property, men who mean to do him harm!'

The guard walked swiftly away through the villa's garden, leaving Albinus to listen with a grim face to the music, laughter and occasional shriek that was emanating from the far side of the wall. He paced up and down while he waited, his anger and impatience growing as the time stretched out, and he was on the verge of approaching the gate guards again when a slightly built man with high temples and a bookish look to him emerged from between the closest of them. He bowed to Albinus with the proper degree of deference, extending a hand to indicate the garden beyond the guards.

'Senator Albinus. Senator Pilinius has asked me to extend warm and convivial greetings to you, and to assure you that you're more than welcome to attend the main party in the house, and to avail yourself of any and all entertainments that take your fancy. The Senator's parties are well known for the promise that nobody ever leaves without having taken their fill of food, wine and the very finest female company.'

Albinus shook his head impatiently.

'That's not what I came for man! If I want to be debauched I'll do it somewhere a damned sight more private than this bloody garden orgy! I came to warn Pilinius that he has imposters attending his private party! I think you know what I mean, the gathering within a gathering where he slaughters slaves for his closest friends' decadent enjoyment?'

The secretary sniffed.

'I really can't comment on the senator's private affairs, sir, but if you tell me these men's names I'll ensure that they don't gain access to the grounds.'

'I'm telling you they're already here! Two men, both close-shaved with military haircuts!' The secretary started, and Albinus jabbed a finger into his chest. 'You've *seen* them, haven't you?!'

The secretary turned and ran, bursting through the surprised gate guards and heading for the house, leaving Albinus open-mouthed in his wake. He made to follow, only to find a wall of muscle blocking his way.

'Here, I've got to—'

One of the pair of men blocking his path shook his head forbiddingly.

'I'm sorry, sir, I can't allow you in unless either the senator or his man there give you permission to enter, unless you have an invitation? The lads at the back entrance will tell you just the same.'

Albinus fumed, raising his voice to shout at the hard-faced guard.

'Of course I don't have a *fucking* invit—' He stopped in mid-sentence. 'Back entrance?'

Marcus sucked in a lungful of the cool night air as he was ushered through the door, looking about him at the house's torchlit rear garden as the guard half turned to close the door behind him. Where the front of the domus had been adorned with groups of trees and bushes, the rear was little more than a well-ordered open space. Its lawns were edged with white stone, and the drive that led to the gate was surfaced with gravel that made a pale grey ribbon in the moonlight. There would be no chance of stealth, he realised, pivoting to grasp the guard's hair and smash his temple brutally forward into the door he had just closed, jerking the head back and knuckle-punching the stunned man in the throat before he could recover his wits to call for help. Allowing his choking victim to slump to the ground, he stamped down hard on the man's exposed neck with his boot's edge, feeling the spine snap beneath his heel. Swiftly stripping off his toga, he manhandled the corpse out of its belt and tunic, dressing himself in the dead guard's uniform before turning to head for the gate with a purposeful stride. The gravel crunched noisily beneath his booted feet, and as he came within a dozen paces of the gate another guard stepped forward from the wall's shadow, his voice thick with the accent of the slums.

'Stop for a wank, did you? I suppose they've started fucking and cutting up the—'

The knife he'd taken from the dead guard's sheath was rammed up into the oncoming bodyguard's throat before he even saw the threat, the point lodging deep in the base of the hapless man's skull, and he sagged bonelessly onto the gravel.

'*What the . . .*'

A second man came out of the gate's shadows with a long spear held out before him, taking in the scene with a snarl of anger, and as he opened his mouth to call for help Marcus threw the handful of dust and gravel he'd scooped up a moment before. Half blinded and choking, the momentarily disoriented guard stabbed blindly out with the spear, but the young centurion dodged to his left as he lunged in with a flat palm that smashed his assailant's nose, throwing him back against the gate with a heavy thud. The dazed guard staggered forwards only to meet his assailant's half-knuckled fist with a crack of cartilage, his windpipe collapsing under the blow's power, dropping to the gravel and choking noisily to death as his killer hauled the domus's back gate open.

'You took your time.'

Cotta stepped out of the gloom to his right, waving an arm in command, and his men rose from their crouching positions behind him. Each of the dozen veterans was equipped with a short infantry gladius and a small round shield, their faces rendered terrifyingly anonymous by the dark shadows cast by their helmets. In their wake Julius walked through the gate, pushing it shut and shooting the bolts while Cotta handed Marcus his belt and swords, looking about him at the villa's garden as his former pupil armed himself.

'Anything we need to know?'

Marcus shook his head at the veteran's laconic question, smiling despite the gravity of the situation.

'Nothing really troubles you, does it?'

Cotta shrugged.

'Not really. You of all people ought to know by now that once a man's faced thousands of screaming murderous bastards across a battlefield and come out of it sprayed with their blood and that of his mates, nothing ever really seems all that serious. So, Centurion, shall we do what we came here for?'

The younger man nodded.

'There are ten or twelve guards inside, lightly armed, and thirty or so guests, most of whom will be carrying knives as well. The slaves they've brought here to slaughter are all wearing either white or black tunics.'

Cotta turned to his men.

'If a man runs at you, put him down. If he's running away but he's not wearing a black or white tunic, put him down. And watch out for the women, they won't be able to tell the difference between those bastards and us, and they may manage to arm themselves. We'll be outnumbered three to one by the sound of it, so we'll do this in the approved manner, in line and by the numbers. You two . . .'

A pair of his men stepped forward, hard-faced and dead-eyed.

'You keep telling anyone that will listen how you could give Velox and Mortiferum a run for their money, here's your chance to prove it. Once the fighting starts you shout the tribune's name, you fight your way through to him and you keep him alive, right? There's a gold piece each on top of what you're already getting if you succeed.' He turned to Marcus. 'You'll be throwing yourself about, I presume?'

Marcus nodded at the question.

'It would be a shame to waste all that expensive education in fancy swordplay our mutual friend managed to drum into me, wouldn't it?'

Cotta's return stare was almost paternal in its concern.

'Just remember that most men who throw themselves into crowds of unfriendly natives tend to pay for the extravagance of their gesture in blood. That rule holds as true here as it does anywhere else in the empire.'

The younger man held his stare for a moment before replying.

'My mother and sisters were brought here, taunted, degraded, raped and murdered, Cotta. So you would do what in my place exactly?'

The veteran put a hand on his shoulder, shaking his head.

'Nothing different. Just make sure that you don't join them before your time, eh?'

Inside the hall, Scaurus and Avenus watched, the former numb with horror while the other crowed exultantly as another piece was removed from the playing board, the woman dragged kicking and screaming away by two of the guards to where another of the guests waited in the shadows, his knife a pale line of grey in the darkness.

'Marius Priscus. A disappointing individual, in more ways than one, given that his distant ancestor was consul no less than three times. Spends most of his time boasting about his achievements in the German War.' Avenus turned to Scaurus with a look of disgust. 'Did you know that he even paid a noted scholar to write a book about the brilliance of his generalship? Not only is he the most ghastly individual, but he has no class whatsoever when it comes to these gatherings. He could have won Perennis's wife just then and still all he'd want would be to open her throat and watch her die. I wonder what on earth it is that makes our host persist in inviting him. In fact, I think I'll go and ask Asinius Pilinius myself. Come on, we'll go and pay our respects!'

Scaurus nodded equably, forcing what he fervently hoped was a cruel smile onto his face.

'Why not? You go, and I'll catch you up in a minute. I just want to see that bitch die.'

Avenus laughed, shaking his head.

'Gods below, not another one! What is it with you soldiers? Very well, go and satisfy your need for blood, but just mind you don't get too close to him while he's holding a knife, he's got a fearful temper!'

He slapped the tribune on the shoulder and advanced into the press of men, making a beeline for their host, while Scaurus walked quickly across to where the retired legatus had clearly won a brief and one-sided fight with his prize. Seeing the younger man approaching him, he froze with his knife ready to strike and barked out a question, his grip on the battered woman's hair enough to hold her quiescent in her semi-conscious state.

'What the *fuck* do you want?!'

Scaurus kept walking, his face set in an expression of respect and his empty palms spread wide.

'Simply to express my respect for your achievements, Legatus. I read your book on the German Wars and was most taken with the brilliance of your tactics.'

Marius sneered and turned back to the woman, raising his knife to make the kill.

'Well now you've expressed them you can fuck off, you brownnosing little b—'

Without breaking stride, the tribune caught his raised knife hand, twisted his wrist and forced the blade down, ramming it into the gap between throat and collarbone.

'What?! You . . .'

Marius's eyes rolled upwards as the expertly placed cut severed the blood supply to his brain, sagging in Scaurus's grip. The tribune put a foot into the battered woman's chest and pushed her over, dropping the legatus's dead weight on top of her and hissing a command that he hoped would penetrate her addled consciousness.

'Lie there and keep him on top of you if you want to live. Scream and move about without throwing him off and they'll think he's raping you.'

She stared at him uncomprehendingly, but her rescuer was already in motion, walking quickly back towards the stairway down which he and Marcus had entered the hall.

Avenus reached Pilinius and clasped his arm, nodding his approval at the evening's entertainment.

'You've surpassed yourself my friend, this is an evening we'll look back on for years to come. I would have come over to pay my respects earlier, but I've been babysitting the two new boys you invited tonight, Scaurus and Corvus. Mind you, I don't think much of either of them, to be honest with you. One of them took umbrage at the nature of our activity . . .' He bent closer and assumed a confidential tone, missing the look of bafflement on Pilinius's face. 'I had your men take him outside, with instructions to deal with him quickly and quietly. The other one just wants to watch people being killed, from the sound of it. A typical legion man, no sophistication at all . . .'

He fell silent, realising that Pilinius was staring at him with a perplexed expression.

'New boys? *What* new boys? Do you really think I'm stupid enough to invite strangers to an evening where we're dismembering the next best thing to the imperial family, you fool!'

Avenus raised his eyebrows in protest.

'But he's just over there watching Marius do his usual stab and stare! He's a tribune from Britannia—'

He fell silent and recoiled a pace at the expression on Pilinius's face.

'Where is he?!'

The senator turned to follow Avenus's pointing hand, but all either of them could see was the legatus's body atop his writhing prize, her screams and cries of pain barely audible over the room's din.

'Well, he was there a moment ago.' Avenus scanned the room. 'Look, *there* he is!'

Pilinius turned and shouted at the men behind him.

'*Guards! To me!*'

Scaurus ran for the stairway, pointing back at the crowd behind him and shouting to the single man standing guard on the exit from the hall.

'There, look!'

His thrown knife served to do no more than distract the man, flying high and wide of its target, but he was on top of the guard too quickly for him to do any better than half draw his sword. Driving him back against the wall, he grabbed his opponent's hair and battered his head against the cold stone and then, while he was still reeling from the concussion, ripped the weapon free from its scabbard and rammed it between the man's ribs. Cries of consternation were filling the hall now, as the guests realised what was happening, and Pilinius stepped out of their press with a pair of his men on either side. A hush fell as he stepped forward, only the incessant cries and moans of those of Perennis's slaves who were being vigorously raped breaking the silence. The senator pointed at Scaurus, his face contorted with anger.

'I don't know who you are, stranger, but I know what I'm going to do to you.'

The tribune grinned back at him, lifting the dead guard's sword to forestall any attempt to rush him.

'Oh, but you do know who I am. Your friend Avenus has already told you, I'm a tribune recently returned from Britannia. And I didn't come back alone, Pilinius, I brought a friend with me. A man called *Marcus*.'

The senator laughed at him, shaking his head.

'Marcus? Is the name supposed to hold some significance for me? And where is this "Marcus" now? Avenus here had my guards take him outside with orders to deal with him.'

Scaurus shook his head, tutting.

'There's me failing to make proper introductions yet again. My apologies, Senator. My name is Gaius Rutilius Scaurus, tribune commanding the First and Second Tungrian cohorts. And my friend? His full name is Marcus . . .' He paused for a moment. 'Valerius.' A smile crept across his face at the sudden widening of Pilinius's eyes. 'But you know his last name, don't you?' He lowered his voice to a harsh whisper. '*And as to where he is . . . ?*'

Pilinius leaned forward slightly in spite of himself.

'*He's behind you.*'

The men facing him turned to find that in the short time that their attention had been fixed on Scaurus, a dozen armed men had filed quietly through the door in the far wall, their shields set in an unbroken line in front of which stood a single man with a sword in each hand. He walked forward, ignoring the three guards advancing on him with their swords drawn.

'Tiberius Asinius Pilinius!'

The first man sprang in to attack with an incoherent scream, but the newcomer barely broke his stride as he pushed the sword wide with the long-bladed spatha in his right hand before punching the shorter gladius in his left deep into his attacker's belly. He shouldered the stricken guard off his blade and continued his advance, staring grimly at the other two men before him.

'Tiberius Asinius Pilinius! My name is Marcus Valerius Aquila! In the name of Nemesis I have come for *you!*'

The two remaining guards attacked together, but their attacks were poorly coordinated and the lone swordsman parried both blades with ease before spinning low and hacking the nearest man's leg off at the knee. The remaining guard backed away with a look of terror, and Marcus called out to his quarry again.

'Surrender yourself, Pilinius! Surrender to me now and these other men can go free!'

The senator turned and ran for the stairs, but in the distraction of Marcus's fight with his guards Scaurus had quietly stepped into the stairway and swung the massive iron gate closed behind him. He slid the heavy bolts home and grinned at Pilinius as he pulled uselessly at the metal grille, shaking his head sympathetically.

'I'm afraid not, Senator. It seems that the time has come for you to face the reality of what happens when monstrous crimes like these catch up with you. And here come your friends . . .'

Half a dozen of Pilinius's guests descended upon him, clearly intent upon taking Marcus up on his offer of clemency. Their host managed to cling on to the gate's iron bars for a moment, but the strength of the men dragging him away was not to be denied. Taking a limb apiece they hauled him kicking and shouting in front of the waiting centurion, one of his guards stepping in to snap a powerful punch into his temple to quieten his protests. Marcus walked slowly forward with his swords raised, scanning the crowd of men before him with disgust.

'Drop your weapons and get back against the far wall. Any man found with a knife will die alongside this animal!'

Guests and guards backed away slowly, their swords and knives clattering to the stone floor, and Marcus looked across the room at the slaves still standing in their places on the robbers board.

'Cotta, get these people out into the garden. All except for Perennis's wife. Bring her to me.'

He returned his gaze to his intended victim, squatting to look into the senator's face.

'You killed my father.'

Pilinius looked back at him with a hint of defiance in his stare, as his wits returned.

'We took your father alive and gave him to the praetorians. Whatever happened to him is on their hands, not mine. I can tell you who else—'

'Save your breath for the screaming. I know who else was involved.' Marcus raised his gladius to silence the senator's attempt to buy his way out of what was coming with information the centurion already possessed. 'You killed my mother.'

Pilinius nodded.

'We did. She took it bravely th—'

The sword's point jabbed towards his face, stopping inches from his eyes.

'Not we. *You. You* built this place specifically for the purpose of the torture, rape and murder of innocent women and children taken from the homes and families of the men Perennis set you to murder, didn't you? These *men* . . .' He swept the sword point up to gesture at the guests huddled against the far wall. 'These *scum* are indeed culpable for those evil acts, but without you they would never have had power over so many innocents. Over my mother.'

Cotta coughed behind him, and Marcus turned to find him holding Perennis's wife by the arm. She was crying, and holding her ripped tunic closed with one hand to cover her nakedness.

'Might we afford the dignity of a cloak for this lady, do you think?'

Cotta nodded, walking across to the wall where the guests' cloaks hung from pegs, selecting a good thick garment and carrying it back to drape over the woman's shivering body. Marcus nodded his thanks and then spoke to the dead prefect's wife in a firm voice.

'Madam, your husband ordered the destruction of my family, the deaths of my father, my sisters and my brother. Doubtless many more members of our household died here, in ways that you can imagine only too clearly given the squalid scenes we have both witnessed here tonight, ways that you and your family would have been subjected to had we not intervened. I hated your husband for that crime, I participated in his downfall and my only regret, to be frank with you, is that he did not die at my hands. However . . .'

He shook his head at Pilinius in disgust.

'I cannot condone such animal behaviour, even when directed at the family of my enemy. You will go free, Madam, although you would be wise to disappear into the depths of the city and never again use the name Perennis, unless you want to fall into the hands of another man like this one. Perhaps your former slaves will help you to survive, if you treated them decently before the end of your former life?'

She nodded helplessly, her face bleak as the terms under which she had been spared from Pilinius's debauched games sank in.

'But before we turn you loose, you have one more decision to make. How should this man die?'

The woman looked at him uncomprehendingly for a moment before realisation dawned.

'You offer me the chance to visit upon him the indignity and agony he intended for me and my daughter.' Marcus nodded. 'Then just kill him. I have no use for the memory of his agony.'

Cotta ushered her away, and Marcus raised an eyebrow at Pilinius.

'If you're ready? You might want to go to meet your ancestors with some small shred of pride intact.'

The senator closed his eyes, screwing his face up against the expected agony, but when Marcus stepped in it was to chop at the kneeling man's throat with the palm of his empty right hand. Pilinius fell choking to the floor, his body writhing as he fought for breath that could not pass his swollen and broken throat, his eyes bulging in horror as he stared up at his killer.

Marcus stepped over the dying man, gesturing to Cotta for the guest's weapons to be collected as he addressed them.

'I promised you men your freedom if you gave him up!'

Avenus stepped out of the throng.

'So let us go! You have no right to—'

He gasped as the longer of Marcus's swords whipped out and opened his throat, dropping to his knees with a horrible bubbling gurgle as his lifeblood ran down into his lungs, then fell forward onto the stone floor in a spreading pool.

'Would anyone else like to debate my *rights* with you, now that we've restored some order?'

Silence reigned for a moment before he spoke again, the spatha's bloodied blade levelled at his aghast audience.

'You bastards have no more *right* to life than he did. How many of you took part that night my family was destroyed? How many of you "*deflowered*" my sisters? And what of my brother, for those of you with a "*taste for a shapely boy*"? Killing you all would remove a canker from this city's heart, a cabal of perverted, sadistic monsters who should have been strangled at birth!'

Scaurus strolled across to join him, hefting his own sword.

'And to strike a more practical note, gentlemen, how many of you will seek revenge for this indignity against your exalted personages, eh? You were quick enough to surrender Pilinius, a man whose friendship you held dear until a moment ago, so is that the measure of your honour? You'll swear to a man to forget all that has happened tonight, I'm sure of that, and yet I expect that tomorrow morning the city will be hunted from end to end by your informants, all of them greedy for the huge rewards you'll offer for the man that provides you with the information that will bring us to bay. You, Secretary!'

Belenus stepped forward, his face an essay in hope, and the tribune hooked a thumb over his shoulder.

'You'll have your freedom, as the reward for betraying your master, but you'll pay half of everything you own into a temple of Mithras as your grateful expression of thanks for Our Lord's intercession on your behalf. Send word to me as to which temple you choose to take the money, and if you fail to do so within a week you can be assured that I'll find you and kill you myself. Get out.'

The freedman hurried past the two soldiers with a look of gratitude, and Scaurus returned his gaze to the remaining captives, knowing that they were close to rampaging forward despite the swords' threat.

'Centurion Cotta!'

'Tribune!'

'What do you think?'

'What do I think, Tribune?'

'Indeed. You strike me as a man with the nerve to order these men's deaths if you feel they deserve it, and the wit to have mercy on them if you feel it deserved. I leave it in your hands.'

Cotta was silent for a moment, as if reflecting on the question, sweeping a cold stare across the men before him. He raised his sword, pointing it at them and raising his voice to shout a command.

'*No! Prisoners!*'

Albinus was waiting when they opened the villa's rear gates, his bodyguards standing in a protective arc around him as the Tungrians walked out into the street. He stared in silence as Cotta's men guided the first of the wagons through the gates, terrified women staring out from between its rear flaps. As the second wagon followed it away down the hill, and the gates were pulled to, he found his voice at last.

'Rutilius Scaurus. I knew if I waited here for long enough you'd saunter out through those gates.'

The tribune gave him a tired glance.

'Centurion Cotta, if that man or any of his party so much as twitch a hand for their weapons you have my express order to kill them all.' He shook his head at the incensed senator, waving a hand as if to dismiss him. 'You're too late, *Decimus*. Centurion Aquila's vengeance on Asinius Pilinius is complete, and all that's left for you is to slip away into the darkness before what's left of the senator and his guests are discovered and it all gets rather more exciting round here than we might like. And remember, my threat to expose you as having stolen a fortune in imperial gold still stands, in case you or anybody in your pay feel like informing on us.'

He turned to walk away and then, as another thought struck him, turned back.

'Oh, and the next time you see our mutual informant Excingus, you might want to do two things – you can give him a message from me and then you can ask him a question for both of us.'

Albinus shook his head in apparent exasperation.

'Still making demands are you? Go on then, what is it you want me to tell the informant?'

'Only the obvious. Not to make the mistake of thinking that he'll get away with this last act of treachery. As of this moment his charmed life is on borrowed time, and the next time I see him I'll have his head!'

The senator nodded.

'And the question?'

'It's the same question you'll be asking him, *if* you get the chance. That greasy bastard contacted you *before* Dorso died in the fire, didn't he? He could have tipped you off to the fact that we were coming for the praetorian that night, but he didn't. Why? Then, when he led the centurion here to Brutus's hiding place, the ideal opportunity for him to have delivered my man to you without our ever having known the truth, he didn't. And lastly, when he tipped you off to the fact that we would be making our move on Pilinius tonight, he failed to mention the one thing you had to have if you were going to take advantage of the information . . .'

He raised a hand to display his invitation, the silver rectangle winking red in the torchlight.

'After all, he knew all too well that you'd never get into one of Pilinius's special parties without one of these. I'm keeping mine as a souvenir of the night when I cleansed this city of some of its worst men. So, *why* didn't he procure an invitation for you, Senator? It wouldn't have been that difficult, given that he had Pilinius's secretary over a barrel.' He turned away again, calling back over his shoulder. 'I think I've worked it out . . .'

6

Marcus rose before sunrise, having slept fitfully. Sitting on the bed, he mused briefly on Scaurus's final words in the officers' meeting the previous evening.

'Last night we did a great service to Rome, gentlemen. We removed a dozen of the most depraved men in the Senate, and with a little luck we will have knocked a large enough hole in their ranks for a little fresh air to get in. And, let us not forget, we have also dealt out justice to the third of the men who slaughtered our colleague's family. However . . .' Marcus had already known what was coming next. 'I can see no way that we'll be able to bring that justice to the fourth of them. For one thing we no longer have the dubious services of the informant Excingus on our side.'

'And for another, the bastard lives in a gladiatorial ludus among hundreds of men who revere him as their unofficial leader.'

The tribune took a sip of the wine he'd broached to celebrate their victory of the previous evening, nodding at Julius's comment.

'Quite so, First Spear. And so it is with regret that I am forced to concede that, for the time being, we will have to wait for an opportunity to arise. I hope you can understand my caution in this matter, Centurion?'

Marcus had nodded.

'I can only profess my gratitude at the support you've given me so far, Tribune. To do anything else would be churlish.'

For a moment he was convinced that Scaurus had not fully believed his show of acceptance, but at length the tribune had nodded, raising his cup again.

'Very well then, gentlemen! To victories gained, and one last victory to come!'

The officers had raised their cups, echoing the chorus, and Marcus had done the same despite his utter clarity as to what he had to do the next morning. He dressed in the darkness, having laid out the tunic and boots he intended to wear the previous night, and silently made his way to the bedroom's door.

'You're leaving without saying goodbye?'

He froze at the door, realising that his stealthy exit had failed, then turned back and sat on the bed beside his wife.

'I thought we said it all last night?'

Felicia sat up and knotted her fingers in his hair.

'Not everything.' She kissed him hard on the lips, her eyes wet with barely restrained tears. 'You know you won't come back this time. You know that once you've killed this man, his followers will tear you limb from limb. You know all this, and still you go to take your revenge no matter what the cost will be, despite the fact that this man Pilinius's death has left you just as empty as the two you killed before him.'

He shrugged helplessly.

'I still have no choice. Any day now we'll be posted away, either back to Britannia or to whichever of the empire's borders is creaking the loudest, and I'll never see this city again, or finish the act of vengeance that I've begun.'

'I know . . .' She sighed. 'I could have stopped you. I could have told Julius what you're planning and he would have confined you to your quarters under guard, but the wall of resentment that would have been erected between us would have been too much for me to bear. So go.' She turned her face to the wall, angrily wiping away the tears that were rolling down her cheeks. 'Go and take your revenge. I hope it brings you some measure of satisfaction before you die . . .'

Marcus shook his head.

'There's no pleasure for me in this. But neither is there any choice . . .'

He stood up, stroking her hair one last time and left the darkened room, pacing silently through the house with his boots held in one hand. The little dog scampered across the tiled floor, eager to play, and he squatted down, submitting to the creature's excited licks and nibbles at his fingers before making his way to the front door with the animal at his heels. Opening the door, he stood in the darkness for a moment before sitting down to pull on his boots.

'You really *are* stupid enough to do this then?'

Marcus started, his hand reflexively reaching for a weapon that wasn't fastened to his belt before relaxing again, as he realised who it was that had spoken.

'Have you been waiting out there all night?'

Dubnus paced out before him, his face all but invisible in the starlight.

'I was hardly going to risk walking up here from the barracks in the dark, was I? If I hadn't been waylaid by thieves, I'd more than likely have slipped in the contents of some dirty bastard's toilet and broken my back.'

The Roman stood, shaking his head at his friend.

'Well you've wasted your time, unless you've got half a dozen men waiting in the shadows, because nothing less is going to stop me from doing this.'

The big Briton laughed quietly, his guffaw rich with dark humour.

'Stop you? I know better than that! I'm not here to *stop* you, you idiot, I'm here to come along with you and watch your back. I've heard what happens to the new boys in these training schools, and—'

Marcus's interjection was vehement, his hands held up in a gesture of flat refusal.

'*No!* You're not coming anywhere with me! This is my fight, and not worthy of your sacrifice!'

His friend put his hands on his hips.

'Oh, you think so, do you? You think I'll stand meekly aside and allow you to march off into the darkness, never to be seen again?' He leaned forward, putting a broad finger in the Roman's chest. 'Well you can think a-fucking-gain, brother, because I'm coming with you whether you like it or not. We can either stand here and discuss the matter until the sun's up, and Julius finds out about this plan of yours, or we can go to this ludus of yours together now. You can choose.'

Marcus eyed him darkly for a moment.

'You realise that you're condemning yourself to almost certain death in the arena?'

The Briton laughed again, but his previously hard-edged jocularity had softened to the fatalistic tone of a man contemplating his own impending demise.

'I'm a *soldier*, Marcus. I face death every time I line my lads up to take their iron to whichever set of blue-nosed bastards it is we're fighting. And besides, unlike most of the other men we'll be fighting with, I've killed more times than I can remember. Trust me, you and I will cut a swathe through those fuckers the likes of which will be celebrated for many a year.'

His friend looked hard into the Briton's eyes.

'And when the time comes to cut that swathe through prisoners of war who've been shipped back to Rome for the purposes of providing the people of the city with a spectacle? Or to kill men condemned to death in the arena?'

Dubnus shrugged.

'I'll put their blood on the sand without a second thought. The barbarians should have kept their heads down, and the criminals either shouldn't have committed their crimes or shouldn't have got caught. Perhaps I'll get to gut the bastard who stole my purse at the baths.'

Marcus smiled despite himself.

'It sounds as if you'll fit right in. And I've no time to be arguing. If you're set on this?'

His friend slapped a huge hand down onto his shoulder.

'I'm set, brother. Now let's get out of here before we're missed. You know that Julius would have us both chained up if he even suspected you might be stupid enough to go after this Death Bringer.'

Marcus shooed the dog back into the house and closed the door, taking a deep breath as he turned away. Dubnus stepped in close, putting his mouth close to the Roman's ear.

'You can still change your mind, Marcus. You've taken more revenge for your family than even I ever dreamed might be possible, and all three of the men you've killed in return for your own loss have died in agony and humiliation. You have a beautiful wife and child who will miss you every day for the rest of their lives. Is one more death worth that much to you?'

The Roman shook his head.

'No. How could it be? But to the shades of my family, with only me to deliver the vengeance that they crave? That's a different question to the one you're asking. Come on, before my nerve fails me.'

They walked up the hill together in silence, Dubnus swearing under his breath as he stepped in the contents of a toilet bucket that had been tossed out into the street from a high window.

'So what happens when we get there?'

'You're asking the wrong man. All I know is that the Dacian Ludus considers applications from potential candidates in the early morning of each working day. What form that trial takes, or what happens thereafter, I have no idea, other than being made to swear an oath that will reduce us to the status of slaves. Worse than slaves. After that they'll give us whatever training we need to make us fit to fight in *that* . . .'

They had reached the hill's shallow crest, and stood for a moment to stare out across the pink-tinged city to where the massive bulk of the Flavian Arena dwarfed the buildings around it, even taller than the towering Claudian aqueduct to its south.

'It holds *fifty* thousand people on a games day, all baying for blood. Facing that will be a little different to taking on the barbarians, eh?'

Dubnus snorted.

'The only difference will be that in there I'll only have to kill one or two men to survive.'

The two men walked down the Aventine's northern slope with the first hesitant bird calls echoing off the walls around them.

'We're sure that this man Mortiferum still lives in the ludus? It'd be a pity to give up your freedom and condemn us both to a lifetime of fighting only to discover that he's packed it in and gone to live with some floozy.'

Marcus shook his head.

'It's not allowed. No matter how exalted a gladiator becomes, until he's freed or buys himself out of his contract, he belongs to the school that pays and feeds him. Besides, why would he want to give up such cosy protection? I doubt he lacks anything . . .'

Staying in the deeper shadows as much as they could, the two men were soon walking past the eastern end of the Circus Maximus, the racecourse's long run of grandstands stretching away to their left into the dawn gloom. Beyond the tiered ranks of seats rose the looming bulk of the Palatine Hill, crowned by the imperial palaces where Marcus had so recently witnessed the death of the man responsible for his father's murder. Dubnus raised a hand, pointing at a sudden flurry of activity in their path.

'Looks like some poor bastard's fallen foul of thieves.'

A hundred paces or so further on, in the light of the torches which illuminated the eastern end of the Palatine Hill, a single man stood in the middle of a group of half a dozen figures, a tight knot of men who were hemming their victim in ever closer and allowing him no chance of escape. As the two friends watched, still advancing unnoticed, the scene exploded into sudden violence, as the gang's intended victim decided that attack was his best form of defence, screaming what sounded like a military battle cry as he sprang forward.

'*Gemina!*'

Lunging at the closest of his would-be assailants, he snatched at the man's arm, neutralising the threat of the blade gleaming dully in the hand at its end, twisting the arm and tearing the ligaments that secured it to his assailant's shoulder.

With a piercing shriek the stricken robber fell to the ground with his arm flopping, writhing in agony with the pain so unexpectedly visited upon him. The men gathering about their intended victim paused in their advance, their apparent leader brandishing his knife in fury, his words clear in the silent street.

'You've fucking maimed him, you cunt! We was just going to

rob you, but now you're going to die slowly with your guts wrapped round your neck. We're going to—'

Dubnus coughed ostentatiously, and the nearest of the robbers turned to find the big man standing less than a dozen paces from them. The gang leader stared incredulously at him for a moment before speaking.

'Who the *fuck* are you?'

The Briton stepped forward another pace, his big hands hanging easily at his sides.

'A soldier, friend. And this morning, it has to be said, a very generous soldier, because right now I'm willing to allow you to walk away from here with nothing worse than one maimed man. Raise a finger against me and you'll all end your days begging for bread because you'll be fit for nothing else.'

'*Take him!*'

If the other gang members heard the shouted command they certainly didn't spring to obey it, and Dubnus raised an amused eyebrow at the furious robber.

'See, here's the thing. You've already picked on the wrong man once this morning, and lost one of your number with an injury that'll never heal, not that *you'll* be feeding him, will you? And there are only six of you now.'

'Six against two. We'll take you down easily enough!'

Marcus stepped out of the shadows of the towering Claudian aqueduct behind the gang leader, having quietly paced around them while everyone's attention was locked on Dubnus. He spoke, his voice hard as he stared at the men before him in disgust.

'Six against *three*. And from the look of it any of us could deal with a pair of you in the time it would take me to scrape a piece of shit off my shoe.' He took a step closer, his eyes roaming across the closest of the robbers, and more than one man took an involuntary pace backwards at the look of hatred that he was playing across their wavering ranks. 'Run now, or you'll have to drag yourselves away with your elbows by the time we're done with you.'

For a moment it looked as if the robbers might still put up a fight, but Dubnus settled the matter by stamping forward with a roar of anger, and in an instant their resolve disintegrated into a panic-stricken rout. Their intended victim looked about him for a moment with the expression of a man who had been cheated of something before turning to the Tungrians with a rueful smile.

'It seems I owe you my life, gentlemen. I doubt that I could have seen them all off . . .'

Dubnus laughed, holding out a meaty hand in greeting.

'You looked sharp enough to have made them work for it alright. Legion man, are you?'

The other man tilted his head, his eyes narrowing.

'Why do you ask?'

The Briton shrugged easily.

'Professional curiosity. I'm Dubnus, and this is Marcus, and we're both . . .' He grimaced at the sudden realisation of their changed circumstances. 'Or rather we were, centurions with an auxiliary cohort in Britannia.'

'*Were?*'

Marcus stepped forward and offered his hand in turn.

'We're on our way to the Dacian Ludus, to sign up as gladiators.'

The man they had rescued shook his head in dark amusement, holding up his hands in the face of Dubnus's growing irritation.

'Forgive me for laughing.' He bowed to them. 'I owe you both my life, and I won't forget that debt. Perhaps I will have the opportunity to pay it off sooner than you think, for I too am bound for the ludus. I had thought to join the Gallic School, but the chance to join alongside two men such as yourselves isn't one to turn up. I'm Horatius, former centurion with the Tenth Twin Legion and now simply a man seeking his destiny.'

Dubnus looked at Marcus, who nodded slowly.

'You would be welcome to join us, although I will warn you, Horatius, that we seek the blood of a man who resides within the ludus, and while his death is nothing less than a sacred duty for me it is likely to end in my own demise, and that of any man that stands alongside me.'

Horatius laughed softly.

'My life is already forfeit. By rights I should have died in Pannonia a month ago, and the gods have doubtless only allowed me to escape for the purpose of revenge. Although how I am ever to achieve that aim is beyond me.'

Marcus nodded.

'Then we have the same aim, you and I. But I must warn you again, my success is likely to condemn us both to death, and quite possibly yourself by association.'

The former centurion nodded.

'I'll take that risk.'

The three men walked in silence beneath the aqueduct's tiered arches, emerging a moment later into the huge open space that was the setting for the Flavian Arena. The massive structure's stonework was catching the first light, its gaudy paintwork gleaming in the pale illumination, and to the arena's left the hundred-foot-high bronze statue of the Sun God that had originally borne the head of the emperor Nero played its blank-eyed gaze down on them. They walked around to the arena's right, and across the open square that stood between its eastern side and the training schools that fed it with gladiators.

'The ludus is up here. And it appears that there are already enough applicants to provide the school with any recruits for a month.'

Marcus led the two men up a long flight of steps, at the top of which two dozen or so men were waiting in front of a gate guarded by a pair of burly men. The rearmost of the group of would-be gladiators opened his mouth to speak to the newcomers, only to be interrupted by the creak of the gate opening.

'Silence! If you want to enter the Dacian Ludus then your first task is to shut up and *listen!*'

A hush fell across the waiting men. Marcus craned his neck, and could just see the stocky man who had planted himself in the gateway. The skin of his shaved head was riven by a long scar that ran from his right eyebrow to his left ear, the top of which was missing.

'My name is Sannitus, and I am the chief lanista of this ludus.

Whatever I say inside these gates is law, with no judge other than me and no right of appeal! If you want the chance to live under my law, you'll have to convince me that you're fit to enter these gates. So, *if* you want to enter the ludus, strip! I want to see your muscles, and I don't have the time for you to undress one at a time!'

He waited for a moment while they pulled off their tunics to reveal bodies of all shapes and sizes, a few preserving their modesty with loincloths while the remainder were naked.

'Now, one at a time, stand in front of me and show me what you're made of.' The men formed a jostling, buzzing queue, presenting themselves to the lanista in turn. 'No, too fat. No, not enough muscle. Lift some weights at your local bathhouse for a month and come back. Yes, you look right enough.' He gestured to the successful candidate to move off to one side, turning a forbidding scowl on the next man. 'No, not you. I told you last time that you're never going to be strong enough for the arena, although it seems I also underestimated your stupidity. Go back to the farm and stop wasting your time and mine here!'

The judgements continued, swift and merciless, with only three men admitted from the twenty or so who had presented them-selves, until the would-be gladiator in front of Horatius was sent away disappointed, and only the three soldiers remained. Sannitus stared at them for a long moment, then shook his head slowly in apparent disbelief.

'Every now and then, once or twice a year, the gods see fit to send something a little bit different to this gate, something I've not seen before. Last time it was a dwarf so vicious that we had to keep him locked in a cell when he wasn't training, such a little bastard that the boys eventually got tired of his antics and decided that he should have the misfortune to fall on a spear during training. Before that it was a high-class aristocrat who'd decided to slum it for a while, and show off his virtuosity with a sword from behind the anonymity of a mask. He was good too, until he pissed off the wrong fish man and ended up with a foot of sharp iron sticking out of his back. And now . . .'

He studied the three men with a pitiless gaze.

'You're all muscles, scars and tattoos, aren't you lads, even you, the wiry one, combat trained and ready to fight at the drop of a handkerchief? Perfect for us, eh? No training needed, beyond a few short sharp lessons as to the dirty tricks that get pulled in the arena. You're all expert with the sword, right, shield trained, and I'll bet you can all put a spear up a cat's arsehole at twenty-five paces. But here's the problem, boys . . .'

He paused for effect.

'You're all spoken for. The army owns you, and any lanista that takes you on is risking losing his licence, his school and most likely his balls into the bargain if he gets caught fielding serving soldiers.' He shook his head. 'Sorry lads, but you're too much of a risk for my liking.'

As he turned away Horatius stepped forward.

'I don't know about these two, but I'm already officially dead.'

Sannitus stopped, thought for a moment and then turned back with a quizzical look.

'You're *dead*? How does that work?'

The former centurion shrugged.

'I got caught up in something that I'd have been best avoiding, if I'd ever known how to stay out of it. Now I'm just another anonymous body with all the right skills to make you a fortune in the arena. Try me.'

Sannitus nodded slowly.

'I just might. You can provide me with your former name and rank, and I'll make some quiet enquiries about you. In the meantime, you can come in with these three, and we'll see if you've got the stones to back up that claim.' He shot a glance at Marcus and Dubnus, neither of whom had moved. 'I don't suppose either of you are going to try to tell me that you're dead as well?'

While Marcus was still weighing the best approach Dubnus stepped forward, his massive frame towering over the lanista.

'We're honourable discharges from the First Tungrian auxiliary cohort, bought and paid for.'

Sannitus frowned up at him.

'Really? At your ages? Neither of you looks a day over thirty, and now you mention it, your mate here looks more like a twenty-year-old.'

The Briton smiled, rubbing his thumb and forefinger together.

'Wars in far-off provinces tend to have some side benefits, once you get past all the obvious stuff like having to kill thousands of screaming barbarians who all want your cock for a belt decoration. Like gold. Me and my brother in arms here . . .' He hooked a thumb back at the impassive Marcus. 'We made it our job as centurions to be out in front of the legions when it came to hunting down the tribal chiefs who were stupid enough to start the whole thing. And when we captured Calgus, the biggest bastard of the lot, he was carrying enough gold to finance our release from service with plenty left over.' He grinned down at Sannitus's look of disbelief. 'Our tribune took our gold and dismissed us honourably as too badly wounded to continue.'

'You can prove this? You both have a diploma?'

The Briton shrugged easily.

'We decided not to bring them with us. After all, you meet some right nasty types on the streets of this city.'

Sannitus pondered the two men for a moment, walking around them with a critical eye.

'Not an ounce of spare flesh on either of you.' He looked closely at Marcus's face, then bent to examine Dubnus's stomach. 'Scars, some of them fresh too. What was that. A spear?'

The Briton nodded.

'My century's line was about to break, so I dived in and got run through for my pains.'

'You? What happened to your nose.'

Marcus shrugged.

'I was too slow winding my neck in.'

The lanista's eyes narrowed, and when he spoke his voice was hard with suspicion.

'He's not from Rome, but you are, aren't you? And I've heard that accent before, I hear it every time the rich boys come down here for their private shows. So what would a man like you have been doing in the auxiliary, eh?'

Marcus bent until his face was inches from the lanista's, his face inscrutable.

'My duty.'

He straightened, waiting for the trainer's verdict with an apparent calmness that he was far from feeling. Sannitus looked up at him for a moment before speaking again.

'Have it your own way. I won't deny that the three of you would make an interesting feature in our shows, but I'm not the ultimate decision maker. Follow me!'

The six men hurried after him as he strode back into the ludus, and the gates closed behind them with a heavy thud, the guards promptly shooting home three massive iron bolts that made the heavy wooden doors well-nigh impregnable. Marcus looked about him, but found no clue as to the school's purpose in its architecture.

'Expecting an arena, were you? We don't need one, rich boy. Let the other schools try to cover all the disciplines, we just concentrate on delivering the best fucking swordsmen anywhere in the empire. And we do it here . . .'

He opened the door into a long, wide hall with an open roof, gesturing for the would-be trainees to follow him.

'One or two of you may be good enough to train for the arena as a member of this ludus, but before you get to sign your lives away you have to pass the test. *Their* test.'

He pointed to a group of men lounging against the far wall, all of them wearing a short tunic that came no more than halfway down their thighs.

'These, gentlemen, are gladiators. They train in this hall, all day every day, until their bodies are like bags stuffed with rocks, and they eat like prize chariot horses, to put that nice layer of fat on them that a man needs in the arena. We train them until they could fight a bout with their eyes closed, so they'll keep going until the last drop of blood has leaked out if they're unlucky or stupid enough get wounded. All you have to do, if you want to join us, is to put up a decent performance against the man I choose from their number. If you put up a reasonable defence, you may just be good enough to win a place in the ludus. In which case you'll swear the oath, reduce your standing in society so low that even the slaves will be sneering down on you, and you will become the property of the school, to be disposed of in any way I choose. So, who wants to go first?'

One of the men who had been ahead of the three centurions in the queue stepped forward, his voice clear and strong.

'I'll have a go, if you please, Lanista?'

The lanista clapped him on the back.

'Good lad. Who shall we get to give you a try out? Pontus!' One of the waiting gladiators got to his feet, picked up a wooden practice sword and walked into the middle of the hall. 'Give this new boy a run around and let's see what he's got! Edius, arm him!'

The would-be trainee took a practice sword from Sannitus's assistant and advanced forward to meet his opponent, who waited until he was within sword's length and then set about him with a series of cuts and lunges which were clearly intended to find the limits of his ability to defend himself, giving the tyro no opportunity to strike back. After a dozen or so attempts to breach the triallist's defence, he stepped up the attack, swinging the heavy wooden blade high and then low, aiming for head and then knees, and then, without warning, leapt forward and shoulder-barged his opponent to the ground, pinning him with the sword's ragged point at his throat.

'Not bad!' Sannitus waited until the gladiator had pulled his defeated victim to his feet with a grin. 'Doesn't matter that he put you on your arse, given he was always going to beat you. That's just one of the more basic tricks of the trade. Decent sword work though. Who taught you to defend yourself?'

The triallist handed his weapon back, standing to attention.

'My father sir; he was a praetorian!'

Sannitus smiled.

'Praetorian, eh? Well he trained you well enough for me to

reckon you're worth giving a chance to. Well done! Now stand aside, and let the next man have a try shall we? Nemo, your turn to show us what he's got!'

The second candidate to step forward looked far less assured, the knuckles of his sword hand white on the practice weapon's hilt, and his brow beaded with sweat despite the morning's chill, and to Marcus's eye it seemed that Sannitus gave the gladiator Nemo a meaningful glance before releasing them to spar. Where the previous triallist had been sufficiently self-assured to defend himself with some degree of proficiency, this man seemed out of his depth from the bout's commencement, and within half a dozen stokes his opponent had tapped him twice on the arm and neck with his weapon's point. Realising that he was rapidly losing his chance to join the school, he leapt forward with a scream and slashed wildly at his opponent, who simply ducked under the blow and jabbed him in the ribs hard enough that he subsided to the hall's sandy floor with a dull groan. Sannitus gestured to his assistants, who collected the practice sword and set the man back on his feet.

'Not for you, I'm afraid, not this time. Go and learn some sword skills if you want to pass this test, and don't come back until you can defend yourself, eh?'

The failed candidate nodded glumly and was led to the gate, followed shortly after by the other remaining civilian whose assessment was equally swift and conclusive. Sannitus turned to face the three soldiers, smiling sardonically at them.

'I'm tempted to get Mortiferum out of his bed to wipe that confidence off your faces, but I doubt he'd thank me, and he can be a right bastard if he don't get his sleep. So . . .'

He turned to look across at the remaining gladiators waiting against the far wall.

'Who shall we use for this . . . yes. Hermes, over here if you will!'

The biggest of them got up and strode across the hall, stopping a dozen paces from the group and folding his arms, waiting impassively for further instructions. Where the previous contestants from within their number had been encouraged by cheers that were only partially ironic, this man's walk across the hall was greeted with nothing more than silence, the other gladiators staring stonily at his back. Sannitus signalled to one of his assistants, who promptly passed the big man a practice sword.

'Let's have shields as well, we don't want anyone getting damaged. You, the legion man. Let's see what you've got, shall we?'

Horatius nodded and stepped forward, taking the sword and wooden shield that he was offered and weighing them for a moment before turning to face his opponent. The gladiator scowled back at him, an angry pink scar marking one of his cheeks, and Marcus was left with the clear impression that he intended making the most of his opportunity to intimidate a potential new entry to the school.

'Fight!'

At Sannitus's command the gladiator leapt forward, eschewing any attack with his sword and choosing to punch with his shield instead, looking to use his superior weight to knock Horatius off balance. The legion man stepped back, barely resisting the blow with his own shield and encouraging the gladiator to step forward again, punching even harder as he sensed that the brutal tactic was unsettling his opponent. Horatius pulled back again, his step to the rear larger than the previous retreat, his right hand sliding back until the point of the wooden sword's blade was almost level with his ear, and Marcus narrowed his eyes as he realised what was coming. Hermes stamped forward a third time, encouraged by the soldier's accelerating retreat to go for the kill, but as he lunged into the attack, bent on smashing the wavering shield out of his way and striking at the reeling centurion with his sword, Horatius sidestepped smartly to his left, hammering his shield's rim against the inside of his opponent's board. Before the gladiator had time to realise what was happening, the soldier had sprung forward off his left foot with his sword arm's elbow held rigidly before him, the blow flattening Hermes and leaving him momentarily stunned as he fell back onto the hard sandy floor.

Horatius reflexively raised his sword to strike at the fallen fighter, but a swift call from Sannitus stayed his hand.

'*Hold!* You might do it that way in the army, but in the arena it's more the done thing to hold a fallen opponent under the point of your sword and ask whoever is chairing the games whether he should live or die. And in this case you can give him a hand since he's your new comrade. Welcome to the ludus.'

The victorious soldier dropped his sword and put out a hand to Hermes, but the gladiator rolled away from him, regaining his footing with an easy grace that belied his size, leaving his sword and shield where they had fallen. Horatius shrugged and handed his shield to Sannitus, exchanging looks with the trainer, who shook his head in mock sadness at the loser's behaviour.

'I know, he's always been a miserable bastard. It's just as well he fights as well as he does, or he'd have had the shit beaten out of him years ago.' He turned away and muttered an additional comment to Edius, intended only for his assistant's ears but which carried as far as Marcus. 'And a good thing we've got Velox and Mortiferum to keep the prick in order, eh?'

He turned back to the remaining triallists, grinning up at Dubnus.

'You, the big bastard. Sure you want to go through this? You look too . . . well built to be quick enough for the arena.'

The Briton raised an eyebrow.

'Would you like to put that observation to the test, Lanista?'

Sannitus shook his head with a wry smile.

'Not today.' He turned to shout a comment after the defeated gladiator, who was already halfway across the hall, glaring hard at his mates and silently daring any of them to make a joke at his expense. 'Hey, Hermes! You don't get off that easily! Come back and take those frustrations out on this.' Shaking his head at Dubnus he gestured to the gladiator, who had turned back to stare at him with an expression that promised violence. 'No, big man, I'll have to pass on your offer, given you've got twenty years' advantage on me. Today you can fight Hermes for the pleasure of our company.'

The Briton shrugged and stepped forward, accepting the practice weapons with a nod to the trainer and rolling his massive bearded head around on his bull neck before stepping forward and dropping into the familiar combat stance he had practised every day for the last fifteen years.

'Come on then, Gladiator. Let's see if you can succeed where ten thousand angry tribesmen failed.'

Hermes stared hard at him for a moment before stooping to collect his weapons, frowning in concentration as he stepped in to sword reach. For a brief moment the two men stared at each other over their shields and then, Hermes took a deep breath, blinked, and then threw himself forward at the Briton. Forewarned by his previous defeat that any attempt to bully the soldier with his shield was unlikely to bear fruit, the gladiator went to work with his sword instead, launching a flurry of blows clearly intended to find a gap in his opponent's defences. Dubnus held his ground, parrying the attacks with sword and shield and watching the gladiator intently, waiting for an opportunity, but after a dozen fruitless attacks, Hermes stepped back, opening his sword hand enough to use his fingers to gesture the big man forward. Sannitus nodded in agreement.

'He's got a point, big man. No one goes to the arena to watch a fighter defend himself, they go for excitement! They want to see—'

With a sudden lunge forward, Dubnus covered the ground between himself and Hermes in a single big step, smashing his shield against his opponent's hard enough to throw the gladiator backwards two paces. Once in motion the Briton's attack was relentless, barging with his shield against his opponent's board again, and a third time, before launching a furious series of sword strokes which took all of Hermes's training and skill to deflect. With each desperate parry he stepped back again, unable to cope with the power of the soldier's incessant sword strokes. Seeing his opportunity, Dubnus struck, swinging his sword high to force the gladiator to parry and then, while the other man's sword was still raised in defence, stamping forward with two quick steps and hooking the ankle of his forward leg, smashing his shield hard against Hermes's to send him sprawling onto his back. The gladiator tensed, ready to roll back onto his feet as he had a moment before, but froze at the hard touch of Dubnus's sword at his throat.

Sannitus strolled forward, raising an amused eyebrow at seeing his man on the hall's floor for a second time. A quiet chorus of sniggers and catcalls from the gladiator's colleagues was silenced by a long stare and a blunt pronouncement from the trainer.

'I'd like to have seen any of you cucumber munchers deal with that, so I suggest you all shut up until you've sparred with this monster . . .' He turned to Dubnus, nodding approvingly. 'Yes, *that's* what the audience want to see! You're in, now let him up.'

The gladiator stood, his face betraying the fact that the ground was clearly moving beneath his feet. Sannitus stepped close, whispering fiercely in his ear.

'Disappointing, Hermes. Perhaps you'll do better with the last of them. He sounds like an aristo, so I doubt he'll have quite the same brutality as those two.'

The gladiator nodded, squaring his shoulders and turning to face Marcus, his teeth gritted in anger at his second defeat. Sannitus waved a hand, gesturing for the last of the triallists to join them.

'Come on then, let's see if you've got as much bastard in you as your mates.'

Marcus stopped just outside of the reach of Hermes's sword and stood ready, both hands hanging easily at his sides and his eyes alert for any sign of an attack. Sannitus laughed, motioning his man Edius to give him a weapon.

'You're not stupid, are you?'

His answer was delivered in a deliberately dismissive tone, but the younger man's gaze never wavered as he stared at Hermes.

'Not stupid enough to let a man who's already been humiliated twice by my brothers in arms have a free shot at me.'

Hermes sneered, but Sannitus nodded his appreciation.

'You've got balls, I'll give you that, Soldier. If you really *are* a soldier?' He pursed his lips and looked the younger man up and down, shaking his head in apparent disbelief. 'You really don't

look the type, do you? Sure you wouldn't be happier up the hill
with the praetorians?'

Marcus shrugged, keeping his eyes fixed on the gladiator.

'I'll let you be the judge of that.' He waved away the shield that
Edius was offering him. 'I'll take another sword, if it's all the same
to you.'

Sannitus shook his head in amusement.

'You can defend yourself with your stick of celery if you like.
I've never had a man elect to fight for his place with two knives
before, and it takes us years of hard work with the best swordsmen
to produce a competent dimachaerus, but if you think you're
good enough to fight that way then you just go ahead.' He nodded
to Hermes. 'Ready?'

The gladiator growled his answer, his gaze locked on Marcus
in a way that was clearly supposed to be intimidatory.

'Let me at him.'

Horatius leaned closer to Dubnus, muttering a question in his ear.

'*Is* he good enough?'

The Briton laughed softly.

'Just watch.'

Sannitus turned to Marcus, who was weighing the two practice
swords in his hands, still watching Hermes intently.

'Ready?'

As he opened his mouth to answer, the gladiator took a deep
breath, and, in that instant for which the young centurion had
been waiting, he closed his eyes momentarily. Marcus stamped
forward with his left leg and lifted his right, bent at the knee,
snapping his foot forward and twisting his body to plant it squarely
in the gladiator's chest. The kick catapulted Hermes backwards
to land hard on his backside, while Marcus stalked forwards with
his swords levelled. His opponent scrabbled backwards, frantically
retreating in the face of the weapons' twin threats, staggering
untidily to his feet with a scowl of fury.

'*Bastard!*'

Marcus grinned for the first time, showing his teeth and
smirking at the gladiator.

'You need to do something about that blink. I doubt it pays for a professional fighting man to have quite such an obvious tell, do you?' He flicked a glance at Sannitus. 'If you really *are* a gladiator? After all, you don't really look the type at the moment, do you?'

The trainer nodded wryly, realising that all he had achieved through his crude attempt to worry the young centurion a moment before had been to sharpen the man's edge, but Hermes had clearly missed the point.

'You cheeky young cunt! I'll have your *fucking* liver out!'

Sannitus stepped forward, raising a hand.

'Enough! We'll—'

Hermes pushed past him with a snarl of rage.

'Fuck off, Sannitus! This turd's *mine*!' He stormed forward, punching with his shield to take advantage of Marcus's apparent lack of any means of defence, and forcing the younger man to dance backwards, away from his lunges. 'Not so fucking clever now, are you boy?' He attacked again, and this time Marcus feinted right before sidestepping left and steering away the gladiator's blade with almost contemptuous ease, looking pointedly down at the gladiator's exposed right leg as he did so. Sannitus shook his head in dismay, turning to look at Dubnus.

'Am I right in thinking this isn't going to end well?'

The Briton shrugged.

'That depends on your man.'

Marcus backed away as Hermes bore down on him again, raising his swords wide.

'It's honours even at this point, Hermes. You've been on your backside, and you've chased me around for a while. We could just drop the weapons and call it a draw?'

The gladiator sneered over the top of his shield.

'*Fuck you!* Offering me a draw when I've got you running scared? I can smell the sh—'

He jerked to his right as Marcus leapt forward, realising even as he did so that the attack was only a feint, twisting desperately to counter the changing threat as his opponent sprang off his left foot and struck at his shielded side, realising too late that this too was bluff as the weak sword stroke merely touched the shield. Far too late, the gladiator realised that his abrupt switch of defence had left the entire right side of his body undefended, his sword nothing better than a forgotten and useless piece of wood in his right hand. The other sword hit his right knee with enough force to buckle his leg, and Hermes found himself lying on his back clutching his leg while his opponent turned away, dropping his swords to the sandy floor.

'*Bastaaaard!* I'll fucking kill you for—'

He fell silent as Marcus turned back and stooped quickly to take his throat in a hard-fingered grip. When the younger man spoke his voice was cold and matter of fact.

'I'll remember that. And if we ever, *ever*, meet in the arena with iron in our hands, you'd be as well to cut your own throat before I get to you, or you'll spend a long time dying.'

'*Enough!*'

Sannitus stepped in between the two men, pushing Marcus away.

'I can usually spot the real animals before they ever pick up a sword, but every now and then I miss one. Like you, you *monster*.' Marcus stared back at him for a moment before realising from the man's tone that the term was intended as a compliment. 'What's your name?'

Resisting the urge to declare his true identity, Marcus replied with the assumed name under which he served in the Tungrian cohort.

'Marcus. Marcus Tribulus Corvus.'

Sannitus nodded slowly.

'Perfect. Every man needs a name for the arena, something that the crowd can shout out when you stand before them with your sword red with blood. Names like Velox, or Flamma, short names that the crowd can punch out in a chorus.'

He pointed to Horatius.

'You'll be "Centurion". And you, Dubnus is it? Yes, "Dubnus", that's a good name for a crowd, short and simple. But you, my lad, since I predict you're going to give my two best men something new to think about, we're going to need something powerful for the fans to get hold of. And I think "Corvus" will do very nicely.'

* * *

'It looks as if the young fool's actually decided to go into the ludus after Mortiferum then?'

Scaurus spread his arms wide with a helpless shrug at his glowering first spear. A messenger sent into the city soon after first light, when Dubnus had failed to make an appearance at the routine dawn officer's meeting, had confirmed what the first spear had strongly suspected.

'And in his place you'd have done what, exactly?'

The fuming first spear shook his head in exasperation.

'And in his place, would you have left your wife and baby son to fend for themselves in the almost certain outcome of your death? Would you have taken your best friend into the bloody ludus to die with you?'

His tribune sat back in his chair, contemplating the ceiling for a moment.

'I doubt he had any choice in the matter. You of all people know just how stubborn Dubnus can be – after all, he put up with you as a centurion for several years, I believe? And in any case, you may be slightly premature in your certainty that they won't—'

A knock at the door heralded the arrival of a soldier sent with a message from Otho, the day's duty centurion. Saluting as smartly as he knew how to, mindful of his senior centurion's ever judgemental eye, he stamped to attention and delivered his message in a breathless gabble.

'Centurion's respects, sir, and he has a man at the main gate asking to see you, sir! Man from the city, sir!'

Scaurus shot a glance at Julius to confirm that his subordinate was as bemused as he felt, nodding his assent. The first spear stood, directing an order to the waiting soldier.

'Very well, Soldier, ask Centurion Otho to escort him here please. Dismissed.'

Once the enlisted man had repeated the stamping and saluting expected of him and left the room, Scaurus sat back in his chair with a thoughtful look on his face, while the first spear paced across the room to look out of its window.

'That's even quicker than I would have expected.'

Scaurus nodded thoughtfully.

'Quite so. Let's hope that this infers good news, shall we?'

Otho himself showed their visitor into the office, his battered face set in a concerned expression. He saluted and withdrew, his hard stare at the back of the man's head speaking volumes for the worry that had spread across the camp once the two centurions' absence had become apparent. Scaurus rose gravely from his chair and paced around the desk, offering the visitor his hand. The newcomer was smartly dressed in a formal toga, his boots shining from the frequent application of wax, and his thinning hair was cut short in apparent defiance of the current fashion. A slave waited behind him with the look of a man who was used to keeping his mouth shut and his eyes and ears open, and he watched in respectful silence as his master bowed to Scaurus and spoke in a confident tone that gave Julius the feeling that he was a man well accustomed to getting what he wanted.

'Greetings, Tribune Scaurus. I can only apologise for making such an unexpected visit, and for not sending a message in advance to request a meeting. I am Lucius Tettius Julianus, procurator of the Imperial Dacian Ludus.'

Scaurus bowed in turn, his disarming smile inviting his guest to share his amusement at the unexpected nature of the visit.

'Greetings, Procurator, and welcome to what is for the time being a small part of Britannia transplanted to Rome, at least until we receive orders to march north again.' They clasped arms. 'This is my first spear, Julius.'

The other man bowed to Julius, and the big centurion gravely lowered his own head in reply. Scaurus gestured to the spare seat and walked back around the desk to his own chair.

'Please do take a seat. Might I pour you a cup of this rather acceptable wine? It's diluted, of course, in due deference to the earliness of the hour.'

Julianus tipped his head in grateful acceptance of the offer, sipping at the drink and nodding his approval. Scaurus tasted his own cup, barely sipping the watered-down wine before raising questioning eyes to his guest.

'So, Procurator, how might we be of assistance to you?'

The visitor took a ring from his finger, passing it to the tribune.

'As I say, I hold the rank of procurator, reporting directly to the imperial chamberlain, and I am responsible for the management of the Dacian Ludus.'

Scaurus inclined his head in recognition of his guest's exalted status, looking at the procurator's badge of office for a moment before handing it back with a respectful inclination of his head.

'A weighty responsibility, Lucius. Especially these days . . .'

He left the statement unfinished, and the procurator took his conversational bait without hesitation.

'How right you are. The emperor's rather close interest in every aspect of the gladiatorial spectacle means that we have to produce the finest swordsmen in the empire if we are to satisfy his expectations.'

'I can only imagine the pressure involved. But then you have those two brothers, do you not? Velox and . . .'

Scaurus looked at the ceiling as if trying to remember the other name.

'Mortiferum. Yes, we do, and by the gods, they're a superb pair of fighters, so good that I've bowed to my lanista's suggestion and named them both as my first rank fighters despite the unusual nature of such an arrangement. However, and as I'm sure you can imagine, we do rather tend to go through the second and third rank men. So, when three candidates for the ludus present themselves together, and proceed, one after another, to comprehensively outfight one of my more effective men, well, I'm sure I can leave it to your imagination to work out what their potential might be. Not to mention their prospects.'

Scaurus smiled his agreement, raising an eyebrow to Julius.

'*Three* men of such skill? I can indeed see what a gift that might seem. But of course, there's always the risk of taking on a man who is in reality still a serving soldier. I can only assume that you examine each ex-soldier's record with the very greatest of care?'

Julianus nodded.

'Indeed I do. Which, as I expect you have already perceived, is what brings me here at such short notice. I have two men from your cohort in my ludus at this very moment, both claiming to have recently bought their way out of their commissions, and therefore claiming the right to take the oath.'

'*Ah.*'

Scaurus's expression went from relaxed bonhomie to shifty discomfort, and Julianus smiled sympathetically.

'Ah *indeed.*' He leaned forwards and lowered his voice, shooting Julius a conspiratorial glance. 'Please believe me when I assure you that your own internal administrative procedures really are none of my business, and to be frank with you both, you've done me a huge service in freeing them up to seek their fortunes in the arena.' He leaned back with an expansive gesture. 'I can see them earning the ludus a good deal of gold. A *very* good deal of it. And some of that gold will, in time, work its way down to them with, I'm sure, the adulation of the crowd, the swooning services of a variety of grateful matrons, and so on. I'm sure we'll all enjoy sharing in their reflected glory – you really haven't lived until your female companion for the evening has spent the day at the arena enjoying the aphrodisiac effect of watching grown men tear into each other with sharp iron!'

He leaned back in his chair with a smug smile, and Scaurus leaned forward with an intrigued expression.

'Now that I would like to see!'

'And you shall, Rutilius Scaurus, as my personal guest when your men fight in the arena for the first time. I suspect that we'll be making them part of a spectacle that will have Rome buzzing for days. Anyway, all I need to be assured of their freedom to take the oath is to see those two precious sheets of bronze that declare them both to be honourably discharged as citizens of the empire, with all the witness seals intact, of course.'

Scaurus shot Julius a swift glance.

'Their diplomas?'

'Yes indeed, that's all. Just show me their diplomas and I'll be on my way. You do have them to hand, I presume?'

7

The morning had passed slowly for the newcomers, obliged to sit and watch the ludus's routine as Sannitus and his men had variously encouraged, chivvied, cajoled, bullied and simply kicked his trainees through their lessons. The sound of booted feet rasping across the floor and the grunts and curses of the would-be gladiators filled the air.

'Ointment.'

Marcus stirred from his reverie.

'What?'

His friend waved a hand at the men exercised before them.

'I was thinking how this isn't very much different to the way we train, and then it hit me.' He sniffed the air ostentatiously. 'Muscle ointment. They're all using it, despite the fact that they might as well be rubbing on rabbit fat for all the good it'll do them.'

The Briton yawned, looking round at the soldier they had rescued from robbers earlier that morning, who had woken from his own doze and was looking around him with weary interest. The three soldiers had been sat down in a corner of the hall with a pail of water between them and told not to move until the issue of their status was concluded, their presence tolerated but not yet accepted by Sannitus.

'You're really listed as dead?'

Horatius nodded at Dubnus, leaning back and taking a sip of water from the pail's scoop.

'As far as the record keepers for my legion are concerned, I died in an ambush a few miles south of Vindobona, in Noricum. Whereas what really happened was that I ran from the fight like a frightened child.'

Dubnus smiled.

'We've all been there.'

The soldier snorted angrily.

'*Not* me. Not until that instant when my feet took me into the forest without me even considering the alternative.' He sighed. 'You won't understand unless you know the full story, and we hardly seem to be short of time for the telling, do we? I was a centurion with the Tenth Gemina, and, let me tell you without any pride at all that I was the best fucking officer in my cohort. The fastest man with a sword, the most accurate with a spear . . . I could kill a man with nothing more than a shield.' He laughed bitterly. 'Oh yes, I was death incarnate, and didn't I know it? As far as I was concerned, every other man in the cohort was inferior to me in the only way that mattered, and I stalked around as though I were the only real soldier in the fortress.' He shook his head sadly. 'Which made what I did that day even worse. I could have killed half a dozen of these bastards before they took me down, and instead . . .'

'How did they manage to ambush you in the first place?'

Horatius nodded.

'Don't think I haven't asked myself that question a thousand times since the day it happened, after all, it's the stuff they teach you in basic training, isn't it? I can still remember that leathery old bugger of a centurion who turned us into soldiers telling us all about ambushes. "Every successful ambush needs two things, gentlemen, one party cunning enough to set the trap and another stupid enough to walk into it!" And gods, you can believe me when I tell you that we really were *that* stupid. Just because the men setting the trap were our own, we meekly allowed—'

'You were attacked by *Romans*?'

Horatius snorted a humourless laugh, raising an eyebrow at Marcus, who was staring at him with a look of incredulity at the revelation.

'Yes, by *Romans*. Is that shocking to you, friend? A praetorian centurion came to the Vindobona fortress, you see, with orders from the emperor. The Legatus was to ride south to Rome immediately, and there was an escort "waiting for us just down the road", so he decided that he only needed a few of his own men for the sake of appearances, me and a half-dozen of my lads that could ride to act as bodyguards. When I asked the praetorian why he'd not brought his own men to the fortress with him, he told me that it was to avoid any unnecessary delay, and that there was "no time to lose". The bastard was right though . . .' The soldier's eyes were cold as he recalled the moment. 'His men were waiting for us alright, they waited at the top of a hill between two steep verges and then, once we were halfway up, they came down the road towards us four abreast and at the gallop, calling out to each other with the excitement of getting to kill a senator. I shouted to the Legatus to ride for his life but he was too slow getting his horse turned about, and they ran him down like a dog. I took my men into them, but there were too many of them for us to do anything but die gloriously.'

He drank from the scoop again, shaking his head in disgust.

'I managed to put my blade's point into a face, punched the man clean off his horse, only to find myself on my back in the road beside him. His spear had caught me in the arm and snagged one of the joints of my manica.' He grunted a mirthless laugh. 'That metal sleeve probably saved my bloody life. I staggered back onto my feet between a pair of horsemen, both of them trying to get their spears lined up on me, and that gave me time to put my swordpoint up into the jaw of the man on my left. Then I slipped on the road's surface, probably from the blood that was running down it in rivulets, and lost my grip on the sword. I knew if I bent down to find it I'd never come back up again, so I drew my dagger and pulled the man on my right out of his saddle.' His eyes closed, and a satisfied smile played across his face for a moment. 'I've always liked my knives long enough to be of some use in a fight, and I hit him so hard that it went right through his neck and stuck out of the other side. And then it happened . . .'

He paused again and shook his head, the disgusted expression twisting his lips.

'I pulled his sword from its scabbard and rolled under his horse. There were four of them surrounding the last of my men, just playing with him before the kill, and as I got to my feet it came over me, the sudden realisation that I could either stand and fight with him, and die with some pride, or run for my life. And I ran, brothers . . .' He lowered his head, rubbing at his eyes with a big calloused hand. 'May Our Lord Mithras forgive me, I *ran*. Coward though I was, Our Lord was still watching me that day, and both of the spears that were thrown at me as I ran missed, one landing so close that I was able to grab it as I jumped the ditch and went for the trees like . . . well, like a man running for his worthless rotten life. I heard a voice shouting orders behind me, whoever was in command of that rabble, "*Get after him! There are to be no survivors!*", and my hope that it was all some horrible mistake went out like a snuffed lamp.

'Those bastards killed the last of my men as I ran from them up the hill beyond the ditch. I heard the scream as one of them put iron into him, and then again as another man finished him. They were after me quickly enough, of course, and I could hear them calling out to me that if I came out nice and meek, and made it easy for them then they wouldn't torment me before the kill, but if I made them wait they'd make me pay for the pleasure, you know the sort of thing.'

Dubnus nodded.

'And that made you angry, right?'

Horatius smiled grimly.

'*Angry*? I was already angry, I was raging! With myself mainly, but it was more than that. They were assuming that I was already a beaten man, because of the way I'd run from them, and until they started shouting for me to come out and die like a man, they weren't far from wrong. No, it wasn't anger, it was fury! It was the need to murder them all to make amends for my own cowardice. There were four of them, laughing and joking to each other as they came up the hill in a line, full of that confidence that a man can't help but feel when he's killed another, whether it's justified or not . . .' He looked down at his hands. 'I just thought "*fuck you*" and stepped out from behind the tree I was using for cover and gave them a moment to realise what they were facing before I threw the spear. I wanted them to know that I was alone, and to come to me.'

He smiled at the memory.

'I always was good with a spear, but I'll tell you this, I've never slung any better than that in all my life. One moment it was in my hand, the point tickling my ear, the next I was looking down my outstretched arm at the closest of them with the bloody thing spitted through him front and back, armour and all. He staggered and fell backwards while the other three just stared at me, come out of nowhere and covered in other men's blood, my teeth bared and my eyes like dinner plates, and I think they knew right then that they were already dead. One of them had a spear, but he was so terrified that he threw it wide of me, and I was into them before they knew what was happening.'

Horatius stared across the ludus's training hall at the men rehearsing their cuts and strokes, and Marcus knew that he was replaying the moment in his head.

'I put the spear man down before the fool even had the chance to pull his own blade free. He was no more than a child, and as I opened his throat I knew I'd made a mistake in attacking him first, but then I had to run straight at him to be able to dodge the spear, if he could have thrown it straight . . .' He shrugged. 'Mistakes we make, eh? Not that the other two were any more of a threat. The man on the right might as well have been trying to fight me with a sausage, for all the good he was with a sword, and in the instant that I looked into his eyes I knew that I was invincible against men like these. I stabbed down with my blade, putting it through his thigh and then ripped it free to open the artery. Gods, you should have seen the blood. So *much* blood . . .'

He grimaced.

'You killed them all?'

The legion man shook his head at the big Briton's question.

'The last of them ran for his life away down the hill screaming for help, and for a moment I considered chasing him down, putting my iron through his spine and then charging into the rest of them to sell my life dearly, but . . .'

He shrugged, and Marcus found the words for him.

'You chose life instead.'

Horatius nodded.

'I chose to make my escape, and ran across the farmland to the next line of trees before they could get their horses onto the open ground. After that I knew that there was only one purpose left for me in life, to discover the reason why my legatus died and to take a cold and bitter revenge for him. It may take me years, or I may never manage it, but this new life will provide me with shelter until that time comes.'

He looked at Marcus and Dubnus with fresh calculation.

'And you?'

The pair looked at each other before Marcus replied.

'Our quest is much the same as yours. We—'

He was interrupted by a shout from across the ludus.

'You three, over here!'

Sannitus was beckoning them over, a toga-clad man with sparse hair the colour of polished iron standing beside him. Disquietingly, several armed men were arrayed behind them, and as the three soldiers approached, the lanista held up a hand in warning.

'Bow your heads in respect, candidates, if you wish to be considered for this school. This man is my master, Tettius Julianus, the man responsible for the Dacian Ludus.'

They stopped and bowed, keeping their heads down as the sword-armed bodyguards fanned out to either side in a protective half-circle about their master that Marcus fervently hoped was routine. With a clear sense for the theatricality of the moment, Julianus waited until his men were in position before breaking the silence.

'Well then, gentlemen . . .' He waited until all three of them had raised their heads. 'Look at you. It's my experience that men like you hardly ever drop into a lanista's hands. We get soldiers, of course, but usually time-expired veterans who can't face the thought of fending for themselves and don't want to sign up again. And now, suddenly, here you are, three of you on the same day, a gift from Fortuna or so it seems.' He looked at the three before him with a wry smile. 'You'll understand then why it was that I wanted to check your bona fides with a little more care than would be the case with the usual class of candidate. Horatius . . .'

The legion centurion snapped to attention.

'Sir!'

Julianus shook his head.

'Don't call me sir, Horatius. That would tend to imply that I have the sort of power that the empire invests in its military officers, and believe me when I tell you this, as far as you're concerned, once you've taken the oath, I'll have far more power over your fate than any officer would ever be likely to exercise. The correct address for you to use for me is "Master". And as for your bona fides, I've done some asking around and, somewhat to my surprise, all seems to be in order. You are indeed, as far as the army's record keepers are concerned, a dead man. I don't know how you achieved such a neat trick and I'm not going to ask, since it's enough for me that I can swear you in to the school legally. So, *Centurion*, do you still want to join the ludus?'

'Yes, Master!'

Julianus nodded, gesturing to the men closest to the soldier, who ushered him away from Dubnus and Marcus. He stared hard at them both in turn.

'And now for you two gentlemen. I went to visit your tribune this morning with the intention of confirming your freedom from imperial service. Obviously the only acceptable proof of this status was for him to produce the diplomas of your honourable discharge, which you told Sannitus would be in his possession.' He looked at them both in turn again, his expression unfathomable. 'And to be frank, gentlemen, my expectation was that he would flatly contradict your story, and demand that I return you to him in chains. And my expectations in such matters, gentlemen, rarely prove to be misjudged.'

Marcus, risking a sidelong glance at Dubnus, saw that his friend's gaze was fixed on a point over the procurator's shoulder, his expression one of supreme confidence. The guards clustered tightly about them shuffled slightly, feet moving to find the best grip on the training hall's floor. Julianus looked at Sannitus with a knowing smile.

'So imagine my surprise when he produced your diplomas from his desk without even a flicker of concern. You, are, it seems legally and honourably discharged from the service of Rome and therefore, without any doubt whatsoever, free to enter this training school. So, gentlemen . . .'

He paused, and Sannitus gestured for them to come to attention.

'The offer on the table before you is this. I will sign you up for a period of five years, no more and no less. I will pay you each five thousand sestertii, half now and half in the event of your death or on completing your term. At the end of your term, if you have risen to the ranks of those men who are celebrated by the crowds and achieve high status within our small world here, you will be able to negotiate a far larger sum for your next period of service. So, do you still wish to swear the sacramentum gladiatorum, and in doing so enter the Dacian Ludus?'

The two men answered together, barking out their answers like soldiers on parade.

'Yes, Master!'

Julianus stepped back, gesturing expansively for Sannitus to come forward and perform his traditional role in swearing in the new men. The lanista motioned Horatius forward to rejoin the other two, and spoke to them in a fierce tone that was loaded with significance.

'The only acceptable answer to the three questions I am about to ask you is '*Yes, Master!*', and I want the men brushing out the sand over there in the Flavian Arena to hear you. Do you understand?'

All three of them bellowed their response at the tops of their voices.

'*Yes, Master!*'

He looked at them for a moment before raising a single finger.

'Will you swear to give your bodies over to the ludus, to be marked with hot iron if necessary?'

'*Yes, Master!*'

He raised a second finger alongside the first.

'Will you submit to being flogged, or beaten, by any member of the ludus's staff, for any reason they deem appropriate?'

'*Yes, Master!*'

A third finger rose up.

'And will you commit yourself to the service of your master Julianus, and any man who may come after him in the role of procurator of this ludus, and vow to meet your fate by cold steel if he decrees it fit?'

'*Yes, Master!*'

The lanista slapped his fingers into the palm of his other hand with a loud crack, shaking his scarred head in amusement.

'Done! You are now officially the property of the ludus, from this day until the day that you earn your release from its service, and more than that, you are now officially gladiators. Think about that oath you just swore, by the way. I really can order any of you to be branded, or flogged, or beaten, and as to cold steel, I can put you to death simply by pairing you with the best men from the other schools when your time comes in the arena, and ensuring your bloody and painful demise. You will have no choice as to who you fight, gentlemen, none at all. We don't usually go to the trouble of branding volunteers, that's for the men who've been condemned to the arena in place of criminal justice, but I've been known to burn the mark onto volunteers who manage to piss me off as a means of making sure they'll never knowingly do it again.'

He looked at them with a pitying smile.

'As of this moment you have the status of *infamis*, the lowest of the low. Every man in Rome will look down on you, unless of course you rise to the status of demi-gods through your exploits in the arena, and even then they will still count themselves as better than you. So welcome to the ludus, gentlemen. Congratulations are definitely *not* in order.'

Felicia and Annia spent a quiet morning in the house, the former's mood too dark for her to do anything much apart from sit and stare at the wall opposite while Appius played with his toys at her feet. Annia bought her a cup of herbal tea sweetened with honey, which she accepted with grace but little enthusiasm, sipping at the drink while her friend fussed around the room tidying what she'd tidied only an hour before.

'I'm sure he'll be fine. After all, he is the fastest man with a sword Julius has ever met, and my man's no slouch when it comes to fighting . . .'

Felicia looked up at her with a weak smile.

'Thank you, Annia. And you're right, of course. He'll beat any man in the city in a straight fight, but then once he's killed this Mortiferum, what's to stop a crowd of angry supporters mobbing Marcus and tearing him to pieces. He's not coming back, and I've no choice but to reconcile myself to that reality.'

Annia looked at her in silence, unable to find any words of comfort in the face of her implacable logic. After a moment her attention was caught by the dog, busy snuffling around the floor in the dining room.

'Come here, Centurion!'

She whistled, and the animal came scampering over to play for a moment before scrabbling away across the tiles again, yapping brightly as he snuffled across the floor around the dining couches.

'Time you went outside, I'd say, since the last time you were sniffing around like that you dropped the contents of your bowels a moment later!'

She scooped up the dog, taking him to the door, but as she opened it Julius was striding up the garden path.

'If I might come in?'

He kissed his wife dutifully, and bowed to Felicia.

'I have news of your husband, Domina. He has been accepted by the Dacian Ludus, and will shortly be fighting in the arena. The school's procurator came to see the tribune this morning to get proof of Marcus and Dubnus's diplomas—'

'Diplomas?'

He nodded.

'When a man leaves the service, he receives a bronze tablet

stating that he has served with honour. We had one prepared for each of them when it became clear to the tribune that your husband wouldn't be dissuaded from seeking this one last act of revenge, whatever the cost.'

She stared at him for a moment.

'You knew he was going to do this? And you did nothing?'

The first spear met her gaze.

'We did. And what should we have done? Locked him up?'

After a moment's thought Felicia shook her head.

'I suppose not. If I couldn't forbid him to go into the ludus, then I can't criticise you for doing much the same. The insult to his honour would have been too much for him to have borne. So now what?'

The first spear rubbed a hand through his hair.

'Now? Now we'll have to wait and see how he does in the arena. Apparently he'll be fighting tomorrow. After all, it's not as if he needs much training . . .' He frowned across the room at Centurion, who was once more snuffling around beneath the table. 'You'd better get that animal outside, before he sh— empties his bowels on your floor.'

One Eyed Maximus strolled into the barber's shop just after lunch, taking a seat against the cool rear wall and leaning back.

'That's better. It's too fucking hot out there, and that's a fact.'

His two companions who, Morban had already noted, usually kept their opinions to themselves, stood on either side of him and glared balefully at the customers having their hair cut, one of whom promptly decided that he had better places to be and left with the job incomplete.

'Think I'll get a haircut, since I'm here.'

One of his minions raised a hand to forestall the next customer who, it had to be admitted, had already looked more than a little hesitant in his approach to the vacant chair. Maximus laughed, grinning at the man as he too decided to pursue interests other than getting his hair cut.

'Very wise too!' He sat down in the chair and twisted his neck to stare up at the soldier who would shortly be cutting his hair. 'Nice and tidy, short at the back and sides and nice and thick on top. Think you can manage that?'

The man with the scissors grunted his assent and set to with vigour, recognising from Morban's face his desire to have the gang leader out of the chair, and for that matter the shop, as quickly as possible. Silence descended for a while, nobody daring to speak while such a delicate operation was in progress, until the gang leader held up a hand to stop his haircut.

'So what's my share today, eh Fatty?'

Morban took a moment to count the coins in his cash drawer. 'Five sestertii.'

Maximus smiled happily.

'You, Fatty, are my new number one client. You're making twice as much as anyone else on my turf, which means that you can afford a small tax rise, can't you?'

Morban winced.

'How much?'

The one-eyed man shook his head, forcing the soldier with the scissors to stop cutting for a moment.

'How much, *sir*?'

The standard bearer fingered the knife that he kept in the drawer behind the piles of coins.

'How much . . . *sir*?'

Maximus grinned with the pleasure of his small victory over the sullen shopkeeper.

'That's *better*! Let's call it a nice round twenty per cent, shall we, just to make sure you're clear on the need to show a little more respect. You won't miss another ten on the hundred, not with the juicy profits you're making now, will you?'

Sighing to himself Morban closed the drawer.

'No sir. I'm sure we'll manage.'

'Good. Now let's have a look at what you've done to me.'

He held up a shining iron blade, nodded at himself as he turned it this way and that to survey his new haircut.

'Not bad!'

He jumped up out of the chair and padded across to Morban, holding out an open palm.

'Collection time!'

The standard bearer handed over a stack of coins, and Maximus dropped one back on the desk with a grin.

'That's to pay for the haircut. It's not like I'm a thief, is it?'

Gathering his men he stalked out of the shop, grinning at the queue outside.

'That's it lads, in you go!'

Morban watched him walk away down the street in silence, ignoring the pointed looks his men were giving him.

'Tomorrow?'

Julianus grinned back at his lanista.

'Drink your wine, Sannitus.'

The trainer raised a jaundiced eyebrow, pointing at the cup before him.

'As I recall it, the last time you told me to drink my wine I ended up agreeing to fight the most successful gladiator this city's seen in the last twenty years so that you could gain favour with the emperor.' Pulling his tunic away from his right shoulder, he pointed at a long pale scar that ran over the muscle between neck and arm before running out of sight beneath the thick wool. 'You made a nice purse of gold, and I got cut from shoulder to belly. If Flamma hadn't been in such a good mood, he'd have smashed my collarbone, and as it was he seemed to find it hilarious to cut my bloody nipple in two.'

Julianus nodded his agreement.

'Ah, Flamma. Now there was a gladiator. Never vindictive in the arena, or at least not unless he was given good reason, and such an artist with a sword, big as a house and nimble as a dancer. And you can stop complaining; it took me enough gold to persuade you to come back for one more fight that a little nick like that was well bought and paid for! Add to that the fact that you were convalescing for long enough to travel to Greece and study for your priesthood in the temple of Nemesis.'

Sannitus smiled darkly.

'And ideas like this one do a lot to convince me that I should have stayed there. You know they're not ready.'

Julianus raised his hands in protest.

'Not ready? All three of them bested Hermes without breaking sweat, and he's *supposed* to be the third best man in the ludus. Why else do you think I went galloping over the hill to see their tribune and make sure they weren't spinning us a story? What more do you think they need to be "ready"?'

The lanista raised his fingers, ticking off the points one at a time.

'They don't understand the rules . . .'

'They're bright boys, all three of them. They'll learn quickly enough, especially with an experienced hand like you to talk them through it.'

Sannitus shook his head, his lips pursed disapprovingly.

'They're still soldiers. Unless we teach them what gladiators do and don't do to each other in the arena then all they're good for is hacking a bloody trail through whatever we put in front . . .'

He fell silent, looking at the man on the other side of the broad wooden desk with a fresh understanding. Julianus nodded.

'Exactly. This emperor isn't like his father, Sannitus. Marcus Aurelius used to insist that we made the most economical use of the lads, and that we turned as many of the prisoners we took in into long-termers as were capable of making the change and learning our ways. All his son wants to see is a series of good fights, ceaseless excitement from the first bout to the last, and above all plenty of blood. I've already been given very clear instructions from the palace to put on something that will make Commodus sit up and take notice, once we've got all the usual animal baiting and bestiality out of the way. Apparently the chamberlain has promised him that we'll be starting this year's Roman Games with a series of fights to make the plebs roar with delight, and you know what that means. Dead bodies, nothing more and nothing less.'

He took a sip of his own wine.

'The Flavian's procurator has promised me a batch of Dacian prisoners, prime men apparently and all still in good condition, and I was going to tell you to put Hermes and Nemo into the ring against them, but I see no reason to risk our better fighters against a bunch of unknowns. Let's see what these centurions are capable of against men with nothing to lose, shall we?'

Sannitus shrugged.

'If you put it like that it doesn't sound as if we have much choice. Two prisoners apiece?'

Julianus inclined his head in gracious agreement.

'You're right, anything more would be pushing our new boys a little too hard the first time out. Two men apiece it is.'

'Life in the ludus ain't all as black as Sannitus likes to paint it.' With the completion of their training for the day, the lanista's assistant Edius was leading the three centurions to their accommodation, talking over his shoulder as he led them into the ludus's maze of corridors. 'Free men, slaves and even the men that scrape out the sewers may all call you scum when they think you're not listening, but women, on the other hand, will see you as their best chance to get a decent portion of cock once their husbands' dicks have shrivelled up and dropped off. And let me tell you from experience, having the nail hammered home by a body the likes of which their men could only dream of drives them wild!'

The school's accommodation took the form of a series of corridors which were lined on both sides with cells barely large enough to accommodate two men, their front walls formed of narrowly spaced iron bars with heavy hinged doors to allow for both access and containment as the situation required. All along the corridor down which he led them, the doors were wide open, and men lounged around both in the cells and the walkway in various states of undress.

'Not everyone in the ludus is quite as happy as you boys are to be here, but since this is the volunteer block we usually keep the doors unlocked. You two will be sharing this one . . .'

He pointed Marcus and Horatius at the doorway of a stone-walled room barely big enough for two straw-filled pallets, before turning back to point at another empty cell, gesturing to Dubnus.

'And you, big man, since we have no one to share with you yet, you get this one to yourself for the time being. One of the slaves will be along with your food soon enough . . .' He paused, looking pointedly at the other two, who had walked into their cell and were looking round the small enclosed space with bemused expressions. 'And you both need to get as much of it down your necks as you can stomach, I'd say. We need to get some fat on you, so that you look like proper gladiators rather than the sad pair of skinny runts you are now, eh? There's only your mate here that's got the look of a fighter!'

The two centurions grinned at each other wryly, Marcus shrugging at his new comrade.

'And there I was making the mistake of thinking that since two years of campaigning in Britannia, Germania and Dacia has left me without an ounce of fat on my body, I'm in perfect condition.'

Edius leaned into their cell with a serious look, wagging a finger at the two men.

'You'll learn better soon enough. If you'd not been so fast with your swords I reckon old Sannitus would have told you both to fuck off.' He shook his head at their baffled expressions. 'Not big fans of the games, are you?'

The two men nodded, Horatius leaning back against the cell's stone wall.

'I was too busy learning my trade to give a toss about a load of fixed fights. There's not one in ten bouts where the outcome's not already arranged before they step onto the sand, and after a while you get bored of watching the same fighters with the same tired moves dancing round each other and waiting for the moment when one of them goes down.'

Edius shook his head knowingly.

'That might be the way where you come from sonny, but this is *Rome*. This ludus is one of the most famous schools in the empire, and our men are expected to put on a show that'll have the plebs roaring and shouting for more. And that means men sometimes get killed, and more often than not even the victors get cut. Of course a decent swordsman can judge the cut just right, and make his opponent bleed like a stuck pig without actually maiming him, or making it so bad the poor bastard bleeds to death in the arena – not unless they're really going for it or they hate each others' guts – but for that to work the other fighter has to have a good layer of fat for him to cut into. See?'

He lifted his tunic, showing the pale lines of scars that crisscrossed his thighs.

'You boys know as well as I do that one good thrust of a sword into a man's upper leg'll kill him inside half a dozen breaths, once you've opened the artery in the thigh, but the men I was fighting knew how to keep their cuts shallow. That way we always used to put on a good show, with plenty of blood, but without too many of us ending up face down. After all, nobody wants the cupboard to be empty when the big games like the ones that start tomorrow come round.'

Horatius started.

'*Tomorrow?*'

The barrel-chested lanista nodded, cracking a wry smile at them.

'I thought that might make you sit up and pay attention. Tomorrow, my lads, is the start of the Roman Games, the biggest series of games in the entire year as far as the major schools are concerned, with hundreds of fights to be staged between now and the end of the celebrations in two weeks' time.' He laughed at their expressions. 'Don't worry, no one's going to throw a bunch of tyros like you into the arena without training you up first!'

Still chuckling, he turned away and left them to it. Marcus and Horatius looked at each other for a moment and then laughed at the same time.

'A pair of skinny runts?'

Marcus shook his head at the other man's incredulous tone.

'It's a label we may have to learn to love. Now I think about it, just about all of the other gladiators in this place are rather better upholstered than I was expecting. Perhaps we will need to fatten up a bit.'

'Or perhaps you *won't*.' They turned, finding a tall, well-muscled man in a tunic of fine red wool standing in the cell's doorway with his arms folded. 'If you've got the speed and skill to keep other mens' blades away from you, then you'll never need to worry about all that padding that everyone else is carrying. They said the same thing to my brother and I when we walked through those gates, but neither of us ever found any need to stuff ourselves.'

He stood and waited for a response, a slight smile on his face, and Marcus looked back at him for a moment before the realisation of who the newcomer was dawned upon him, a snatched memory of a face seen in the light of torches in the city weeks before, the hairs on the back of his neck rising.

'*Mortiferum?*'

The other man grinned back at him, shaking his head.

'No, I'm his brother, as it happens.'

'You're Velox?'

The gladiator nodded.

'You'll have to forgive the rather bombastic nature of my arena name, but it's so much easier than trying to persuade anyone to use my real name that I've more or less stopped trying.'

Horatius stepped forward and offered his hand to the gladiator, who clasped it and then reached out to repeat the greeting with Marcus, who realised that he was giving a good impression of being awestruck by the man's presence, even if his main emotion was in reality simple hatred. He took the hand, looking into the other man's eyes as they clasped.

'Forgive me, it's not often that a man gets to meet an arena legend.'

Velox shook his head.

'We'll have none of that nonsense in here. Within the ludus we have no adulation, whether contrived or not . . .' He paused, looking at them both with a sombre expression. 'After all, any of us might meet the other on the sand at some point. In here, my friends, we are brothers, from the youngest tyro to the most experienced and deadly man in the place.'

Marcus inclined his head in recognition of the generous sentiment, turning to introduce Dubnus only to find the big man staring over his shoulder down the corridor. Looking round to see what had caught his attention, he realised that a group of three men had gathered around a single woman at the far end of the run of cells. She was wiry, and as tall as the shortest of them.

'Ah yes.' Velox's voice took on a sardonic note. 'Those of us not disposed towards enjoying each others' bodies have the choice of either taking a handful of grease and closing their eyes or forcing themselves on the slave girls, which is, after all, what they're here for. Apparently.'

As they watched, it became clear that the gladiators gathered around the woman were playing with her as a prelude to something much more direct, taking advantage of the fact that she was carrying a bucket of meat stew with both hands and unable to prevent their lewd groping. Dubnus shook his head, his anger evident to Marcus in his narrowed eyes and tight lips.

'Is that woman assigned to this corridor?'

Velox nodded, speculatively eying the hulking Briton.

'She is. But if you fancy taking her for a ride you may find there's something of a queue. You should—'

The Briton brushed past him, striding purposefully down the run of cells with a set in his shoulders that Marcus had seen before.

'Excuse me brothers, I suspect that this is about to get nasty.'

He slipped past the champion gladiator with a nod, padding quietly after his friend who had stopped a few feet from the scene of the servant girl's molestation.

'Get your dirty fucking hands *off* her!'

His booming command silenced the hubbub in an instant, and the three men who were now dragging the woman towards a cell swivelled to face him, one of them the gladiator who had been bested by the three friends that morning. In an instant they were lined up across the corridor with their fists clenched. Hermes stepped forwards, raising his right hand to display his scarred knuckles in an unambiguous threat.

'And who the fuck do you think you are, *tyro*?'

Dubnus straightened his back, folding his massive arms.

'I think I'm the man who's going to put his fist through your face so hard you'll have to reach back to blow your nose, unless you back down and leave the woman alone.'

Hermes walked forward until he was within a foot of the Briton, who allowed his hands to fall to his sides.

'Beating me with a *wooden* sword doesn't give you any rights in here, Briton. Until the day I can meet you with iron and put you in your place, you'd better keep your head down, unless you want to get a quick reminder of just how far down the ladder you are from me. That woman is ours. *Mine.* I've fucked her before, and I'll fuck her again, any time I like. She's a slave, so I'm free to do whatever I want to her. And when I'm done, these other men will take their turn with her. We're happy, 'cause we get to empty our balls, and the master's happy because a happy gladiator is a quiet gladiator.'

'And the woman?'

Ignoring the dangerous note in the Briton's question, Hermes threw his arms out wide, turning his head to grin at his audience.

'The woman? Well she doesn't get a choice, does she boys? She just gets a regular load of our—'

He didn't see the punch coming until it was way too late, a fast left-handed hook that smacked him full in the face and bounced him off the wall to his left. The gladiator tottered, groaned once, the long, slow moan of a man who was already no better than semi-conscious, then slumped gracelessly to the corridor's floor. In the instant before violence erupted, while the men around him were still goggling at the speed and ferocity with which the Briton had put their comrade away, a bellow of command froze them in place.

'*Hold!*'

Marcus started at the snapped order, realising that Horatius had advanced down the corridor half a step behind him, but before he had time to register any gratitude for the other man's support, the gladiators gathered about them stirred angrily at the sight of their friend sprawled across the stone floor.

'*Fuck* you! You're not in the bloody legion now, *Centurion*. We're going to kick the fucking shit out of all three of you, and then—'

'No . . .' Velox's voice cut through the rapidly escalating anger with ease, silencing the rumble of threats with his first word. 'You won't.'

The gladiator stalked down the corridor, easing past Marcus and Horatius and planting himself in front of Dubnus with self-assurance oozing from every pore.

'You won't raise a finger against these men. Not just because I reckon they'd give half a dozen of you a good hiding and come looking for more. And not even because if you do, and trust me on this, I will personally kill, slowly and with the greatest pleasure I can squeeze from the act, the man who makes the first move. And you know how much I like to live up to my arena billing.' He looked around him, his face hard, and Marcus saw more than one of the men around them flinch at the overt threat. 'They don't call me "The Master of Carnage" without good reason, do they? Be the first one to step forward against these men and tomorrow morning it'll be just you and me, with sharp iron and no question of mercy.'

He looked about him with an expression of disgust.

'It's not even because I'm tired of you dirty bastards degrading these poor helpless bitches just because you *can*. No, the reason that you're not going to touch these men is because, as I was just about to tell them, is that they're fighting in the morning. So right now you can consider this as an instruction from Sannitus himself, since he asked me to give them the good news. And knowing Sannitus as well as I do, and the expectations he has of these three, I can assure you all that the first man to raise a fist will have an easy enough exit from this life at my hands, compared with what'll happen to the others when I tell him who else participated.'

A moment's silence stretched until first one, and then another of the men who had squared up to Dubnus looked down at their feet, and the tension ebbed from the situation like water from a split skin.

'We keep the woman though.'

Velox smiled at the petulant mutter, shaking his head slowly from side to side as he went face-to-face with the man who had spoken.

'No. You *don't*. I really am sick to my guts of your depravity. Wait your time, earn your passes into the city, and then take out your need to fuck on the multitude of women who actually want you between their legs. And, let us be clear about this . . .'

He stepped forward, reaching out a hand to grasp the culprit by his ear, whispering something that was inaudible to the Tungrians, grinning as the subject of his attentions blanched at whatever it was that he'd said. He turned away with a last contemptuous stare at the surly group still gathered around him, an act which seemed to be the cue for the man to whom he'd just spoken to start herding his fellows back down the corridor to their cells.

'You, on your way.'

The slave girl turned and fled at the command, leaving the buckets of food on the floor, and Velox nodded in satisfaction, raising his voice to ensure his words carried down the run of cells.

'It's a good thing I was here for all concerned, I'd say. Remember what I've told you, and don't imagine that my threats won't hold good if any stupidity starts once I'm round the corner!'

Turning to leave, he threw a final comment over his shoulder.

'And you three had better make sure you get a belly full of food. You'll probably not have any appetite in the morning.'

Later, with their bellies full of bread and meat, the three men went to their beds and lay in the barrack's darkness. Listening to his comrades breathing, Dubnus heard first one and then the other fall asleep, the pattern of their respiration slowing and deepening. The big Briton smiled up at the cell's invisible ceiling, quietly satisfied at having guessed his friend's reaction to the tribune's suspension of their attempts to kill Mortiferum.

'I won't let them kill you, brother, not unless they come through me f—'

A finger on his lips silenced him, and before he could react it was replaced by a mouth, the woman whispering into his lips as she crawled onto his body.

'Be still. I thank you for save me.'

The Briton was still pondering a response when she put a hand on his phallus, the warm body atop his slithering down until he felt her moist sex press down against the suddenly erect organ. After a moment's resistance his member slipped inside her as the woman pressed herself insistently against him.

'*What . . . ?*'

She kissed him hard, twitching her hips to widen his eyes at the sudden unexpected pleasure.

'Told you, quiet. Only way I can thank. And better you than six men same time.'

The Briton lay in silence as the slave moved over his body, her suddenly urgent rhythm and questing tongue bringing him to his climax with unsurprising ease, given his months of abstinence. She lay on his body for a moment longer, kissing him one last time, then lifted herself off his rapidly shrinking manhood and touched his lips again, drawing a knife from inside her clothing as she stood, preparing to return to her quarters through the sleeping ludus.

'Wait!'

The slave shook her head.

'I go. I catch here, I be flog.'

'But . . . what's your name. At least tell me that much.'

Her smile was a line of white in the darkness.

'My name Calistra. Go now.'

'I will free you, Calistra . . .'

His words fell on empty air, the woman having slid round the cell's door and darted silently away down the corridor.

'Good evening, Gaius.'

'Senator.'

Scaurus bowed deeply, holding the position as his host stepped forward and embraced him warmly, waving a hand to his butler to dismiss him. He'd been summoned earlier that evening and had attended to the invitation immediately, taking only Arminius and a pair of Cotta's men with him across the city.

'There's no call for you to bow to me young man. While I've been kicking my heels here in Rome for the last three years, you, I hear, have been making a name for yourself in the north of the empire?'

Scaurus inclined his head to accept the older man's praise.

'I have enjoyed a fair degree of good fortune.'

The senator rubbed at his heavily bearded chin with a look of polite disbelief.

'Good fortune? A man makes his own luck in this world, as well you know! Your "good fortune" has seen you win more than one victory in Britannia, capture a notorious bandit chieftain in Germania and rescue an emperor's ransom from a gold mine in Dacia. Not to mention restoring the honour of the lost standard of my old legion, Sixth Victorious, or so I hear. I would sacrifice to Fortuna every day for the rest of my life if I could be assured of that degree of success. Wine?'

The two men retired to the senator's private office, and Scaurus accepted a cup of excellent falernian from the man who, in the absence of his dead father, was the closest thing he had to an authority figure.

'You've excelled yourself, Gaius, and about time too! I was starting to wonder if you were going to dedicate the rest of your service to taking ever more ridiculous risks out beyond the empire's boundaries. I can only thank the gods that Ulpius Marcellus took some notice of what I'd told him about your abilities and put you in command of an auxiliary cohort.' The senator paused to sip his own wine. 'My only concern now is whether you'll live beyond the end of next week.' He stared levelly at his protégé, waiting for the younger man to reply.

'I was wondering why you sent for me. I presume you're referring to my recent visit to the palace?'

'*Yes.*' The tribune looked up, surprised by the sudden vehemence in his sponsor's voice. 'I am indeed referring to your most *recent* attempt to commit suicide.'

'*Suicide?*'

'You heard me, young man. You may lack the necessary degree of self-awareness to know what game it is that you're playing, but I'm more than astute enough to compensate for your wilful refusal to confront your demons. I know all too well why you spent as long as you did *scouting* the northern tribes, with only that big German slave of yours for company'. Your reputation is that of a danger seeker, a man driven to take risks for the thrill of it, but we both know better, don't we? And now here you are doing just the same thing, and in Rome of all places.'

Scaurus raised a hand, but the senator waved away his nascent protest.

'I'm more than a little disappointed in you, Gaius. Were you actually planning to visit me at any point while you're in Rome? I've waited patiently for you to come and present yourself, and yet you've shown no sign of doing so, forcing me to summon you as if you were a wilfully disobedient nephew.'

'Instead of which I am . . . ?'

The older man grimaced.

'A brilliant, brave and occasionally wayward young man who, given the right guidance, might yet still aspire to the empire's highest ranks.'

'Really?'

'Indeed. If I can rise from teaching Latin grammar to the position of provincial governor then there's clearly hope for you!'

The younger man shook his head.

'But my father . . .'

'Indeed, let's get to the root of it, shall we? Your father's disgrace in Germania, and his honourable suicide.' He shook his head. 'In case you'd forgotten, young man, I served with your father. Indeed, if it wasn't for my promise to watch over you, made to him before an altar to Mars before he took his own life, I might have despaired of you years ago.' He shook his head sadly. 'The German War.

Triumph and disaster all rolled up into one dirty little package. Your father, Gaius, didn't have to fall on his sword, as I told him even as he was binding me to my oath to act as your sponsor after his death. His over-developed sense of honour led him to do so in the face of utter indifference from those above him. And you show all the signs of having the same instinct towards self-destruction. Don't you?' He waited, but Scaurus made no response. 'Did you *really* interrupt Commodus when he was in a state of some agitation, and in his own throne room?'

The younger man shrugged.

'I can't deny it. But I had good reason.'

'Good enough reason to risk having your tongue cut out?'

A long silence settled upon the two men. At length the older man spoke again.

'And now?'

Scaurus looked at his mentor with a hint of the defiance which had been the hallmark of his boyhood years.

'And now I'm assisting a man who has been ill-used by the empire to regain his lost honour.'

'This would be the Aquila boy, if the whispers I hear are to be trusted?'

'Yes.'

The Senator was silent for a moment.

'You do realise that his father was executed for treason?'

Scaurus laughed without any hint of humour.

'And you do realise that his accusation was false?'

'Gaius, the ice upon which you're standing couldn't be any thinner. And if you fall through it I will have no power to save you.'

'I know. Nor would I expect you to do so.'

'It might be worse than that. This new man Cleander, egotistical power monger though he is, has one redeeming feature. He seems to see some value in restoring me to favour, apparently on the grounds that if Perennis distrusted me enough to force me out of public life, I must in reality be of some value to the empire. There's talk of Britannia.'

The younger man raised an eyebrow.

'As governor?'

'Apparently so. Although any revelation as to your involvement with this Aquila might well see us both condemned, given that my role in your life as a guardian isn't exactly a secret. It won't be Britannia for me, but rather a place in the Palatine dungeons alongside you.' Scaurus nodded slowly. 'But you can't help yourself, can you?'

'No, sir.'

'I already knew as much. Very well, we'll face the risk together, you on the streets of Rome and myself here in my gilded cage, while Cleander decides whether to use me for my abilities or put me down as the mentor of quite the most dangerous man in the city. But there is some small compensation you might offer me for this risk.'

'Senator? Whatever I can do for you, if it is in my power, I will.'

The older man smiled.

'I know. There is a colleague of mine, an old friend who has fallen from favour. I can do nothing overt to assist him, as he is, I hear, already marked for betrayal and death, when the time is right. But a man like you, a man with the right resources and lacking in conventional scruples – not to mention any sense of self-preservation – might just be able to spirit him out of Rome?'

Scaurus bowed again.

'I will do everything in my power. His name?'

The senator smiled knowingly.

'You've already made his acquaintance, I believe. His name is Gaius Carius Sigilis. Save him from the executioner for me, young Gaius. Extend just a hint of your improbable daring and outrageous good fortune to my friend, before he becomes another victim of this regime's thirst for blood, will you?'

The ludus woke before dawn, its inhabitants summoned from their beds in the usual manner, the volunteers encouraged by the jibes and sarcasm of their trainers while the ranks of condemned men were escorted out into the torchlight by guards armed with clubs. The ranks of yawning, farting fighters were unusually quiet, collectively digesting the fact that the coming week would see most of them fighting for their lives in the arena. Sannitus walked onto the parade square, looked up and down their ranks and nodded to himself.

'You apes look shit scared! Which is good!'

He strolled up the front rank, meeting each man's eyes in turn.

'Today is the first day of the Roman Games! The *Great* Games! Two whole weeks of chariot racing, boxing, athletics, acrobatics and, of course, enough blood on the arena sand to keep our discerning public happy! So, during these next few days we will be sending more than two hundred fighters over there . . .' He waved a hand at the Flavian Arena's top tiers, visible over the ludus's walls. 'You'll be fighting men from the other schools, all of whom will be looking to put one over on us by winning more of their fights than we do!' He lowered his voice to a growl, forcing them to strain for the words. 'In all the years that I've been the lanista of this school that hasn't happened, and gentlemen, trust me . . .' He looked up and down the lines of men again with a grimace that made his feelings on the subject crystal clear. 'That will *not* change this year. Whatever you find yourself facing: fish men, net men, hoplites . . .' He shrugged, pulling a face that neatly summed up his contempt for the other gladiatorial disciplines. 'You *will* win. You'll win to bring glory to the ludus. You'll win to bask in the adulation of sixty thousand screaming plebs, and to get the women vying for your straining pricks. And you'll win because you know that I'll be waiting for you if you lose and manage to escape with your life. So, pairings . . .'

He stood in silence as Edius stepped forward and, one man at a time, read out the waiting gladiators' destinies.

'*Mortiferum!*'

Marcus started as the champion swordsman stepped out from the front rank, staring at the back of his father's killer's head through narrowed eyes.

'You will fight a pair of fish men from the Gallic School as the last bout of the day in two days' time!'

The champion gladiator nodded with a look of indifferent confidence and stepped back into his place.

'*Velox!* The Gallic ludus have sent their number one man in the vain hope that he'll be able to regain them some pride after last year's pathetic display. He's a hoplite, apparently!'

'Not for long he isn't!'

A ripple of laughter ran across the waiting fighters, knowing that their champion had the skills required to back up his bravado.

'Very funny. You've got the last fight of the day on the last day of the games.'

The roll call lasted until the horizon had turned from purple to a rosy shade of pink, as individuals and small groups of the less capable men were briefed as to their pairings for the first week of the games. When the last of them had stepped forward and heard his fate, the rotund lanista barked out one last set of names.

'Centurion, Dubnus and Corvus!'

The three men looked at each other and stepped forward. Edius looked over to his lanista with a questioning expression, and Sannitus walked down the line of gladiators in silence, pushing through to the rear rank.

'You three will be taking a mid-afternoon slot today. Come the middle of an afternoon's fighting the plebs need something special to wake them up for the big fights to come, and Procurator Julianus has volunteered the three of you to provide that spectacle.'

Turning away, he raised his voice in a bellow of command.

'All men fighting today, stay here. The rest of you, get back to your training. *Move!*'

The twenty-eight men who were due to fight mustered around the lanista, who took a swift head count, frowning at one man who had strolled over to join the group.

'You're not fighting today.'

Velox shrugged, smiling easily back at him.

'I thought I'd come along for the parade, and then perhaps take them into the arena to have a look around and get used to the noise.'

Sannitus thought for a moment and then nodded.

'It's not as if a day's missed training is going to trouble you over much. Right then, go and get your equipment, everything you'll be wearing later on. Let's give the plebs a show, shall we? You three can stay here, your armour will be provided by the arena staff since you'll be fighting in military equipment.'

The friends waited in silence for a moment, until Horatius sniffed something familiar and yet unlikely on the air.

'Smells like . . .'

He looked at Marcus, who shrugged and took a deep breath.

'Now you mention it . . .'

Both men looked at Dubnus, bursting into uncontrollable laughter at his sheepish expression.

'You *lucky* bastard! It wasn't that slave girl was it?' Horatius goggled at the Briton's nod. 'Mithras above us! She came to you in the night? Remind me to be a bit quicker off the mark next time those apes try to mess with her, that's the sort of gratitude a man could use in here!'

Marcus raised an eyebrow at his friend, seeing less amusement in his face than he might have expected.

'Her name is Calistra. And I'm going to free her.'

'Now *that's* impressive.' Both of them turned to Horatius, who was shaking his head in new-found respect. 'She's only done the love thing to him, and all in the space of one quick bunk up. She must come like a fully wound bolt thrower . . .'

Once the gladiators slated for that day's entertainment had returned, most of them dressed in what seemed to be more or less the standard fighting equipment for the ludus, the lanista looked about him with a hint of approval in his faint smile. The gladiators were equipped for the most part in wide-brimmed helmets adorned with griffons or crests, each with a face mask perforated by holes large enough to allow clear vision. Their sword arms were wrapped in heavy padding beneath sleeves of segmented metal of the type worn by legionaries on the Danubius frontier, and each man's leading leg was protected by a metal greave strapped over heavy padding to protect their ankles from the harsh bite of the metal shin guard's edges.

'Very nice, gentlemen, you almost look like gladiators! Swords and shields will be issued in the arena, just to make sure nobody decides to start the fighting early, or looks to use their weapons in some desperate bid for freedom! And for those of you who are here as condemned men, let me remind you that the guards accompanying us will beat the blood-stained piss out of you if you so much as look like making a run for it. Come along then!'

The lanista led the group down a stairway and into a sloping tunnel lit at intervals by freshly set torches. Velox laughed at the look of bemusement on Dubnus's face.

'You didn't think we were going to stroll over to the Flavian through the sort of crowd that will already have gathered, did you? We'd be mobbed the second we set foot outside the gates, and it'd take an age to push our way through. This is much quicker . . .'

The tunnel ran downhill at a slight gradient for fifty paces before joining another, larger underground corridor, and Marcus realised that they had reached a junction of several such concealed walkways.

'This is where the tunnels from all of the schools meet. It's not far from here to the arena.'

The group marched on in a direction that Marcus judged to be eastward, and after a moment's walking the dim light ahead of them resolved itself into a stairway leading upwards into the morning sunlight, while the dimly lit tunnel ran on to the west and, he presumed, into the bowels of the arena itself. At the top of the stairs they stepped out into a crowded space filled with gladiators of all types, the city folk kept at a respectful distance on all sides by a ring of arena guards, and Sannitus raised his voice as he pushed his way into the crowd.

'Now then you Gauls, you beast men, you fighters of the Great School, make way for the greatest gladiators in the world! Make way for the men of the Dacian Ludus!'

A barrage of ribaldry and foul language met his apparent bombast, but Marcus could see that most of it was good natured despite the obvious nerves on display among the men that would fight and possibly die that day. Another man of roughly the same age as the veteran lanista stepped forward, a giant of a man with a bald head whose scalp was scarred as if by the claws of some vicious beast, and with one eye socket concealed by a patch. He wrapped the Dacian lanista in a bearlike hug, lifting Sannitus clean off his feet with a growl of welcome, and two more men crowded in to make their greetings, mutual respect evident on the faces of all four.

'We're not too late then?'

The one-eyed man laughed.

'With this lot organising the parade? Not likely.'

Sticking together in their tight group, the Dacians looked around them with the understandable curiosity of men who might well be looking upon either their victims or their killers to be. One or two of the more experienced veterans recognised previous opponents, and stepped out of the huddle to make the clasp and enjoy a moment of conversation with men who, mortal enemies though they might briefly have been, were now simply fellow professionals, subject to the same hopes and doubts with which they themselves were struggling.

'Gladiators!' A strong voice rang out over the throng, snapping heads round as the fighters anticipated the command to move. 'Follow the usual path to the starting point please . . .'

The three friends went along with their group, most of whom clearly knew where they were going, walking around the towering arena past the eastern gate.

'That's the Gate of Life.' Velox hooked a thumb over his shoulder. 'Win your bout, or lose well enough to avoid a fatal wound and win the emperor's favour, and you'll make it back to the ludus even if they have to carry you back.' They walked on around the amphitheatre's curved walls, and at length he pointed forward at the gate in the amphitheatre's western side. 'On the other hand, if you die, or lose so badly that you have to receive the mercy stroke, or simply incur the big man's wrath for not fighting hard enough, then you'll be carried out through *that* gate. The Gate of Death.'

He was silent for a moment, as the straggling procession passed under the infamous arch in silence.

'There, see?' He pointed to a tunnel opening close to the gate. 'From here that tunnel runs back to the east, under the arena all the way from here to the spolarium on the far side of the Morning School. If you die in the arena, then the staff take your corpse in there to be stripped of its weapons and armour, and to keep the poor sods that weren't good enough or fast enough from putting off the lads that haven't fought yet. And here's the worst part of it . . .' He pointed to the crowds gathered about the gate. 'They've been waiting there most of the night, making sure they get the prime spots, and get to see the dead men as they're carried out.'

'Fucking ghouls.'

A fighter walking before them in the smooth egg-shaped, full-face helmet of a secutor spat the words over his shoulder, and Velox laughed in response to the venom in his voice.

'Ghouls they are, that's true enough. But if you couldn't take a joke then you shouldn't have joined!'

The anonymous gladiator laughed bitterly, his face hidden by the helmet's smooth iron face and his eyes invisible in the holes cut into the mask to allow him some limited vision.

'As if I had any choice in the matter.'

'Ah yes, that was true for the first few years, wasn't it Glaucus, but it's not quite the case these days. You're no longer the bankrupt who was forced into the arena to pay off your creditors, are you? How much did it take to tempt you into the games this time round?'

Glaucus, who Marcus supposed was easy enough to identify despite the anonymity of his enclosed helmet given the absence of the little finger of his sword hand, turned his head to be better heard, a wry note in his muffled voice.

'Not as much as they're paying to see you, eh "Master of Carnage"?'

Velox grinned back at him.

'Probably not, but I'll bet good money that getting a nice big payment isn't all the attraction, is it? Some of them may be ghouls, but there's something about their adulation that just hooks us back into the game, isn't there, even though we know we might end up leaving the arena feet first that last time?'

The gladiators marched through the Arch of Titus and down into the Forum, through crowds gathered on either side of the road behind a barrier of praetorians. In the shadow of the Capitoline Hill, the remainder of the procession was gathered awaiting the order to march.

'Acrobats, dancing girls, musicians, gladiators, dwarfs pretending to be gladiators . . . *Fuck me!* What in the name of Cocidius are *those*?!'

Velox smirked at Dubnus's stunned reaction.

'Elephants. They come from far to the south of Africa. Big bastards, aren't they? Imagine facing a dozen of those on the battlefield.'

The Tungrian stared up at the closest of the beasts as they walked past, grimacing at the sizeable heap of dung that had accumulated beneath its hind quarters.

'I reckon a few hundred well-thrown spears would give them something to think about.'

Velox raised an eyebrow.

'And I reckon all you'd do with your spears would be to get them angry. Do you really think you'd want to see something that big angry at close quarters?'

Dubnus shrugged.

'I'll worry about it when I have to deal with it.' He looked up and down the parade. 'They do this for every day of the games?'

'Every day. It gives the public a chance to see the gladiators, to prove that they're in good condition for the fight and to see what's in each man's face. Does he look ready to fight for his life, and to kill, or does he just look like a victim? That and the elephants. Everybody loves elephants . . .'

Dubnus shook his head in wonder, then noticed something else that made him frown.

'And the big man with the hammer? Is he going to fight with that?'

The gladiator smiled.

'That's Charun, or at least it's the man who plays his part. If you die in the arena, then before you're carried away to be stripped that bastard gives your head a sharp tap with the hammer and stoves in your skull, just enough to make sure you really are dead. I suppose it's the quickest way of making sure that no one's faking it, and to put anyone that's still breathing out of their misery, but even so . . .'

They joined the tail end of the parade, watching as a group of a dozen lictors pushed their way through to the front with the customary bundles of fasces resting on their shoulders. Marcus saw his friend's baffled look and explained their function, while Velox accepted the plaudits of those members of the crowd who had realised who he was.

'They're a sort of state bodyguard, although the twelve men assigned to escort Commodus when he goes out and about are really there to look after the emperor's dignity rather than act as bodyguards. The bundles of rods they're carrying represent their right to beat some respect into anyone who's stupid enough to get in their way and by association impede the great man's progress, and they're here to make sure that the parade progresses to schedule, once he's entered the arena. It's not just the emperor that gets them, most senior public officials have a few to make sure that nobody gets away with showing them any disrespect. Even a Vestal Virgin will have a lictor to escort her to a ceremony, if her attendance is requested—'

'Although that's more to safeguard the men of the city than to prevent her from being ravished!'

They laughed at the old joke and Glaucus bowed, clearly enjoying himself behind the faceless helmet.

A moment later the distant arena erupted in a roar of approval, and Glaucus turned to hail Velox, who was chatting with several excitable-looking matrons at the crowd's edge.

'That's the emperor's arse in his seat then! Come on Velox, stop trying to make the women wet! It's time to go walkies again! And make sure you don't step in any elephant shit, that stuff's three-feet deep!'

8

Once the parade of the gladiators was complete, the procession having made its way through the Forum to the Gate of Death, and onward into the amphitheatre for the ritual circuit of the fighting surface, the day's combatants were dismissed back to their schools while the beast fighters took their turn in the sun. Sannitus summoned his men to him, pointing towards the Gate of Life.

'Come on then, let's have you back down the tunnel, you can channel all that frustration from marching behind the dancing girls into some serious practice for a change!'

Velox walked over to him and bent to whisper in his ear, tipping his head at the three centurions, and after a moment the lanista nodded and came across to them.

'Your new best friend here thinks he ought to give you a tour of the arena, show how it all works so that it's a bit less of a shock this afternoon when the time comes to fight. Behave yourselves, and remember that you've signed your lives over to the ludus. If you run, then when we catch you we'll crucify you over the gate as a lesson for others. And you . . .'

He pointed at the champion gladiator.

'Don't go pushing your luck with the arena staff. You may be golden bollocks at the moment, but there'll be a few of them who'd happily screw you over, especially if they're still nursing their losses from that fight with the net man last month. Right, I'm off to find the procurator and make sure that we know exactly what it is that those three will be fighting later on. Edius, you're in charge, get the rest of them back to the ludus without anyone getting any clever ideas about taking the rest of the day off, eh?'

He turned away and led his men away towards the Gate of Life, and Velox grinned at them with the look of a man excused duties for the day.

'Come on then, let's get off the sand before the beast fighting starts.'

'Greetings, Tribune. I had not thought to see you again so soon, given your preoccupation with the pursuit of the Emperor's Knives?'

Scaurus bowed to Sigilis, the men behind him copying the gesture as they had been instructed. The Senator had received them without any delay, despite the unannounced nature of their visit, and looking about himself Scaurus noted that his vestibule was empty of any clients despite the relatively early hour.

'You are my first guests of the day, Tribune, you and your men. My usual constant flow of clients has dried up to nothing, now that the word is out as to my pending fate, it seems. Nobody wants to associate with a man under threat of death, do they? You and your people are welcome visitors, to break up the monotony of an otherwise empty day.'

The tribune had once again been accompanied by the same trio of barbarians and his first spear, the latter accompanied by a pair of soldiers.

'I thought you might appreciate a little news on that very subject, Senator. After all, I suspect that you've seen little of your erstwhile informant in the last few days?'

Sigilis nodded, gesturing for the tribune's party to follow him.

'Indeed. I take it as yet another sign that the throne's fingers are tightening around what's left of my allotted lifespan. My people are followed whenever they leave the domus, and men watch the house around the clock. This morning both of my supposedly hidden exits from this property were found to have been broken in, with armed guards set to prevent their use. I do not have long left, I suspect. Anyway, tell me your news, Tribune, and hopefully bring a little pleasure to these grey days.'

Scaurus inclined his head respectfully.

'I believe that my tidings would be best delivered in a setting that would ensure privacy, Senator. Might we perhaps repair to your garden, as we did the last time I came to visit?'

'Well now, Julianus, here's a cup of wine for you. It's the Sicilian, the one you enjoyed so much the last time, and it's already watered.'

The procurator accepted the drink from the servant who had approached him at his host's signal, took a sip and nodded his approval.

'Delicious! Every bit as good as the last time I tasted it, if not even better!'

He waved a hand at the packed and buzzing arena that rose high above their place on the first floor, adjacent to the imperial box. The emperor himself was relaxing at the far end of the area reserved for his court, a pair of young women vying to feed him from the table of delicacies laid out before them, while his chamberlain Cleander was standing not far from the party of senior gladiatorial officials which Julianus had joined, looking about him with his usual expression of calculation.

'And am I to take this apparent state of relaxation as a sign that all is as it should be for the first day of the games?'

His host, the man responsible for the arena's operation, shook his head dismissively.

'As it should be? I *very* much doubt it, but then what else does a man have staff for? They'll be running around like men whose backsides have been stung by hornets at this very minute.' The men standing around the table laughed appreciatively at the affected insouciance in his aristocratic drawl. 'Just as you procurators have your lanistas, I have a small number of very capable and in one or two cases ruthless individuals whose specialisation is the art of making things happen, no matter what it takes. So the show, gentlemen, will go more or less to schedule, and nobody not intimately familiar with the way in which the organisation that runs this arena operates will ever know the difference. Let us just hope that your gladiators will be able to live up to the magnificence of the setting, shall we?'

'There's no fear of anything else!' Novius, procurator of the Gallic Ludus, raised his cup to point at Julianus. 'We've raised a fine crop of fighters this year, hard as nails all the way down to the tenth rank and not, as some schools seem to be, dependent on a few big names to carry their reputation.'

He sniffed loudly, and the other procurators sniggered at the barb, sinking it even deeper into Julianus's thin skin.

'There's more to the Dacian Ludus than Velox and Mortiferum!'

'*Is* there?' His counterpart raised a disbelieving eyebrow. 'Who do you have in the third rank? I hear the name Hermes, although I hear little to encourage a belief that he'll give my own third-rank man a decent workout. Face it, Julianus, once we're past your admittedly lethal one and two, the rest of your ranking is decidedly ordinary.'

Julianus bristled at the slur, waving his rival's words away with an extravagant sweep of his hand.

'Which shows how little your sources within my school really know. I'd advise you to stay for the mid-afternoon livener, colleague, rather than sloping off to your favourite brothel after the first bout of the afternoon as seems to be your usual habit. You might see something from which you'll learn a thing or two about the finer arts of finding good fighting men.'

Novius narrowed his eyes, turning to the arena's procurator with a questioning look, and the administrator waved a languid arm at Julianus.

'Procurator Julianus has entered a new team of commoners for the last non-ranking fight of the day, something to get the crowd shouting again before we send in the big names. We're going to match them with an appropriate number of Dacian prisoners of war and see if they're as good as he makes out.'

'And how many of these mob fighters do you have, Julianus? Ten. A dozen?'

The Dacian procurator smiled back at him.

'Only three. But three men of such a quality that I expect them to go through their assailants without any problem whatsoever.'

'And how many Dacians will you throw at these newcomers?'

Julianus shrugged, affecting to neither know nor care, despite his lanista's very careful instructions on the subject.

'That's a level of detail somewhat deeper than I usually bother myself with, although I do recall Sannitus muttering something about a two to one fight.'

He looked at his fingernails, but Novius saw an opening and went for it.

'Two to one? But if they're as good as you say, surely they can cope with stronger odds than that? Perhaps we need to make a wager on the subject?'

Julianus looked up at him from beneath hooded eyelids.

'A wager? But Novius, surely the last time we gambled on the result of a fight you lost a—'

'And now's my best chance to make it back, from the sound of it. A thousand sestertii, eh, but on a *three* to one fight?'

Unable to back down, Julianus decided to attack.

'A thousand? No, *five* thousand.'

Novius recoiled.

'*Five?*' He looked about him, realising that he'd manoeuvred himself into a corner from which there was no escape. 'Very well, five.' He waved a hand at the arena's procurator, and Julianus smiled at him while a small part of him started worrying as to how Sannitus was going to react to the change of plan. 'With our colleague here to ensure fair play, eh? And, before you leap to your feet to scurry off and warn that animal of a lanista of yours, that bet's good just as long as there's no warning for these new commoners of yours. Let your men discover that the odds against them have changed when the Dacians jump out of their pits, eh? Or will that be too much for them?'

Julianus shrugged, knowing that having raised the stake so high he had little choice in the matter.

'As you say, let's see how real gladiators cope with surprises.'

Sigilis led the small party into the domus's garden and took his seat under the shade of the circle of trees that protected his outside dining area.

'Do sit down, Tribune, and tell me your story.'

Scaurus took his seat.

'Forgive me, Senator, if I detail one of my men to take an interest in this magnificent garden. It would not do for us to be overheard.' The senator nodded, and one of the two soldiers who had accompanied Julius paced away steadily towards the massive wall that guarded the property, while the other walked steadily towards the house. 'So, you will be pleased to hear, three of the four men who have terrorised Rome for the last few years have been dealt with by my vengeful centurion.'

He briefly detailed the deaths of Dorso, Brutus and Pilinius, and with the mention of the last of the three Sigilis smiled slowly.

'With regard to that particular disgusting specimen of twisted humanity and his cronies, I'm genuinely pleased to hear your news. I knew that something had happened to them, from the rumours sweeping the city, but for the delivery of their justice to be so fitting . . .' He looked across the immaculate garden to where the soldier set to search for any eavesdroppers had reached the wall, turned about and was walking back towards them in the same slow, deliberate manner. 'But what of the fourth? Which one of them still survives?'

'Mortiferum.'

'I should have known it . . .' He shook his head knowingly. 'And how do you expect to get to him, might I ask?'

'So there you see it. The Flavian arena in all its glory.'

Velox gestured to the view through the closely spaced iron bars that protected the viewing point out onto the arena's sand, grinning as Dubnus and Horatius crowded forward to peer up at the tiered rows of seats on the amphitheatre's far side. Their window out onto the fighting surface was at ground level, the room in which they stood part of the arena's labyrinth of underground passages and chambers. Looking up, they could see that every seat was filled, the packed galleries teeming with a mass of humanity whose sole instinct seemed to be to bay for the blood of the men pacing forward across the fighting surface before them. With their heads only five feet above the arena's surface, the four men's view out across the sand was unimpeded, although there were only two fighters on show and neither of them was showing any sign of hostility towards the other. Armed with long rectangular shields and what looked like smooth wooden cudgels, they were advancing slowly towards a hastily installed grove of small potted trees in the amphitheatre's centre.

'You've seen all this before, haven't you?'

Their escort's quiet question in Marcus's ear was couched in a knowing tone of voice, and his answer was equally amused.

'Yes. But I was usually sitting in the expensive seats.'

The champion gladiator grinned wryly.

'Gives you a different perspective, eh?'

The Roman nodded, pointing up at the low ceiling above their heads.

'And the noise!'

The packed stands over them were booming with a raucous cacophony, as the crowd yelled, bellowed and hooted their preferences for the fight underway before them, the massive structure seeming to shake with the reverberations. Dubnus shook his head in amazement.

'What are they shouting?'

Velox put a finger to his ear.

'Listen carefully and you'll make it out.'

The big Briton tipped his head, and after a moment realised that the crowd were shouting two words in a seemingly unending chorus.

'*Black Brutus! Black Brutus! Black Brutus!*'

'Black Brutus?'

The gladiator pointed at the arena before them, indicating an iron cage large enough to hold two men at best, its door open wide in anticipation of a prisoner of some nature.

'You see the empty cage? Those two are beast fighters. It looks like they're playing a rather dangerous game that was only invented last year, which I suppose you might call "putting the blood-crazed man-eating cat back in his box without becoming his lunch". Any minute now there's going to be—'

A trapdoor within the circle of trees swung upwards, and out of the yawning gap in the fighting surface a glossy black feline monster sprang out onto the sand. Driven to fresh paroxysms of excitement by the animal's sudden appearance, the sixty-thousand-strong crowd came to its collective feet, bellowing the same two words over and over again as the two men facing the cat eyed it unhappily over the rims of their shields. Dubnus shook his head in disbelief.

'What the fuck sort of animal is that?'

Mortiferum shook his head in amusement at the Briton's awed question.

'You don't get many leopards in Britannia then? That, my friend, is a four-legged killer of men. He's a rarity, being black, but he's just as deadly as his spotted brethren, if not more so. Apparently most black leopards are smaller than usual, but not only is that bastard bigger than the norm, he fights with just as much cunning as my brother Mortiferum, if not a little more viciously. Just watch what happens next . . .'

As he spoke, the midnight-black cat sprang forward, hooking its claws over the rim of the closer of the two shields and using its two-hundred-pound weight to drag the defence down. Finding himself face-to-face with the beast's snarling maw, the fighter hastily released his grip on the shield's handle and stepped back with his cudgel raised to strike, but by mischance managed to find the edge of another trapdoor with his heel, tripping backwards to land hard in the sand, the cudgel spilling uselessly from his hand as he hit the hard surface.

With a coughing growl that was audible over the crowd's own bloodthirsty roar, the leopard pounced, springing forward again and landing on the fallen beast-fighter's body as he struggled to rise, its head snapping forward to bury long incisors deep into his throat. As the dying man struggled ineffectually beneath his assailant's weight, the other man stepped in, swinging his cudgel in a long arc to connect with the leopard's hind quarters, smack of its impact raising a fresh cheer of approval from the crowd, but the cat, as if inspired by the blow's stinging power, turned and stepped off its victim with a chunk of his windpipe visible in its mouth. Spitting out the grisly evidence of his partner's demise, it stalked towards the remaining man with the slow self-assured pace of a killer, eying its victim for the weak spot at which it would strike.

Tossing away his shield in an abrupt movement that sent the crowd into fresh raptures, the sole remaining bestiarius took a two-handed grip of his club, rotating his wrists until the weapon's heavy head was behind his neck, seeming to rise onto his toes as he waited for the leopard to attack. In a flurry of motion the beast pounced forward, but where it had struck the fighter's partner on the chest, the surviving fighter swayed to one side with a dancer's grace, snapping the club round in a vicious arc that smashed its very tip into the big cat's head with enough force to send the beast sprawling onto the sand, its paws twitching as it clung to consciousness.

Looking at the club in his hands the bestiarius tossed it to one side, walking to where his mate's discarded shield lay flat on the sand.

'*No!*'

The bellowed command from another of the viewing positions away to their right had no apparent impact on the bestiarius, and he took up the shield, turned on the spot and walked back towards the semi-conscious animal with a purposeful stride. A dozen or so animal handlers burst from doors set in the arena's walls, hurrying across the fighting surface with their nets and restraining poles, but it was clear to the audience that they would be too late. A barrage of catcalls and imprecations rained down on the fighter as he raised his fallen colleague's shield as high as he could before pounding its brass-rimmed edge down onto the stunned leopard's throat.

The big animal's back arched convulsively as its windpipe was smashed, the bestiarius landing a second vicious blow to ensure that it would die of asphyxiation before he was wrestled away from the doomed creature with the crowd's boos ringing around the amphitheatre. Velox shook his head as the bestiarius was dragged away kicking and shouting.

'Let's hope that his revenge was worth it, because he'll be paying for it with his life. And that monster was a crowd favourite, which means that they'll still be baying for blood when the first proper fight of the afternoon starts. I pity the poor bastards who've drawn that slot, because one of them's dead for certain with the mob in that mood. Come on, let's go and get some food.'

He led them back into the huge building's depths, torch and lamplight swiftly replacing that provided by the windows into the arena.

'Mind you, there's a lesson there. Always keep your feet flat to the ground, and shuffle step, feeling the way with your toes. If you fall over in the middle of a fight like he did, then your life is likely to be equally short and unpleasant. Now, here we are.'

He led them through a doorway into a scene that resembled something from the underworld, organised chaos by torchlight as dozens of cooks worked to complete the meals that would be taken up the long staircases to feed the dignitaries perched high above them.

'And you can fuck off as w—' The nearest man to them stared hard at Velox for a moment before cracking a broad smile. 'Welcome, champion! I won a gold aureus on your last fight! Here, have a pie!'

He handed the gladiator a hot piece of pastry, staring past him at the three friends. 'I suppose you want these three feeding as well?'

Velox shrugged and smiled conspiratorially.

'That depends on whether you want my tip for this afternoon to be supported by well-nourished fighters or not.'

'Here!' The cook passed them each a pie with almost indecent haste, looking over his shoulder to the other end of the kitchen where the master cook stood watching his men's progress. 'Now, tell me quickly and get away, before that old sod sees me feeding you!'

The champion gladiator winked, taking a mouthful of the pie. 'Mmm. Excellent . . .'

The cook lifted a clenched fist with a snarl that was only partially playful.

'You'll get me—'

A shout from the kitchen's far end warned them that they had been spotted.

'Oi! Get the *fuck* out of my kitchen!'

The cook raised his fist in earnest this time, advancing on them with a pleading look.

'I'm seeing them off, never fear!'

Velox took pity on him.

'The mid-afternoon wake-up bout. Bet on the three centurions!'

Allowing the winking cook to hustle them out of the kitchen, the four men ate their pies, blowing on the hot filling as they nibbled at the pastry.

'Come on, we can eat these as we go. Follow me and I'll show you a place you only want to visit once.'

Once outside the domus's sprawling property, Scaurus raised an eyebrow at his first spear.

'Well then, did you get what you needed?'

Julius looked in turn at the men who had accompanied him, and the older of the two nodded happily.

'Everything, Tribune.'

Scaurus nodded grimly, indicating the two men lounging brazenly on the next street corner.

'Good. Make a start as quickly as you can. I fear the senator has very little time left.'

'Well then, Tettius Julianus, I hear that you're giving us all a bit of a treat at the end of the day?'

The procurator started at the quiet voice in his ear. While his attention had been on an attractive young woman in the company of one of his fellow senators, the imperial chamberlain had left the imperial box and strolled onto the senatorial podium that ran alongside it, his approach silent until he'd spoken in Julianus's ear.

'Yes!' His voice sounded high-pitched, and he cursed Cleander's ability to make him feel guilty in even the most innocent of situations. 'We had a trio of walk-ins yesterday, three former centurions all of whom seem to be as capable as the best of my men.'

'Really?' The chamberlain arched an eyebrow, clearly enjoying his discomfiture. 'As good as the Death Bringer?'

Julianus shrugged.

'Maybe not *that* good, but . . .'

'Good enough for you to risk their lives against three desperate prisoners of war apiece though?'

Julianus smiled weakly.

'My lanista tells me—'

'Your lanista? Surely as the procurator of an imperial gladiatorial school you take a close personal interest in the abilities of the men you send into the arena? After all, as I'm sure I hardly need to remind you, Caesar takes a very dim view of things when the men sent onto the sand to amuse him are proven to lack the necessary skills and bravery to entertain him. After all, he is exceptionally skilled with any weapon you might care to mention . . .' Cleander raised both eyebrows in mock question. 'We'll just have to hope that your lanista has sufficient discernment to ensure that Commodus will be entertained on this occasion.'

He waited for a moment expectantly and then, just as Julianus was about to speak, smiled widely.

'I'm just having my fun with you, Senator, don't pay me any attention. I'm sure your new men will be sudden death personified once they come face-to-face with a handful of underfed Dacians. Tell me though, I am curious – where did these three men come from? I'd hate to think that serving soldiers might have sought refuge from their duty in your school, no matter how risky an alternative it might make . . .'

Julianus gabbled an answer into the chamberlain's long pause, relieved to find himself on firmer ground.

'No fear of that, Chamberlain, no fear at all! One of them's a legion man listed as dead – I had my slave check with the military records – and the other two are Tungrians, honourably discharged. I checked that with their tribune in person, because I . . .'

He fell silent, waiting for the Chamberlain's intrigued expression to turn into speech.

'*Tungrians*? I see. And the legion man, what's his name?'

The procurator wracked his memory for a moment.

'What did he call himself . . . ah, yes, his name is Horatius.'

Cleander's smile broadened.

'Is it indeed! Well there's a happy coincidence! I've been hearing tales of a centurion with the same name who gave some men of mine a most thorough display of his fighting skills only a few weeks ago. Let's hope that *your* Horatius shares his skills, for if he does we're in for the most gripping performances for a good while. Now, do carry on considering that young lady's finely turned ankle . . .'

He patted Julianus on the shoulder and turned back to the imperial box, the guards' crossed spears opening to admit him to the emperor's presence. The procurator realised that he was sweating profusely despite the day's unseasonal cold, his appetite for covert examination of the city's aristocratic females suddenly absent.

Velox led the friends through the tunnel's cool gloom, the floor sloping gradually downwards before levelling out to run under the arena's length to the east, its walls lit by blazing torches that provided just enough illumination to see. A familiar tang filled the air, and their guide inhaled deeply.

'There it is. That's the smell I associate with the arena. Blood.'

The tunnel started to climb, and he gestured to an opening on the right. They followed him in and found themselves in a torchlit chamber some thirty feet square and ten feet high, its floor filled with tables large enough to accommodate a man's corpse.

'This is the spolarium's lowest level. Once Charun's stoved their brains in, the bodies are carried down here to be relieved of their kit. Corpses go out of the building on carts for disposal, equipment goes to the armamentarium to be reconditioned for the next man to use it. Efficient, isn't it?'

On one of the tables lay the body of the dead beast fighter, stripped of his clothing and in the process of being washed clean of the blood that had poured from the dreadful wound in his throat. In one corner a man was crouched over something large and dark, and Velox led them over to stand beside him.

'Cheer up man, nothing lasts for ever!'

The animal trainer looked up from the dead leopard's corpse with bitter, tear-filled eyes.

'He had dozens of fights left in him, *dozens*! And now he's dead because one stupid bastard lost his temper! All because the two of them were fucking each other, the pair of tunic-lifting b—'

'Now now, let's not say something we might regret, eh? You'd be surprised at some of the people who prefer the company of other men . . . my brother, for example.' The trainer's eyes widened as he realised how close he was to offending the champion, but Velox patted him gently on the shoulder. 'And never mind, I'll sell you a secret that will help you towards some of the money you'll need to replace him, in return for something you've no need of any more.'

The trainer looked up at him suspiciously.

'What are you offering?'

'Only a sure-thing bet on the mid-afternoon fight.'

'How sure?'

The gladiator smirked at him.

'Totally. You can put as much as you like on the result in the certainty that it'll come back to you in style.'

The trainer pursed his lips.

'And what do you want from me? His cock, I suppose.'

Velox shook his head.

'That's more my brother's style. No, I want the teeth, or more to the point, his fangs.'

The other man pulled a face.

'I was saving those to sell to a lucky charm dealer I know, they're worth at least—'

'Not as much as the information I can give you for them. Put an aureus on the right side of the fight I've got in mind and it'll come back as three, I'm telling you.'

'An aureus? Where am I going to get a bloody aureus from?'

The gladiator reached out with the toe of his boot, nudging the dead leopard's underbelly.

'You already know the answer to that one. Any one of half a dozen potion dealers will give you good money for his family jewels. So, do we have a deal?'

The trainer nodded, ignoring the commotion as a pair of dead beast fighters were carried into the room and dumped without ceremony onto tables next to the first corpse.

'Deal. So what's the big secret with this fight then?'

'Procurator? You have two guests, sir, military men.'

Julianus nodded with relief, grateful for the welcome distraction from the revolting scene playing out in the arena below him, although he was careful to keep a smile plastered across his face given the emperor's apparent rapt attention. Gesturing to the podium's entrance for the Tungrian tribune and his senior centurion to be admitted, he walked across to greet them and acknowledged their respectful bows with one of his own.

'Tribune Scaurus! I'm so glad that you and the centurion could join us. Your men are set to fight this afternoon, and I think you're going to find what we've got planned perfectly attuned to your military tastes.'

The crowd roared with apparent delight at the lunchtime entertainment, and the two soldiers peered over the podium's parapet, Scaurus raising an eyebrow at Julianus and shaking his head in apparent bemusement.

'I see the Flavian arena hasn't lost its touch for the bizarre while I've been away in the north.'

His senior centurion had managed to keep a straight face, but Julianus sensed that he was less than happy at what he'd witnessed. The tribune was clearly aware of his man's discomfort, his question filling the awkward silence.

'So, some sort of military-themed bout, from the sound of it? Will our two men be fighting together?'

Julianus smiled, doing his best to ignore the shouts of encouragement that the crowd were showering down upon the object of their attention.

'Better than that, Rutilius Scaurus, they'll be going into the arena with another soldier, a man called Horatius. My colleague who runs this place has dug up some Dacian prisoners for them to fight, so it ought to make for a spectacular piece of entertainment.'

Scaurus nodded, and was about to reply when the crowd roared in sudden delight.

'Thank Our Lord Mithras for that, the poor beast must have finished.'

Julianus turned to look briefly over the parapet.

'So it seems. It never ceases to strike me how degrading that must be for all concerned, but of course the audience here do like their depravity. There, the beast handlers have him under control . . .'

A blast of horns blew to warn the crowd that the first fight of the afternoon was about to begin, and Julianus turned back to the sand with a note of relief on his face.

'Thank the gods for that. I haven't seen such a lacklustre lunchtime show for years. A few tired-looking clowns, and a drunken baboon being made to couple with a young woman tied to a post isn't really my idea of entertainment.'

'Watch the net. With a retarius you always have to watch the net, because that's what does the damage. The trident's dangerous alright, but if he puts the net over the secutor then the fight's over unless the other man's very, very lucky. Mind you, this should be easy enough for Glaucus. Trust me, a good chaser will beat a good net man almost every time, and Glaucus is still just about as good as they come.'

Looking through the closely spaced iron bars, the friends watched as the first bout of the afternoon was announced, and the veteran secutor Glaucus walked proudly into the ring with his sword and shield held up in recognition of the booming applause that showered down on him from all sides. His smooth-fronted helmet, whilst it was designed to frustrate the net in his opponent's hand by providing it with nothing to catch on to, also had the effect of bestowing an anonymity upon him that was far more unnerving to an opponent than a snarling face. Velox nodded his head with a fond expression.

'Look, even the emperor's up and shouting. That old bastard Glaucus may be getting long in the tooth for all this, but he's earned all the adulation he's getting. Thirty-six fights, and against every decent net man to have come out of the Ludus Magnus in the last ten years, and he's never once been defeated. And in all that time he's always been decent enough to make his opponent look good, so that he's only had to put a handful of them to the sword.'

He stared speculatively at the veteran's opponent, nodding approvingly as the retarius padded across the sand to take up his position ready for the fight to begin.

'Nice feet. See how he barely disturbs the sand as he walks? That boy's as light-footed as a mountain goat. Let's see if his skills with the net and trident are as good as his footwork.'

The retarius padded up to his starting position and took guard, the trident held underarm and ready to fight, while the Master of the Games announcer bellowed out the names and fighting records of the two men. Velox frowned as the net fighter's list of fights and victories was detailed, and looked out at Glaucus with a bemused look.

'His opponent's only had a handful of fights from the sound of it, and none of them were in Rome, which makes him a bit of an unknown quantity.' He stared pensively out across the sand at the waiting retarius, stroking his chin thoughtfully. 'Glaucus must be wondering what's going on, given the stupendous amount of money he was offered to make one last appearance . . .' He turned away with a determined look, throwing a swift comment over his shoulder. 'Stay here!'

In his absence the chief referee strode out between the two men, resplendent in his white tunic and carrying the long stick with which he could marshal cooperative gladiators, while his heavily built assistant loomed behind him, his iron-tipped quarterstaff ready to deal with anything that required more direct methods. Behind them the arena slaves waited by a red-hot brazier, which contained several long irons already sufficiently hot to make them visibly glow red and leave trails of smoke when they were pulled out and shown to the crowd, their threat more than enough to persuade any reluctant fighters to get on with their bout. Velox was only gone for long enough that the preliminaries to the fight were all but complete by the time he returned, his face set in an angry scowl and his voice dangerously controlled as he raised it to be heard over the announcer's shouted introduction of the two fighters and the cheers that greeted them in turn.

'It's a bloody *fix*. I tried to get odds against Glaucus from one of the gamblers who makes odds for the senators up on the podium, but he told me he's not been taking bets on the net man for an hour or so, ever since someone in the Ludus Magnus spilled the beans to someone who was good enough to warn him off in turn. Apparently this "new boy" isn't a new boy at all, but some talent whose skills have been sharpened up on the arena circuit in Hispania over the last year. Not that they needed much sharpening, from the look of him . . .'

They turned their attention to the two gladiators who were now squaring up to each other under the referee's command, Glaucus's blank iron face seemingly locked on to his opponent as the retarius bounced on the balls of his feet, ready to fight. At the shouted command he leapt forward, and from the first moves of the bout it was clear that the veteran fighter was in trouble.

Dancing in with quick, darting steps that made a mockery of the usual practice of shuffling forward to avoid tripping on an unseen obstacle, the retarius struck first. His attack was lightning fast, stabbing his trident at the other man's head with such speed and force that it was all that Glaucus could do to get his shield in the way of the blow. As the unbalanced secutor stepped back to regain his footing, the retarius stabbed his trident in low, its long central prong scraping down the hastily lowered shield's painted face until it snagged the brass rim, forcing Glaucus's defence down until it hit the sand. He flicked the weapon back and up to strike again with the same seemingly divine speed, jabbing it over the shield's rim at Glaucus's helmet faster than the secutor could raise it. The brass-sheathed iron stopped the blow, but Glaucus's head was punched backwards with a clang that was audible at fifty paces, violently rocking the veteran with its crashing impact.

Velox sucked in a swift breath, shaking his head as the older man staggered backwards, and the crowd were suddenly silent as the reality of what was happening to their beloved champion sank in. Before the veteran chaser could re-establish his defence, the retarius hooked his trident over the top edge of Glaucus's shield, leaning back and whipping the weapon backwards with all the strength in his finely muscled torso and thighs to tear the heavy layered board from the secutor's stunned grasp. The crowd, already shocked at the indignities being visited upon their hero, were reduced to horrified silence as Glaucus staggered forward, dragged off balance from the abrupt removal of his defence. As he teetered on the edge of another involuntary step forward, the retarius took a single pace forward, disdainful of any threat from the secutor's sword, and plunged the long middle prong of his trident into the veteran's leading foot.

'*No!*'

A single voice in the otherwise silent crowd denied what was so clearly happening before them. The veteran gladiator threw his head back in a scream of agony that was clearly audible despite the helmet's face mask, the muscles of his chest tensing like whips as the agony of the cold metal's punching intrusion through the bones of his foot hit him. After a moment's disbelieving pause, the crowd found their voices, screaming a single word again and again.

'*Habet! Habet! Habet!*'

'Yes, he's had it alright.' Marcus looked across at Velox as the champion spat out his disgust at the crowd's exultant reaction. 'It didn't take you lot long to decide which side you'd rather be on, did it?'

Stepping back from the reeling chaser, the retarius cast his net at the stricken veteran with such confidence that he barely even looked at his target. Released by a practised twist of his hand, that opened the net out from a tight ball into a six-foot-wide spinning snare, it wrapped around the older man to seal his doom. Crippled and ensnared, Glaucus toppled over with the inevitability of a falling tree, not even bothering to struggle against the net's bonds.

'Poor bastard.'

Velox looked over at Horatius, his eyes hard with anger.

'Poor betrayed bastard, you mean. They're both from the same school, and yet he clearly had no idea what was about to hit him. That net man is the cream, and the ludus have clearly put him in without giving Glaucus any warning. Either it was a bet set up to let them place some very hefty money on a result that only they could predict, or he's upset someone important and rich enough to pressure the school into setting the whole thing up. I don't suppose his fee was ever a problem, whatever was at the root of the matter, given that a few well-placed wagers will have more than paid that back . . .'

He fell silent as the referee walked out to look down at Glaucus, who had wearily raised a finger in surrender. The official paused for a moment, as if he were unable to believe the evidence of his own eyes, then turned to look up at the imperial box.

'He's already dead. There's no way that Commodus will let him live after that poor a display, and even if he were minded to show some respect to the man's long and distinguished record, this crowd are baying for blood.' The champion fighter shook his head sadly. 'And who can blame them? Many of them probably put more than they could afford to lose on Glaucus, given what a safe bet he's been for so long, and now the professional gamblers are walking away smiling while the average man is already down on the day. See, Charun knows . . .'

The arena slave dressed as the spirit guide of the underworld, whose task it was to finish off dying gladiators with a heavy double-headed hammer, was walking slowly forward as Commodus rose to his feet and looked about the arena for a moment. He was clearly taking stock of the number of cries of '*Mitte*' he was hearing, entreaties for the defeated man to be spared death. Velox smiled sadly.

'Listen. I told you so.'

The number of people shouting for the killing stroke echoed around the arena in a ceaseless, vindictive chorus of '*Igula! Igula! Igula!*', utterly overwhelming those few sentimentalists who had been swayed by Glaucus's glorious record. The emperor paused for a moment to bask in the waves of sound and the power that they gave him, making a show of considering the fallen secutor's fate. His hand rose, the thumb pointing upwards for a second before he jerked it towards his own throat, and the crowd's roar descended into a wordless, frenzied cacophony of screams as the retarius stepped forward, taking a sword from an arena slave and raising it in readiness for the delivery of the killing stoke.

Snared in the net's deadly embrace and unable to stand, his opponent managed to lever himself up onto his knees, fiddling with the fastenings of his helmet and pulling away the face mask to stare up at his opponent with unveiled hatred. His words were inaudible over the crowd's continuous roar, but the effect was immediate, as the referee waved the brazier minders forward to free the condemned fighter from the net's folds. Unable to put his weight on the shattered and torn remnant of his foot, he reached forward and took a firm grip of the retarius's thigh, staring up at the imperial box for a long moment before releasing his hold and opening his arms wide, his lips moving again as he spat whatever defiance he had left at the man who would be his killer.

The retarius struck with the same mercurial speed that he had used to defeat his opponent, sinking the sword's blade deep into Glaucus's throat, and the dying veteran sank to the sand in a fresh gout of blood. Bowing to the referee, and then to the emperor, who was still graciously applauding his victory, the retarius dropped the sword and turned away without a second glance at Glaucus's corpse, walking away towards the Gate of Life with the hysterical shouts and screams of the crowd still echoing around the arena.

'And a new hero is born.' Velox shook his head in disgust. 'But whoever came up with the idea of sacrificing a man to make it happen, that man should be praying that I never find out his name. Come on, I'll take you to the armourers. After that disgusting charade, we'd probably be best making sure that they haven't been instructed to kit you three out as dancing girls.'

'I presume that rather hapless chaser had done something to offend, or is that just the way the Great School does business these days?'

While the arena slaves scattered fresh white sand over the blood spilled by Glaucus, and the next pair of fighters entered to yet more thunderous applause, Cleander had strolled across the imperial box to direct an apparently casual question at the Ludus Magnus's procurator. Much as the man clearly wanted to take umbrage, the chamberlain's reputation for making and breaking both careers and men went before him.

'In truth, Aurelius Cleander, the man's demands for money had become rather tiresome. He knew only too well that he was expected to be on the bill, and in consequence he was asking for a hundred thousand just to put his feet on the sand.'

The chamberlain nodded.

'I'm familiar with the mind set. Men decide that they are indispensable, and in doing so make it essential that they are dispensed with.'

The procurator dipped his head to acknowledge the point.

'Not only that, but he was clearly past it. My lanista was having to hand-pick his opponents, and it was only a matter of time before he became a laughing stock when people realised that we were putting no-hopers in front of him.'

Cleander inclined his head in recognition of the point.

'Which would never have stood. Especially given that our

beloved Caesar is such an attentive follower of the games. And besides . . .' He raised a conspiratorial eyebrow. 'I presume that you managed to find a way to turn the whole sorry situation to some small advantage?'

The procurator had the good grace to colour slightly.

'I . . . made sure that the ludus wouldn't be financially disadvantaged in the matter, as is my responsibility.'

Cleander's smile hardened.

'I'm sure you did. After all, most of the men here have probably lost a few sestertii on the match, and I doubt the professional gamblers will have scooped all of that rather splendid sum. Shall we say ten per cent? Not from the Great School's profit of course, that would be unfair to the throne, just from whatever small wager you might have placed yourself?'

The procurator bowed, opening his hands to gesture his assent to the suggestion.

'It would be my pleasure to donate such a sum to the imperial treasury.'

Cleander nodded.

'Excellent. And now I really must get back to my duties. I think it's time we ran an audit of arena gamblers' takings and losses. I do so like to know exactly what monies are changing hands, and where the throne might request a small percentage as a means of meeting its incessant outflow of gold to safeguard the empire's frontiers.'

He turned away but then, exactly as Scaurus had expected, he turned back with a faint smile.

'Tribune Scaurus, you do get around.'

Scaurus bowed.

'I make a point of introducing my officers to as many new experiences as possible, Chamberlain, and Julius here has never seen the Flavian amphitheatre.'

Cleander raised an eyebrow.

'And how do you find our entertainment, Centurion?'

Julius smiled wanly.

'Informative, sir.'

'Informative!' The chamberlain guffawed. 'I'm sure you do, given the bestial nature of the lunchtime show. But never fear, there's nothing more in that line planned for the rest of the day, although I suspect that dear old Glaucus's death will have left the crowd in the mood for some red meat. Let's hope your men can provide them with a good-sized portion! Oh, and Scaurus?'

'Chamberlain?'

'I really do think it's time your men were given a break from all that tedious sitting around and waiting for their next set of orders. I'll send a man to you in the morning to detail the time of a meeting and we'll find you something more interesting to do. Something involving travel . . .'

9

Velox led the three friends through the Gate of Life, his face still betraying the fury he was feeling at the death of his friend Glaucus. The gate guards on duty did no more than nod respectfully as he escorted the three soldiers out into the open space between the arena and the gladiatorial schools clustered around its eastern side. The square was almost empty, most of the people who had thronged it a few hours before now in their seats high above the arena's sand, and those few who remained were easily turned away by the pair of ludus guards walking before them with their heavy knobbed wooden clubs.

Leading them across the square, his mood seemed to soften slightly as he pointed out each of the gladiatorial ludi in turn, from the Ludus Gallicus's comparatively humble establishment, to the Ludus Magnus's massive square-sided barracks, the height of its walls fully two-thirds of the arena which faced it across the intervening open space.

'They've got a full-sized arena in there to make the training realistic for the horse boys, and big enough that they can stage chariot fights and massed battles when the aristos want to pay for some private bloodshed. It's always been the same. The Great School turns out most of the mainstream acts, and so it has all the money and all of the power. The rest of us are always running to catch up.'

He led them up a side street and into a huge stone building.

'But here's a place where that doesn't matter, because these boys are managed by the Flavian procurator, and they treat everyone with exactly the same disdain. You'll be here a lot over the next few years, getting your gear sorted out before a fight.'

If the champion's reputation had the power to open almost any door, there was little sign of that influence in the dour-faced man who confronted them when they reached the arena's armoury, protected by three sets of heavy iron-studded oak doors.

'Equipment for these three? I was told about it less than an hour ago, so you'll just have to make do with what we've got in store. It's not as if we've not already got enough work to keep us busy for the rest of the week!'

The chief armourer waved a hand at the ordered chaos behind him, half a dozen muscular men with their heads down over their work, hammering at armour and sharpening the weapons required to equip the men who would fight in the Flavian arena. The air in the workshop was heavy with the stink of sweat, and the four men were barely spared a second glance by the toiling craftsmen. Velox put a hand on their overseer's shoulder.

'Don't worry about it, I know your store well enough to find what we need. We'll bring it back to show you before we carry it off, never fear. After all, if we wait for those idiots upstairs to come and sort it out, these lads'll be going out onto the sand naked.'

The armourer nodded, happy to have the problem taken off his hands, and turned back to his workshop with a final admonishment.

'Off you go then, but no trying to sneak off with any of the good stuff!'

The store was cooler, if no better lit than the workshop through which they had walked to reach it, and the four men walked down its long central aisle looking at the equipment stacked in both sides with an eye for anything military. Velox picked up a sword, testing its edge with his thumb.

'Let's hope this is going to feel the touch of a stone before it's used in anger. Of course, once a man's fought and won a few times he gets to use his own gear, since it makes him more recognisable to the crowds and encourages them to gamble on him, with the arena taking a healthy cut of course, but most of the tiros get something from this rather dull collection thrust at them just as they're about to go out onto the sand, poor bastards. A few practice swings and suddenly you're out there face-to-face with another man who has to go through you if he wants to make his way back through the Gate of Life. No wonder so many of them don't survive their first two or three . . . Ah, here we are then!' He waved a hand at the racks of gear that ran the length of the storeroom. 'Designed by veteran soldiers, tested to destruction in foreign wars and then eventually made by the lowest bidder with the cheapest materials possible, so you'd better make sure that anything you choose isn't ready to fall to pieces!'

The soldiers looked up and down the racks of equipment before them, each of them selecting what they needed in their own size. Horatius paused in the middle of buckling on his armour, realising that the Tungrians had both chosen to wear mail rather than the legion standard-issue body protection.

'You're sure you want to wear that stuff? Plate armour's better protection against a spear point, because the plates are layered two and three thick. And see, the shoulder guards will hold off a sword blade better as well . . .'

His voice trailed off as Dubnus turned a strained smile on him, fastening a thick leather belt tightly about himself to carry some of the heavy mail shirt's twenty-pound weight.

'On the other hand, see how the shirt protects my thighs, nearly as far down as my knees. And I'm used to this, whereas it could take me days of practice to be able to fight as well with that thing on.'

Velox reappeared from the back of the store with three helmets piled in his arms.

'Here you go, these look like they'll do the job.' He passed one to each of them, watching as they pulled on arming caps to pad out the space between head and helmet, then dropped the heavy iron headgear into place. 'Now you look like soldiers, and not just particularly well-muscled tourists. Find yourselves some military-looking shields and I think that'll more or less be you three ready for the sand.'

Picking out a sword and spear for each of them, he led them back into the workshop. The armourer stared at the three men as they walked through his toiling men, his head shaking slowly from side to side as they stopped in front of him for inspection.

'First time?'

Marcus nodded, frowning down at the man.

'Yes, but—'

'How could I tell? It's in the eyes, lad, in the eyes. You lot are looking about you as if this is some sort of big adventure, rather than the never-ending bloodbath that it really is.' Having noted the equipment they were wearing and made each of them sign for it, he detailed a slave to carry their spears and swords. 'If you walk out into the streets carrying that lot you'll start a bloody panic.'

He turned back to his work, leaving Velox to lead them out of the workshop and back into the sunlight. Their appearance excited somewhat more comment than had been the case earlier, and a small crowd quickly gathered about them as they strode back towards the arena. Their guards pushed through the gathering throng, re-inforced by a half-dozen men sent out from the Gate of Life to escort them in, and Velox grinned broadly at Marcus as they pushed and shoved their way to the gate, his previous dark mood forgotten.

'If you've ever wondered what keeps men who've won their wooden sword coming back, other than they don't have any other skills, this is it. They love us, these poor bastards with little else to brighten their lives, they worship us and they adore us. And soon enough they'll be chanting your names . . . *if* you win this afternoon.'

The gate supervisor hurried up to him with a look of near-panic.

'Thank the gods you're back! One of the men who was scheduled to fight this afternoon has fallen down the steps and broken three fingers of his sword hand and the others aren't here yet. Once this fight's finished we've got no one else to put onto the sand, so you've been moved up the order. Get your lads ready to fight!'

Velox led them down into the tunnels beneath the arena floor, grinning at the cacophony that reverberated around the dark, enclosed space.

'Just be grateful you're not down here when the place is packed with animals. All that grunting and roaring, not to mention the stink of their shit . . .'

He delivered them to their holding cell with a smile of re-assurance. Waiting until they were inside the iron-barred cage whose stone back wall had a succession of heavy wooden beams set into it to form a stairway, he pointed at the spot where the roughly formed stair met the cell's stone roof.

'When that trapdoor opens, climb the steps and you'll find yourselves in the sunlight. Take a moment to adjust your eyes to the light before moving forward, or they'll release the Dacians before you've got your bearings. The announcer will probably want to tell the story of what's going on before you get started in any case, so just stand there looking tough until he's finished spouting whatever nonsense they've made up to justify the three of you facing a bunch of barbarians. Now, when they attack you they'll come out of the ground just like you will. Let them get out of their cell and once they're all above ground, anything goes.'

He paused and looked at them, opening his arms wide and tilting his head with his eyebrows raised for emphasis.

'*Anything*. All the rules that we follow when it's gladiator versus gladiator? Forget them, if you ever knew them. If you wound a man and you have the time, finish him. All that stuff about stepping back and waiting for the referee to start the fight again is out of the window as well, because for one thing he's not going to come anywhere near half a dozen blood-crazed Dacians, and for another, these men have been brought here to provide a little entertainment for the rabble as they die. So get it done anyway that works, kill them all and take the adulation of an adoring crowd. Simple, eh?'

He grinned at them again, nodding his head as he turned away.

'I'll drink a cup of wine with you when it's done, eh? Just make sure you do the Dacian school proud!'

Velox strolled easily through the barely illuminated passages beneath the arena's floor, crossing from one side of the broad oval to the other and looking briefly at each holding cell he passed until he found what he'd been looking for. The Dacian prisoners were being herded disconsolately into a cell which was the identical match for the one in which the three centurions were waiting to fight, and for a moment the gladiator stood and looked at them with appraising eyes, until with a start he realised that there were more men being driven into the cell at spear point than he had expected.

'There should be six of them!'

The arena slave guarding the cell's door shook his head flatly.

'I get new order. Another three men put into fight. We only just fetch from cells in time.'

Velox looked at the Dacians for a moment longer, then turned on his heel and ran, hearing the blare of trumpets and the roar of the crowd from the arena above him as the fight in progress came to whatever end the emperor had decreed. Passing a party of arena guards escorting a pair of heavily armoured murmillos to their cell, he recognised one of them and skidded to a halt.

'Nilo! You still owe me a favour for that tip I gave you on that net man at the last games! Lend me your spear! And you two!' Seeing the incredulity on their faces he fished out his purse, pulling out a gold aureus and holding it up for them to see. 'I'll rent them! An aureus for one fight's worth of rental! It's not as if you need them to control this pair of amateurs.'

They dithered for a moment, looking at each other in bemusement while the murmillos bristled at being described in such harsh terms, and with a snort of impatience he tossed the coin at their feet, snatched the weapons from their unresisting fingers and ran, the wooden shafts clattering in his grasp. Skidding round the corner he saw a rectangle of golden sunlight in the holding cell's farthest corner, and realised with dismay that the cage in which he had expected to find the three soldiers was empty.

The trapdoor had risen from its recess with a slow creak, and after a moment's pause Horatius had led them up the steps, moving to the opening's left as Dubnus climbed out behind him, turning to the right and leaving the way clear for Marcus. The three men stood blinking in the sunlight, momentarily stunned by the roar of fifty thousand voices beating down on them as the crowd greeted their appearance with the usual barrage of noise. The arena's tiered seats towered over them on all sides, the waves of sound from their occupants washing down on the dazzled comrades.

'*Citizens! Citizens!*'

A man was bellowing out at the crowd from a place beneath the imperial box, and the crowd swiftly fell silent, accustomed to the arena's pre-fight ritual. When the announcer spoke again it was into a hushed silence, with only the susurrations of quiet conversation and a few coughs to distract from his portentous announcement.

'*Citizens, the Flavian Arena and the Dacian Gladiatorial School will now bring you a spectacle unlike anything you have ever seen before!*'

'*Corvus!*'

The Roman turned, looking about him before realising that the urgent voice addressing him was coming from beneath his feet. Peering down into the trapdoor's black rectangle he realised that Velox was looking up at him.

'Take these!' Three spears clattered onto the sand at his feet. 'You've been set up! There aren't six men coming out to fight you, there are nine of them!'

He vanished into the gloom, and the trapdoor swung shut as the arena slave who had been waiting behind him pulled at the rope and dropped it back into place, leaving the arena's surface unbroken.

'*For the first time in arena history we bring you not one, not two, but three former centurions from the imperial legions, battle-hardened veterans who have come to test themselves against whatever might be thrown against them! Behold, the finest fighting men of the finest army in the world!*'

The crowd erupted in a bellow of delight, forcing the announcer to fall silent for a moment.

'What did Velox say?'

Marcus looked at the other two men, reaching down to pick up one of the spears before answering Dubnus's question.

'The odds against us have been changed. There are nine prisoners waiting to be sent against us.'

Dubnus nodded, passing a spear to Horatius.

'We've fought worse. Here's your chance to show us whether you could really hit a cat's arse at twenty paces.'

The legion man grinned back at him.

'Twenty-five.'

'*Citizens!*' The crowd fell quiet again, although this time they were still buzzing with chatter, speculation as to what might be about to happen before them. '*We are watching a scene from the divine Emperor Trajan's war against the Dacians, a piece of history well known to any man who fought in that bitterly fought campaign. We are watching the story of . . . "The Three Centurions!"*'

'What the fuck is the man prattling on about?'

Horatius raised an amused eyebrow at Dubnus.

'I suspect we're about to find out.'

'*The Emperor sent three centurions out with orders to find and kill the general commanding the Dacian forces facing his legions, three men who were the greatest champions in his entire army! Their names were Horatius, a man of Noricum . . .*'

The crowd roared, and Horatius raised his shield and spears in salute, grimacing at the other two.

'*Dubnus, a barbarian from the far-off island of Britannia converted to the emperor's service!*'

Again the roar, and Dubnus pulled a wry face as he raised his arms.

'Fuck me, a man could get used to this.'

'*And Corvus, a citizen of Rome skilled with every weapon and devoted to his emperor!*'

Marcus shook his head at the unintentional irony, lifting his shield and spears to acknowledge the crowd's roar of approval.

'*Together, these three brave men journeyed deep into the heart of the enemy's territory, unaware that they were in their turn being hunted by the enemy!*'

The announcer fell silent, and Horatius looked at the other two with a grim smile.

'I suspect that it's time to journey deep into the heart of the enemy's territory. Heads up! And since the rules seem to have gone out of the window, I suggest we strike first!'

They stepped forward, pacing towards the arena's centre with their shields raised, each with a single spear ready to throw and the spare held in their shield hands.

'*And then, without warning, the enemy struck!*'

With the announcer's last words, almost shrieked above the crowd's rising growl of tension, a trapdoor in the sand before them flipped open. Men armed with swords and small round shields started to stream up the steps and out into the light, their bearded faces screwed up against the sunlight, long, dank hair tied back into braids in readiness for the fight. While they were still blinking at the sudden bright daylight, clustered around the trapdoor while more men mounted the steps behind them, Horatius stamped forward and slung his spear into their midst. He clenched his fist as the weapon's iron head slammed through a man's shield and gutted him, sending him staggering backwards, the ground beneath his feet dropping away as his third step found the door's empty space. Chaos reigned in the barbarians' ranks for a moment, the cries of the men still trying to ascend the steps as their comrade's spitted body fell into their midst barely audible over the crowd's roar of delight.

Marcus and Dubnus stepped forward to throw their own spears, and the Dacians' battle experience showed as three men stepped forward in front of their comrades and raised their small shields to meet the weapons in flight. One threw down his shield, having managed to stop one of the flying spears, holding the board away from him to prevent the protruding blade from striking his body. The other was less fortunate, as a massive throw from Dubnus slammed its iron head through the shield and then, as if the layered wooden boards were no more substantial than smoke, cleaved deep into his face. He staggered backwards to fresh cheering from the crowd around them, and while the barbarians were still attempting to order themselves, Horatius bellowed a single word at his fellow centurions.

'*Phalanx!*'

They went forward to meet the Dacians quickly, their paces synchronising as Marcus and Dubnus fell in on either side of the legion man, their shields locking together as they accelerated to a run.

'*Hit them hard, before they can flank us!*'

Marcus picked a target as they closed with the milling

barbarians, drawing his second spear back as the three men smashed into the Dacians, then snapping it forward to strike at his opponent's face. The other man managed to deflect the blow over his head with his shield, but the centurions' charge had blasted through the Dacians' straggling line, and as his target staggered backwards Marcus struck again, leaping high into the air with practised grace and punching his shield's iron boss down into the reeling man's face. As he landed, he stabbed the spear's iron head into the stunned barbarian's neck, wrenching it free in a shower of the dying man's blood as the prisoner slumped to his knees.

The flicker of a shadow made the Roman flinch backward, turning his body to gain some protection from the shield and raising his spear to meet the new threat, but before he could bring the weapon to bear something hit the spear's shaft hard enough to almost tear it from his hand, the blade hammering at his shield an instant later. Looking down the weapon's length he realised with a shock that the blade was missing, cleaved away by the blow intended for his head, and he threw it at the man in front of him to make him duck away, springing back to get some space as he drew his own sword. A pair of tribesmen were advancing on him with murder in their eyes, while his friends were deep in their own fights. He hefted the unfamiliar shield momentarily, before shaking his head and throwing its unwieldy weight at them. Stepping back swiftly to the twitching corpse of one of their fellows, he scooped up the dying man's sword with his left hand and turned to face the pair as they battered the shield aside and came for him.

The man to his right was leading his comrade by a pace, having deflected the flying shield into his path, and the Roman met him blade to blade, allowing the Dacian's long sword to skate harmlessly out to his left while the barbarian shaped to smash his small shield into the Roman's face. As he punched the shield forward, Marcus pivoted backwards on his right foot and leaned back to allow the blow to spend itself on empty air, as he wristed the sword in his right hand high into the air above his shoulder. Hacking it down at the hapless Dacian's extended shield arm, he severed the limb cleanly below the elbow, tearing a bloodthirsty roar from the crowd.

The maimed tribesman staggered backwards, dropping his sword and cupping the brutal wound with his right hand in a futile attempt to stop the blood that was pouring from the stump. His comrade quailed at the look on Marcus's face as the Roman pushed the helpless man aside, tearing his throat out with a swift thrust and twist of his left-hand sword without ever taking his narrowed eyes off the surviving Dacian. Stalking forward, Marcus barely broke his stride as the prisoner charged forward with an incoherent scream, smashing away the Dacian's sword and hacking a lump out of the rim of the terrified man's shield, sending him backwards with blood leaking from a cut down the front of his rough prisoner's tunic where the sword's point had torn his flesh as it ripped through the layered wood of his tattered shield.

Their eyes met again in that instant before Marcus struck again, the Dacian's gaze suddenly calm as if he knew for a certainty that he was facing his death. The Roman's long sword swept out again, cleaving the shield almost in two, while the prisoner's attempt to counter-attack was child's play to parry. He stepped back and raised the shield's boss and the remnant of board clinging to it with a look of terrified resignation, his sword's blade barely level with the ground, and Marcus knew his opponent would not survive another attack.

His anger abruptly burned out, he reached out with his left-hand sword and tapped hard at the prisoner's weapon, jerking his own blade to one side to indicate that the other man should discard it. For a moment the Dacian was confused, but then a look of understanding crept onto his face, his eyebrows rising in puzzlement as he looked back at Marcus. Before he could comply with the Roman's silent instruction, the hapless prisoner staggered forward a pace, his face contorting in agony as Horatius dropped him to the ground with the blade of his spear buried in the prisoner's lower back. He stared at the Roman for a moment before speaking, his words almost inaudible over the crowd's roar.

'Hasn't anyone told you it's not right to play with a man you're about to kill?'

Marcus looked back at him with an expression of mystification, but before he could reply the crowd's tumult coalesced into a one-word chant that had them staring at each other in surprise.

'*Corvus! Corvus! Corvus!*'

Horatius raised an eyebrow, looking up at the mob of humanity bellowing out Marcus's name.

'I was wrong, it seems. Apparently playing with the man you're about to kill is exactly what these bastards want from us.'

The three centurions turned as they were hailed by the referee, who was careful to stay outside the reach of their weapons.

'*Sheathe your swords and drop your spears!*'

They did as they were bidden, arena slaves hurrying past them with buckets of white sand and scattering it across the blood that had been spilled during the fight. Other men were dragging the dead Dacians away towards the Gate of Death, each of the corpses receiving a shattering blow to the head from Charun's hammer before they were carried away towards the tunnel that led to the spolarium. Relaxing a little, the man in white stepped closer, pointing with his hand to direct their steps.

'Now go and make your bow to the imperial box. And don't be fooled by the archers. They may look bored, but they'll turn you into pin cushions if you give them the slightest excuse.' He pointed up to the spot where Commodus stood, having risen from his seat to applaud when the last of the barbarians had fallen to Horatius's spear thrust. 'Bow nice and deep and wait for him to signal for you to leave, then walk to the Gate of Life. You'll be disarmed by the guards and then someone from your school will take you back there. Move.'

Obeying the commanding note in his voice, the three men walked across the sand until they were close enough to the imperial box to make their bows, seeing the threat implicit in the archers who were staring at them from openings in the arena wall below the box with arrows nocked to their half-drawn bows. Bowing deeply, they waited until Commodus raised a hand in recognition, turning to speak to the man at his side who Marcus instantly recognised as his chamberlain Cleander, before raising their heads. The chamberlain looked down with a knowing smile, and Marcus knew immediately that the man who guided the emperor's every decision had without any shadow of doubt identified him despite the heavy iron helmet's partial disguise.

Turning away as bidden, they marched in step towards the Gate of Life, allowing themselves to be disarmed by the arena guards who, clearly used to men still seething with the potent emotions stirred by combat and bloodshed, kept their spears to hand as they accepted the three men's bloodied swords and battered shields.

'Well then, it seems that I had no need to worry on your behalf.'

Velox was waiting for them beyond the guards' cordon. He gestured to the man in charge of the gate.

'I'll take them from here, if your men can just see us through to the tunnel.'

They waited while a party of guards was mustered to get them from the gate to the tunnel's mouth, and, looking out through the tall, arched opening, Marcus realised that it was going to take more than the half-dozen who had seen them across the gap between amphitheatre and tunnel an hour before. Where there had been no more than twenty fans waiting in the open space previously, there were now more than two hundred, all chanting the same chorus that had greeted the fall of the last prisoner.

'*Corvus! Corvus! Corvus!*'

The champion gladiator shook his head at Marcus.

'They're strange creatures, the sheep that flock to watch us wolves tear at each other. They'll pick a man that takes their fancy and turn him into the next best thing to a god. And you Corvus, well you've taken their fancy in a big way. They think you were toying with those poor bloody Dacians, when you maimed and then killed one of them, and held the other at sword point so that he could take a spear in the back. They think you're the next big thing, a man blessed with all the skill and brutality needed to become a hero of the arena. And perhaps you are, except . . .'

He looked at the three men for a moment, then pointed at Horatius.

'You, you were born for this. You're quick, ruthless, skilful . . . I can see a great future for you, my friend. And you . . .' He looked at Dubnus with a smile. 'What you lack in sophistication you make up for in brute force, and the will to apply it without hesitation.'

He turned back to Marcus with a quizzical expression.

'But you? You're something else, Corvus. Fast, blindingly fast, and as good with two swords as my brother, if not quite up to my standard, and yet . . .' He shook his head. 'You're just not a killer, are you?'

Marcus looked back at him without answering, and Dubnus guffawed quietly.

'Not a killer? Our boy here's killed more men in the last three years than you'll ever fight.'

The gladiator shook his head, holding Marcus's stare.

'Not the type of killer that makes for a top-class fighter. You can kill alright, but you can't do it in cold blood, can you? You have to be angry, or threatened, and if you're not then the fire that drives you dies out like that.'

He clicked his fingers, raising an eyebrow to elicit some response from the Roman.

'I saw you with that last Dacian, I was watching your face while you were fighting, and right up until you killed the poor bastard whose arm you'd hacked off, you were terrifying, relentless. Even I'd have been nervous if I'd been facing you. But when the last man pissed himself, you stopped fighting, just like that.'

He pursed his lips and stared at Marcus for a moment.

'And here's the thing. Right now, Julianus is up there on the senatorial balcony with the other procurators slapping him on the shoulder and telling him what a find you three are. He'll be misty-eyed at the thought of a couple of dozen fights from you, with all the opportunities to make a profit every time you set foot on the sand. I just hope that *you* can deliver on that promise.'

'Well then, what a show!'

Cleander had crossed the imperial box again, breezing past the guards to plant himself firmly in the middle of the small crowd congratulating Julianus on his men's seemingly effortless victory.

The pleasure of watching his colleague Novius's face as the tiros had ripped through their hapless opponents was wiped away in an instant by a sinking feeling as the imperial chamberlain inclined his head in a deep bow of respect, his mouth twisted in a half-smile.

'Quite stunning, Julianus, even by the redoubtable standards your school has set down the years. And the breathtaking cruelty displayed by that man Corvus! The emperor is more than impressed, and you know that's not something that happens every day, given his titanic prowess with any weapon you care to name.' He leaned close to Julianus, raising a hand to whisper confidentially in his ear. 'He's asked me to convey my congratulations on a superb performance, and to assure you that it hasn't gone unnoticed.'

Julianus allowed his breath to hiss slowly and almost inaudibly from between his teeth, the tension slowly ebbing from his body as he realised that Cleander was doing no more than passing on the thanks of a delighted patron. But as he tilted his head ready to bow in return, the chamberlain spoke again, his voice edged with the iron that he'd been expecting.

'He also asked me to make a *request* of you.' The emphasis was accompanied by a twist of the other man's lips and a raising of his eyebrows that left the procurator in no doubt as to the binding nature of the request. 'Caesar was so impressed by these three men, and by Corvus in particular, that he instructed me to request a small favour of you, a chance to see them at work from a slightly closer perspective . . .' He paused for a moment, and Julianus realised with a further slump what was coming. 'A private bout, Procurator, a blood match in the privacy of your school premises. This man Corvus matched against one of your best men to provide Caesar with a more adequate display of the man's talents.'

Julianus nodded slowly.

'A blood match? I have just the man, Hermes, a fast and lethal fighter from—'

'Mortiferum.'

The procurator frowned.

'I—'

Cleander shook his head, his lips wreathed in a sardonic smile.

'Caesar was most specific. He wishes to see this new boy's skills tested against your deadliest fighter, and his instruction was for the match to be fought with your best. With Mortiferum.'

Julianus spread his hands.

'Not that I have any place arguing with my Caesar . . .'

Cleander smiled again, but this time the expression was thinly stretched.

'How very wise of you, Procurator.'

'But surely Velox must be my deadliest man?'

The chamberlain shrugged.

'Not in the emperor's view. So, Corvus and Mortiferum, tomorrow evening.'

'Tomorrow? Mortiferum fights a pair of fish men the day after!'

Cleander shook his head dismissively.

'Not any more he doesn't. That bout's been rescheduled for next week, plenty of time for him to get over his exertions. It's amazing how quickly these things can be resolved when an emperor's wishes are involved, isn't it?'

Recognising defeat, Julianus bowed again.

'In which case I will be delighted to host Caesar in the Dacian School tomorrow evening. Please convey my delight and gratitude at having my fighters selected for such an honour.'

Scaurus stepped forwards, nodding his respect to the chamberlain.

'With your permission, Aurelius Cleander, I'd very much like to see that fight. Might I beg the emperor's indulgence and be allowed to attend?'

The chamberlain's mouth twitched into a smile.

'It seems that you will persist in this habit of putting yourself at risk by interposing yourself into situations where you really have no business. You got away with it the last time by the skin of your teeth, didn't you?' He raised an eyebrow at Scaurus, who acknowledged the point with a nod. 'Indeed. How many men can say that he's had an emperor's knifepoint under his chin and escaped without a mark? It's something of an exclusive club, I can assure you.' He smirked, his expression taking on a knowing look. 'Are you sure you want to take the same risk twice?'

'To see my centurion fight a renowned champion gladiator? Of course . . .'

Cleander shrugged.

'Very well, Tribune. After all, it is, as they say, your funeral . . .'

He turned away with the ghost of a smile playing on his lips, and Scaurus turned to his first spear with a slow exhalation.

'Every time I deal with that man I have the feeling that I'm teasing a poisonous snake with a very short stick. I think perhaps it's time to let Cotta do what he's been suggesting ever since your centurion decided to abandon his new life and go after Mortiferum.'

Julius nodded, watching the chamberlain as he walked through the guards and back into the imperial box.

'I'll go with him.'

Scaurus smiled.

'Curious, First Spear?'

Julius nodded with a snort of suppressed laughter.

'Curious? Too bloody right I am, Tribune. Aren't you?'

The slave girl Calistra came to Dubnus again that night, her visit lasting little longer than the first time. Again, having silenced the Briton, she worked his manhood into her, ground herself against his body until he lost the ability to hold himself back and then climbed off his body with a gentle smile.

'That two time. One more time and thank is done.'

Gripping her hand, he restrained her flight, pulling her close to him.

'My name is Dubnus. And I will free you Calistra. I promise.'

Her smile broadened, but her head shook emphatically.

'You never free me. I here all my life.'

He stared up into her eyes.

'I swear. I will free you. The next time you lie on top of me it won't be in this place, and you'll be free to choose whether to lie with me or seek another man. I have sworn this.'

10

The imperial chamberlain swept into the ludus's formal reception hall the next evening at the head of a small party of two praetorian guardsmen and a single slave, looking about him at the mural-decorated walls, the intricate mosaic floor and the statues depicting gladiators in fighting poses. Julianus stood in the hall's centre ready to greet his emperor, dressed and barbered to perfection, the other ludi's procurators and Scaurus waiting to one side.

'Greetings Chamberlain!'

Cleander nodded regally to Julianus's colleagues, then smiled wryly at Scaurus.

'I see you've persisted with your urge to watch your man Corvus in action, Tribune Scaurus. How fortunate that you'll be able to witness one of the most *interesting* gladiatorial contests in the city for many a year.' He looked about at the lavish decor. 'Very nice, Julianus. Very nice indeed. You clearly believe in providing your more aristocratic clients with the feel of quality?'

Julianus nodded, gesturing at the walls with an air of self-deprecation.

'We operate a spartan enough school, staying as close to the traditions of the founders as we can, but we do always try to make our private clients feel at home when they come here. We hope that a little luxury will differentiate our offering from that which they might experience elsewhere, and encourage them to favour us with their presence on future occasions. I presume that you've come in advance of the emperor?'

Cleander shook his head, waving a dismissive hand at the question.

'Regrettably, Tettius Julianus, Caesar won't be joining us this evening.'

'There's probably nothing that I can tell you about my brother that will be of very much use to you. He's been fighting in the arena for just as long as I have, he's every bit as good as me, and even with your obvious talents we both know that you're not going to stand a chance of beating him. After all, you only really fight when your temper's lit, don't you?'

Marcus nodded, keeping his eyes averted as Velox paced across the room towards him with a knowing look to Dubnus and Horatius, who were leaning against the far wall watching the impromptu training session.

'No, you'll be fighting to minimise the damage he could do to you if you manage to get his back up. Fight defensively, make sure you always have a space to retreat into, and at some point be prepared to take your three cuts and end the fight. Not too quickly, mind you, or Commodus might just order the pair of you to keep going until he's satisfied that you've given your best. Show me your blades . . .'

He examined the swords, shaking his head in disgust.

'You're fighting the Death Bringer, and Sannitus arms you with this rubbish? Fetch my swords!'

One of the junior gladiators ran for the weapons, and while the four men waited, Velox raised the blades he'd taken from Marcus before him, their points inches from the Roman's face.

'Now watch carefully. My little brother may be as fast as a striking snake, but he has his habits just like the rest of us, and there are a couple of them that you'll need to watch out for. Firstly, there's this . . .'

He wristed the right-hand blade in a flashing arc, stopping its swing just at the point where it was poised for a chopping blow at Marcus's head.

'He threatens your head, you respond with a sword raised to catch the blow and he lunges in . . .' He pushed the other sword forward with a swift stamp of his leading foot. 'And before you know what he's doing, he's sliced your forearm open or, if he's in a really bad mood, he's cut a chunk out of your armpit and your life's running down your arm.'

Velox stepped backwards, resuming his previous position.

'And here's another little trick he's particularly fond of.'

He danced back, his eyes taunting Marcus and drawing the Roman forward, as if they were fighting for real, and as his opponent approached, he took another step back. As Marcus raised his foot to step forward again, the other man sprang off his back foot, his blades suddenly in the Roman's face in a move so fast that Marcus didn't know if he could have countered it even if he'd had swords of his own.

'Be ready for that one too. He uses it in most of his fights with men who don't know his style. Ah, here are *my* swords . . .'

The champion gladiator took his weapons, drawing both blades and discarding their elaborately decorated scabbards. He handed them over and then stepped back, making space for the Roman to swing them. Marcus ran through a swift series of practice cuts and lunges, nodding at the weapons' excellent balance. Looking closely at the blades, he raised an eyebrow at the gladiator, his eyes hard with concentration.

'These are . . .'

Velox grinned.

'I think the word you're looking for is *incomparable*. And you'd be right. They're a pound lighter apiece than the usual weapons we're issued with, and they're edged with some special iron that stays sharp longer in a fight. They're my arena swords, saved for occasions when I need to put on a bit of a show, but perhaps they'll help to even up the advantage my brother will have over you.'

Edius appeared in the training room's doorway and beckoned to Marcus.

'Time to fight.'

In the ludus's arena, Cleander was putting on a show of apology for Julianus and his guests, but if his words were those of a contrite man, neither his tone nor his expression were doing very much to support them.

'My apologies, Julianus. What can I say? When I left him the emperor was somewhat . . . *preoccupied*, shall we say? I felt it best not to interrupt the important matters that were demanding of his full attention.'

Julianus nodded, knowing all too well the sort of 'matters' that the chamberlain was describing, but any distaste he might have been feeling was submerged in a deep-seated sense of relief so profound that it was all he could do not to sigh.

'I completely understand, Chamberlain. And, under the circumstances, I'm sure the emperor will be happy to save his money, given that he's not here to see the—'

Cleander shook his head briskly, with a smile that made it all too clear how well he understood Julianus's short-lived relief.

'Far from it, Procurator. Far from it! Knowing that I am possessed of an excellent recollective skill, Caesar simply implored me to bring him back the most precise account of the fight possible. I shall therefore take a seat here . . .' Cleander pointed to the ornately gilded wooden seat that had been positioned ready for the ludus's exalted guest. 'And attempt to do such a titanic bout some small degree of honour with my description.'

Julianus's mouth opened in consternation.

'We're to continue *without* the emperor?'

Cleander's response was delivered in a cheery tone, but there was no mistaking the command implicit in his words.

'Indeed we are, Procurator! After all, the price for the bout has been set and paid, and the fees that will be owing in the event of either the serious wounding or indeed the death of either participant are equally clear and, I should add, ready to pay out.'

He glanced behind him at the shaven-headed slave, still flanked by a pair of praetorians, at whose belt a good-sized pouch bulged with coin.

'Dacian gold, Procurator, freshly minted. And after all, Julianus, who are either of us to risk the wrath of our emperor by disregarding his instructions? Bring on the contestants, and let us see what it was that Caesar had in mind when he commanded this match, shall we?'

Marcus was led into the arena first, looking around the surprisingly small fighting space with an expression of wary appraisal. Finding Scaurus in the group of imperial officials, he nodded his recognition, then stared back at the gladiators who were standing behind the ludus's guests. Hermes was one of the men favoured with the opportunity to watch the bout, and he grinned at Marcus without any trace of humour in the expression.

'Not quite what you were expecting, eh Centurion?'

He turned to the small group of men gathered at the opposite end of the room, recognising the chamberlain's urbane tones. Walking towards them, he stopped ten paces short and bowed as he had been instructed by Edius, digging his toes into the sand.

'It's not as grand as some other places I've fought, Chamberlain, that's true, but it makes a pleasant change to have clean sand underfoot rather than what I'm rather more accustomed to.'

'And what would that be?'

He smiled bleakly.

'Mud that's been stamped into foam so deep that a man who falls wounded is likely to drown before he bleeds to death, stinking with the blood, piss and shit of the men who are fighting and dying around me. This is a holiday, by comparison.'

A door in the arena's wall opened, and Mortiferum stepped out onto the sand, walking easily across the fighting surface until he was standing half a dozen paces from where Marcus stood waiting for him. A mirror image of his brother in both height and musculature, his hair had been greased back to give him a sleek, deadly appearance. Sannitus stepped forward with a forbidding look, his usual rough tunic replaced by the white garb of a referee and the customary long stick held in one big hand.

'Gladiators, this bout has been commanded to be a blood match, with the first man to cut his opponent and draw blood three times being named as the winner. The prize is one thousand sestertii, ten gold aurei donated by the emperor himself. When a cut is inflicted you will step apart and allow me the time to make an examination of the wound. If I deem the wound to be too serious for the fight to continue then I will declare the wounded man to be the loser, and the fight will be over. However, in the event of such a serious wound being inflicted, the winner's prize will be retained by the ludus, as his punishment for damaging valuable property. This is to be a display of gladiatorial skill, not a fight to the death. Do you both understand?'

Both men nodded, and the lanista turned to look to his master.

'If you and our guests are ready, Procurator?'

Julianus nodded tersely, still preoccupied with the potential for needless injury to either man.

'Continue!'

Sannitus stepped backwards, smartly waving his hands for the gladiators to close on each other.

'*Fight!*'

The two men eyed each other over the blades of their levelled swords, Mortiferum raising an amused eyebrow as he slid his feet across the sand, crabbing round to his right and eliciting a matching response from Marcus.

'So, *Corvus*, how does it feel to be blade to blade with the most famous gladiator in Rome? How long do you think you can stand against me?'

Marcus stared back, his face expressionless as he matched the other man step for step, the two of them slowly circling, watching each other with eyes narrowed in concentration.

'I thought your brother was the most famous gladiator in Rome?'

The champion opened his mouth as if to speak but leapt forward instead, wristing his right-hand weapon in a savage arc aimed at his opponent's head, just as his brother had predicted. Rather than lifting his own blade to parry, Marcus spun to his right, slicing his right-hand sword at the other man's thigh, forcing Mortiferum to hop neatly backwards with a delighted laugh.

'Nicely done! Perhaps this won't be quite as boring as I'd exp—'

Something in his complacent smile triggered a response in Marcus, a sudden kick in the pit of his stomach, and he found himself going forward with a growl of anger, meeting his opponent's waiting blades and driving him backwards in a flurry of cuts and parries. Staring into the other man's eyes, his swords seeming to move of their own volition as he hammered at the retreating gladiator's defences, he saw the first hint of concern in the other man's face. And then, as if his opponent had simply decided enough was enough, he glared at Marcus and stopped retreating, fighting back with a speed and skill the Roman had rarely experienced.

Cleander clenched his fist as the fight's tempo escalated, banging a palm on his chair's arm in approval.

'Now we can see what these men are made of! *This* is a fight!'

As they watched, Mortiferum parried a flurry of blows and then, in the brief moment when Marcus's defence was opened by his ferocious attack, sprang forward in a straining lunge and jabbed the very tip of one of his blades into his opponent's leg just below the knee. The gladiators lining the walls cheered loudly at the first blood, and Sannitus stepped forward, bellowing a command at the two men.

'*Stop fighting!*'

At the ludus's main door a heavy fist banged twice on the woodwork, jolting the slave on duty out of his comfortable reverie. He slid open the thin vision slit carved into the thick beams, speaking though it without even bothering to see who it was that had disturbed his doze.

'Fuck off and bother someone else. The ludus is closed to the likes of you for the night.'

'Really, Piro? Closed to the likes of *me*?'

The doorman started, half recognising the voice from a memory that he hadn't revisited for years. It was deep and commanding, filled with an arrogant disregard for anyone else, the voice of a man who had faced death a hundred times and walked away unharmed.

'It's *not* . . .'

'It is.'

'*Fuck* me . . .'

'Not while there are dogs on the street. Now open this door and let me in, unless you're keen to see the colour of your own liver before you go to the underworld.'

Sannitus stepped in between the fighters, prodding at Mortiferum with his long stick to push him out of sword reach before bending to examine the wound. A slow seeping runnel of blood was oozing down Marcus's leg, and the lanista nodded with a look that spoke volumes as to his desire to get the fight finished before one of them badly hurt the other.

'*Blood! One to Mortiferum!*'

He stepped back, waving the two men together.

'*Fight!*'

'*Go on Death Bringer, put the tyro in his place!*'

The veteran gladiator nodded at Hermes's shout and stormed into the fight, his face set in determination at the realisation that nothing other than the best of his skills and commitment would be enough to defeat this new and unexpectedly effective opponent. Their swords flickered and clashed with such speed that the watching audience could scarcely follow the fight's progress, but it seemed to Velox's trained eye that while his brother was attacking with all of his ability, Marcus had retreated back into himself again, and was fighting on the defensive without any sign of the necessary impetus to go forward and take down his enemy.

The ferocious duel continued, the two men entirely focused on each other's faces as Mortiferum constantly probed for an opening, Marcus comfortably parrying his blows without any sign of taking the fight back to him. Procurator Novius pulled a disparaging expression, shaking his head slightly.

'Your man Corvus seems to have rather lost interest since taking that cut. I must profess myself a little disappointed. I thought your new boy had a little more in him . . .'

'Oh, I'm not so sure . . .' They looked around at the seated Cleander, his eyes still intent on the fight. 'This looks more like strategy than tactics to me.'

He waved away their bafflement, watching as Marcus allowed himself to be manoeuvred around the small arena. At length Mortiferum managed to lever an opening in the Roman's defence, more by brute force than any subtlety with his blades, whipping a blade in under Marcus's defence to prick a skilful cut into the top of his thigh to the renewed cheers of the gladiators lining the walls.

'*Stop fighting!*'

'Well now, Edius.'

The assistant lanista whipped round, his eyes narrowed at the sound of his challenger's voice. He stepped closer to the newcomer, screwing up his eyes and staring hard at him in the corridor's gloom. The ludus slave standing behind him put a startled hand to the hilt of his sword, then froze at the look of wolfish anticipation on the stranger's hard, scarred face as he wagged a forbidding finger.

'If you air that iron, one of us will die before your next breath is expelled. Do you choose to die, here and now?'

The terrified man eased his hand away from the weapon's hilt, swallowing audibly.

'Wise. And you, Edius? Do you and I have to fight?'

The lanista shook his head, raising his empty hands before him.

'I'm no more of a fool than I was the last time we met.'

The big man nodded, putting out a hand.

'I'll be needing weapons, Edius. I'll make a start with your man here's blade, and I'm sure you can find me another quickly enough, eh?'

The lanista turned, taking the sword from the guard's scabbard and pointing down the corridor.

'Fetch him another. Quickly. And tell no one else.' He turned back to the big man. 'I'll not get in your way. But why come back now?'

The newcomer's answer was accompanied by a shake of the big man's head.

'I've been asking myself the same question.'

Sannitus put himself between the two men for a second time, examining the puncture with swift professionalism.

'*Blood! Two to Mortiferum!*' He looked at Marcus, perturbed at the unconcerned look on the Roman's face. 'Nearly there. Just behave yourself and take the third cut and we'll have this done.'

He stepped back from them.

'*Fight!*'

Mortiferum, smugly secure in the certainty of his impending victory, frowned as Marcus held his hands up to raise his swords until they were level with his face, forcing the other man to look him in the eye. The gladiator shook his head in bemusement, his lips twisting in the grin of a man who knew he already had the fight in the bag.

'You're good, Corvus. Very good. You're the only man I've ever met, other than my brother, who can watch his opponent's eyes and leave his swords to their own devices. But you're not quite good enough to stop me, are you? No one's ever come back against me in a blood match once the first hit was called, never mind two. So be a good boy and—'

Marcus cut him off, his voice hard with hatred and disgust.

'Do you recognise these? You *should.*'

Mortiferum shook his head.

'Why should I recognise some pair of swords I've never seen before?'

'Because they used to be the property of one of the first families you and your fellow murderers destroyed in the name of *imperial justice*. And now here they are, hungry for your blood.'

Sannitus stalked up to the two men with a look of anger clouding his face.

'Get on with the fight, or I'll—'

Marcus's voice was suddenly as cold as stone, as he overrode the lanista's warning without turning his gaze from his opponent.

'Get off the sand, Sannitus, or *I'll* cut you down alongside this piece of shit.'

Julianus took one look at the Roman's face and took a pace backwards with an eye on the door. He stopped abruptly as it opened in his face and a massive figure squeezed through the gap with a sword held in each hand.

'Nobody leaves. Not until this fight is done.'

Cleander looked over at him with a beatific smile that made Julianus's blood run cold.

'Ah, *there* you are! There's a sight to make a man proud to be a citizen of this great city. Greetings, champion, and welcome to the emperor's blood match! You're just in time, it seems . . .'

The big man nodded to him and then turned his attention to the sand.

'Sannitus.'

The lanista was still staring at him, as if unable to believe the evidence of his eyes as his erstwhile nemesis walked forward, brushing past the gathered procurators as if they weren't there.

'*Flamma* . . . Of all the men I never expected to see in this ludus again.'

The big man shrugged.

'Sometimes a man can't ignore the things that need to be done. Even if I've managed to turn a blind eye for the last few years.'

He turned his attention to the two men crouched in their fighting stances.

'Well then young Marcus, how much longer are you going to play with this fool? Didn't I always tell you to get the job done as soon as you found your opening?'

Mortiferum shook his head, his eyebrows raised in disbelief.

'Fuck you old man, whoever it is you think you are! This blood match is over! I'm going to carve this upstart into—'

He staggered backwards as Marcus launched himself bodily into a ferocious attack, frantically defending himself as the Roman remorselessly drove him back with a strength born of the fury that was pulsing through him. The rage that had festered inside him during the years of his exile was abruptly, terrifyingly free, unthinking, unquestioning, raving for the blood of the man who had slaughtered his family.

'My sisters were raped and murdered, and left for the crows on a rubbish dump!'

He smashed through Mortiferum's reeling defence, but rather than use his blades on the man he pivoted with the speed of a striking snake, hammering the point of his elbow into the gladiator's face and punching him backwards.

'My mother bled to death at the hands of men who called my father their *friend* until you did their dirty work for them!'

Mortiferum rallied, but his wits had been shaken by the blow, and Marcus's swords were momentarily too fast for him to counter. He chopped at the gladiator's sword hand, and Julianus shrieked in horror as three of his champion gladiator's fingers dropped to the sand. Velox started forward, only to find himself looking down the blade of one of Flamma's swords, the big man's attention fixed on the fight but the sword's point unwaveringly aimed at his throat.

'One more step . . .' He raked his gaze across the men lining the back wall, his face twisted in contempt. 'Any of you who want to die here, try me!'

Frozen in place by the threat, the champion gladiator watched in horror as his brother, unable to hold the sword in his ruined hand, attempted to hurl it at his tormentor. The blade merely tumbled uselessly to the ground, and Marcus pushed it aside with his foot as he advanced upon his stricken enemy.

'My brother was sold into slavery!'

He battered aside the remaining blade with one sword, then stabbed the other down into his opponent's thigh, his long blade skewering through the muscles as it pierced the limb to protrude from between his hamstrings, a thin trickle of blood running from the point onto the sand. Mortiferum stared into Marcus's face in hollow-eyed disbelief, and the Roman leaned in close, whispering in his ear as he twisted the blade, dragging a groan of agony from the gladiator.

'My father was tortured until he confessed to a treason he had never committed. But he never gave up the secret of where he'd sent me, to escape you and your fellow scum.'

Pulling the sword from Mortiferum's leg, he kicked the staggering gladiator's feet from under him, whipping down the other blade to pin him to the ground and dimpling his bare chest with the weapon's point.

'And my name is not *Corvus!* My name is *Marcus!*'

He leaned on the blade, sinking the first inch of metal into his helpless opponent's chest. Mortiferum stiffened, fighting the iron's cold intrusion.

'*Valerius!*'

Slowly, surely, Marcus pushed the sword's blade deeper until it pierced his opponent's heart, shouting the last word the doomed gladiator would ever hear.

'*AQUILA!*'

The gladiator stiffened, his eyes rolling back as he lost consciousness, his back arching as Marcus thrust the sword through his body. He stared down at the dead man's corpse for a moment before turning back to face the men staring at him, dropping the other sword.

'My vengeance is complete.'

'No. It *isn't* . . .'

Velox stepped forward, glaring at Flamma as if daring him to use the swords that were still pointing at him. His voice was thick with hatred, his stare loaded with menace as Marcus turned to face him.

'You've killed the wrong man, *Marcus Valerius Aquila.*'

Marcus shook his head.

'Mortiferum was the last of the Emperor's Knives, the men who destroyed my family. I have taken vengeance . . .'

Velox shook his head, his face contorted by a savage, distraught rictus of a grin.

'Yes. You have your revenge. On the *brother* of the man who carried out the deeds you just described.'

Cleander stood, his voice matter of fact as he looked across the sand at Mortiferum's blood-spattered corpse.

'It's true. I had the records of the whole matter of your family's liquidation retrieved from Perennis's private files, after your revelation with that stolen gold led the emperor to put the butt spike of a spear through the praetorian prefect's guts, and ordered his sons to be murdered before they could mobilise their legions. It seems that on the night in question, Mortiferum was somewhat preoccupied with a more than usually shapely boy. He persuaded his brother here to take his place, and, it has to be said, the stand-in seems to have performed his duties with commendable vigour.'

He waved a finger, and the praetorians waiting behind him stepped forward, levelling their spears at Marcus and Flamma.

'And now, I suppose you might be tempted to do something heroic, given that your revenge has been a little flawed in its execution, but I'd advise against it. I'm happy enough to pay Julianus here the blood price for Mortiferum, but his brother was never part of my plans . . .' He smiled at the expression on Marcus's face, as the realisation of exactly what it was that he was saying sank in. 'When the Knives started dying, *apparently* for no reason other than either their own stupidity or weariness with the life that they had chosen, I thought it sensible to undertake a little recruitment of my own. These men may wear the praetorian uniform, but they're mine, bought and paid for. And who knows, with the demise of the last of the originals, I may find it necessary to make use of them to fill the gap that's been left by their loss. The only question now is what to do with you, now that your usefulness to me seems to have run to a natural conclusion?'

Velox stepped forward, growling out a response to the question.

'I treated this man as an arena brother, and he has repaid me with the death of all that was left of my family! Give him to me. I'll rip out his spine and hang it from the ludus gates!' He looked at Flamma with disdain. 'Think you can get in my way, old man? One word from me and you'll be arse-deep in gladiators, all of whom will be vying to be the man who kills you.'

Cleander pulled a thoughtful face.

'It would make for a nice tidy end to this whole thing . . .'

Flamma shook his head and leaned closer to the chamberlain.

'I'll tell you what would be even neater. Imagine a fight between this *boy* and myself, eh? The reigning champion against a man who retired unbeaten as the darling of the crowd? Imagine being able to tell your gladiator-obsessed emperor that you've procured Flamma the Great for one last fight.' He winked conspiratorially at Julianus. 'And to sweeten the cake, what if I guarantee to take the fall? There'll be a lot of money washing around for a fight like that, and there'll be a lot of it on me, retired or not. I'll even stay here in the ludus until the fight if you like, so that you'll have no fear of me backing out. What do you say?'

'*No!*'

He turned and looked at Marcus, who was staring at him with a look of desolation, then back at Cleander.

'Do we have a deal?'

The chamberlain nodded, his eyes alive with the profit to be had from the veteran gladiator's offer of self-sacrifice. Flamma bowed.

'Very well. And now if you'll excuse me for a moment, Chamberlain, I think I can make the lad see sense. It would be better if he were to leave here quietly, I presume?'

He walked slowly across the sand to where the younger man stood shaking his head.

'There's no other way, you can see that?' Marcus opened his mouth to retort, but Flamma shook his head with a sad smile. 'There's that look I never thought I'd see again. Every time I used to put you on your arse as a twelve-year-old you'd give me that same stare, as if you were working out how to fuck me up, given half a chance. And look at you now . . .' He smiled apologetically at Marcus. 'I owe you this, Marcus, you, and your family. I should have done something when they were taken, but to my shame I kept my head down. This way I can get you out of here and find some peace for my conscience. And trust me, that little shit Velox won't be walking out of the arena unscarred.'

Marcus shook his head in bafflement.

'But if you think you can beat him, why offer to let him kill you?'

The big man smiled, putting a hand on his former pupil's shoulder and leaning in close. He spoke into his dejected friend's ear for a moment or so, until Marcus nodded slowly with a look of resignation on his face. Flamma turned back to Cleander with his hands spread wide.

'See, I told you I could persuade him. He leaves, with his brothers in arms, and I stay, to fight just as soon as you like. Tomorrow might be best, to give the gamblers the least amount of time to brood on this unexpected match.'

'Eager to die, are you old man?'

Flamma smiled into the face of Velox's obduracy.

'Eager to put your skills to the test, more like. You're a dancer, boy, I've seen you fight, and all you do is jump around and wave your swords about like the womanising lightweight you so clearly are. I come from a different school. And I will educate you, before I die, I promise you that.'

Marcus stalked up to Velox, his body stiff with unresolved rage.

'You crave revenge for your brother. I *will* have revenge for my family. We will meet again . . .'

The gladiator nodded tersely.

'And when *you* least expect it.' He tossed a trinket onto the floor between them, a panther's tooth on a fine gold chain, pointing to an identical pendant around his own neck. 'I had that made to offer as some form of consolation for your defeat this evening. Take it, and wear it for the rest of your life, Aquila, to match the one round my neck. Every time you touch it remember that I'll be hunting you down. You're marked for death at my hands.'

Marcus knelt, picking up the pendant.

'I'll wear it. Feel free to come and test your desire for revenge against mine, *if* you can get past Flamma.'

Cleander spoke before the gladiator could make any further retort.

'And if we're done with these slightly tiresome demonstrations of undying enmity, I think it's time for the emperor to have an opinion on the matter of this proposed death match. I would ask Procurator Julianus what he thinks, but he is after all an employee of the state, and I can assure you that the state very much likes the sound of what's on offer. Your proposal is accepted Flamma, and you'll be accommodated in the imperial palace until the time comes for the fight. I'd imagine that Commodus will be keen to meet you in the morning, given his penchant for your trade. Which means it's time for us all to be on our way.'

Dubnus and Horatius stepped out of the shadows, and Marcus realised that his fellow Tungrian was wearing a look verging on distress. He turned to the procurator, putting a hint of iron into his voice.

'Julianus!'

The procurator turned to him, clearly affronted at being

addressed in so pre-emptory a manner by a man he had considered to be his property until a moment before.

'Corv—.' He corrected himself. '*Aquila*. What more do you want from me, having murdered my champion?'

'There is a woman, a slave girl, called Calistra, who has formed an association with my brother here. He will not leave her behind to face a life of abuse at the hands of your men.'

Flamma nodded.

'Call her a down payment on my cooperation if you like.'

Julianus looked at Sannitus, who shrugged, his bafflement with the turn of events evident from his nonplussed expression.

'She's no loss.'

The procurator shook his head, then closed his eyes and waved a hand in apparent surrender.

'Fetch the woman.'

An awkward silence fell on the group, and Horatius walked across the sand to where Marcus had dropped one of his swords. Stooping, he picked the weapon up and stood for a moment looking down at the dead gladiator before turning away with an unreadable expression. As he walked back across the arena Dubnus caught his eye momentarily, frowning at the unexpected look of hatred his comrade shot at him. Opening his mouth to say something, he realised that his friend's stare was focused on the back of Marcus's neck as the sword's blade slowly rose from its place at his side. Before he could react Horatius was upon his erstwhile brother in arms, wrapping his arm around Marcus's face as he put the sword's point under his chin, the weapon's shining iron length laid against the Roman's chest, ready to thrust up into his jaw.

'*What . . . ?*' Flamma reacted first, raising his own sword to strike at the former centurion, but Horatius swivelled, pulling his helpless victim with him. 'I'll have your liver out for this!'

Marcus's captor sneered over his victim's shoulder, pushing the sword's point up into the Roman's throat until the skin around it was white.

'All in good time. First I have a score to settle with this bastard!'

A tiny movement to Dubnus's left caught his eye, an almost

imperceptible movement by the guardsman closest to him. He caught the man's eye, frowning as he realised that the soldier was smiling faintly as he edged away from his fellows. Flamma raised his sword, clearly calculating whether he could kill Marcus's captor without condemning his friend to death as well.

'What score would that be, Horatius?'

Horatius snarled at Cleander's question.

'I think you know, Chamberlain! It was you who ordered the murder of Legatus Perennis!'

The older man nodded.

'In point of fact, it was the emperor who ordered your commanding officer's execution, but yes, I gave the detailed orders. It comes as something of a disappointment to discover that you managed to make it all the way to Rome, despite my having ordered that you were to be hunted down and killed.'

Horatius laughed tersely.

'Your men were looking for a military officer, not a shit-encrusted farm worker. I stole a horse and took my chances, riding by night for the most part, and then when I was close enough to Rome I swapped it for a ride into the city with a farmer delivering his crop. Just another thick bastard brought along for his muscle, or at least that's what the men on duty at the gate saw.'

The praetorian to Dubnus's left took another slow, sliding step, his movement barely discernible, reversing his hold on the spear at his side from the underhanded carry to an awkward overhanded grip. Cleander shook his head, waving a hand at Marcus.

'And now you intend to murder this man, for no apparent reason?'

'I heard what you said! It was this man that condemned my legatus to death!'

Horatius bristled, scowling at the chamberlain and, with another slow, stealthy movement, the praetorian next to Dubnus slid his booted foot forward, easing his body back and tensing the muscles of his shoulder in readiness to throw the spear. The soldier tightened his grip on the helpless Marcus's throat, his scowl daring any of the men around him to make a move. Dubnus stepped forward, crossing his meaty arms.

'Before you kill my friend, know two things. Your legatus wasn't the first of Perennis's sons to die at our hands. His older brother was a fucking traitor too, he betrayed an entire legion in Britannia and we made him pay the price. I put an axe through his spine, and stamped on his head while I tore it free. I left him twitching and drooling blood, so I doubt his death was a quick one. And when you've killed my brother, I'm going to do the same to you, only this time I'll do the job with my bare fucking hands!'

In the instant that Horatius turned to snarl defiance at the big Briton, Cleander nodded smartly at the praetorian, and the soldier took one quick pace forward to hurl his spear at Horatius with nerveless accuracy. The weapon's long iron shaft penetrated the soldier's neck right up to the point where it flared to join with the thick wooden shaft, its impact snapping him away from Marcus with the abrupt force of a brutally delivered punch. Choking and spitting blood he sank to the floor, dragged down by the spear's weight and his grievous wound.

The Roman turned to see the agent of his delivery, as the praetorian stared at the dying man with a look of satisfaction, recognising his face immediately despite the helmet's disguise.

'Yes, it's the retarius who made such short work of Glaucus yesterday.' Cleander had stepped forward and was standing beside him, looking down at Horatius's twitching body. 'When I see the very highest skills on display I'm quick to recruit them to my service.'

He looked down at the dying man with a dispassionate expression.

'Irony stacked upon irony, it seems. Centurion Aquila looks for revenge on the last of the Knives only to discover that he's killed the wrong brother. And you, the only man left alive who gives a damn about the fate of the Perennis family, put your sword to a man who has suffered exactly the same loss and wasn't even the one who killed your sponsor the legatus. And as a consequence for that act of stupidity you end up with a spear through your neck and your existence receding down life's drain hole. It just goes to show that the thirst for revenge can lead a man to drink some bitter potions, doesn't it?'

I I

The next morning Morban and his barbers opened up soon after dawn, as usual, and if some of them looked a little bleary-eyed it had no effect on the usual swift-forming queue of men who had decided to take advantage of their continuing generosity. Morban strolled out to address them, shaking his head sadly.

'Sorry gentlemen, but we won't be cutting hair today as a mark of respect to Flamma the Great, who fights in the arena this afternoon!'

For a moment the men waiting in line assumed that he was joking, but when the burly soldier remained where he was, arms folded and clearly not for moving, an angry clamour broke out. Morban waited for a moment, then cleared his throat ostentatiously before shouting his next words at the top of his voice.

'*Shut the FUCK up!*' His would-be customers stared at him in amazement. 'That's better. Now I'll only say this one more time. We're. Not. Cutting. Hair. Today. Got it? Now you can either fuck off now quietly or I'll be forced to tell the lads inside to come out and deal with you. You choose.'

As if on cue, the window shutters were thrown open, and half a dozen irritated Tungrians looked out at the queue, several of them holding heavy wooden clubs. Realising that they weren't going to be getting a cheap haircut or a shave any time soon, the disgruntled customers dispersed, leaving Morban looking out into the street with a grin.

'Don't know what you've got to smile at.'

The standard bearer turned to find his neighbour the potter at his side, his expression rather less happy than the last time they'd spoken.

'Oh, I don't know. Everyone likes a day off work every now and then.'

The potter shook his head in bemusement.

'A day off work? You do realise that you'll have the Hilltop Boys up here within the hour, once the story gets round that you've told your customers to piss off?'

Morban's smile broadened.

'That's what I'm counting on. Perhaps you should probably close up your shop and go upstairs for an hour?'

The shopkeeper nodded, his expression telling Morban that had been his intention all along, and the standard bearer glanced along the line of shops to see that his neighbours had all come to the same conclusion, goods hastily withdrawn into their premises and shutters unceremoniously closed to provide the occupants with some semblance of security. Smiling to himself he turned and walked back into the shop.

'Right then, it's all gone quieter than a mute with her mouth full out there, so let's have the weaponry upstairs, shall we?'

He watched impassively as the soldiers lifted the floorboards that covered the stairs down into the cellar, each of them fetching a shield and sword. The last man up the stairs handed him a spear, watching impassively as the standard bearer strolled back out into the afternoon sunshine, propping the weapon up against the wall in the shade of a brick pillar where it was invisible to a cursory glance. A pair of Maximus's enforcers hurried round the corner, having clearly heard the rumour that the shop had failed to open for business.

'What the fuck's going on?'

Morban grinned broadly at the gang member addressing him.

'A day's holiday is what's happening, my old son. We just thought we'd—'

'Get back to fucking work, you fat bastard!' The gangster leaned close, putting a finger against Morban's chest. 'You've got taxes to pay, and if you don—'.

The standard bearer grinned up at him lopsidedly, shaking his head gently as he interrupted.

'Not really. We've decided not to pay any more protection since, to be honest with you, we don't really need it.'

The man looked at his mate with an amused smile, inviting him to join in the joke.

'That's fifteen per cent. Keep talking and I'll have to go and get One Eye.'

Morban shrugged.

'You clearly don't get it. We're not paying.'

The gangster's patience snapped, and he jabbed the finger into Morban's chest with an angry snarl.

'And you "clearly don't get it". We're the fucking Hilltop Boys. We take whatever we want, and right now what I want most is to stick your fucking head right up your fat arse, smart mouth. So give us the cash or I'll have to—'

He stopped talking abruptly, as a sliver of cold metal touched the area between his belly and his penis. His comrade was suddenly equally still, his attention fixed on the daggers that had appeared in the hands of the two men behind Morban, their evilly sharp blades glinting in the morning sunlight. Morban pushed the finger away.

'Yeah, well you may be the Hilltop Boys, but we're the imperial Roman army. You've cut the occasional poor sod that made the mistake of getting in your way, whereas we've fought in pitched battles against barbarians who all wanted to skin us alive. So I'd advise you to fuck off, and not come back unless you want to leave with your cocks in your hands.'

The enforcers fled, and Morban turned back to his supporters.

'Start counting. I'll give two to one we're toe to toe with them in less than five hundred. And no gabbling it either, nice measured counts. Those odds working for anyone? Two to one? Five to two?'

After a few moments of waiting in the morning's growing heat, they heard the sound of footsteps echoing distantly up the hill, swelling quickly from a mutter to a clamour of leather slapping on stone, and Maximus rounded the corner at the head of a dozen of his men. Seeing Morban waiting for him he spread his arms wide, gesturing to his companions to spread out to either side.

'Well now, *here's* Fatty enjoying the sunshine. Isn't that nice boys? It's a shame that every fucking shop in the street's had to close as a result though.' He stopped in front of Morban, an angry sneer plastered across his face. 'I ain't got the heart to slap you about, Fatty, 'cause I reckon if I do you might just burst. I'll have to make do with a temporary increase in your tax rate to say . . .' He made a show of thought. 'A hundred per cent for the day. If you open that door right now, and put your boys back to work, I'll settle for a day's takings as your fine. How's that, Fatty, or do I have to make my point even clearer? Even the fucking "imperial Roman army" can't be that stupid.'

Morban nodded slowly, putting a hand on the shop's door handle, and the enforcer turned to his comrades with a triumphant grin.

'Like I've always said, you let them get out of line and you always end up having to slap them around to compensate for being too lax in the first place!'

He turned back as Morban swung the door open and stepped aside, his eyes widening as he saw the first of the Tungrians come through the opening with his shield raised, the polished tip of his sword's blade winking in the sunlight, and another man at his heels. In the moment of the gangster's distraction, Morban reached for the spear propped up beside him and stabbed the weapon's sharp pointed head down into the gang leader's sandal-clad foot, feeling the crackle of small bones parting under the iron's remorseless thrust. Maximus screamed in agony, and while his mouth was hanging open, the standard bearer released his grip on the spear with his right hand and swung a bunched fist into the helpless man's gaping jaw, hard enough to break the bone with a rending crack.

'*Hold!*'

The gang members, caught between the obvious need to fight back and the overwhelming urge to flee, froze at Morban's bellowed command, their eyes fixed on him as he pointed to the soldiers facing them.

'If you fuckers run, these lads will chase you down and stab you in the back. D'you want that? *Drop* your fucking knives!'

The gangsters looked from the standard bearer's implacable mask to the writhing body of their leader, then back at the hard faces of the soldiers, clearly ready to spill their blood at the slightest excuse. One weapon fell to the floor, swiftly followed by another, and then the rest of them allowed their iron to drop to the cobbles, their faces red with the shame.

'On your way then. And no looking back, or you might just find it brings us down on you!'

He waited until the last of them was round the corner and out of sight, then took a firm grip of the spear's shaft, experimentally tugging at it. Maximus groaned with the pain.

'No . . .'

'Well as it happens . . . *yes!*'

Morban wrenched the spear from his victim's foot, tearing a moan of agony from the thug's shattered mouth, then squatted down to speak conversationally.

'Well now, One Eye, my old mate. All this time you've been calling me nasty names and taking my money, and suddenly here we are with the roles reversed. Now you're the one with the problem, aren't you, with one foot all torn up and your face in pieces. I don't suppose it could get much worse, not unless . . .' He put a finger to his chin and adopted a pensive expression. But surely nobody would be *that* inhuman. Would they?'

He levelled the spear at the helpless gang leader, easing it forward until the blade was an inch from his eye.

'We do get an amazing amount of training in the army, of course, especially with this little beauty. I can hit a man with it at thirty paces, or I can just stick it into him an inch or two and watch him bleed to death. I bet I could pop that other eye of yours without killing you, if I wanted to.'

Maximus moaned again, but this time it was more from fear than pain.

'And you know what they say, don't you, about bad things coming in threes?'

Morban looked down, his face wrinkled with sudden disgust. He jerked the spear sharply, driving the point into the good eye.

The gangster screamed, his entire body rippling with the pain, while the standard bearer looked down at him dispassionately.

'Consider that as your payout for all the extortion, and rape, and murder you've visited on these people over the years. Let's see how compassionate they feel towards a crippled, blind beggar who can't even chew his own food, shall we?'

He gestured to his men.

'Right then lads, pick up those knives, drop the weapons back into the shop and let's be away to leave old 'No Eyes' to consider the error of his ways!'

He turned to find the potter standing close behind him.

'You're going to leave all those swords in the shop?'

Morban nodded.

'They'll be safe enough until someone comes to collect them. I'll lock the place up and I can't see anyone being brave enough to break in given the obvious penalty for crossing me and my lads.' He offered the shopkeeper his spear with an impetuous grin. 'Want to finish him off? Be my guest! After all, think of all the times the bastard's taken money off you, or pawed your wife.'

The other man shook his head.

'Part of me wants to, wanted to the second I saw you put the iron into his foot . . . but I can't.'

Morban nodded, giving the weapon to a passing soldier.

'I know. I would have been the same, a long time ago . . .' He sighed. 'And now I'm just a murdering animal. Only every now and then I get to do some killing that actually feels good. Be lucky, friend, and when Maximus's replacement turns up, and you know he will, you just remember that the only thing keeping them on top of you is your willingness to be stood on. Show 'em your teeth and they'll soon fade.'

He locked the shop and headed off down the hill towards the Ostian gate with the last of his men, a grizzled veteran from his own century who had waited for him while he chatted to the potter.

'You think they'll stand up for themselves, do you, next time the protection boys come knocking?'

The standard bearer shook his head sadly.

'Not a chance.' He was silent for a moment. 'See, I've worked out what it is I like so much about this place. It's *civilised*. Good food, good wine, whores wherever you look. It's just *nice*. Problem is, you introduce animals like us to somewhere nice and before you know it everyone's paying a percentage just to keep their guts on the inside, or to avoid having their daughters fucked in the street. And that's sad, mate, more than sad, it's a fucking tragedy. All we can do is console ourselves that at least we did a little bit of good today, and gave them one less horrible bastard to worry about.'

His fellow soldier nodded.

'And not only that, you also gave me something to tell the lads back in barracks.'

Morban puffed his chest out.

'You mean when I put that spear to him?'

The soldier shook his head.

'No mate, when you told him you could kill him from thirty paces with it. You couldn't hit a barn door with a bolt thrower!'

Scaurus and Marcus made their way through the crowds surrounding the Flavian arena with their usual escort of barbarians and Cotta's men in close attendance. Both men were immaculately turned out, Scaurus wearing a toga bearing the single narrow stripe that indicated he was of the equestrian class, while Marcus was dressed in a simpler garment and walking a careful half-pace behind him. Striding up to the guards barring the entrance that led up to the senatorial level, the tribune announced his invitation by the imperial chamberlain himself to witness the afternoon's bouts. After a swift reference to the list of guests for the day, they were admitted, leaving their escort to wait for them in whatever shade they could find, while Cotta made his way over to the next entrance to take his seat in the section reserved for army veterans. Climbing up to the senatorial balcony, they were greeted at the entrance to the imperial box by Cleander himself.

'Rutilius Scaurus! It was good of you to make the effort. I wasn't sure that you'd take me up on the invitation, given the fact that your young colleague's mentor will die on that sand very shortly.'

Marcus returned his smile with an impassivity that he was far from feeling, allowing the tribune to answer on his behalf.

'My officer recognises the inevitability of the situation, Chamberlain, and has sworn to Mithras to witness Flamma's last bout with the dignity and reserve expected of a Roman officer. It's not as if we're barbarians, after all.'

Cleander nodded, raising his eyebrows at the younger man.

'Impressive discipline, Centurion. Accept my sympathy, if you will, and my respect for your stoicism. You're an example to some *other* members of the imperial establishment.' He looked pointedly across the box to where Julianus stood wringing his hands. 'If a certain procurator isn't careful, he'll find another man occupying his office. You'd think he'd be happy, given the fact that I gave him permission to place a few thousand on his own man, but apparently his lanista is convinced that Flamma will rip Velox apart in short order, agreement to take the final dive or no. What do you think, Centurion? After all, you know him best of anyone here?'

Marcus stared at him bleakly for a moment before finding his voice, the words numb in his mouth.

'The Flamma who taught me to fight was a man of the greatest honour, and I see no change in him despite the brevity of our reunion. If he says that he'll lose the bout, then you can be assured that he'll die here this afternoon.'

Cleander nodded.

'As I thought. Certainly the man gave me no indication of anything but the strongest of intentions to go through with his offer. It'll be over soon enough and we'll all be able to get on with our business, me to running the empire and you two gentlemen to defending its frontiers. I have something in mind for—'

A blare of trumpets interrupted him, and the three men turned to stare down at the arena's sand as the referee led out a pair of lightly armoured figures. Both men were wearing a manica on their right arms with the mail-sleeve-secured straps running to a heavy leather pauldron on their left shoulders. Velox had chosen to fight bare chested, while Flamma had donned a light mail shirt to provide some protection against the edges of his opponent's swords. Both men had eschewed a helmet, their heads left bare to grant them the breadth of vision necessary for the fluid fighting style of the dimachaerus, and each had a pair of swords strapped to their waists on wide leather belts. Flanked by an honour guard of a dozen spearmen with brightly plumed helmets and shining breastplates, they strode out towards the arena's centre, gazes fixed forward as if neither was willing to recognise the other's presence. The announcer was struggling to be heard over the crowd's sudden deafening roar of appreciation, and after two futile attempts at introducing the bout, he fell silent, waiting as the two men strode out across the clean white sand. At some prearranged signal they stopped, both turning to acknowledge the crowd's fevered applause with raised arms. After several moments of shouting and clapping, the crowd gradually fell silent in the face of their heroes' patient inactivity, allowing the announcer to make another attempt. Raising his voice to a hoarse bellow, he shouted his scripted introduction to the fight over the audience's continuing hubbub.

'*Beloved Caesar! Noble senators! Roman gentlemen! Citizens! People of Rome! The Flavian Arena bids you welcome to this, the third day of the Roman Games! Today we are doubly blessed by the presence of the two greatest fighters of our age!*'

The hysteria erupted again, and the two gladiators once more raised their arms to acknowledge their respective supporters.

'*Fighting for the Dacian Ludus, the current champion gladiator, a man with the proud record of never having been wounded in all his career!*' The announcer paused portentously, allowing the fact of Velox's apparent invincibility to sink in. '*The master of carnage! The fastest man with two swords in the city of Rome and with nineteen victorious fights to his record and no draws or defeats! Citizens, I give you . . . Velox!*'

The crowd went wild, and looking around the arena Marcus realised that a good three-quarters of them were on their feet and waving their fists in support of the champion. Velox stepped forward and raised his hands for a third time, turning a circle to salute every side of the packed stadium before stepping back and lowering them to his sides, close to the hilts of his swords.

'*The Champion's opponent this afternoon needs little introduction! A hero of the recent past, the greatest gladiator of our time, with the record of thirty-eight victories and one draw . . .*'

'*And that was a fix!*'

The anonymous shout from the crowd drew a gale of laughter, and Flamma bowed to the side of the arena from which the interjection had been thrown, his face clearly fixed in a broad grin.

'He looks rather more happy than I'd expect from a man facing his end.'

Scaurus turned to look at the chamberlain, seeing the calculation in his expression.

'You'd be surprised, Chamberlain. Sometimes it's easier for a man to accept certain death than to strive for life in the face of overwhelming odds.'

If Cleander had been minded to reply, the announcer beat him to it.

'*Citizens, welcome back to the Flavian Arena, an old favourite . . . Flamma the Great!*'

The eruption of noise was little less violent than that which had echoed from the arena's high walls a moment before, the crowd clearly expressing a genuine fondness for the veteran gladiator, who turned a swift circle with one hand in the air to acknowledge their sentiment. Waiting until the applause had died down to a gentle roar, the referee stepped forward, waving away the customary escort of his hulking bodyguard and the slaves who usually flanked him with hot iron to encourage the fighters to commence their brutal entertainment, as Velox and Flamma unsheathed their weapons.

'Quite right too!' The Tungrians and Cleander looked over to where the emperor had been lounging on his couch to find him up on his feet and leaning over the balcony, clearly brimming with enthusiasm. 'These two men don't need to be driven to fight!' The two gladiators bowed to the emperor, each of them spontaneously raising his swords in salute, and Commodus turned to address his court. 'The two most talented dimachieri in living history are about to fight to the death for *my* entertainment! How thrilling!'

Cleander shared a wry smile with Scaurus.

'As I said, he's rather enthusiastic about the whole thing.'

They watched as the referee spoke to the two fighters briefly, Velox bouncing lightly on the balls of his feet as he stared at Flamma with a deadly intent that was evident even at fifty paces. With an exaggerated gesture for the fight to begin, the official stepped backwards, and with a lunge the younger man went for his opponent, his swords flashing in the sunlight as he set about his assault. For a moment it seemed that not even the Flamma of Marcus's memory could resist the terrible speed and purpose in the younger man's attack. That Flamma would have danced away from his opponent's swords so lightly that he would have appeared to float across the sand, ready to turn his fleeting retreat into a vicious scything counter-attack, but the intervening years had evidently gnawed hard on his body. Marcus winced in anticipation as Velox slapped aside the sword that the older man had raised to parry his strike, stabbing forward with an audacity born of his apparent supreme confidence. The crowd held its collective breath for a moment, then gasped in amazement.

'How the fuck did he do *that*?!'

The emperor was on his feet again, pointing in amazement at Velox, suddenly wrong-footed as his veteran opponent summoned whatever measure of his massive strength that still remained and hit the thrusting sword so hard with his other blade that it was smashed to the ground. While Velox's defence was still open, he threw a looping punch with his left fist, fingers still wrapped around the hilt of his other sword, the blow connecting squarely with Velox's temple and sending him reeling away on legs suddenly robbed of their strength. The crowd were on their feet, half of them howling indignation at the tactic while the remainder were jubilant at Flamma's escape from what had looked like certain death a moment before. Scaurus shook his head.

'He's shown his hand too early, if his plan is to overwhelm the man with brute strength, because he won't get that close again. Velox will just stand off, and cut Flamma to ribbons.'

The younger fighter was indeed suddenly giving a good deal more respect to his opponent, intent on taking the time he needed to recover from the enervating blow he'd taken a moment before. As if he knew that his opportunity would be a fleeting one, the veteran stamped forward to attack, moving faster than the champion could retreat in his momentarily shocked state. Some hint of the fleetness of foot that had combined with his bestial strength to make the veteran fighter invincible in the days of his pomp still remained, and he covered the distance between them in half a dozen swift steps to attack with a furious purpose of his own. Velox retreated in the face of his fury, his swords flicking out to punish the big man for his assault with first one cut to his thigh and then another, but Flamma was too quick and wary to allow a killing blow to open the femoral arteries, which his opponent was aiming for, and as the younger man tarried an instant too long to make the second cut he seized his chance and lunged forward on one bleeding leg, punching Velox between his eyes so hard that the champion flew backwards to land full length on the sand.

'Can you see what he's doing? He can't kill Velox if he's to keep his word, but he's damned if he's going to allow the man to best him.'

Scaurus nodded agreement with Marcus's words, his gaze riveted on the bloodied veteran as he stood waiting for his opponent to rise, his chest heaving from exertions that would barely have troubled him five years before. While the disoriented champion climbed to his feet, the older man bowed ironically to his crestfallen opponent, wringing a chorus of laughter from the fascinated crowd who were now silent for the most part, recognising that they were watching arena history being made.

The younger man shook his head, taking a moment to steady himself before he attacked again, driven forward by his pride, and

Marcus shot a glance to where Julianus was watching, his face aghast as his most valuable asset moved back into sword reach one heavy step at a time, where previously he would have stepped lightly forwards. As if he recognised that Flamma could not kill him without impugning his own honour, the champion threw himself into one last frenzied attack, his swords swinging almost incoherently as he stepped forward. And then, as Velox made his final attempt to win the bout, the man Marcus had known throughout his youth surfaced in what was left of Flamma in one last glorious, fleeting display of the almost divine gifts that had seemed routine in the big man's heyday. Strutting forward with the same grin that had advertised his apparent immortality to the crowds who had roared him on over the years of his glory, he parried half a dozen wild sword strokes, any of them enough to tear out his life as the champion's blades raged wildly at his defence, indifferent to their deadly threat as he closed remorselessly in on the younger man. Parrying one last desperate lunge aside, he flicked his blades aside in a trick he'd taught to Marcus years before, snapping out his left hand to grip Velox's tunic and drag him bodily into close range. Once, twice, three times he twisted at the waist to sink his massive right fist into the helpless gladiator's stomach, then stepped back as the younger man bent double, gasping for air with his lungs brutally emptied, smashing one last titanic back-fisted blow into the side of Velox's head to send his opponent spinning senseless to the ground.

A stunned silence reigned for a long moment before the crowd found its collective voice, a cacophony as they screamed and bellowed their conflicting pleasure and rage at the result. Marcus looked over at Commodus who was holding on to the balcony rail, his knuckles white with the force of his grip. Before the emperor had chance to even begin to consider the verdict the crowd was howling for, Flamma bent to pick up one of his swords, raising it over his head and waiting until the hubbub had reduced to a puzzled hush in reaction to the unprecedented nature of the bout's end.

'*People of Rome!*' The hush became silence, as the sixty thousand men packed into the arena strained their ears to hear what the former champion had to say. '*I came here today not to fight, but to die! My strength is used up . . .*'

Voices rang out begging their idol to deny his own words.

'*It's true! I have an affliction that I would wish upon no man, not even this murderer lying at my feet devoid of any honour.*'

Commodus stirred himself from his amazement.

'*Archers!*'

Cleander was at his master's side in an instant.

'It might look bad, my Caesar, were you to have one of the greatest champions of the Roman arena that has ever been known shot down like a dog in the moment of his victory. Riots have begun over less, and the flames of public unrest are so much easier to ignite than to quell. And if you were to allow Flamma a moment more, I suspect there'll be no need . . .'

Flamma looked up at the imperial box, as if he knew where to find the man he had trained to fight while still a boy. Marcus looked back at him through his grief-stricken tears, the big man's words of the previous evening still echoing in his mind, the answer to the horrified question he'd blurted out when his mentor had agreed to give Cleander one last fatal day in the arena.

'Why? Because, my lad, there's a crab gnawing at my bones.'

Marcus had frowned, shaking his head.

'A *crab*?'

'I've paid the doctors the best part of a year's winnings to understand what's happening to me. If I were to take off this tunic you'd be revolted by the growth on my back, black and lumpy . . .' He shook his head. 'It was the last man I consulted, a man called Galen, who treats the emperor and takes the occasional case on the side when they're "interesting", that made my blood run cold. He told me that I am afflicted by what he calls "the Crab", our translation of the Greek word "Carcinos". He tells me that the growth will kill me inside half a year, and that I will die in agony as it invades my organs and destroys them. I can feel it eating me sometimes, a hot pain deep in my chest. My last fight is already lost, Marcus. The only question is whether I go out on my feet, or on my knees in supplication to the pain that grows stronger every day. Would you deny me a swift death, and a glorious exit from this life?'

He'd stared at his former pupil imploringly, and at length Marcus had nodded his understanding, his eyes wet with tears.

'Good lad. And promise me one thing? Will you see to it that I'm buried with honour? Have a nice stone carved in my memory, so that my name will live on?'

As the former champion stared up at him, Marcus nodded slowly, raising a hand in salute. Flamma nodded to himself, turning back to address the now silent crowd.

'*And now, my friends, my time to leave this life is upon me! Remember me with kindness, if you will!*' His voice lowered, and the words barely carried to Marcus's ears. 'For a while you were all the life I ever wanted.'

Lifting the sword he placed its point upon his chest and tensed, then rammed the blade through the thin mail whose only purpose had been to disguise his ailment, pushing the point between his ribs and deep into his body, his agonised grunt the only sound in the awestruck arena as he tensed himself for one last effort. Cupping his hands around the weapon's hilt he drew one last long whooping breath with blood pouring from his open mouth, bellowing an incoherent cry of pain, anger and, to Marcus's ear, release from torment that echoed around the silent arena. Then, his body jerking in its death throes, he pulled the blade towards him until its hilt rested against his chest, the weapon's point first tenting the thin mail that lay across his back and then ripping through it, a stream of blood running from the point to paint a haphazard pattern on the sand at his heels. Swaying on his feet for a moment, gazing around the arena with a silent rictus, Flamma the Great tottered and then fell face down, his body twitching.

Utter silence reigned in the arena, and Marcus clearly heard the chamberlain's voice as he leaned forward to mutter in Commodus's ear.

'A little applause would set the right tone, my Caesar. A magnanimous gesture from the city's foremost patron of the gladiatorial art?'

To his evident relief the emperor rose, clapping his hands together and looking about him at the crowd with an expectant expression, and the arena erupted into wild applause as their ruler's gesture broke the spell that Flamma's suicide had momentarily cast over them. Cleander turned to the Tungrians, his hands clapping in an imitation of the emperor's gesture.

'Well then, who could have predicted such a thing? It seems that at least one of our associates has exposed himself to such a result rather more than might have been deemed wise.' Marcus and Scaurus looked round at a surprisingly sanguine Cleander, who was in turn looking with amusement at Julianus's white face and twitching fingers. 'My father taught me at an early age never to risk money I couldn't afford to lose on any gamble where I couldn't be quite sure of the outcome, but clearly the procurator there failed to heed any such advice.'

Scaurus smiled, nodding his head in reluctant respect.

'You didn't bet on a victory for Velox, did you, Chamberlain?'

Cleander smiled mirthlessly back at him.

'Of course not. I've been waiting for Flamma to surface from wherever it was that he buried himself after the Knives took down his patron Senator Aquila, and in the meantime I've made it my duty to know everything I can about the man. Of course, it helped that the emperor's physician had just diagnosed him with an incurable disease, a fact that inevitably came to my attention through one of his assistants who serves to keep me informed of the physician's movements. Men who know they're dying are capable of great self-sacrifice, and once Flamma knew that he had the chance to meet the senator's killer in the arena, it wasn't hard to guess what he had in mind. Velox may have escaped with his life, but his career as a gladiator is over, in Rome at least. And, since you ask, half of the throne's money went on a Flamma victory while the other half was wagered on Flamma dying in the arena today – regardless of the result.'

'The throne wins.'

The chamberlain smiled again.

'In my experience, Tribune, the throne always wins in the end.

And now, with that valuable lesson imparted for you to do with as you please, I think it's time for you both to leave, before Commodus recovers from his upset sufficiently to recognise *you*, Rutilius Scaurus. He still talks about the tribune who had the gall to interrupt him in his own throne room, and were he to realise that you were here I wouldn't put it past him to whip out that knife he carries everywhere and renew the discussion. And today is not your day to die. Perhaps tomorrow . . .'

Cotta met the two men at the bottom of the stairs that led from the imperial box to ground level, his eyes shining with unshed tears. Marcus paused, looking towards the Forum to the arena's west.

'Excuse me Tribune, I promised Flamma an honourable burial.'

Scaurus nodded.

'He's earned it.' He looked at Arminus, who nodded briskly in reply to his unspoken question. 'We'll come with you. For once there may be some small value to be had from our inevitable escort of barbarians other than their entertainment value every time we see a working girl.'

Marcus led them to the Gate of Death, stopping at the cordon which restricted access to the tunnel leading to the spolarium. The arena guards moved to block their path, and Scaurus raised a hand to forestall any conflict.

'I am Gaius Rutilius Scaurus, and I am here on the orders of imperial chamberlain Cleander to provide the body of Flamma the Great with a decent Roman burial.'

The leading man shook his head, his voice appropriately respectful but firm nonetheless.

'I'm sorry, sir, I'm forbidden to allow any unauthorised access to the spolarium. You'd be amazed at the number of people who try to—' He fell silent, having caught a glimpse of Marcus standing behind Scaurus. 'Here, you . . . you're Corvus, aren't you? The gladiator who put on such a good show in the arena the day before last?'

Marcus nodded, smiling wanly.

'I was.'

The guard's face split in an unexpected smile.

'I thought I recognised you! I was on duty when you came down here before your fight. My mates on duty in the arena said you put on quite a show! Did you know Flamma?'

Marcus nodded, a tight smile touching his lips at the thought of all the hot afternoons he'd spent having his sword skills drummed into him by the big man.

'I knew him. He trained me to fight.'

The guard looked about him, his expression turning conspiratorial.

'In that case, since you're one of the family, so to speak, I'll allow you and your friends to pass this once. Flamma was one of the old school, if you know what I mean, a true gentleman for all the years he was champion, and he deserves better than the nameless grave he'll get here without anyone to look after him.'

'And you're sure that they'll be coming this way?'

Excingus nodded, pointing down the hill past the Great Circus to where the Flavian Arena's brightly painted walls caught the afternoon sun's rays.

'My spies saw Scaurus and Aquila walk down there earlier with no more escort than a few of Centurion Cotta's men and a handful of hairy barbarians, none of them armed with anything more dangerous than whatever they can conceal under their tunics. It seems pretty certain that they'll be coming back up the hill at some point, and when they do . . .'

Senator Albinus nodded grimly.

'When they do, they'll find me waiting for them at the head of twenty hand-picked men. Just pray to your gods that you're right, Informer, or you'll find that you've reached the end of my tolerance for your mistakes and misinformation. And don't think you're going anywhere in the meanwhile. You can join me for a refreshing cup of wine, and while we wait for my former friends to walk into the jaws of their fates, you can contemplate what I'm going to have these bloodthirsty individuals do to you should they fail to appear.'

The informer looked around him at the men Albinus had

recruited to replace Cotta's veteran soldiers, finding their stares locked on him like cats gathered around a mouse. He shrugged, doing his best to project an air of indifference.

'I'm sure you'll do whatever seems best to you, Senator. Although what my other client will think of my sudden disappearance might make for interesting conjecture.'

He allowed the comment to hang in the air, knowing that Albinus would be unable to resist the bait.

'Your *other* client? You told me that you had abandoned Senator Sigilis, as he will imminently be arrested for plotting against the throne.'

Excingus allowed the ghost of a smile to creep onto his face, enough to establish some small edge of advantage without looking as if he was condescending to the senator.

'Indeed he is. But it's very rare for an informant to have a single client, especially a successful man such as myself.' Albinus snorted his amusement, and the ring of men gathered around them smirked at Excingus's irritated reaction. 'In point of fact, I have two other clients.'

'And if the doomed Sigilis is one of them, the other is . . . ?'

The informant was unable to resist a smirk of his own, fighting hard to control his urge to shake his head at the senator's lack of insight.

'I'm not at liberty to disclose the name, but I'm sure you'll work it out in due course, Senator.'

Albinus shrugged.

'I don't care who else you work for, Informant, just as long as the information I buy from you turns out to be a little more accurate than has been the case until now.'

Marcus walked out of the spolarium ahead of the four men carrying Flamma's body, Scaurus bringing up the rear with Cotta's men. The gladiator's corpse had been washed clean of blood, the wounds that marred his legs and trunk tightly bandaged to prevent the escape of any more blood, and a coin placed in his mouth to pay his passage across the river Styx. Then, once the dead man's body had been dressed in the armour he had worn for his last fight, the Tungrians had rolled it into a tightly wrapped thick linen shroud, and Dubnus, Arminius, Cotta and Lugos hoisted it onto their shoulders in readiness for its final journey. At the building's entrance the guards stood aside to make room for the impromptu funeral procession, but Marcus found his path blocked by half a dozen men with Sannitus at their head.

'We came to provide Flamma with an honourable burial.' The lanista looked at Marcus and the men behind him with a grimace of distaste. 'And instead I find the man who killed one of the finest fighters the Dacian school has ever seen carrying our brother away. What do you think you're playing at, Corvus?'

Marcus stepped forward and went toe to toe with the lanista, his face hardening.

'You heard what I told Mortiferum last night.'

'I did. You mistakenly believed him to have been part of the murder of your family. What does that have to do with Flamma?'

'Flamma was the man who taught me to fight. What you saw me do in the arena was pretty much all the result of his training, and in the process of teaching me those skills he became as close to me as my own father. Closer in some ways.' He leaned in, his gaze locked on the lanista's eyes. 'You're welcome to join me in providing him with a burial befitting his fame, but if you step into my path I will walk *through* you.'

Sannitus looked back at him for a moment, then nodded.

'I believe you would. Very well, you and I will lay our friend to rest together then.' The gladiators formed up around the men carrying the corpse, while Sannitus looked at Marcus thoughtfully. 'It seems that ours weren't the only lives that Flamma touched. So where were you thinking of laying him down to sleep?'

'In a quiet garden close to the top of the Aventine Hill. Any member of the Dacian school will be welcome to visit his grave for as long as my wife owns the house.'

Sannitus nodded, pulling a roll of cloth from his belt, opening it up and draping it over his head, shrouding his face in shadow.

'That sounds ideal. In truth I had little idea of where to take him. All that was in my head was to avoid his being dumped into a nameless grave along with all the other corpses from today's fights. I will intercede with the goddess on Flamma's behalf.'

They headed south, past the great circus, and began the ascent of the hill's shallow rise in silence. As they approached a tavern on the hill's crest a familiar figure stepped out in front of them, Albinus's face red with the effects of the afternoon sun and the wine he'd clearly been drinking. Excingus remained in his seat opposite the one the senator had vacated, his amused smile slowly fading as he took in the hard-faced and well-muscled men escorting the Tungrians.

'This is becoming a little routine, isn't it, Decimus?' Scaurus had strolled past the corpse bearers with an amused smile, shaking his head at the look of anger on his former sponsor's face. 'Are you sure you want to delay a solemn funeral procession like this?'

Albinus shook his head.

'Not this time, Rutilius Scaurus. This time there'll be no surprises, no unexpected rescue. This time you end up face down in a puddle of your own blood. With your lapdog centurion and that viper Cotta alongside you. Tonight, young man, I will open a jar of my very best wine and celebrate the removal of three particularly difficult thorns from my flesh.'

He clicked his fingers, and a score of muscular men who had been lounging against the walls around them straightened their stances and closed in around the corpse bearers. Scaurus looked about him appreciatively, nodding at Albinus.

'You're a persistent man, Decimus, I'll give you that. Thin-skinned, a little lacking in the perceptive skills, bad tempered, a venal opportunist and slow witted, but certainly persistent. But are you sure these men will do as you tell them?'

Albinus grinned back at him in anticipation of his long-awaited revenge for the indignities the Tungrians had heaped upon him.

'Oh yes, I'm more than certain. After all, they're gladiators. They'll do anything for money.'

'Anything?'

The senator swaggered forward, putting a finger on Scaurus's chest.

'Anything! Their profession has removed any scruples they might have, and any status they once possessed, and now all they have left is the pursuit of riches. Riches which I will bestow on them in such quantity that they will never have to fight in the arena again. This time, Rutilius Scaurus, I have you by—'

Sannitus, his head bowed and his face invisible, lifted his gaze from the cobbles to reveal his identity, looking about him with a challenging stare.

'Do you men know who I am?'

The man closest to him performed a double take of almost comedic intensity, shaking his head in disbelief.

'*Sannitus?*'

The lanista turned slowly, looking at each man in turn.

'I'm committing your faces to memory, brothers, so that I can have you hunted down and murdered. Those of you who do not know me should be aware that I am lanista of the Dacian Ludus and a priest in the worship of the goddess Nemesis, taking the body of our renowned brother Flamma for his inhumation. Those of you who are not delivered a swift and bloody justice by the members of my ludus for desecrating his memory will surely face judgement in the afterlife.'

Scaurus raised an eyebrow at Albinus, who was staring at Sannitus with a horrified expression.

'Undone once more, eh Decimus? Or are you sure enough of the legitimacy of your quest for justice that you'll risk ordering the death of a priest, especially one to a deity as unforgiving as Nemesis?'

The gladiators' apparent leader, a big man with one eye covered by a length of cloth wrapped around his head and knotted at the back, stepped forward and held his empty hands up before him.

'No fear. We're not about to incur the anger of the goddess and have her pursue us for the rest of our lives. Come on lads!'

Albinus watched open mouthed as his escort melted away.

'So, Decimus, once again you've come after me with murder in your heart, only to find yourself in my power. Is there any good reason why I shouldn't order my barbarians to deal with you once and for all, here in the street? That big lad there might just be strong enough to rip your arms off, which would make for an interesting spectacle.'

Lugos grinned savagely down at the senator, who visibly blanched.

'I . . .'

The tribune leaned close to his former legatus, casting a glance at Excingus who, still seated at the tavern's table, was doing his best to appear inconspicuous.

'I won't sully this solemn occasion with your blood, but the next time I see you one of us will die, you can be assured of that. And given that you've been stupid enough to let yourself be led around the city by that snake of an informer, I'd say the odds are on my being the one to step out of the shadows unexpectedly.'

Excingus stirred, getting to his feet and dropping a coin on the table.

'Led round the city? Isn't that a little harsh, Tribune?'

'Is it? Is it really? Decimus here may not be bright enough to have seen through your game, but I've worked it out.' Scaurus raised his hands in a self-deprecating gesture. 'I'll admit that I'm somewhat later to the realisation than might have been ideal, but I can see it now.'

'See *what*?'

He turned back to Albinus, shaking his head.

'You've had Excingus in your pay for what, a fortnight? Ostensibly working for your senatorial colleague Sigilis, whereas in reality he's been your creature, passing you information about our doings and helping you to plot your revenge on me for having the temerity to threaten you with the proof that you embezzled a fortune in gold from the throne in Dacia.' He paused, raising an interrogatory eyebrow. 'So would you say that's gone well, Decimus? Your first attempt ended up with your would-be murderers siding with us, and since then you've either been too late to the party or not even been aware of the opportunity until it's been too late. Has it ever occurred to you that your informer here might just be in the pay of someone else? Someone too big for him to refuse, even if the payment on offer hadn't been quite so tempting? How much is Cleander paying you, Excingus?'

Albinus blanched, his ruddy face losing its colour in an instant. '*Cleander?*'

'Cleander. I told you Decimus, that night outside Pilinius's domus, that I'd worked it out. Too late to have been anything other than the chamberlain's puppet, with this devious bastard pulling the strings on his behalf, but at least I *do* understand what's been happening.'

The informant shook his head with a half-smile.

'You give me too much credit, Tribune.'

'On the contrary, I think you've played a masterful game. Allowing my rather slow-witted colleague here to believe himself to be your master, while all the time you were doing the chamberlain's bidding and feeding us the information we needed to kill the Knives on his behalf.' Scaurus shook his head in amusement. 'And I was taken in by your act, I'll admit it. I genuinely believed you were working for Sigilis, motivated by his apparently bottomless pockets to betray the emperor's team of assassins to us one at a time. Even when I realised that you were working for this oaf on the side – and you can close your mouth and keep it shut, Decimus, unless you want me to have a change of heart as to the desirability of shedding your blood here and now – I still failed to perceive what should have been as plain as the nose on both of your faces.'

Excingus's eyes narrowed theatrically.

'Well done, Rutilius Scaurus. But tell me, what was it that led you to realise I was working for the senator here? What mistake did I make?'

Scaurus laughed, gesturing to the red-faced Albinus.

'You know very well that you made sure I knew about your employment by Decimus here, as a smokescreen for your rather more influential employer. And I note you're not denying your link to Cleander.'

The informant shrugged.

'Given it's probably the only thing that's keeping me alive, I'm happy enough to admit the truth of your assumption. Cleander was never going to tolerate the Knives, once he'd replaced the praetorian prefect as the man behind Commodus's throne. They had outlived their usefulness, and what was worse, they were getting greedy and, of course, they knew too much. Killing them would have been simple enough, but he needed his hands to be clean in the matter.'

Scaurus nodded.

'Indeed he did. Imagine the excitement that would have ensued if the emperor had caught even a hint of his complicity in their deaths. Not to mention the fact that he needs their replacements, his own men, to trust him absolutely, right up to the moment that he has them killed in their turn to ensure their silence. So he used you to point us at them, one at a time, and sat back with a quiet smile while Centurion Aquila did his dirty work for him.'

Excingus shrugged.

'Men like Cleander don't reach the top of the dunghill without treading on a few faces on the way. It was made crystal clear to me that any failure to cooperate in his scheme would result in a protracted and distinctly unpleasant exit from this life for me, so of course I did as he told me.' He bowed to Scaurus, and then to Marcus. 'And now, gentlemen, with my thanks for your assistance, I really must be away. I have one last small task to perform, and then I shall slide away into the shadows. I suspect that Rome will shortly become inhospitable to a man with my twisted loyalties. And for you I have only one piece of advice . . .'

Scaurus cocked his head and waited, watching as Excingus turned away and spoke his parting words over his shoulder.

'Beware the Knives, gentlemen. All of your efforts have only served to make way for a deadlier collection of murderers than the men you killed ever were . . .'

He walked swiftly away down the hill with the purposeful stride of a man with things to do.

12

'And you swear not to seek vengeance on this man Velox?'

Marcus looked down into his wife's eyes and nodded.

'I swear it. My thirst for revenge has been slaked, and with every mouthful the taste became more bitter than the last. Although I cannot say what will happen when Velox recovers from the beating that Flamma gave him.'

Felicia had examined the veteran gladiator's body before Marcus and Cotta had dug a deep grave in the walled garden and carefully lowered the corpse into place.

'That poor man was in agony, I can tell you that much just from the size of that part of his growth that was protruding from his body. It must already have consumed most of his lungs, and how he was able to fight a bout in that condition is a mystery to me.'

Marcus smiled sadly.

'You should have known him ten years ago. And thank you for giving your permission to bury him here.'

She smiled, stroking his cheek.

'Nobody will ever know, so the prohibition on burials within the city walls will never be a problem. And besides, how could I refuse you when it was clearly his intervention that saved your life. The altar looks nice . . .'

Sannitus had sent his men out to purchase a suitably ornate memorial, and with several hefty gladiators standing round him, the stonemason had been inspired to take up his chisel and carve the required words into the white marble without delay. Each of the fighters had vowed to return and make the appropriate sacrifice before heading back down into the city, and

Julius had half persuaded and half dragged Dubnus away to the barracks, leaving Calistra in the care of the two ladies of the house. Felicia had spent an hour speaking quietly with the Dacian girl who, it transpired, had been captured in the same campaign the Tungrians had fought in the previous year.

'That poor girl seems to have been through a lot, but I sense iron in her. She'll need some time to get over her hardships though, she's been raped enough times to have driven a gentler spirit to suicide. Your friend will have to demonstrate more patience than he's known for.'

Marcus nodded, gesturing to the little dog Centurion as he gambolled around their feet.

'And now, I think, it's time for you to get ready. Julius and the tribune will be back soon, and you'll have to go down to the barracks for a while.'

'You think?'

Her husband smiled.

'I don't think, I know. Excingus had the look of a man with unfinished business when we last saw him, and I think that business has to do with you and I.'

The streets of the Aventine were quiet, the taverns and brothels having mostly closed for the night. The informant made his way carefully up the hill with the wine jar cradled in the crook of one arm, stepping round dark puddles of human waste poured from the higher floors of the insulae on either side, half a dozen protective figures skulking through the shadows at his back. He had purchased the container several hours before at a cut price, its contents having spoiled as the consequence of an imperfect seal between jar and plug. Pouring its contents away down the nearest drain to the highly animated disgust of half a dozen beggars, he carried the empty jar away to replace its previous contents with a different liquid altogether.

'*Here!*'

The informant stiffened at the challenge, relaxing again as he realised it was the child Gaius, hidden in the shade of a doorway.

The informant slid into the shadow alongside him, his whispered greeting edged with the usual sardonic tone.

'I'm impressed. Most children of your age were in their beds hours ago.'

The boy showed his teeth in what might just have been a smile.

'Most children of my age ain't on the promise of a gold coin just to watch a house until you turn up. Where the fuck have you been? I've had to show my knife to two dirty old men while I've been sat here looking at nothing. And what's in the jar?'

'I've been sorting a few things out ready for going away. The jar contains one last gift from me to an old friend. Well, an acquaintance.'

The child looked past him at the man who had materialised from the shadows.

'Hello, Dad.'

Silus grinned at his son, his teeth a slash of dull white in the darkness.

'Hello, Son. All quiet?'

Gaius nodded.

'All quiet. Them soldiers was up here earlier, but they only went to that shop, loaded some stuff into their cart and then buggered off back down the hill.'

Excingus frowned.

'I still don't see why they bothered with the whole barbering idea. Presumably they were carrying off the weapons they'd left in the shop. I hear they took the Hilltop Boys to pieces this morning.'

The child laughed without humour.

'Didn't do no good though. There was another gang on the street soon enough, telling the shopkeepers what's what and putting them back in their place.'

Excingus smiled sadly.

'It will ever be so, I'm afraid. Ah well, to business. You're sure nobody's been in or out of the house since the gladiators left?'

'Nobody at all.'

'And all of the gladiators left?'

Gaius nodded emphatically.

'Hours ago. I counted them. All the soldiers went off down the hill too, that bloke in the toga and all his barbarians, and the officers that usually hang around with him.'

'Which means that Marcus Valerius Aquila and his family are enjoying a quiet night after what must have been a joyous reunion. Plenty of wine taken, no doubt, which ought to make your task easier, Silus. Off you go then!'

The hired thug gathered his men to him with a grunted command, leading them across the road to the house's wall. They paused for a moment in its shadows, then climbed swiftly over its smooth cap stones one at a time, dropping out of sight into the garden.

'We'll give your father a few minutes to do what has to be done, shall we, and then I'll wander over and finish the job.'

Gaius nodded, looking with curiosity at the leather satchel on his employer's back.

'What's in the bag?'

Excingus smiled at him benevolently.

'Exactly the same question your father asked me not an hour ago. And the answer, young thief, is that it contains more money than you could ever imagine.'

The boy's face screwed up in disbelief.

'What, in that little satchel? Not likely . . .'

'Ah, but that's where you're wrong. Listen and learn, you revolting little monster. There is money in my bag, enough to pay you and Silus for your services, and a further sum by way of a reward for getting me to my ship in Ostia later this morning. But since I'm not entirely unaware of the risk that Silus, being a direct sort of man, might simply murder me here and take his bonus without having actually earned it, it is in the form of a banker's draft.'

'A what?'

Excingus sighed.

'A banker's draft. A piece of paper that details the money I have given to my banker, a man of undoubted trustworthiness as evidenced by his membership of his profession's guild. I'm carrying two such drafts, one to give to Silus when I'm safely aboard my ship, and another which allows me access to my total fortune, which, I should add, is considerable, at any city large enough to merit the presence of other bankers. All I have to do is prove my bona fides to the banker in that far off place, and he will provide me with money against that draft. The proof is a word, something known to both bankers, which I will tell Silus once my safety from his somewhat acquisitive nature—'

'His what?'

'His fondness for killing people and taking their possessions.'

The child nodded, familiar with both his father's choice of career and the enthusiastic manner in which he pursued its rewards.

'So my old man takes this piece of paper, says this word to the banker, and he gets paid?'

'Well done, you've grasped the concept. Further proof that your intelligence stems from your mother. Do your best to help Silus grasp the concept will you? I suspect he still has a yearning to knife me on the road to Ostia and claim my fortune for himself, which would be a shame for both of us. And no, since I know the way your devious little head works, I don't know the word. It's written on a piece of paper which I placed in my travel chest without reading it, a chest which has already been delivered to the ship in question. It really is quite foolproof, as long as you can persuade your father not to upset the apple cart and in doing so cheat himself out of his reward. And now, I think, Silus has had more than long enough to deal with a sleeping family. Stay here. He rose from the doorway's concealment, padding carefully across the road and trying the door that led into the garden of Felicia's house, gratified to find it unbolted.

'You really are confident in your own abilities, aren't you, Centurion. That must be the pride that took root just before the gods decided to punish you.'

The knock at the front door was soft, barely loud enough to be heard. After a moment, the signal was repeated, slightly louder than before, and Marcus opened the door to find Excingus standing there with a triumphant grin on his face and a large wine jar in the crook of his arm. The scene was illuminated by a small torch that had been placed in the sconce an hour or so before, its flames casting an orange tinge on the informant's momentarily horrified face.

'Ah . . . Centurion! I've . . . come to celebrate your miraculous escape from the very jaws of a slow and painful death!'

Peering over Marcus's shoulder at the darkened room beyond, he frowned in apparent admonishment at the younger man.

'Surely you won't deny me a crumb of hospitality, Valerius Aquila? Can we let the past lie where it fell, and at least part company on civil terms?'

Marcus looked at him for a moment before replying.

'My wife is asleep. Come in, say what you have to say and then leave us in peace.'

Excingus stepped into the house and Marcus pushed the door closed, the informant starting in surprise as he shot the bolts to secure it. Excingus looked about himself owlishly, unable to see very much as his eyes struggled to adapt to the room's sudden darkness after the torch's bright light. He tapped the wine jar with his free hand and spoke loudly into the darkness, praying that Silus and his men were close at hand.

'Surely you'll allow me the honour of offering a toast to your continued good fortune, for Fortuna must be looking at you with more than a little jaundice given the reliance you've put in her over the last few days? Fetch a pair of cups and we'll take a drink to your long life and happiness.'

Marcus walked past him and then turned, shaking his head.

'I don't think the goddess would be all that impressed with the jar of rather badly spoiled Iberian red which you purchased in the market earlier, given that you spent rather less than would have been the case were it actually drinkable.'

The former grain officer's eyes narrowed, and Marcus leaned forward to speak quietly in his ear.

'You're not the only person in Rome who knows how to have

a man shadowed, Excingus. Our men not only saw you purchase the cheapest wine possible, they also watched you tip it out. You caused quite a commotion among the beggars, if you think back . . .'

His voice had taken on a confidential tone that failed to distract Excingus's attention from the dagger that had appeared in the young centurion's hand, and whose point was pressed against the inside of his thigh. Something moved in the shadows behind him, and the informant started as a rough voice muttered in his ear.

'*Come on, sir, spare us a sip of the good stuff!*'

'The *beggars*?'

Marcus nodded.

'You've been using those children to watch us, Excingus, so it felt only reasonable to return your interest. We've had eyes on you, Informant . . .'

Julius stepped out of the darkness, the indistinct lines of his shadowed face resolving into hard, angry features. He nodded to Marcus, taking Excingus by the throat.

'It was a neat enough plan. Your hired thugs slip into the house and butcher my centurion in his sleep, kill his son, rape and murder his wife, and then let you in with your jar of *wine* so that you can torch the place. Or perhaps you planned for your victims to burn alive, their screams telling the story of a house fire with horrible consequences?'

He gripped the informant's throat harder, pulling him closer with inexorable strength and grinning savagely into his face, and, now that the informant's eyes had adapted to the room's near darkness, he realised that he was surrounded by silent figures whose armour gleamed in the pale lamplight. His skin crawled at the implications of their presence, his mouth opening wordlessly as Julius's words sank in.

'It's funny how things work out, isn't it? You've doubtless been trying to understand why we went to all the bother of setting up as barbers, especially after that little weasel of a child took a look at the new cellar our engineers dug under it, and told you it was just an empty room.' He signalled to one of the soldiers, who stepped forward and handed him a tiny dog. Julius took the animal in his big scarred hands with surprising delicacy, using a finger to scratch behind one cocked ear. 'The strange thing is, while we were digging out the cellar we found a woman's body, recently murdered by her husband the landlord. It seems she had a little dog, a scrap of a thing which by some whim of Fortuna ended up being adopted by my wife. This little dog, in fact. And once this little dog had adapted to his new surroundings, he kept on coming back to one place in the house, scratching at the floor tiles and yapping. He was so persistent about it that we decided to take them up and see what it was that was attracting him . . .'

He stared at Excingus for a long moment.

'But of course you know what we found, don't you? You planned to slop the naphtha in that jar you're holding . . . You, take it off him before he drops the bloody thing, he's shaking like a standard bearer who's been caught with his hand in the burial fund.' A soldier stepped forward and took the jar from the informant's unresisting fingers. 'That's better, now we can all relax. Yes, you were going to pour that stuff all over the house, except for one special spot, weren't you? And when the urban watch came to investigate the fire, to poke in the ruins and pull out the twisted bodies, the unmistakable stench would have led them to five corpses buried under the dining-room floor, wouldn't it? Sextus Dexter Bassus and his wife, and their slaves, the previous inhabitants of this house who you killed less than a fortnight ago. It would have been simple enough to work out, I suppose. Bassus and his household would clearly have been murdered, a crime obviously carried out by Centurion Corvus as a means of reclaiming his wife's house, without the bother and delay of legal proceedings. The deceased centurion would have been adjudged to have buried them under the floor with a nice thick coating of quicklime to dry out their flesh and stop them from rotting.' His voice took on a note of respect. 'It was smart thinking, I'll give you that. If we'd looked like getting too close to guessing what your real game was you could have tipped the Watch off to search the house at any time, and got us off your back in hours. And as a convenient means of completing your last revenge it's brutally efficient. Worthy of me, in fact.' His voice hardened. 'Except, you piece of shit, and this is the bit where I get to see you sweat . . .' He leaned in close and whispered savagely in the informant's ear. 'They're not *there* any more.'

Scaurus walked forward out of the darkness, his face appearing almost demonic in the half light. He stopped in front of the informant with his hand out.

'Give me the bag.' He took the satchel that Excingus handed over with such clear reluctance that the nature of its contents was easy to guess, speaking conversationally as he pulled everything out and examined them. 'The bodies were there, Varius Excingus, until just a few hours ago, and then while all that excitement down in the Flavian had everyone distracted, they were exhumed, given a blessing to ease the passage of their tormented souls, and then carried through the tunnel to the shop. My men carried them out when there was no one about and placed them in a cart under the cover of several sheets of canvas and yet more quicklime. They *stank*, Excingus, they smelt worse than anything you could ever imagine if you hadn't walked a battlefield a week after the shouting was finished, which means that your neighbours will already be starting to wonder if you died a few days ago and are lying undiscovered as you rot.'

The informant started again, his eyes widening at the implications of the tribune's words.

'Did I forget to mention that our spies followed you back to your house pretty much straight after we set them to tailing you round the city? All that looking over your shoulder doesn't seem to have been much use, does it? They've been enthusiastically hailing you from the gutter whenever you've come out of the front door ever since. Anyway, your neighbours are probably considering whether to kick your door in even now, given that your rooms will be squarely implicated as the source of such a revolting odour, and they're going to find five very dead people who clearly didn't die of natural causes. Unless, of course, you manage to get back there first and dispose of the bodies before it comes to that.'

He grinned at the horrified informant.

'I could just release you, of course, but you'd probably only make a run for it, given the contents of this bag.' He held up the banker's draft, unrolling it and reading the detail with a low whistle. 'That's a very large sum indeed, Varius Excingus. Clearly the informing game is a lucrative one. There's enough money here for a man never to have to worry about where his next loaf of bread is coming from ever again, no matter where in the empire he went. Where were you planning to run to, eh? Iberia? After all, the wine's good. Asia Minor? I do hear the Greek islands are very nice though . . .'

'You already know.'

Scaurus nodded sanguinely.

'You're right, I do. It's amazing just how much more cooperative a ship's master can be when the questions are being asked by a bad-tempered centurion like Julius here. So you don't have to worry about missing your boat, since your boat isn't really your boat any more. And yes, to answer that question lurking in the back of your mind, we do have your chest, and yes, I did find the password for your banker's drafts. Your contribution to my cohorts' burial funds will be much appreciated.'

He stood back and waited for the informant to speak, but Excingus simply stared back at him with hate-filled eyes.

'And now, I suppose, you're wondering whether this can get very much worse. Sadly, I'm afraid the answer to that unspoken question is most definitely *yes*.'

Senator Sigilis walked out into his garden at the hour which Scaurus had nominated with such firmness, looking about him in the starlit darkness with no more idea what he was supposed to do next than he'd had when the tribune had proposed his flight from Rome. Earlier in the day, he had dismissed the last of his staff, giving each of his slaves a statement of manumission, which had been witnessed by a judge so prominent that no one would think to challenge their freedom in his absence. Thanking his butler for the man's devoted service, and pressing a more than generous purse upon him as a reward for his loyalty, the senator had sent him on his way with the instruction to lose himself in a part of the city where he was unlikely to be unearthed by any search for those members of the household who had been close to their master.

'There will be men coming for me soon, perhaps tonight, and if by chance they fail to find me here, they will naturally turn to those of my staff who might have some knowledge of my whereabouts. And I fear that no amount of denial would blunt their willingness to dig so hard for the truth that your exit from this life would be a matter of some considerable discomfort.'

The bemused servant had surprised him by embracing him before turning away.

'Farewell, Senator, may Mercury speed your flight. And I must now pass you a message that Tribune Scaurus left with me for this moment. The tribune wants you to wait in your garden once the moon has risen, and listen for a man calling your name.'

Sitting in his accustomed place within the ring of trees that sheltered the garden dining area, he waited with the patience of his years, musing on the events that had brought him to the point of imminent disgrace and execution, wondering whether his wry acceptance of looming death would survive the moment of his apprehension by the emperor's murderers.

'*Senator! Senator Sigilis!*'

The call was so quiet as to be almost inaudible, and for a moment Sigilis wondered if his overwrought imagination had conjured the sound from nothing, until it was repeated. Standing, he walked slowly towards the place from which he believed the sound had come. And then, with an abruptness which made him take a step backwards, a figure detached itself from the gloom, seeming to rise out of the earth itself. Grasping at the amulet given to him by his wife decades before for strength, he found his voice, a reedy whisper of challenge that sounded like another man's.

'*What are you!*'

The response, disquietingly, was a laugh, the earthy chuckle of a man who had seen too much of life to take very much seriously.

'What am I? I'm tired, Senator, and keen to be away from here. Here, put this on.' Sigilis reached out automatically to take the garment that was thrust at him, pursing his lips at the coarse material, and the anonymous man from the shadows spoke again with the same amused air. 'Yes, sir, it's rough, and if there were light you'd see that it's dirty too. And it smells of sweat. Strip off that fine tunic and leave it here for the men hunting you to find, eh?'

Sigilis stripped, pulling on the rough garment as bidden.

'So what now, stranger, now I look and smell like a working man?'

'Now? Follow me, sir. And I ain't no stranger. My name's Avidus. I was here the other day, measuring up this lovely garden.'

The mysterious figure turned away, taking a few steps before seeming to literally vanish into the earth, and while Sigilis dithered, fighting to master his fear of the unknown, he called out to him again, his voice muffled.

'Come on then, sir! Just a few steps more! Here, you, pass me that lamp!'

The senator paced forward slowly, his eyes widening as the light revealed the nature of his apparent salvation.

'Ahhhh. I *see*.'

Almost an hour after his father had jumped over the garden wall into the centurion's garden, an increasingly impatient Gaius heard voices from the other side of the street. The garden gate opened, allowing a single figure to exit onto the darkened street with the quick, uncontrolled steps of a man who had been pushed. He stopped, looking about himself with swift, jerky movements, cradling something in his hands as if he were reluctant to put it down.

'*Oi, Excingus!*'

The furtive figure started with the child's whispered challenge, backing away with what sounded disturbingly like a muffled whimper. Gaius rose from his hiding place, crossing the road on quick feet as the informant backed away in apparent terror, still holding whatever it was that he was so unwilling to relinquish.

'*What's that you've got th—*'

The child's question died in his throat as he stared down at the round object in his employer's hands, shaking his head in shocked disbelief and reaching out to pull the knife from the informant's belt. Excingus, his mouth bound with a tightly tied gag, shook his head frantically as the boy lifted the blade over his head with a shout of rage.

'You *cunt*!'

He slashed at the reeling informant, whipping the blade back up over his head ready to strike again in a scatter of blood. Excingus staggered, his bellow of pain muffled by the gag, dodging the blow with a frantic sidestep before taking to his heels with the desperate speed of a man who knew that he was facing his death. Gaius ran after him, the knife held ready to strike again, his child's voice raised in a piping shriek of rage.

'Come back, you bastard! Come back and face me!'

Marcus opened the door the next morning in response to a firm knock, finding a quartet of men in praetorian uniform waiting in the small garden, the foremost of them wearing the plumed helmet of a centurion.

'Marcus Tribulus Corvus?'

He nodded, looking at their faces one at a time until he found the man who had put his spear through Horatius's neck the previous evening.

'You're to come with us.' The speaker looked at him levelly for a moment. 'By the order of the emperor.'

Scaurus stepped up alongside his centurion.

'I presume this invitation also requires my presence?' His only answer was an imperturbable nod. 'Very well, in which case I suggest we go?'

The two men walked down the hill towards the Great Circus and the Palatine's sprawling palaces in silence, their escort ignoring the inquisitive glances of the pedestrians who cleared from their path willingly enough when they laid eyes on the soldiers' grim faces and glinting spear heads.

'All in all, Centurion, and whatever it is we're walking into, I'd have to say we did the right thing. You spent an untroubled night, I presume?'

Marcus smiled wearily.

'Untroubled by my family's ghosts? Yes, Tribune. The doctor tells me that my acts of revenge have in some way assuaged my guilt at being my family's only survivor . . .' He sighed. 'All I know is that where I expected exultation and the joy of bloody revenge, I found only emptiness and self-loathing.'

The tribune put a hand on his shoulder.

'You did what you had to do. And now my advice would be to let the whole thing go. Put any thought of completing your revenge from your mind.'

Marcus stared up at the looming bulk of the imperial palaces.

'I have. Although I doubt that Velox will take the same attitude . . .'

They were escorted through the ring of iron that protected the Palatine, the officers supervising each successive praetorian checkpoint deferring to the dagger-shaped emblems on their escort's dangling belt ends with an alacrity that made Scaurus smile quietly.

'As ever, Cleander seems to have taken Perennis's informal expedient and turned it to his own ends.'

The four soldiers guided them through a waiting room filled with supplicants waiting their turn to speak with the chamberlain, many of whom shot them the venomous glances reserved for those who pass unchecked where others are forced to wait their turn. Walking through the door into the chamber beyond, they were greeted by the sound of the chamberlain's unmistakable voice.

'Justice? If you want justice, Senator, you know what the price is. And now, I'm afraid, your time is at its end. You choose, either make the necessary payment or wait for the wheel of imperial justice to finish its slow and unpredictable revolution. Who knows, you may be lucky enough to draw a magistrate who will sympathise with the injustice that appears to have been dealt out to you . . .'

He gestured to an aide, who took the senator in question's arm in a firm grip, leading the man away while he continued to protest his innocence in whatever matter it was that he had come to bring to the chamberlain's attention.

'And now . . . Ah, good, I've been looking forward to this all morning. Tribune. Centurion. I see you've made your acquaintance with the Emperor's *new* Knives? I say "the Emperor's", of course, where in point of fact I mean "mine" . . .'

He smiled at them, encouraging them to join in his joke, and Scaurus smiled wryly back at him.

'And of course, our pursuit and murder of their predecessors was only ever possible with your active assistance.'

The chamberlain nodded, his expression sanguine.

'Of course. As I'm sure you've worked out by now, Varius Excingus was my creature from the very start, the agent of my helping you on to the scent of each of them in turn. How long did it take you to make the realisation?'

'It was the moment that I found Senator Albinus waiting for us outside Pilinius's villa. We already knew that Excingus was feeding information to him, but despite his having every opportunity to give us up to his apparent sponsor, he seemed reluctant to do so. Why, I wondered, would he not complete his betrayal of us, unless there was some bigger dog with his throat in its jaws? And what bigger dog could there be than a Roman senator with more than enough gold to buy the loyalties of a single informant? I didn't have to look very far for the answer.'

Cleander conceded the point with a smile.

'You've played quite a game, haven't you, Tribune? While it seemed to all appearances as though you were simply supporting this man's revenge-crazed rampage through the ranks of the man who killed his father, you were in truth once again dabbling in Roman politics, weren't you?' Scaurus looked back at him with a nonplussed expression, drawing a reluctant laugh from the chamberlain. 'Come now, you're not going to expect me to be taken in by your silent protestation of innocence?'

Cleander sat back in his chair, waiting for the tribune to answer.

'You do me too much credit, Chamberlain. I am no more than a simple—'

The other man guffawed loudly, shaking his head in amusement.

'A simple soldier? I don't think so. I sent my new Knives out yesterday evening for their first task, with orders to remove a substantial problem from my already heavy burden of difficulties. They attended the residence of Senator Gaius Carius Sigilis who, as I'm sure you know, has recently been under something of a cloud for his pronouncements in the senate glorifying the former republic and demonstrating grievous and unforgivable disdain for the imperial cult. Expecting to find the senator in residence at his domus, since his movements have been tracked for the last few weeks to ensure that he didn't attempt anything foolish to further undermine imperial rule, they were disappointed to find him absent, and the house completely empty.'

He fell silent, playing a hard stare across the two men's faces.

'I trust your men managed to recover the senator's estate as some means of reparation for his crimes?'

The chamberlain nodded slowly, clearly unable to fault the concern in Scaurus's voice.

'For the most part, Tribune, although the fugitive seems to have escaped with a significant fraction of his wealth, which he appears to have been quietly converting into liquid assets for the past few weeks.'

Scaurus's tone hardened, a note of disgust entering his voice.

'And presumably he's been doing that in such a way as to make it untraceable? These people leave me speechless, seeking to undermine the throne and then running away with their money when an attempt is made to bring them to heel!'

Cleander stared at him for a moment longer before speaking again.

'A more detailed investigation of the senator's domus this

morning revealed the means by which he escaped, a tunnel that had been dug from a shop in an adjoining street, and which ran a full one hundred and ten paces into the senator's garden before coming to the surface. A tunnel which, I'm told by those that know what to look for, displayed all the hallmarks of military engineering . . .' He allowed the silence to play out, waiting for some response from Scaurus. 'Nothing to say, Tribune?'

Scaurus shook his head.

'There's nothing I can say, Chamberlain, without sounding disrespectful to the emperor's own legions, and therefore I shall say nothing.'

Raising an eyebrow, Cleander resumed his story.

'And so we come to the facts surrounding a man with whom we're both well acquainted, our mutual associate Tiberius Varius Excingus.' He waited in silence again, but Scaurus made no more attempt to comment than before. 'Excingus was found on the street in the Aventine district this morning, close to death as a result of several knife wounds of varying severity, apparently delivered by his own weapon since it was missing from the scene. Held in his hands . . .' One of his aides leaned forward and whispered in his ear. 'I stand corrected. *Nailed* to both of his hands was a severed man's head, that of one of several men who were also found dead in the same area at much the same time. They had, apparently, been killed with long bladed weapons of the type used by your Tungrians. The head in question has been identified as belonging to one of Excingus's closest associates, a man by the name of Silus, and it seems that it had been secured in place by means of the type of nails usually used for military crucifixions, two of which had been driven through each of his hands and into the dead man's head in an X-shaped pattern, making it impossible for him to pull them out without assistance.'

Scaurus shrugged.

'I won't pretend that the man was any friend, Chamberlain. Let his family mourn for him, I have no tears to waste on the man.'

Cleander's voice hardened.

'Excingus was at the point of death when he was discovered, having been mortally wounded by some street scum or other, but he did manage to say one thing before expiring.'

The tribune smiled slowly.

'Killed with his own knife? That seems poetic . . .' He shrugged. 'Did he say anything of note?'

Cleander stared at him for a long moment.

'Not really, on the face of it. He was rambling, it seems, unmanned by loss of blood. Apparently his only discernible statement before he died was a single word. The word "impossible". Having mused in the subject for a short while, I found my thoughts wandering back to the tunnel through which Senator Sigilis was spirited away under the noses of the men who were watching all of the exits from his property, including the two previously secret doors in the walls of his domus. A tunnel to the senator's estate, which it seems was dug by men who had the gall to pose as workers refurbishing a shop. And it struck me that our mutual acquaintance, for all of his cunning, might have been tricked by something as simple as just such a tunnel? Perhaps, I mused, in overzealous pursuit of the centurion here, and in defiance of my orders, he led this collection of street thugs in seeking furtive access to the house in which your colleague's wife has taken up residence, only to find several heavily armed men waiting for him? A tunnel would have been an excellent way for your men to take up their positions to wait for his intrusion without their presence being obvious to anyone watching the property on his behalf?'

'A tunnel?' Scaurus shrugged. 'It's a little far-fetched, Chamberlain. We're infantrymen, not engineers. And besides, a tunnel from where?'

The chamberlain leaned forward with a hard smile.

'From a certain recently opened barber's shop, perhaps? I forgot to mention that the landlord of the property whose tunnel abetted Senator Sigilis's escape from justice is the very same man who owns, or rather owned the shop in which your men have been practising the tonsorial arts for the last week or so. A landlord who appears to have sold up his properties for a bargain price and vanished, quite possibly on the same ship which I think it safe to assume carried Sigilis away on this morning's tide. And by some strange coincidence, it seems that the entire block in which this shop of yours was located collapsed this morning, rather fortuitously without any loss of life. It seems that the occupants heard the structure creaking and fled the building before it caved in.'

He shook his head at the two men.

'Doubtless, were I to order a sufficiently thorough investigation, my men would find some form of evidence as to your involvement in the senator's escape and my informant's regrettable demise. The former occupants of the collapsed insulae will doubtless surface soon enough, having spent whatever coin they were given in return for their absence when the block was pulled down by the same engineers who dug the tunnel in question as a means of disguising its presence. Were I to order this collapsed apartment block to be removed, piece by piece, I suspect that my men might well find its remnants, running from that shop straight to the house owned by Centurion *Corvus* here. Further, were I to order the fleet at Misenum to sea, with orders to overhaul and search every ship that left Ostia in the last day, I suspect that both senator and landlord would be back in Rome and awaiting their eventual punishments within another day or two. And were I to have you tortured, Tribune, or you, Centurion, or better still your doubtless wholly innocent wife and child, I expect the whole clever little deceit would be laid bare with remarkable speed.'

He sat back, waiting in silence for a response.

'And the reason why we're *not* being tortured at this very moment is . . . ?'

The chamberlain nodded.

'I thought that might provoke some comment from you, Valerius Aquila. The reason you're not being tortured for your tribune's transparent scheming – yet – is twofold. Firstly, I'm grateful for the brutally efficient manner in which you personally performed a series of badly overdue executions on my behalf. The Emperor's

Knives were an embarrassment waiting to happen, too secure in their positions for any other solution, given the need for their depredations to remain a closely guarded secret. And, to be frank with you, Excingus's death is no more than the tying up of another loose end which would otherwise have required the attention of the men standing around you. So let me turn your question around, Centurion, since you've found your voice at last. Why is it, do you suppose, I haven't ordered my men to slit your throats and dump you in the city sewer?'

Marcus shook his head in dark amusement.

'That's easy enough to work out. In less than a month, we've been instrumental in the death of the one man who was standing in the way of your absolute grip on power, destroyed a cabal of assassins who still owed some degree of loyalty to the emperor himself, and opened the way for you to replace them with your own men. We're useful to you, aren't we, Chamberlain?'

Cleander nodded.

'Exactly. You're resourceful, cunning, and, it has to be said, you take a rather more direct approach to whatever gets in your way than most of the men in my service. But as my father used to say to me, a man needs to be careful what he wishes for, given that wishes are rarely granted in exactly the form that we hope for. You came seeking the destruction of the men who killed your family, to release you from the unbearable pressure of your wounded honour, but was the end result really to your liking?'

He turned his attention back to Scaurus.

'You leave me with only two alternatives, Tribune, given that I won't be the only person with the wit to connect the events of the last few days and come to an accurate conclusion. I can wrap the protection of the state around you, and make you part of the organisation that runs the empire for a ruler who is, to be brutally honest with you both, far more interested in the contents of his bed than the incessant demands of governing one hundred million people. Or I can unearth your conspiracy to murder imperial officials and assist a known traitor in evading justice, with the inevitable result that you and your officers, and their families, will all be subjected to the full weight of the emperor's justice. What do you think?'

Scaurus pursed his lips, looking back at the chamberlain with a steady gaze.

'If it were my choice, I'd be tempted to take the hard way out.'

Cleander nodded.

'I can see it in your eyes. But it isn't simply *your* choice, is it, Rutilius Scaurus? And even you, seemingly without dependents, still have a sponsor whose eminence in Roman society might be more than a little dented were I to make it my business to take an interest in his doings.'

'No, it isn't my choice.' The tribune shrugged. 'What is it that you want from us, Chamberlain? I think I can speak for my officers when I tell you that we won't be party to any "confiscatory justice".'

The other man smiled wryly.

'Oh no, I have something rather better suited to your particular collective skill set in mind.' He held out a hand to his secretary for a pair of scrolls. 'Here.'

Scaurus took them, opening the first and staring at it for a moment before looking up in genuine amazement.

'*Legatus?*'

Cleander smirked at him.

'It's a strange feeling, I'd imagine, to have your life's impossible ambition offered to you as an alternative to execution, and by a man for whom you feel nothing better than contempt? And the other scroll?' He waited while Scaurus opened and read the second order, grinning at the look that the tribune shot him after a moment's perusal of the contents. 'And I think your young colleague's somewhat charmed life as a fugitive from his father's crimes should be put on a slightly more regular footing. I've therefore decided to appoint him to the tribunate, under your command of course, Legatus Scaurus, and by doing so to confirm that Marcus Tribulus Corvus is a trusted servant of the throne. Or rather, of mine. His previous life shall be our little secret, and shall remain so just as long as you both provide the emperor, and more importantly myself, with the appropriate combination of loyalty and effective service. He will be formally elevated to the Equestrian order, and thereby enabled to act as a military tribune under your command. As long as the pair of you perform effectively, you will be under my personal protection. Fail to do so, or display even the slightest sign of biting the hand that has chosen to protect you, and your falls from grace will be spectacular.'

'What . . .'

'You? Lost for words, Legatus?'

Scaurus shook his head.

'No, Chamberlain. I've long since passed the point of amazement, I was simply gathering my thoughts. What is it that you want from us?'

'There is a legion, Rutilius Scaurus, in a distant and rather warm part of the empire, that needs a firm grip on its collective neck. You are to relieve the current legatus, take command, and act as you see fit to restore Roman authority to that legion's operational area without delay. Our frontier is being disregarded, Legatus, and I want those men who find it entertaining to display their contempt for us stamped flat, as an example for their kindred that won't be forgotten for the next fifty years.'

Legatus and tribune stared back at him for a moment before Marcus found his voice.

'And my family?'

'Your family, *Tribune* Corvus, will stay here in Rome under my personal protection. And in any case, I wouldn't have thought you'd want them with you, not where you're going.' Cleander stood, smoothing his toga out with his hands. 'As to your men, Legatus, you can decide what to do with your Tungrian cohorts. Send them home, take them with you, it makes no odds to me, although I think having some friendly faces at your back might be a sensible idea, given the depth of venality to which your new command has succumbed of late. Who knows what form their resistance to your assumption of command will take? And now, gentlemen, you'll have to excuse me. The emperor does so hate it when I'm late for our meetings. I'll be sure to stress to him just how pleased I am to have delegated this small matter to such consummate professionals.' He nodded to the leader of his freshly assembled group of assassins. 'Escort the legatus from the palace.'

Scaurus and Marcus were led back through the palace's maze, finding themselves on the steps of the Palatine Hill once more. Both men stared out over the Great Circus's grandstands with mutual bemusement for a moment before Scaurus spoke, his voice flat and emotionless.

'Legatus.'

Marcus looked at him, seeing the disgust in his face.

'You do have a choice.'

The older man laughed, his amusement hollow.

'Do I? Think about it for a moment, and you'll come to another conclusion. If I refuse this honour, this pinnacle of a military man's career, this *impossible* honour for a man of my class, then I make hostages to fortune of every man under my command. You will be executed, be under no illusions about that. Your family . . .' He shook his head, unwilling to speak the words. 'And the fifteen hundred men we brought here? I can imagine numerous ways to make every last one of them wish he'd never volunteered, and none of them will ever see their homeland again. Nor can I leave them here, at the mercy of every officer with a gap to fill in his ranks. There's no choice for either of us, Tribulus Corvus. I must accept this position, and smile at the taste of ashes it will leave in my mouth, and you must accept the reality that you may never again use your family name in public.'

Marcus nodded, looking up at the sky above them.

'In which case, Legatus, I suggest we go and break the good news to my brother officers. What was it that Cleander said? "Distant, and rather warm?"'

AFTERWORD

Gladiators. Even now, with the apparently elevated moral perspective of modern society, the word still carries a resonance far beyond that which might reasonably be expected for a concept as barbaric as the gladiatorial arts as exercised under the Romans. The iconography of this archaic blood sport is as vital now as it was then, and a constant flow of books, television and even films attest to its enduring popularity, although few of us would find the Flavian amphitheatre's entertainment (we call it the Colosseum these days, named after a huge statue that used to stand alongside its walls) an easy spectacle to watch, were we given the opportunity to view such contests in their full bloody pomp.

The Romans seem to have borrowed the concept, as was so often the case with their ideas, weapons, tactics and ways of life, from their defeated neighbours. The first mention of gladiatorial combat, recounted by Livy – over two centuries later – as having taken place in 264 BC, seems to have been exceptional, but the dominant powers in Italy before Rome, the Etruscans and Samnites, seem to have constructed purpose-built arenas long before that. Etruscan sacrifices to their gods seem to have involved an element of combat, and when Rome and its Samnite neighbours squared up for domination of the Italian peninsula between 343 and 290 BC it is likely that prisoners of war on both sides would have been forced to fight to the death. But if the Romans were late to adopt gladiatorial combat as a form of public spectacle, they were as quick and morally uninhibited as ever to take that concept and develop it to its ultimate expression.

The first Roman gladiatorial fights on record were a relatively small affair, with three pairs of men chosen from among twenty-two prisoners of war to fight in a Roman cattle market to honour the memory of the *consul* Decimus Junius Brutus Pera, human sacrifices to appease the gods to the dead man's arrival with that extra thrill of men fighting to the death. Sacrifices at funerals were always likely for exactly this reason, but the idea of making the men who were doomed to die fight each other was, from the Roman perspective, inspired. At first the games were restricted to funeral rites, although there was a steady escalation in the number of men involved, and therefore the prestige of the man hosting the event, until in 216 BC the death of a man called Aemilius Lepidus was celebrated by twenty-two pairs of fighters. The number of fighters at an aristocratic funeral had become a mark of prestige, and nobody who considered himself to be a prominent member of Roman society could afford to be seen to skimp on such an event. It was Scipio Africanus, the famous republican general and politician, who started the move to disassociate the games from death rites when he held such a *munus* – the term means 'obligation of honour' – for his father and uncle several years after their deaths. An ambitious *aedile* by the name of Julius Caesar took the practice to a new level by holding a games for his dead father twenty years after his death, unashamedly presenting the public with no fewer than 320 pairs of gladiators in single combat in a move that paid him back with success at the next elections. The *munus* had been translated from a show of devotion to a departed relative to something far more cynical and calculated, the expenditure of large sums of gold, frequently borrowed by the politician in question, to buy public favour as the would-be office holder's 'duty' to his constituents. The immediate result was that the hosting of games was banned for anyone seeking office within the two years of the event, and limiting the number of armed fighters to remove the risk presented to the republic by what were effectively highly skilled private armies.

As the popularity of the games spread, schools were established to train gladiators for the spectacles, which proved handy when the empire was under pressure and needed military training in a hurry (but troubling when an escaped gladiator called Spartacus

ran amok at the head of an army of freed slaves for two years).
As the republic became increasingly unstable, it became normal
for the aristocracy, especially those with political ambitions, to be
escorted around the city by teams of gladiators who were paid
to protect them from the potential intimidation of their rivals. In
short, with purpose-built arenas – amphitheatres, from the Latin
word '*amphi*' (oval) – starting to spring up, and with Caesar
hosting the first state-sponsored games in 42 BC, the gladiatorial
munus had become an established feature of Roman society.

For men who exercised such a strong influence on Rome's society,
the life of the average gladiator wasn't all that enjoyable for the
great majority of men lacking in the skills and single-minded
brutality to fight their way through to the *rudis*, the wooden sword
that released a man from his contract. The gladiator, for all that
many respectable married women seem to have been drawn to
their presence – and brutal 'bad boy' sexuality – like moths to a
flame, were nevertheless (and quite possibly in partial consequence),
considered to be the lowest strata of Roman society, openly despised
by even the empire's slaves even while the latter were all but
worshipping the best-known fighters. Not that every man who
fought in the arena will have had very much choice in the matter.
Criminals, if they were lucky enough not to find themselves
condemned to participate in the gory lunchtime shows by being
ripped to pieces by hungry animals – *damnatio ad bestias* – could
simply be condemned to the games – *damnatio ad ludos* – a form
of punishment from which a determined, skilful and above all lucky
man might still win his freedom. Worse than this was to be
condemned to the sword – *damnatio ad gladium* – a genuine death
sentence, whether in the condemned man's first fight or his thirty-
first. Inevitably, however, reasonable numbers of both suitably skilled
and quite unsuited men volunteered to fight in the arena in return
for financial reward. Whether to pay off a particularly unpleasant
debtor – who would quite likely be using gladiators as the means
of collecting what he was owed – to impress a girl, or simply to
make his fortune, men voluntarily sold their bodies into the ludi,
the gladiatorial schools. In doing so, and quite apart from lowering

their status to that of infamis, the scum of society, unable to vote, hold public office or even buy a burial plot, and shunned by all and sundry for fear their status might be communicable, they submitted to an oath which put their lives utterly at the mercy of a *lanista*, the man who owned them until they were killed, invalided or freed. The great majority of them would eventually leave the arena with either a life-threatening or fatal wound, in which latter case their skulls would have been stoved in by a man with a large hammer, dressed in the costume of an ancient Etruscan god and whose job it was to ensure that a man who looked dead really had nothing more calculated on his mind.

One last class of men fought in the arena, the *auctorati*: men who came to exercise their need for danger. These days thrill seekers jump out of aircraft or climb mountains to get their kicks, but in ancient Rome the lure of the games seems to have exerted a powerful pull on those men (and perhaps the occasional woman) determined to demonstrate their *virtus causa*, their skill at arms. This was barely acceptable, as long as the man was careful to preserve some degree of anonymity behind a faceless helmet and spare his family and friends the shame of his degradation, although the emperor Commodus shattered that social convention by appearing in what were presumably carefully rigged contests late in his ill-starred reign.

Over a dozen different types of gladiator fought and died in the empire's arenas over several centuries, one class of fighters who were effectively heavy infantrymen taking on another group of nimble small shield fighters, who depended on their speed and skill to defeat slower and better protected opponents. The classic combination was that of the *retarius* – the net man – who sought to snare his opponent the *secutor* – the chaser – with a net, keeping him at arm's length with a trident, while the *secutor* pursued him with every intention of battering and hacking him to death.

Speciality acts also abounded, like the *andabatae* – two fighters blinded by helmets covering their faces – and the dimachaerus, fighting without a shield but using two swords to mount a constant assault on his would-be victim. Chariot fighters were popular while Rome's conquests over the barbarian tribes of the north – Gauls,

Germans and Britons – provided a ready supply of suitably trained captives. Indeed the arenas thrived on prisoners, Rome's wars providing a constant flow of raw material from around the empire's periphery, men unsuitable to be sold into domestic slavery due to their aggressive natures or simple lack of any saleable skill being used instead to provide the population with bloody entertainment. After his huge victory in the war with Dacia, the emperor Trajan hosted 123 days of games in which over 5,000 pairs of gladiators, many of them captured Dacian warriors, fought to the death. It was no coincidence that two of the four gladiatorial schools were named after the styles of fighting that these men brought with them, the *Ludus Gallicus* (Gaulish School) which produced heavy fighters like the *secutor* and the *murmillo* (fish man, after his crested helmet, usually armed much like a legionary) and the *Ludus Dacius* (Dacian School) which turned out the more nimble *retarius* and *thracian* (a highly mobile fighter whose best hope was to stab his lumbering enemy in the back with his curved blade).

And, by the same token, it was no coincidence that as the empire slid into the chaos of the third century, the games became less grand, due both to financial crises and a lack of the previously abundant prisoners of war. But for all of the reduction in expenditure on the games, and the empire's vaunted conversion to the more apparently ethical Christian religion, the popularity of the gladiatorial ludi was largely unchanged. Despite the higher moral standards espoused by the state, the games proved remarkably stubborn in their continuing popularity, although theatrical shows and chariot races gradually rose to prominence, not least, one suspects, because they were quite simply cheaper to stage and therefore held more frequently. The end seems to have come with the death of an Egyptian monk by the name of Telemachus, martyred while protesting at the games held to celebrate defeat over the Goths during the reign of the emperor Honorius, his death proving the catalyst for the emperor to outlaw the games – although it still took more than one imperial decree to put a conclusive end to the munera. The last fight was held on the first day of January in the year AD 404.

I hope *The Emperor's Knives* will provide the reader with some feeling for the glory and terror that accompanied the many thousands of gladiators who endured their new status of infamis in order to fight for money, for their freedom or simply to see another sunrise.

EMPIRE

The story began in

Wounds of Honour, Arrows of Fury, Fortress of Spears, The Leopard Sword, The Wolf's Gold, The Eagle's Vengeance
and
The Emperor's Knives

It continues in

Thunder of the Gods

By the late second century, the point at which the *Empire* series begins, the Imperial Roman Army had long since evolved into a stable organisation with a stable *modus operandi*. Thirty or so **legions** (there's still some debate about the Ninth Legion's fate), each with an official strength of 5,500 legionaries, formed the army's 165,000-man heavy infantry backbone, while 360 or so **auxiliary cohorts** (each of them the equivalent of a 600-man infantry battalion) provided another 217,000 soldiers for the empire's defence.

Positioned mainly in the empire's border provinces, these forces performed two main tasks. Whilst ostensibly providing a strong means of defence against external attack, their role was just as much about maintaining Roman rule in the most challenging of the empire's subject territories. It was no coincidence that the troublesome provinces of Britain and Dacia were deemed to require 60 and 44 auxiliary cohorts respectively, over a quarter of the total available. It should be noted, however, that whilst their overall strategic task was the same, the terms under the two halves of the army served were quite different.

The legions, the primary Roman military unit for conducting warfare at the operational or theatre level, had been in existence since early in the republic, hundreds of years before. They were composed mainly of close-order heavy infantry, well-drilled and highly motivated, recruited on a professional basis and, critically to an understanding of their place in Roman society, manned by soldiers who were Roman citizens. The jobless poor were thus provided with a route to both citizenship and a valuable trade, since service with the legions was as much about construction

The Chain of Command
LEGION

LEGATUS ---- LEGION
CAVALRY
(120 HORSEMEN)

BROAD STRIPE
TRIBUNE

5 'MILITARY'
NARROW
STRIPE
TRIBUNES

CAMP PREFECT

SENIOR CENTURION

10 COHORTS
(ONE OF 5 CENTURIES OF 160 MEN EACH)
(NINE OF 6 CENTURIES OF 80 MEN EACH)

CENTURION

CHOSEN MAN

WATCH OFFICER   STANDARD BEARER

10 TENT PARTIES OF
8 MEN APIECE

The Chain of Command
Auxiliary Infantry Cohort

Legatus

Prefect

(or a Tribune for a larger cohort such as
the First Tungrian)

Senior Centurion

6-10 Centuries

Centurion

Chosen Man

Watch Officer   Standard Bearer

10 Tent Parties of
8 Men Apiece

– fortresses, roads and even major defensive works such as Hadrian's Wall – as destruction. Vitally for the maintenance of the empire's borders, this attractiveness of service made a large standing field army a possibility, and allowed for both the control and defence of the conquered territories.

By this point in Britannia's history three legions were positioned to control the restive peoples both beyond and behind the province's borders. These were the 2nd, based in South Wales, the 20th, watching North Wales, and the 6th, positioned to the east of the Pennine range and ready to respond to any trouble on the northern frontier. Each of these legions was commanded by a **legatus**, an experienced man of senatorial rank deemed worthy of the responsibility and appointed by the emperor. The command structure beneath the legatus was a delicate balance, combining the requirement for training and advancing Rome's young aristocrats for their future roles with the necessity for the legion to be led into battle by experienced and hardened officers.

Directly beneath the legatus were a half-dozen or so **military tribunes**, one of them a young man of the senatorial class called the **broad stripe tribune** after the broad senatorial stripe on his tunic. This relatively inexperienced man – it would have been his first official position – acted as the legion's second-in-command, despite being a relatively tender age when compared with the men around him. The remainder of the military tribunes were **narrow stripes**, men of the equestrian class who usually already had some command experience under their belts from leading an auxiliary cohort. Intriguingly, since the more experienced narrow-stripe tribunes effectively reported to the broad stripe, such a reversal of the usual military conventions around fitness for command must have made for some interesting man-management situations. The legion's third in command was the camp **prefect**, an older and more experienced soldier, usually a former centurion deemed worthy of one last role in the legion's service before retirement, usually for one year. He would by necessity have been a steady hand, operating as the voice of experience in advising the legion's senior officers as to the realities of warfare and the management of the legion's soldiers.

Reporting into this command structure were ten **cohorts** of soldiers, each one composed of a number of eighty-man **centuries**. Each century was a collection of ten **tent parties** – eight men who literally shared a tent when out in the field. Nine of the cohorts had six centuries, and an establishment strength of 480 men, whilst the prestigious **first cohort**, commanded by the legion's **senior centurion**, was composed of five double-strength centuries and therefore fielded 800 soldiers when fully manned. This organisation provided the legion with its cutting edge: 5,000 or so well-trained heavy infantrymen operating in regiment and company-sized units, and led by battle-hardened officers, the legion's centurions, men whose position was usually achieved by dint of their demonstrated leadership skills.

The rank of **centurion** was pretty much the peak of achievement for an ambitious soldier, commanding an eighty-man century and paid ten times as much as the men each officer commanded. Whilst the majority of centurions were promoted from the ranks, some were appointed from above as a result of patronage, or as a result of having completed their service in the **Praetorian Guard**, which had a shorter period of service than the legions. That these externally imposed centurions would have undergone their very own 'sink or swim' moment in dealing with their new colleagues is an unavoidable conclusion, for the role was one that by necessity led from the front, and as a result suffered disproportionate casualties. This makes it highly likely that any such appointee felt unlikely to make the grade in action would have received very short shrift from his brother officers.

A small but necessarily effective team reported to the centurion. The **optio**, literally 'best' or **chosen man**, was his second-in-command, and stood behind the century in action with a long brass-knobbed stick, literally pushing the soldiers into the fight should the need arise. This seems to have been a remarkably efficient way of managing a large body of men, given the centurion's place alongside rather than behind his soldiers, and the optio would have been a cool head, paid twice the usual soldier's wage and a candidate for promotion to centurion if he performed well.

The century's third-in-command was the **tesserarius** or **watch officer**, ostensibly charged with ensuring that sentries were posted and that everyone know the watch word for the day, but also likely to have been responsible for the profusion of tasks such as checking the soldiers' weapons and equipment, ensuring the maintenance of discipline and so on, that have occupied the lives of junior non-commissioned officers throughout history in delivering a combat-effective unit to their officer. The last member of the centurion's team was the century's **signifer**, the **standard bearer**, who both provided a rallying point for the soldiers and helped the centurion by transmitting marching orders to them through movements of his standard. Interestingly, he also functioned as the century's banker, dealing with the soldiers' financial affairs. While a soldier caught in the horror of battle might have thought twice about defending his unit's standard, he might well also have felt a stronger attachment to the man who managed his money for him!

At the shop-floor level were the eight soldiers of the tent party who shared a leather tent and messed together, their tent and cooking gear carried on a mule when the legion was on the march. Each tent party would inevitably have established its own pecking order based upon the time-honoured factors of strength, aggression, intelligence – and the rough humour required to survive in such a harsh world. The men that came to dominate their tent parties would have been the century's unofficial backbone, candidates for promotion to watch officer. They would also have been vital to their tent mates' cohesion under battlefield conditions, when the relatively thin leadership team could not always exert sufficient presence to inspire the individual soldier to stand and fight amid the horrific chaos of combat.

The other element of the legion was a small 120-man detachment of **cavalry**, used for scouting and the carrying of messages between units. The regular army depended on auxiliary **cavalry wings**, drawn from those parts of the empire where horsemanship was a way of life, for their mounted combat arm. Which leads us to consider the other side of the army's two-tier system.

The **auxiliary cohorts**, unlike the legions alongside which they fought, were not Roman citizens, although the completion of a twenty-five-year term of service did grant both the soldier and his children citizenship. The original auxiliary cohorts had often served in their homelands, as a means of controlling the threat of large numbers of freshly conquered barbarian warriors, but this changed after the events of the first century AD. The Batavian revolt in particular – when the 5,000-strong Batavian cohorts rebelled and destroyed two Roman legions after suffering intolerable provocation during a recruiting campaign gone wrong – was the spur for the Flavian policy for these cohorts to be posted away from their home provinces. The last thing any Roman general wanted was to find his legions facing an army equipped and trained to fight in the same way. This is why the reader will find the auxiliary cohorts described in the *Empire* series, true to the historical record, representing a variety of other parts of the empire, including Tungria, which is now part of modern-day Belgium.

Auxiliary infantry was equipped and organised in so close a manner to the legions that the casual observer would have been hard put to spot the differences. Often their armour would be mail, rather than plate, sometimes weapons would have minor differences, but in most respects an auxiliary cohort would be the same proposition to an enemy as a legion cohort. Indeed there are hints from history that the auxiliaries may have presented a greater challenge on the battlefield. At the battle of Mons Graupius in Scotland, Tacitus records that four cohorts of Batavians and two of Tungrians were sent in ahead of the legions and managed to defeat the enemy without requiring any significant assistance. Auxiliary cohorts were also often used on the flanks of the battle line, where reliable and well drilled troops are essential to handle attempts to outflank the army. And while the legions contained soldiers who were as much tradesmen as fighting men, the auxiliary cohorts were primarily focused on their fighting skills. By the end of the second century there were significantly more auxiliary troops serving the empire than were available from the legions, and it is clear that Hadrian's Wall would have been invalid as a concept without the mass of infantry and mixed infantry/ cavalry cohorts that were stationed along its length.

As for horsemen, the importance of the empire's 75,000 or so **auxiliary cavalrymen**, capable of much faster deployment and manoeuvre than the infantry, and essential for successful scouting, fast communications and the denial of reconnaissance information to the enemy, cannot be overstated. Rome simply did not produce anything like the strength in mounted troops needed to avoid being at a serious disadvantage against those nations which by their nature were cavalry-rich. As a result, as each such nation was conquered their mounted forces were swiftly incorporated into the army until, by the early first century BC, the decision was made to disband what native Roman cavalry as there was alto- gether, in favour of the auxiliary cavalry wings.

Named for their usual place on the battlefield, on the flanks or 'wings' of the line of battle, the cavalry cohorts were commanded by men of the equestrian class with prior experience as legion military tribunes, and were organised around the basic 32-man **turma**, or squadron. Each squadron was commanded by a **decurion**, a pos- ition analogous with that of the infantry centurion. This officer was assisted by a pair of junior officers: the **duplicarius** or **double-pay**, equivalent to the role of optio, and the **sesquipilarius** or **pay-and- a-half**, equal in stature to the infantry watch officer. As befitted the cavalry's more important military role, each of these ranks was paid about 40 per cent more than the infantry equivalent.

Taken together, the legions and their auxiliary support presented a standing army of over 400,000 men by the time of the events described in the *Empire* series. Whilst this was sufficient to both hold down and defend the empire's 6.5 million square kilometres for a long period of history, the strains of defending a 5,000- kilometre-long frontier, beset on all sides by hostile tribes, were also beginning to manifest themselves. The prompt move to raise three new legions undertaken by the new emperor Septimius Severus in 197 AD, in readiness for over a decade spent shoring up the empire's crumbling borders, provides clear evidence that there were never enough legions and cohorts for such a monumental task. This is the backdrop for the *Empire* series, which will run from 182 AD well into the early third century, following both the empire's and Marcus Valerius Aquila's travails throughout this fascinatingly brutal period of history.

The Centurion

A short story by Anthony Riches

ALEXANDRIA, EGYPT: 175 AD

Centurion Cotta walked through the darkened streets of his legion's camp with the swift, purposeful pace of a man with a task to perform, ignoring the curious glances of the sentries he passed as they muttered to each other at the unusual circumstance that would prise any centurion without guard duty from his bed in the early hours of the morning. At the boundary of the Third Gauls' encampment with that of their neighbours he greeted the Egyptian legionaries guarding the entrance to their territory with a wave of his vine stick, and a tersely barked command.

'Stand aside! I carry a message for the emperor from my legatus!'

Striding through them and out into the Second Legion's camp, he grinned as his strutting confidence drew muttered curses behind his back, deliberately pitched just loud enough for him to hear. Following the line of torches that marked out the road which led to the sleeping legion's heart, he whistled softly as the dark bulk of the new emperor's headquarters tent rose high above the camp around it. A swathe of empty ground surrounded it on all sides, a sensible precaution to prevent an unobserved approach through the sea of tents, but stealth and secrecy were not what he had in mind. Marching straight across the open space, he walked a direct path towards the two men guarding the headquarters' entrance. They turned from their brazier with the reluctance of men who had spent too long enjoying its heat, the more senior of them, his helmet's crest identifying him as a chosen man, raising a hand to block Cotta's path.

'There's no entry to the emperor's tent after dark, Centurion. State your business.'

Ignoring the disrespectful tone of the man's voice, Cotta tapped a finger on the wooden message tablet under his belt, answering the bombast in the chosen man's challenge with a growl of command.

'I carry an urgent message for the emperor from my legatus.'

The chosen man held out a hand.

'We have orders that the emperor is not to be disturbed. I'll see he receives it.'

Cotta shook his head with a hard smile.

'Not likely, Chosen. My legion's commander told me to deliver this to the emperor in person, and to carry back the reply immediately.' He leaned close to the chosen man and rapped the man's armour sharply with his vine stick, taking the offensive with his undisputable seniority. 'And you can show me a bit more fucking respect if you don't want my first spear to have a chat with yours in the morning and get you put back in the ranks! As to this message, it bears urgent news of enemy troop movements. A horseman has ridden through the night to bring it here with all the speed it deserves, and on reading it my legatus instructed me to bring it to the emperor *immediately*. Not to some fucking jumped-up grunt with ideas above his station. So I'll tell you what, I'll just wait here until the big man strolls out for his morning shit and give it to him then, shall I? And when he asks why the fuck there are enemy legions ashore and marching to attack us without him being aware of it, I'll just give him *your* name.'

The chosen man stiffened at the prospect of being held responsible for any delay to such evidently vital information, and did exactly what the centurion had guessed he would.

'Wait here.'

He turned away and disappeared into the tent, leaving the other man to watch the unexpected messenger while he went in search of someone more senior on whom to dump the problem. Pulling off his helmet, and putting it carefully down on the ground, Cotta stretched his arms out and yawned extravagantly in evident disgust at the unusual hour. Rolling his head on a neck thickened by constant physical exercise, he rotated his shoulder blades beneath the finely-scaled armour that both demonstrated his rank and protected his torso with a grimace at the watching sentry, throwing his arms back and arching his chest to relieve the stiffness in his muscular frame. Then, in a move so fast that the soldier had no time in which to react, he unwound from the tension position with whiplash speed, smashing the tip of his vine stick across the other man's throat and rupturing his larynx with the force of the blow. The legionary staggered backwards, unable even to choke with his throat smashed flat, and Cotta plucked the spear from his victim's twitching fingers as he eased the dying man to the ground, stepping catlike through the tent's doorway into the lamp-lit gloom of the headquarters' outer chamber.

'Well now. . .'

The formal nature of the interview an hour before had been plain to Cotta from the moment that he'd marched into the legatus's office behind his first spear. Standing to attention in front of the senior officer's desk, the glossy waxed surface completely empty save for a cloth-wrapped object in the exact centre of its generous expanse, he'd waited impassively as the legion's commander had leaned back in his chair and looked up at him with evident curiosity.

'I can't say that you look like a particularly dangerous man, Centurion Cotta. In fact you barely look like a centurion, if you'll forgive my observation. You stand before me in the full glory of a legion officer's uniform, and yet you resemble nothing more than a veteran soldier who happens to be somewhat more lavishly equipped than the usual. I very much doubt I would have picked you out of a group of your peers for the job I have in mind, not without your first spear's recommendation.'

Turning his head, he'd nodded to the first cohort's senior centurion, the most powerful man in his legion below the rank of tribune, who was standing behind the legatus with his vine stick held behind his back. The veteran soldier had barely hesitated before naming Cotta on hearing his superior's intentions, once he had recovered from the initial shock of their implications. Having acknowledged his most experienced officer's part in selecting Cotta, the legatus had sat back and waited for an answer to his observation, intrigued by the fact that the man in front of him seemed happy enough to take his time responding, so long in fact that he had sensed his first spear's discomfort in the slight shuffle of the man's feet behind him. Just as the senior centurion had drawn a sharp breath to bark a command at his man, the answer had come, and in a tone so apparently relaxed with the situation that the speaker might as well have been ordering a round of drinks in the officers' mess.

'You're not the first man to have said as much. Sir.'

The legatus had leaned forwards, putting his elbows on the desk and steepling his fingers.

'And do you find that to be a problem, Centurion?'

Cotta's dismissive shrug was neither bombastic nor insolent, simply matter-of-fact.

'Appearances can be deceptive, Legatus. Most centurions in this man's army are big nasty bastards, if you'll forgive my language. They have to be if they're going to deal with any insubordination in the approved manner, which is to put your fist through the face of the offender. But I'm different, Legatus. I don't need all that weight to throw around.'

The officer had smiled despite himself, shaking his head as if in polite disbelief.

'You seem very sure of yourself.'

Cotta's words had given the lie to his lack of facial expression.

'That, sir, would be because I am. *Very* sure of myself.'

The legatus had looked up at him for a moment longer, faintly embarrassed at his need to string out a silence of his own.

'The first spear here told me much the same thing, but when I asked him to elucidate he simply suggested that I should meet with you, and ask the question of you myself. So, in your own time, why don't you tell me what it is that makes you so special?'

Cotta had pondered the question for a moment before finding the right reply.

'When I joined the legion, Legatus, every man in my tent party took one look at me and put me to the top of their list as a good man to go to for an extra share of rations, or a non-refundable loan, or a nice easy hole to use when tossing off got boring . . .' The senior officer had raised a hand to forestall his first spear's rebuke.

'I asked the question as you suggested, Decimus, so I think we ought to allow the Centurion the dignity of answering it in his own way. I'm sure the answer will continue to be . . . *entertaining.* So, Centurion, your fellow soldiers all took you for an easy man to bully, did they?'

He'd gestured to the man standing before him to continue.

'Every tent party has one victim, Legatus. The weakest man, the man that gets all the abuse, unless the soldier in control refuses to allow it to happen. But good men like that are rare in the legions, any kindness soon gets beaten out of us by the training, and my tent party was bossed by a right bastard. Or at least he was for as long as it took him for come after me that first evening, and for me to break his arm.'

The senior officer had shaken his head in disbelief.

'You . . . *broke* his arm? In a fight?'

Cotta had shaken his head.

'Not really, Legatus. The fight was pretty much over by then. I jabbed my fingers into his eyes, and while he was busy screaming and rubbing at them I put my boot through his elbow. *Right* through it.'

With the same hard clarity that always washed over him when the time came to either spill blood or take a blade himself, Cotta assessed the odds he was facing as he stepped through the tent's door flap, raising the spear ready to throw. The chosen man had his back to the tent's entrance, and was talking to a tribune dressed in a sculpted muscle cuirass in hushed but urgent tones, while a pair of hulking legionaries was dozing on a bench to his left. Drawing the throwing weapon back until the shining iron blade was almost level with his ear, he stamped forwards and slung it into the chosen man's back with an explosive exhalation of breath. The weapon's brutal impact punched through his armour and deep into his body, pitching him forward into the officer's arms. The tribune dithered for a moment before pushing the dying man off him, giving Cotta the time he needed to pull the dagger from his belt and step forwards, shouldering the dying chosen man aside and springing at the officer with the ferocity of a man fighting for his life.

The younger man was commendably fast to unsheathe his own dagger, but from a lifetime of fighting experience the centurion knew he was easy meat simply from his awkward stance and poor foot positioning. Not giving his opponent time to reach the conclusion that the best defence would be to shout for help, he took a swift pace forwards, blocked a half-hearted stab of the other man's dagger and then shot his arm out in a lightning-fast thrust, burying the knife deep in the tribune's neck before grunting with the effort of tearing it out of his throat, severing the thick veins that fed the man's brain in a spray of hot blood.

With a guttural challenge the first of the sleeping soldiers was on his feet and fumbling for his sword with sleep-addled fingers while the other simply stared at Cotta in disbelief. The centurion drew his hand back and hurled the bloody dagger at the more alert of the two, the heavy impact of its handle on the man's forehead rocking him back for long enough for Cotta to cross the tent with three quick strides, reaching behind his head with one hand to pull a second knife from the sheath hanging down his back beneath the scaled armour shirt. The weapon's blade was longer than the standard pattern dagger, its edge rough-sharpened to inflict the most horrendous wounds. Coming back to his senses, the man on the bench made to leap to his feet, and Cotta paused in his advance on his momentarily dazed comrade to put a hobnailed boot into the soldier's face, hard enough to catapult him back into the canvas wall behind him with a crack of bone.

The first soldier was on him quickly, shrugging off the effects of the dagger's impact with impressive speed and coming forward again with his sword drawn, grinning wolfishly at the centurion's knife and tapping the blade of his sword.

'Now I kill you!'

The legatus had raised his eyebrows, considering the act of violence Cotta had described and the obvious consequences for both victim and assailant.

'You didn't just break his arm then, you wrecked it beyond repair. My word. You were punished, I presume?'

The man behind him had spoken for the first time.

'I was his century's chosen man at the time. Since he'd been defending himself against an unprovoked attack we decided to show some leniency. He was lashed to a post and flogged, twenty strokes.'

The legatus's wince had not been affected.

'Twenty strokes? Gods below, I've seen men die after that sort of beating.'

The senior centurion barked out a soft laugh.

'Not this one! He walked away. Stiff-legged I'll grant you, but he *walked* away to the medicus, with his back opened up like a piece of meat and blood running down his legs, and I marked him down as a nasty little piece of work who just might make an effective centurion.'

'I see. And did you have many more challenges, Centurion?'

Cotta had shaken his head with a wry smile.

'No, Legatus.'

The first spear behind him had snorted his dark amusement again.

'He made it known publicly that the next man to try him would have his nose bitten off. Funnily enough, not one of them was brave enough to put the threat to the test, not given that he'd robbed his first victim of the use of his right arm for the rest of his life.'

The legatus had nodded, rubbing his chin thoughtfully.

'And here you are, all these years later, a highly regarded centurion in the Third Gauls.'

'Thank you, Legatus.'

'Don't thank me. You may end up regretting your notoriety soon enough. Tell me Cotta, what are your views on the events of the last three months? And stand at ease man, this might take a while.'

Cotta's eyes had narrowed, genuinely surprised by the senior officer's unexpected line of questioning.

'You mean . . . ?'

The question had hung in the air for a moment, until the legatus had answered his question in a weary tone.

'I mean, Centurion, the events that have taken place since news of the emperor's death in Germania reached Egypt.'

'Well sir, we were all clearly distraught to hear – '

'Just the facts, man, don't feel any need to cover it in honey for me.'

Cotta had paused for a moment, considering the unusual nature of his superior's request.

'As you wish, Legatus. You want to know what I think? I think it was one great big fucking fraud.' He'd shaken his head in evident disgust. 'I couldn't have set it up any more obviously myself, not if you'd paid me to do the job. You should know well enough, you were there alongside Governor Cassius. Once the news had got around, and everyone knew that the emperor had died from the plague, it wasn't exactly unexpected when we were paraded, along with the men of Trajan's *Valiant* Second . . . ' Having managed to invest their sister legion's name with all of the scorn he could muster, he continued in a sarcastic tone. 'And then, *what* a surprise, a group of senior centurions step forward and demand that their beloved Avidius Cassius take the throne. Not that any of us wasn't expecting it, given all the mutterings we'd heard beforehand.'

'He *did* initially refuse to countenance the idea.'

The legatus's retort had been voiced so mildly that it was clear even he was struggling to credit the events of that morning with any dignity. The man standing before him had shrugged, knowing that no man in the room harboured any illusions as to the nature of their leader's elevation to the purple.

'Yes, he did sir. And that lasted for about as long as it would take me to lace my boots. A brief show of reluctance was all it was, and then he couldn't get that purple cloak on his shoulders quickly enough. And he was happy enough to be acclaimed by the men of the legions, to sit on his horse and wave his hand while the Egyptians shouted that he was the master of the world.'

'Not just the Egyptians, Centurion, you men of the Third Gauls acclaimed him too. It seems to me that the idea of a nice hefty imperial donative was on everyone's minds.'

Cotta had shrugged again.

'No offence intended Legatus, but I didn't hear you speaking out against the idea.'

The senior officer had laughed, shaking his head at the point.

'Very true, Centurion, and I feel no shame at the fact! Any reluctance on my part would have required a good deal more heroism than I possess! Can you imagine what nature of accident would have befallen me, if I'd found the nerve to gainsay a process that had been days in the preparation? All those quiet meetings between the governor's men and *certain* senior centurions . . . ' He'd fallen pointedly silent, the feet shuffling behind him again. 'Of *course* it was a foregone conclusion.'

He'd waited for a response, but the centurion, clearly determined to outlast him, had locked his gaze on the wall behind his first spear. He'd sighed.

'You won't understand it properly unless I tell you the story behind those events.'

The Egyptian sprang forward and lunged with his long sword, intent on running the intruder through with the weapon's point, but where he might have expected his target to jump aside, Cotta did no more than turn his torso sideways, leaning back as the soldier attacked him. The sword's blade skated harmlessly across his armoured chest, and at the point that the soldier's body was fully extended in his lunge Cotta, having passed the long knife from his right hand to his left, gripped his attacker's extended sword arm at the wrist to prevent him from stepping back and stabbed down at the pale flesh of his attacker's right thigh. He wrenched the knife upwards and then tore it free of the horrendous wound that was already pulsing out thick gouts of the man's arterial blood. The soldier staggered, groaning at the sudden pain, and in an instant the centurion took his opportunity to make the kill, drawing the blade back over his right shoulder before whipping it round in a deadly arc and burying the ragged edged iron in the soldier's neck.

'You see, Centurion, the truth of it is that when the eastern plague took hold of Marcus Aurelius he was so close to death, it seems, that no-one could say with any confidence that he wouldn't go to meet his ancestors within the hour. He lay unconscious for a day, barely breathing and with no pulse to speak of, and it seems that his doctors were unanimous in their opinion that all hope of his recovering was lost. At which point his wife sent a messenger, all the way from the German frontier, to our very own Gaius Avidius Cassius here in Egypt. And yes, to answer the unspoken question that's written all over your face, Avidius Cassius is indeed rumoured to have enjoyed the pleasures of the empress's bedchamber, despite her husband's high regard for him. The message she sent to the governor said that her husband was dead, and that she feared for her life, and that of her son Commodus, if another man seized the throne. She wrote to Cassius to beg for his help, a plea to declare himself emperor written to a man who, let us not forget, was already ruling the eastern provinces under a decree of *imperium* issued by Marcus Aurelius himself. He was practically an emperor already. She entreated him to take the throne, to rescue the empire from the threat of usurpers and civil war. She also doubtless offered to be his empress.'

Cotta had nodded his understanding.

'That all makes sense, Legatus. But. . .?'

The legatus nodded grimly.

'*But* indeed. *But* the emperor didn't die. He lives.' The officer had smiled at his centurion's reaction. 'Believe me, I was as amazed as you, when I first heard the news. Word of this miracle reached Avidius Cassius three weeks ago, which is the reason why he marched both legions out here, to get himself away from the city, now that the news has reached the populus. And which is also the reason why he's taken to hiding in his tent, brooding on what he is to do to get off the enormous hook on which he finds himself swinging in the breeze. The only realistic answer to which is that he can do nothing at all.' He paused to emphasise the point. '*Nothing*. The entire army, with the sole exception of the seven eastern legions, have immediately and very wisely declared their undying loyalty to the throne. Let's face it, given the choice between a blatant usurper far away in Egypt or the true emperor, only a few weeks' march away and in command of a dozen legions made bone hard by ten years of war with the Marcomanni, it wouldn't have taken them long to work out the right choice.'

He'd paused, looking at the cloth-wrapped bundle on the desk in front of him.

'I think it likely that Cassius's seven loyal legions will have shrunk to two by the time the legions from the Rhenus and the Danubius arrive to violently demonstrate the error of our ways, ourselves and the Second, since we're the only two legions here in Egypt. The legates of the other five will doubtless find it more prudent to fall on the emperor's mercy, and quite possibly their swords, than to face the sort of punishment that the throne reserves for members of the aristocracy who choose the wrong side at times like these. I doubt the emperor will have them killed, though. He's a rational enough man and has, it appears, already forgiven his wife for her "understandable error of judgement". The only man who can't change sides at this point is Cassius himself. He's a dead man whatever he does from now, and the only freedom of action he has is to decide where to meet Marcus's legions in battle. All he can hope for is some kind of divine intervention, such as the emperor getting in the path of a ballista bolt, and for providence to drop a victory in his lap. Which isn't beyond the bounds of the possible, but I wouldn't be squandering any money to bet on the result . . . '

He'd waited for the centurion to speak, which he eventually did with obvious and somewhat bitter reluctance.

'All this seems very interesting, Legatus, but I can't help feeling that you're revealing things to me that aren't merited by my status. Things I might not have wanted to know?'

The senator had sat forward, his smile pitilessly hard, and the first spear behind him had smirked at his centurion knowingly.

'It's time for the truth, Centurion, and although you certainly won't want to hear it I'm afraid that we all have to face up to our responsibilities to the empire sooner or later. And yours are about to become a little more onerous that you might have been expected. You see, there's rather more to my role with the Third Gauls than meets the eye. Indeed if Avidius Cassius had even a hint as to my real purpose here, he'd put a dagger in my throat with his own hands, just to be sure of my death.'

'You're . . . '

'Go on. The first spear here had the same revelation not an hour ago.'

'You're an imperial spy!'

'Gods, no! Nothing so *crass*! What I am, Centurion, is an old-fashioned Roman gentleman, of impeccable breeding. There are a dozen death masks of exalted ancestors in my father's house, men clever and ruthless enough to have guided our family's fortunes through the death throes of the Republic. Men who survived civil wars by always managing to choose the right man to be aligned with, who kept their heads down when the more deranged of our rulers were on the throne, and men who master-minded the carnage of campaigns that have left our armies as the last men standing in a brutal world. I am as much a weapon as you, Centurion, just not *quite* so much of a blunt instrument, and I am here to perform a task, at the request of my emperor, a task I intend to carry out at whatever cost to myself. And, Centurion, to be brutally frank, to you . . . '

He'd pushed the cloth parcel across the desk towards the centurion.

'Go on, I know you've been dying to know what's in it.' His voice had hardened, and taken on a commanding tone. '*Open it.*'

Turning away from the stricken guard, the Egyptian shuddering as he choked on the blood spurting into his throat and lungs,

Cotta paused to put his iron-shod boot into the semi-conscious soldier's face again just as the man was starting to regain his wits, stooping to recover the dagger that he'd thrown at the dying soldier before turning back to the doorway into the tent's inner chamber. It had been waiting for him on the legatus's desk, unmistakable in shape for all that it was wrapped in cloth, a legion issue weapon drawn from the 3rd's armoury that same evening and quickly but expertly punch marked with *II TR FORT,* military shorthand for their sister legion's formal title. A lamp was burning by the doorway to the inner chamber, its dim light easily extinguished by Cotta's wet finger and thumb, plunging the tent into total darkness.

The legatus had been adamant on the necessary manner of the usurper's death.

'Kill him, Centurion, and if you manage to escape with your life I'll see you safely away from here before the sun rises. *If* you do it the way that I've told you.'

After a moment's thought the centurion had nodded his agreement.

'Not like I have much choice in the matter, is it Legatus? You'll only find someone else to do it, and they won't be half as likely to succeed. But I want – '

The legatus waved a dismissive hand.

'Money? Nothing I couldn't predict, Centurion. If you manage to do the job and get away cleanly then there's enough gold waiting for you to recompense you for your lost wages, and your share of the burial club, and more besides. There'll be a cart waiting for you at the gate with whatever you want to take with you, ready to take you to the docks. You can be anywhere in the empire inside a month or two, and rich enough to start a new life, happy in the knowledge that you've served your emperor and saved thousands of men from futile death in a needless battle.'

Cotta had shaken his head.

'I'm sorry, Legatus, that's not enough. If I'm to do this I need to know that my closest friends are safe. If I simply vanish it won't take this lot long to put two and two together, and there are men whose lives I value who'll take the brunt of any attempts at revenge.'

The legion's commander had raised an eyebrow.

'That's surprisingly noble of you. How many men?'

Cotta had watched the legatus's face as he reeled off the names.

'They're all long-service men, most of them joined about the same time I did, so I'm not robbing the legion of much. We'd all have been retiring in a year or so.'

His superior had shaken his head in dark amusement.

'You're expecting me to retire a dozen veteran soldiers? That's audacious, Centurion.'

The man on the other side of the desk had shrugged.

'You're expecting *me* to kill an emperor armed with nothing more than a stolen dagger. I'd say we're about equal when it comes to the audacity of our demands. Enough gold to get us all away and allow us to set up new lives, and I'll do it just the way you want.'

'And you trust me to see my side of the bargain through?'

The centurion's smile had resembled a wolf's snarl in the dim lamp light.

'Yes, Legatus, I do. For one thing you're a Roman gentleman, and your word is bound by your honour. And for another, if I as much as sniff the suspicion that you're going to break your word, I'll raise a commotion that half the camp will hear. And I think you can guess whose names I'll be shouting.'

He'd shot the first spear a hard glance, waiting until his immediate superior had nodded his acceptance of the point.

'Very well. Your friends will be waiting for you at the gate. If you're not back by sunrise I'll send them on their way without you. Best not hang about once you're done with the "emperor", eh, Centurion?'

Cotta eased through the doorway to the tent's inner sanctum cautiously, hearing nothing in the silence other than the thunder of his own pulse. If the man within had been awakened by the sounds of the struggle he'd chosen not to shout for his guards, reasoning perhaps that he was better served by the immediate tactical advantage of remaining undetected than calling for help and giving away his position within the tent. The legatus had given him one last piece of advice before he'd walked away across the camp to carry out his orders.

'He won't try to cut his way out of the tent, I'm sure of that. Not knowing what might be waiting for him on the other side of the canvas, and being so very sure of his own ability with a sword, he'll stand and face you. If there's one thing we can all agree on, Avidius Cassius has balls the size of a bull's.' The officer had shaken his head sadly. 'Rome's greatest general, and probably its best replacement for Marcus Aurelius too, and he has to die like this.'

'Having second thoughts, Legatus?'

'Don't be so fucking cheeky, Centurion. And no, I'm not having any second thoughts. Now go and do your bloody duty.'

Pacing slowly through the doorway into the inner chamber,

Cotta stopped suddenly as a tiny sound reached his ears. The hobnails on his boots were making the faintest of clicking sounds on the wooden floor with each pace. A sound that would ordinarily have been lost in the general hubbub of the place during the day was, he suddenly realised, loud enough to be heard from the other side of the canvas-lined room. Stopping in mid-pace he sank down on his haunches in the darkness, listening intently, guessing that Cassius's feet would be bare and therefore almost soundless. A faint movement of air was all the warning he got, cringing as his would be victim swung a sword in a lethal arc at the last place from which he'd heard the sound of hobnails on timber, the blade's edge hissing only inches above his bowed head. Knowing that Cassius would simply retreat back into the darkness given time to do so, the centurion took the only chance he knew he was going to get in such a one-sided fight, diving full length into the gloom with his arms outstretched, hoping to catch his quarry unawares.

Hitting Cassius low, he wrapped his arms around the man's knees and bore him to the floor, reaching up and gripping his hair to smash the usurper's head back into the hard wooden boards. The emperor attempted to use his sword to defend himself, but the weapon's three foot length, such a potential advantage in the darkness, was suddenly a liability when the two men were at each other's throats. The first attempt to cut at his attacker did no better than to bounce off the centurion's scale-armoured back, and while Cassius attempted to change his hold on the weapon to a two-handed grip, ready to stab at the rear of his assailant's thighs, the fighting instincts honed in Cotta over almost two decades of training and combat snapped him into action. Raising the dagger high, he plunged it blindly into the emperor's groin, clawing at the other man's tunic and pulling himself up his victim's body as the usurper sucked in a long whooping breath, clamping a hand over his mouth before he could scream out his sudden agony. Pushing Cassius's head back, he thrust the dagger up into the soft skin of his jaw, ramming the ten-inch blade into his head as the emperor contorted with the searing agony, then stiffened and went limp.

Rolling away from his victim, Cotta lay panting on his back for a moment before climbing back to his feet and finding the dead usurper's corpse by touch. Pulling the stolen legionary dagger free he bent to his grisly task, dropping the knife as he'd been instructed when the job was done. A bed-sheet from the emperor's couch served to remove the worst of the blood from his hands and face, although his armour remained spattered with the gore of half a dozen men's violent deaths. Crossing the outer chamber he crouched at the door to pick up the helmet he'd discarded before killing the first of the guards and his fallen vine stick, then looked out into the Second Legion's camp, still deep in the silence of the night. A swift kick sent the unattended brazier flying into the tent's side, hot coal spilling out across the trailing canvas where it lay smouldering, wisps of smoke rising as the thick material momentarily resisted the embers' heat.

Turning away, he walked swiftly into the camp, looking back at the tent once he'd crossed the open space that surrounded it. The canvas had taken fire, flames licking up the wall by the door, and he filled his lungs with the night's cold air before bellowing out a warning across the camp.

'Fire!'

After a moment's delay answering shouts were raised, and men started to poke their heads out of the tents around him.

'Fire! Get yourselves out of your pits and get some fucking water on it! Move!'

In an instant the camp was fully awake, dozens of men running at the blazing headquarters with their tent parties' water buckets, and Cotta turned away, using the confusion to make his way back towards the Third Legion's camp. The sentries he had blown through moments before were fully awake now, snapping to attention at his shouted command.

'What's happening, Centurion?'

Cotta laughed bleakly.

'Some stupid prick knocked over a brazier. It'll be out by now.'

One of the closer of the sentries sniffed, wrinkling his nose at the stink of blood rising from the centurion's armour.

'What's that smell?' He spotted a bundle hanging from the centurion's left hand. 'And what's in that—'

He recoiled with a grunt as the end of Cotta's vine stick thumped into his gut with an expert aim born of long practice.

'Don't be so fucking cheeky. And pray to your gods that you never smell anything like this again boys, because if you do then a sad collection of goatfuckers like you lot are going to be in the deepest shit of your lives.'

He marched on through the salutes of his own legion's sentries, waiting for a challenge from behind him that never came. The legatus was waiting for him outside the command tent with an escort of half a dozen legionaries, all armed with spears. He smiled grimly as he spotted the centurion walking towards him.

'Well then, Centurion Cotta. There seems to be something of a clamour being raised in the Second Legion's camp?'

Cotta raised the blood-soaked sheet in which he'd wrapped his grisly prize.

'It was a fire to start with, but I expect they've discovered a bigger problem by now.'

The senior officer shook his head slowly.

'That old rogue Decimus said that if anyone could do it, it was you.' He took the bundle, opening it to reveal the dead usurper's contorted features on the severed head that Cotta had carried through the Second Legion's camp, shaking his head sadly at the sight. 'How very distressing. I doubt the emperor will be all that happy to see this either, but at least we'll have prevented a civil war, however brief it might have been, and saved Mithras knows how many lives in the process. You left the knife behind?'

Cotta nodded tiredly, as the desire to fight leached out of his exhausted body, looking at the soldiers flanking their legatus on either side with an inkling of what was likely to happen next.

'Good. No matter how much they might suspect us of being at the root of the matter, the discovery that Cassius was beheaded with a dagger marked with their legion's name will be enough to put the official blame squarely on them. Doubtless the Second legion's legatus will make up some story or other about a lone assassin striking the emperor down, probably on the march and when he least expected it, rather than admit that the deed was carried out in the supposed safety of their camp. Which leaves only you, Centurion.'

Cotta looked up, his face expressionless.

'And this is where you remove the last threat to this whole thing being a complete mystery, right? I might talk, after all, if not, then at some point in the future, under the influence of drink, or desperate for money? I suppose my brothers are already face down and stiffening as we speak?'

The legatus looked at him for a moment with a cold expression.

'Even if you really think so little of my honour, Centurion, I can assure that I value it somewhat higher than to stoop to the murder of a good and loyal officer. Besides, who would ever believe you, once this thing blows over and normality has been restored? And do you know, I actually believe you've got more sense. No, Centurion, this isn't where you get a blade in the back, or even the front. Go to the main gate, and you'll find your brothers in arms waiting for you, along with your effects and the money you'll need to get yourselves set up in your new lives. The carter will take you as far as the city, and from there you'll be able to take a ship anywhere around the edge of Our Sea. I wish you good fortune.'

Cotta nodded wearily, saluted for the last time in his military career and turned away, only to stop in his tracks as a thought occurred to him.

'I've a mind to see Rome, Legatus, if only for a month or two. Would you have any advice to offer on the city?'

The officer nodded.

'Advice? That's simple enough. Treat every man you meet in Rome with the caution you'd apply to a thief, and you won't go far wrong. Keep one hand on your purse, and . . . ' A thought occurred to him, and he pondered on it for a moment before coming to a decision. 'And if you've a mind to stay in Rome for any length of time, go and see my older brother. He lives on the family estate to the south-east of the city, it's not hard to find if you walk down the Via Appia for a few miles. Tell him I told you to seek him out, and that I recommend you to provide skill at arms training for my nephew. Tell him that you provided me with some service in the matter of Avidius Cassius, and he'll understand you clearly enough.'

Cotta's brow furrowed.

'You want me to train a *child*? To do *this*?'

He raised his hands, black with dried blood, and the legatus shook his head.

'My nephew isn't a child any more, he'll be a man soon enough. My uncle has a gladiator working with him already, but you, Centurion, you're something else. You might rough up a few of the smooth edges he's been given by all those Greek tutors his father insists are necessary to make him into a gentleman. Besides, the boy has promise, a gift with the blade that would benefit from the application of a little of your talent. Say you'll at least go to meet him?'

Cotta wearily raised his hands again in surrender.

'Yes, Legatus. If I get the opportunity I'll make the trip down this Via Appia, I'll go and see the boy. If I can find the place.'

The officer smiled.

'I think you'll find it easily enough. Just ask for the villa of the Aquila family, you can hardly miss the place, given it's big enough to have its own aqueduct. My brother's name is Appius Valerius Aquila. And my nephew's name is Marcus.'